The Falls of Erith

A Medieval Romance

By Kathryn Le Veque

D1714838

Printed by Dragonblade Publishing in the United States of America

Text copyright 2012 by Kathryn Le Veque

Cover copyright 2012 by Kathryn Le Veque

Library of Congress Control Number 2014-016

Other Novels by Kathryn Le Veque

Medieval Romance:

The Wolfe * Serpent
*

The White Lord of Wellesbourne* The Dark One: Dark Knight
*

While Angels Slept* Rise of the Defender* Spectre of the Sword* Unending Love* Archangel* Lord of the Shadows
*

Great Protector* To the Lady Born
*

The Falls of Erith* Lord of War: Black Angel
*

The Darkland* Black Sword
*

Unrelated characters or family groups:
The Whispering Night * The Dark Lord* The Gorgon* The Warrior Poet* Guardian of Darkness (related to The Fallen One)* Tender is the Knight* The Legend* Lespada* Lord of Light

The Dragonblade Trilogy:
Dragonblade* Island of Glass* The Savage Curtain
     -also-
The Fallen One (related)* Fragments of Grace (related prequel)
*

Novella, Time Travel Romance:
Echoes of Ancient Dreams
*

Time Travel Romance:
The Crusader*Kingdom Come

Contemporary Romance:

Kathlyn Trent/Marcus Burton Series:
Valley of the Shadow* The Eden Factor* Canyon of the Sphinx

The American Heroes Series:
Resurrection* Fires of Autumn* Evenshade* Sea of Dreams* Purgatory

Other Contemporary Romance:
Lady of Heaven* Darkling, I Listen

<u>Note:</u> All Kathryn's novels are designed to be read as stand-alones, although many have cross-over characters or cross-over family groups. Novels that are grouped together have related characters or family groups. Series are clearly marked. All series contain the same characters or family groups except the American Heroes Series, which is an anthology with unrelated characters. There is NO particular chronological order for any of the novels because they can all be read as stand-alones, even the series.

CHAPTER ONE

North of Castle Erith, Cumbria, England
Year of our Lord 1305
The month of August

She could hear the screaming.

Like a dagger through the chest, physical pain bolted through her slender body at the sound. She knew it was her daughter; it could be on one else.

They were quite alone out in the wilds of Cumbria, harvesting fat purple berries from a bumper summer crop. All had been peaceful this morning, a warm summer day that had dawned soft and sweet upon the land, and she had allowed her daughter to separate from her in search of additional edibles. As another scream pierced the air, she was coming to regret that decision immensely.

"Brooke!" she screamed in return. "Brooke, where are you?"

The woman began to run; she wasn't even sure which direction the screams were coming from but she began running nonetheless. Panic bubbled in her chest as she heard screamed words off to her left; they were incoherent but unmistakably urgent. The woman plowed through the heavy foliage that stood between her and the screams; the branches scratched and the grass was wet with humidity, causing her to slip in her haste. She charged through the bushes, bleeding scratches on her arms, as she emerged into the clearing on the opposite side.

She drew closer to the towering falls of Erith, an oasis of crystal pools and roaring water about a dozen yards away. The thunder of the falls grew louder as she raced towards them, the piercing screams of her only child penetrating the mighty roar. The woman could hear the cries but she couldn't see her child; only the green, moist foliage surrounding the falls and the spray of the water greeted her. Heart pounding, she yelled again.

"Brooke?" she cried.

"Mama!" Came the call. "Help me!"

The Lady Gray de Montfort Serroux could hear the cry again, like a nightmare, but she still didn't see anything.

"Where are you?" she began to move towards the falls, a towering thunder of water that emptied into a crisp pool some fifty feet below its zenith. "I cannot see you!"

"Here!" came the cry. "I slipped! I am here!"

Gray raced to the edge of the falls, as close as she dared, seeing her slip of a daughter dangling from a ledge about ten feet below her. She couldn't help the terrified yelp that escaped her lips as she fell to her belly, struggling to reach out a hand down to her daughter.

"Take my hand!" she stretched as far as she could go, reaching, begging. "Grab my hand, Brooke. Take it!"

Brooke was terrified, clinging to slippery rocks as the falls roared behind her. She was weeping hysterically, lifting a hand but too terrified to reach too high. After a half-hearted effort, she stopped trying altogether and clutched at the rocks again.

"I cannot," she wept. "I will fall."

Gray was biting back tears, having no idea how she was going to reach her child. Her heart sank as she realized that the girl was just too far out of her reach. All she could think to do was to untie her apron and yank it over her head, trying to use it as a rope as she awkwardly tossed it in her daughter's direction.

"Sweetheart," she tried to keep the terror from her voice, knowing calm heads would better prevail. "Try to grab hold of my apron. I will pull you up."

Brooke was sobbing, terrified, clinging to the wet rocks. "I cannot!"

"Aye, you can," Gray struggled to calm herself for her daughter's sake. "Please, Brooke; grab hold of my apron."

Brooke shook her head, crying, but eventually lifted a wet hand in the direction of the lowered apron. Gray tried to feed it down to her, lying on her belly and reaching over as far as she could go without slipping herself. The seconds were ticking. As Brooke reached up and took the tail-end of the apron ties, she lost her grip on the wet rock and she screamed, sliding another foot or so away from her mother down the slippery, grassy rocks.

"I am falling!" she screamed. "Help me!"

Gray's tears returned, filling her eyes as she hurried to gain a better position now that her daughter had slipped further. She lay on the wet grass, trying to lower the apron to her, struggling against panic to coax her daughter into making another try for the apron.

But Brooke was paralyzed with fear, clutching the wet rocks and weeping hysterically. Gray couldn't get her to look up at her or even make another attempt at the apron rope. As the great falls of Erith thundered only a few feet away, dousing them with spray, Gray sat up and yanked off one of her woolen hose.

It was full of holes but sturdy. With shaking, panicked hands, Gray tied the hose to the end of the apron and tossed it over the side of the cliff. It hit Brooke in the head and the girl shrieked; any little movement had her terrified she was going to fall the remaining forty feet into the churning water below.

Gray lay on her belly again, trying to coerce her daughter into taking hold of the hose, when the wet ground beneath her suddenly gave way. Gray let out a piercing scream, positive she was going to go crashing down on her daughter and, in turn, sending both of them to their death. The ground was sliding and dirt was falling, and Gray struggled to pull back, away from the sliding earth. But she was caught in the avalanche and there was nothing she could do. Just as she neared the edge to the point of no return, someone grabbed her ankle.

Whoever it was yanked hard, sliding her back along the wet grass that was now more like mud. Stunned, and slightly numb that she wasn't already in a watery grave, Gray looked up to see a fairly big knight bolting past her, dropping to the edge of the cliff to peer down the side of the rushing falls. As she watched him, bewildered, a soft, deep voice from behind caught her attention.

"My lady?" he asked. "Are you injured?"

Gray turned in the direction of the voice; a knight was kneeling beside her, his handsome face glazed with concern. He was fair, his blond hair cropped close and graying at the temples, and his square-jawed face held an intelligent, angled edge. He was perhaps ten or more years older than her twenty-nine, but he wore his age well upon his striking features. He was average in height but he was very broad; she could see the thickness of his arms and legs, heavily muscled from years of warring. All in all, he was a big, handsome man, something she hadn't expected to see out here in the wilds of Cumbria, and she struggled to find her tongue.

"I... I am well," she suddenly scrambled to her knees. "But my daughter has fallen. I was trying to pull her up when the ground gave way."

The knight rushed to the edge of the cliff, beside the other knight, and as Gray joined them, the three of them peered down at the very frightened young lady about twelve feet down. Gray's amber eyes filled with tears as she gazed down at her frightened daughter.

"Please," she turned to the men. "Please help her. I fear I have done all I can."

The words hadn't even left her mouth before the knights were swinging into action. She didn't even have to ask, truly; they had already decided they were going to assist. They had heard the screams, too, and had followed the cries until they came across the source. Even now, the older knight was directing the younger.

"Take your mail off," he instructed quickly as the man hurried to do his bidding. "This ledge cannot take the additional weight."

The mail coat came off and the younger knight, a lean and attractive man with shoulder-length blond hair, fell on to his belly and slithered to the edge. The other knight got in behind him and grabbed his ankles.

"I will lower you down," he said. "Tell me as soon as you have hold of her and I will pull you up."

The younger knight nodded, waiting until his liege had him by the ankles before plunging forward. Muddied, wet and terrified, Gray leaned over the edge of the cliff, as far as she dared to go.

"Brooke!" she called over the roar of the falls. "Take hold of his hand!"

Brooke was clutching the rocks, her eyes closed and face pressed into the wet granite. But when her mother called to her, she dared to open her eyes, looking up to see that someone was descending towards her. She started to scream.

"Nay!" she wept loudly. "He will make me fall!"

Gray tried to soothe the terrified girl. "Nay, sweetheart," she assured her. "He is here to help. Take hold of him."

Brooke sobbed loudly as the knight was lowered. Gray glanced over at the older knight; he had a good grip on the younger man's ankles but it was taking all of his strength to lower him. Just as it looked as if he was having a rough time of it, more men burst through the foliage and the older knight snapped orders to them; a tall, red-haired knight went to his aid, grabbing hold of the legs of the other and helping to lower him while two men –at-arms stood by the man who was now lowered over the edge of the cliff by about three—quarters of his body length. The knight dangling over the side called back to the others.

"She is too far out of my reach," he called. "I need another seven or eight feet to get to her."

Gray suddenly remembered the apron and hose rope in her hand and she thrust it at one of the men-at-arms.

"Here," she gave it to him. "He can use this. She can grab hold of it."

The soldier took it, handing it down to the knight as the others struggled to hold him. The knight wrapped one end around his forearm securely as he dangled the end to the girl.

"My lady?" he called to her, oddly formal under such peculiar circumstances. "Take the rope. Grab hold!"

Brooke peeped an eye open; the rope had fallen against her arm and she instinctively grabbed it. But in doing so, she suddenly lost her balance and, with a mighty scream, slipped right off the rocks. She had a strong hold on the hose rope, but she screamed like a banshee as she dangled forty feet above the foaming waters of the falls.

The knight had the other end of the rope wrapped several times around his forearm. He wasn't concerned that he would let go, but he was very concerned that the young girl would let go. She was thrashing about, screaming, and he called down to her steadily.

"Stop kicking, my lady," he commanded. "Hold fast and we will pull you up."

Gray, standing at the edge of the cliff, watched the scene unfold with her heart in her throat. "Brooke, stop thrashing!" she begged, looking to the men who were struggling to pull her up. "Please; pull her up quickly!"

The older knight knew that; God help him, he did. But the grass beneath his feet was giving way as he and the tall, red-headed knight pulled back steadily. The tall knight lost his footing in the slick grass and ended up on his knees, but together, they managed to pull the knight and the lady back from the boiling brink of madness. Once the younger, blond haired knight was able to get his footing, he pulled the young lady to the edge of the cliff where the two men at arms grabbed her by both arms.

They hauled the hysterical girl onto the grass where her mother collapsed beside her, pulling her into her arms. The young girl wept loudly as her mother comforted her with compassion, with gratefulness. Everyone could breathe again now that the girl was safe and if one listened closely, a collective sigh of relief could be heard.

"You are safe now, sweetheart," Gray whispered, holding her daughter tightly. "Stop crying. You are safe."

The knights were winded, wiping sweat and mud from their faces, watching the exchange. They were spent but relieved they could contribute to a happy ending; when they had first heard the screaming from their encampment to the south, they had no idea what they would find. Truth be told, screaming women were never a good thing. Not one of them would deny that there had been a bit of apprehension as they had followed the sounds.

"Is she all right?" the older knight asked.

Gray allowed her daughter to weep for a few moments longer before pulling back, holding her child's face between her hands and looking hard at her. "Are you well?"

The girl sniffled, sobbed, wiped at her cheeks. "I... I am not hurt."

"What happened?"

Brooke shrugged. "I am not sure," she gasped. "I was looking at the water and suddenly I slipped. I guess I drew too close to the edge."

Gray smiled gently, feeling quite weak with relief. She honestly hadn't been sure she would ever share a moment like this again with her child, the tender embrace between a mother and her offspring. It was heavenly, something that renewed her spirit.

"I would say that is a fair assessment," she murmured, kissing her daughter's wet cheek. "Now, stop weeping and thank these brave men who have come to your aid, for without them, you and I would have surely been in a predicament."

Brooke was struggling to calm. As the minutes passed and she realized she wasn't dead at the bottom of the falls, she simply felt ill and somewhat shocked. She allowed her mother to pull her to shaky legs, all the while turning her focus to the three knights standing a few feet away. Her gaze found the big knight with the long blond hair, the one who had risked himself to save her. Shaken, she tried to curtsy but it came out quite unsteady. She almost tipped over in the attempt.

"Th-thank you," she sniffed. "You saved my life."

The young knight smiled at her. "It was my pleasure, my lady."

"What is your name?"

"Sir Dallas Aston," he indicated the men standing next to him. "This towering man with the red hair is Sir Geoff de Mandeville and the third knight is our liege, Sir Braxton de Nerra."

Brooke regarded the three of them carefully; her savior, with his striking good looks, the tall knight with the dark red hair, and the muscular knight with the graying blond hair. They gazed

11

back at her with varying degrees of kindness and curiosity, which began to stir Brooke's spirits. It was rare when she was exposed to men, and certainly rarer still with men of this caliber. She knew just by looking at them that they were chivalrous, powerful knights that all ladies dream of. Her heart stirred a little more at the thought of these strong men saving her. It almost made the memory of the event pleasant; it would certainly make a good story in years to come.

"I am the Lady Brooke Serroux," she seemed to be perking up a little. "Perhaps you will share sup with us tonight so we can properly thank you. Can we invite them, Mama? Please?"

With the focus suddenly on her, Gray was uncomfortable. She hesitated in her reply. "Of course we should, but perhaps Sir Braxton and his men have other plans. I am sure they are very busy and we have taken enough of their time."

Brooke turned her sweet face to Braxton, the leader of the knights. Her eyes lit up.

"Do you have other plans?" she asked hopefully. "Could you come and stay with us tonight? Perhaps you could tell us about your dangerous adventures."

"Brooke," Gray chided softly, quieting her. She looked at the knight. "I am sorry, my lord. She is an eager young girl and has not learned the art of tact yet. I am sure you are far too busy to sup with us."

Braxton met her gaze. "My men and I are on our way to Kendal. But we would be honored to sup with you tonight if you would be kind enough to have us."

Brooke looked thrilled. Gray looked pale. "We... we do not set a fine table, my lord," Gray insisted weakly; she knew it was a losing battle. "I am sure you must be accustomed to much finer accommodations."

Braxton did not pick up on her reluctant tone. "My lady, the woods are our usual accommodations. Supping beneath a roof would be as grand as we could imagine."

She just looked at him. Then she forced a smile. "We would be honored, my lord."

Her disinclination suddenly came clear to him. Not wanting to be a burdensome guest, he sought to make his presence more attractive. "We have all manner of bounty that we have hunted from these woods. Just this morning, we downed a three point buck. It should be enough food for an army. We shall bring all that we have and share it with our gracious hosts."

Brooke clapped her hands. "Meat!" she said gleefully. "It has been a long time since we've had such a treat. Oh! I must retrieve my berries. I dropped them when I slipped."

She was off. Gray tried to stop her, to at least admonish her from getting too close to the edge again, but Brooke wasn't listening. The falls roared, drowning out the mother's pleas. Brooke collected her basket, near the edge of the cliff, and quickly backed off. But off to her right she caught sight of a bush with fat black berries and she darted in that direction. Gray watched her daughter, looking to the knights after a moment with some uncertainty.

"My thanks to you again, gentle knights," she said in her soft, sultry voice. "I... I suppose I should collect my own basket. I dropped it somewhere in the trees." She looked back over at her daughter, now busy several feet away yanking berries off the bush. "Come along, young woman; 'tis time to leave. Do you hear me?"

Braxton put up a hand. "I will collect your daughter, madam. You go and find your basket."

Gray was a little unsure about leaving the minding of her daughter to a stranger, but she reckoned that the mere fact he had just saved Brooke's life warranted some amount of trust. Still, she couldn't help her natural suspicion; she wasn't trusting by nature, especially with men.

She hesitated and Braxton saw it; in spite of their altruistic intentions, he was well aware that they were all strangers. Now that the terror of her daughter's predicament had passed, an odd suspicion was settling. He was positive the woman would turn and run from them given half a chance and it occurred to him that he had not particularly eased the situation. Now that the chaos had settled, he realized that he didn't even know her name.

Braxton's gaze lingered on her. "To whom do I have the pleasure of addressing, madam?"

She looked puzzled. "My lord?"

"Your name, lady. I do not know your name."

Embarrassment crossed her lovely face. "My apologies, my lord," she said. "I am the Lady Gray Serroux."

"Gray? Of the Northumberland Grays?"

She nodded her head. "My mother is of the family. She named me Gray in honor of the House."

He understood more clearly. "Gray is your Christian name?"

"I was christened Gray Isabella."

It was as unusual and beautiful as she was. Somehow, she didn't look like an Elizabeth or Elinor or Anne. He studied the woman for a moment; he simply couldn't help himself. Her features were angelic with her lusciously smooth skin, round cheeks and pert nose. She had long blond hair, lush and pillowy lips, and eyes of the most amazing amber color. He could have gazed into those eyes forever; in fact, the only word that came to mind when he looked at her was exquisite. Like a goddess descended, she had him in her spell whether or not she knew it. Like a baited fish, Braxton was hooked.

"Lady Gray," he smiled at her, not realizing his men were looking between him and the lady, realizing their liege was quite smitten with her. "It is a pleasure making your acquaintance even under these harsh circumstances. If you will permit me, I will collect your daughter for you and escort you both back to Erith."

He sounded so sincere; Gray would have had a difficult time refusing him in any case. Although her natural suspicion and reserve screamed for her to resist the man and his attempts, somehow, she wasn't able to. Perhaps it was because he had saved her only child or perhaps it was simply because she was growing stupid in her old age. Whatever the case, she went in search of the basket she had dropped on her wild run to Brooke's aid, all the while thinking on the broad knight with the blue-green eyes.

Braxton watched Gray wander back into the trees, whistling softly at one of his men to go with her for protection. Geoff took the order and followed the lady as Dallas and the men at arms moved back in the direction of their encampment. With everyone on the move, Braxton went after Lady Brooke.

She was yanking berries off a stubborn branch that refused to give way. Braxton walked up beside her and she glanced over at him, smiling as she popped off a resistant berry and put it in her basket. Braxton returned her smile politely.

"Are you ready to go, my lady?" he asked. "A feast awaits you."

Brooke's delicate eyebrows lifted. "Feast? What feast?"

He pointed at the basket. "Those are a start."

She looked at the berries and shrugged. "Berries are not a feast, although these berries are very sweet. We return here every year." She glanced over her shoulder toward the direction of the roaring falls; she could see the spray billowing up over the tops of the foliage. "Although I suppose now we will never return here. My mother will be afraid I will end up in peril again."

Braxton lifted his eyebrows. "You were indeed in a quandary. How did you slip, anyway?"

Brooke shrugged irritably; for someone who was close to dying just a few minutes earlier, she had bounced back admirably, which was a tribute to her young resilience.

"I do not know," she said with some irritation, as if he had asked a probing question. "What matters is that my mother will no longer trust me now. She already treats me like a child. Now she will never let me out of her sight again."

He wriggled his eyebrows. "It is only because she does not want to see you come to harm. As you have discovered, wandering alone out here in the woods can more than likely invite that."

Brooke lifted an eyebrow. He could read in her expression that she believed he was siding with her mother. "I am not a child," she said indignantly. "My grandmother says that I am a woman. And I am."

Braxton didn't dare smile, though he wanted to. "I see. And

15

what does your father say?"

She jutted her chin in the air. "My father is no longer alive but, if he was, I am sure he would agree that I am a woman grown. And I do not need my mother to nursemaid my every move."

She was certainly a spitfire. But he realized that her statement brought him pleasure; so her mother was a widow. Braxton didn't know why he felt joyful about it, but he did.

"Be that as it may, I am sure your mother is only doing what she feels is best," he glanced over to the distant tree line where Lady Gray and Geoff had disappeared. "Shall we go and find her?"

Brooke frowned, shrugged, and then finally relented. Braxton took her arm gently, escorting her towards the tree line and away from the treacherous falls. Brooke stole glances at him when she thought he wasn't looking.

"What are you doing here?" she asked; there was nothing greater than the curiosity of a fifteen-year-old. "Where do you come from?"

His blue-green eyes fixed on her. "My men are camped on the other side of the trees down there to the south," he said. "And I come from Northumbria."

"Does your family live there?"

"My father lives there."

"Do you live with him?"

He shook his head. "I do not live anywhere."

She was puzzled. "But you are a knight. Surely you have a House."

They approached the edge of the trees where Braxton had last seen Lady Gray. "I am a knight bannerette," he said simply. "I am not sworn to one particular liege."

Brooke was quickly forgetting about her near-death experience, now focused on Braxton's life story. "You are a bachelor knight?" she asked, awed. "So you travel everywhere and fight for whomever you wish. How exciting! Have you been to many wonderful places?"

"Nay, lass, I am not a bachelor knight," he corrected her. "I said that I am a knight bannerette; there is a difference. Bachelor knights do not have men sworn to them. I have one hundred and eighty. And yes, I have been to many wonderful places."

She was gazing up at him openly. "I would like to travel someday," she said. "I would like to go to Paris."

The corner of his lips twitched. "It is a grand place. Surely your husband will take you there someday."

She looked away from him with a haughty expression so suited to young adults. "Aye, he will take me there, and anywhere else I want to go. I will marry a very rich man."

"Is that so? Tell me; have you already selected this mountain of wealth?"

She shook her head. "Not yet," she looked at him, pausing, her gaze alternately eager and hesitant. "Do you want to know a secret?"

"What is that?"

"My grandmother has already invited several houses to vie for my hand. My mother does not even know!"

It was scandalous; he could tell just by the way she was smirking. "Why would your grandmother not tell your mother?" he wanted to know.

Brooke was still playing the haughty young lady. "I already told you; because my mother would keep me a child for the rest of my life."

"You *are* young."

Her delicate features clouded with defiance. "My mother was only fourteen years of age when she married my father. I am a whole year older."

"A whole year," he repeated, his tone laced with sarcasm. "Practically an old woman."

"Aye," the girl insisted, missing the patronizing lilt. "Besides, my grandmother wants me to assume my rightful place."

"As what?"

She looked at him as if he were daft. "As a great nobleman's wife, of course. Grandmother says I am the only hope our family has."

It didn't make much sense to him, but then again, very little pertaining to women ever did. Before Braxton could reply, they began to hear movement in the trees and looked over to see Gray and Geoff approaching.

Braxton's blue-green gaze fixed on the luscious woman approaching, feeling such a strong attraction to her that he couldn't begin to describe it. Brooke, apparently unwilling to wait for her mother, began to follow Geoff as the man walked past them, heading towards the south in the direction that the other men had taken a few minutes earlier. But Braxton waited for Gray, smiling politely as she approached with the big basket of fruit on her arm.

Gray returned his smile weakly, hesitantly; as the minutes ticked by and the realization of guests at tonight's meal weighed more heavily upon her, she had been scrambling to think of an excuse or a reason to discourage Sir Braxton from attending. For a family that subsisted on only the very basic necessities, guests were out of the question. An army was impossible. Before she could speak, however, Braxton interrupted her thoughts.

"I will again thank you for your generous invitation to sup, my lady," he said pleasantly. "It is not often we are afforded the luxury of a private home."

Oh, Lord, she thought to herself. *How can I ^ the man and not offend him?* But her smile grew at his statement, forced as it was.

"As I said, we do not set a fancy table," she replied. "We live… simply."

He waved her off. "Not to worry," he reiterated. "The buck we have can feed an army and then some. "

She was still resistant, struggling not to insult his generosity. "Truly, my lord, you are too kind," she said. "You do not have to provide us with food from your precious stores. Surely your men will require that food on your travels."

"My men have more food than they can eat," he said. "Hunting is something of a sport for them. We are glad to share what we have."

"If you are certain it will be no hardship."

"Not at all."

18

There wasn't much more that Gray to say to that. Feeling somewhat ill and resigned, she began to walk with Braxton taking up pace at a respectable distance next to her. They walked in silenced for a few moments before Brooke suddenly re-emerged from the trees, heading in their direction. Gray looked curiously at her daughter as the girl approached.

"What is it, sweetheart?" she asked. "I thought you walked on ahead."

Brooke shrugged. "There are gangs of soldiers down at the bottom of the hill and I assumed you would become angry if I just walked into the midst of them, so I came back."

Gray's brow furrowed. "Gangs of soldiers?"

Braxton was looking at the young girl, so defiant of her mother yet inherently obedient in spite of herself. "My men," Braxton explained. "We camped down the hill to the south."

Gray nodded in understanding, watching her daughter take up position on Braxton's left side as they trudged through the trees. Brooke wasn't looking at her mother, however; she was focused on Braxton.

"You said that you have traveled a great deal," she said eagerly. "Have you ever been to Rome? I have heard that there are buildings made with gold. Is that true? And is it also true that the streets are made of white marble?"

Gray thought her daughter was being rather pushy with her demanding tone. "Brooke Elizabeth, you will mind yourself," she said quietly but firmly. "Sir Braxton is our guest and I will not have you hound him."

"But I was simply asking him a question, Mama," Brooke insisted. "Why can I not ask him a question?"

A faint smile on his lips, Braxton focused on the young lady. "Lady Brooke," he said in his deep, quiet voice. "I will speak until the dawn on whatever you wish to know, but we must make it back to your castle first. If you will direct me to your palfrey, we can be along our way."

"We do not have a palfrey," Brooke said before her mother could reply. "We walked."

"Walked from where?"

"Castle Erith," Gray said, watching his piercing gaze turn to her. "It is a few miles to the south."

A light of awareness came to his eyes. "The fortress that sits on the rise near the crossroads?"

"Aye."

He didn't say what he was thinking; the structure they had passed on their way north was massive and derelict. He thought it had been abandoned and was rather surprised to discover it was their home. From the outward appearance of the structure, he was sure they did not have the means to feed almost two hundred men. But all he could manage to say was: "That was a long walk."

Gray shrugged. "It was a lovely morning. It was no hardship."

He looked away, back in the direction of his encampment. "My men and I will escort you home."

Braxton took hold of Gray's elbow with his free hand, a gentle and knightly gesture. Gray, unsure how to respond, simply did as he bade.

The past several minutes had been slightly odd, given the knight's sudden appearance and Brooke's strange attraction to him. She did not want to be rude, but she also did not want to invite trouble into her home. It wasn't just the fact that they couldn't feed two hundred men; it was the simple fact that Erith had no army and no protection. With Braxton's army flooding her castle, they would have no way of defending themselves against one hundred and eighty soldiers. She could have spanked Brooke silly for her suggestion. But on the other hand, as a properly bred woman, hosting weary travelers was part of her calling. She could not turn them away.

Trapped, she attempted to think of a plausible explanation as to why his men could not enter the gates of Erith. She could not think of anything that did not sound rude or suspicious. Even when Braxton mounted her on his own fine charger for the ride home, she continued to think of a way out of this. The closer they drew to Erith, the more panicked she became.

By the time they entered the crumbling ward, she had lost the battle completely.

CHAPTER TWO

Braxton's first impression of the massive and imposing Castle Erith was that it had once been a beautiful place that had aged very badly. It appeared to be a few hundred years old with its mossy stones and degenerating façade, but he knew that it was not as old as it looked.

The castle had been built by King John during the early part of the last century to seduce a northern baron for his support. When the allegiance had fallen apart and the castle abandoned, it had eventually fallen into the hands of Simon de Montfort during his relationship with Henry III. As Braxton and his men rode upon the massive, crumbling walls, he drew in the view of what had once been, for a short time, a mighty place.

The castle had been named Erith after the waterfalls three miles to the north, the very falls that had almost claimed Brooke's life. The fortress possessed the unusual feature of concentric walls; a shorter outer wall encircled a taller inner wall with five towers built into it. The place was oddly shaped, too, with five sides to it.

Passing through the non-existent outer gate and an equally rotted inner gate, the ward was fairly small and there was a single keep to the northwest side, soaring three stories to the sky. Other than the keep, the ward was fairly devoid of structures but for haphazard stables built against the western wall. There were a few servants milling about, dressed in rags, terrified of the army now entering their domain.

Although the entire picture was a sobering sight, Braxton did not voice his opinion to the lady. It would not due to insult his hostess. He positioned his men near the outer gates and placed his five massive provisions wagons up against the outer wall. Each wagon had its own force of men to protect the contents. He made sure to settle his men and wagons before helping the lady off his charger.

"Your men may make themselves comfortable where they will," Gray told him. "I am afraid the keep is not big enough for all of them, though some may find shelter in the great hall if they wish."

"Your hospitality is very much appreciated, my lady," he said. "I will have my men bring the meat around to the kitchen."

"The kitchen is to the rear of the keep."

He nodded his thanks and she excused herself along with her daughter. Braxton's gaze lingered on her shapely form as she made her way across the bailey and up the rotted wooden stairs into the keep. He thought it rather comical how Brooke kept pausing to look at him and Gray kept shoving her daughter onward.

"Any orders, my lord?"

A voice from behind broke him from his thoughts. His next in command and the man who had saved young Brooke's life, Dallas, had asked the question. Braxton thought a moment before replying.

"Make sure the men are properly settled and the wagons guarded. And have someone bring that buck around to the kitchens."

Dallas moved smartly to do his lord's bidding. He was young, quiet, immensely strong and capable. He was also quite handsome with shoulder-length blond hair and blue eyes, sending many a maiden's heart fluttering. But he was more focused on his duties than on women at this point in his life, something that worked well in Braxton's favor. As Dallas began barking orders, the men moved towards the inner wall to set up camp within its shadow. With a final glance at the entrance to the keep, Braxton gathered the reins of his black charger and moved off after his men.

They were a hard-core bunch, used to travel, and therefore quite efficient when it came to setting up camp. Braxton had two squires, orphaned brothers, who would tend to his personal set up. One of them, the younger brother called Edgar, took Braxton's charger and led the animal away to feed it. Braxton alternately watched his men settle in and observed the keep.

"The men will set up camp as directed, my lord," came a voice. "Are there any further orders?"

The inquiry came from Sir Graehm de Leron, another of Braxton's knights. Graehm's question lingered in Braxton's mind as his blue-green eyes roved the inner wall of Erith. Ideas were beginning to take hold.

"There might be," he said after a moment. Then he started to walk. "I shall return."

Braxton crossed the compound, leaving Graehm staring curiously after him. The stables were several yards before him, ramshackle but serviceable. There were a couple of horses, three goats and a cow. He was moderately surprised to see livestock in such a poverty-stricken castle. The four big chargers that belonged to Braxton and his knights were being watered by the squires and made the other animals nervous. He could hear the bleats of fear.

Braxton inspected the stable supports and studied the roof. It was thatched adequately, and had obviously been repaired many times. He moved on, finding his way around behind the keep and into the kitchen area. There was a fairly large garden off to his left and an exterior oven built into the wall several feet to the right of the garden. There were at least four kitchen servants going about their tasks, all women, and two of those were tied up tending the buck that his men had just delivered. It was a heavy thing and the old women were having trouble handling the weight, but they managed.

There was a ground floor entrance to the keep from the kitchen. It opened into the bottom story of the structure, divided into two rooms, which were used for stores. A ladder led up to a trap door in the ceiling, which presumably led to the hall above. Peering inside the gloomy, cool store room, Braxton could see that what little they had was neatly stacked and carefully covered. It was coming clear to him why Lady Gray had seem so reluctant to offer a meal to him and his men; it was apparent they barely had enough for themselves. Now they would have to, literally, feed an army. With that thought, he went back to where his men were camped.

A couple of fires were already started in the shadows of the outer wall. Braxton found Dallas, Graehm and Geoff standing together and talking quietly between them. He motioned his men to him, away from the others.

"My lord?" Dallas asked in response to Braxton's furrowed expression.

Braxton threw a thumb in the direction of the keep. "I believe we've made a mistake in coming here," he said. "Do any of you notice anything unusual about this place?"

The knights looked at each other. "Other than the fact it is crumbling around us?" Graehm asked.

"These people can hardly afford to feed us," Braxton lowered his voice. "From the looks of it, they can barely feed themselves. Our presence here is burdensome and presumptive."

His knights still weren't sure what he was driving at. "Should we leave, my lord?" Geoff asked tentatively.

Braxton's pale gaze drifted across the wall over their heads. "Nay," he said after a moment. "But we will make our stay here worth their while."

"What do you mean?" Graehm asked.

Braxton crooked a finger and his men gathered close.

***

Constance Gray de Montfort had been a beauty in her time. A slight woman with graying blond hair piled high on her head, the family resemblance to her daughter and granddaughter was apparent. She was a cool woman, bluntly so, bred from the high nobility of England. Though her circumstances had been reduced to poverty over the years, she still retained a haughty manner and a piercing gaze that could drill holes through walls.

As Constance gazed out of the lancet window facing the section of the bailey where the mercenary army was settling in, her mind was working in a thousand different directions. If nothing else, Constance had learned over the years to be very resourceful to ensure her family's survival. And she had learned not to discount any opportunity.

"What do we know of this knight?" she asked her daughter.

Gray was seated on the only chair in the room, mending in her hands. Once her father's solar, it was now a sad reflection of its glorious past. Anything of value had been stripped and sold, even things of sentimental value. But Gray had long gotten over the sorrow that selling her father's items had provoked.

"His name is Braxton de Nerra," Gray said as she struggled with an uncooperative piece of thread. "He told Brooke that he is a knight bannerette. Beyond that, I do not know."

Constance's cool gaze lingered on the men in the distance. "A knight bannerette," she snorted softly. "Hardly a man of noble breeding. Why on earth did you not refute your daughter when she offered him shelter and sup?"

Gray was used to her mother's disapproval at her actions. That was normal. "I told you; it would have been rude to do so. The man had just saved Brooke's life and I felt as if we had to do something to thank him. Moreover, they have brought their own food. It is not as if we shall be feeding them from our stores. We shall even eat meat. Do you know how long it has been since we have eaten meat?"

Constance turned away from the window, pulling her tattered shawl more tightly around her thin shoulders. "I shall not join you for sup," she said imperiously. "I will take my meal in my room."

Gray did not look up from her mending. "Though we rarely have visitors, Mother, you have always taught me that the true mark of nobility is impeccable manners. It would be unmannerly of you not to at least greet our guest."

"You'll not lecture me," Constance snapped softly. "I know more of nobility and manners than you could ever hope to."

"Then you will attend us."

"I shall do as I please."

The last exchange was spoken sharply, the words overlapping.

Gray would not acknowledge her mother's disdainful words. She had long learned to deal with her supercilious mother who still fancied herself a fine lady of wealth and power. In tense silence, Gray finished mending the girdle, one that had belonged to her and she now modified for Brooke. Her daughter was growing by leaps and bounds, developing the figure of a woman that must be property outfitted. Though it was an old girdle, it was still serviceable. They certainly could not afford to buy another one. Biting off the thread, she collected her things and stood up.

"Then I shall excuse myself to see to the preparation of the meal," she knew her mother would not fight her for the task. "I would hope you change your mind about attending us."

Constance didn't reply. Her silence was her dismissal. She listened to her daughter walk from the room, her well-worn shoes making scuffing noises along the boards. She continued to gaze out over the ward, watching the men in the corner of the bailey, noting that they did not appear ragged or impoverish as traveling armies sometimes did. In fact, she had counted four big chargers adorned with expensive saddlery. Poor knights could hardly afford a horse much less lavish tack. And the knights themselves, that she had been able to see, were clad in well-made armor. These mercenaries were well-supplied and apparently with some means of wealth.

Men such as these did not usually take wives, but with the promise of a fortress as the dowry, even a traveling soldier might consider. In fact, being that these men fought for money, the lure of monetary or material gain was their primary motivation. Constance began to see a positive side to their presence.

She reconsidered her decision not to join them for sup.

***

The great hall of Erith had once been a fine place back in the days when men of power inhabited its stone walls. It was still the nicest room in the keep, but that wasn't an overwhelming statement. The hearth had been built as in the olden days, a massive fire pit in the center of the room that emptied smoke into the ceiling. The hall itself was two stories tall; consequently, the second and third floors of the keep butted up along the south side of the hall and were a single room a piece. Both rooms were reached by a narrow spiral stair case, one stacked upon the other.

Gray had spent a good deal of time preparing the great hall for their visitors. The grand old dame would once again come alive with guests, as it had in ages past. Though still wary of the mercenary army's presence, she found herself increasingly excited as she prepared the room. It wasn't often they had visitors, and she was looking forward to having someone new to talk to. Perhaps there would be news of the happenings through the realm. Isolated as Erith was, information was few and far between.

As far as they knew, Longshanks still ruled, though he had been in poor health for some time. The Scots were creating issues as far south as York, but had thankfully missed Erith, to the west of York although still considered a part of the disputed north. The landscape of their region of Cumbria was thickly wooded and off the beaten path. In spite of their regional location, they were protected by the barrier of the Pennine Mountains from the turmoil that gripped the rest of country.

The buck that Braxton's men had brought had been roasting over an enormous pit in the kitchen yard for several hours, creating a heavenly smell of roasting venison. Gray had been in the kitchen when two of the knights who had helped rescue Brooke brought in other supplies – dried fruits, jerky, barley meal, and a large sack of flour. And not just any flour; it was finely sifted white flour. Gray had been momentarily speechless, but quickly found her tongue and graciously thanked the knights. Dallas and Geoff bowed graciously and left the kitchen yard just as swiftly as they had entered it.

The cook, a fat woman with a strange habit of howling like an animal, was delighted with the supplies. She hooted for her daughter and immediate began preparing the flour to bake fine white bread for their sup. The woman's equally bizarre daughter joined her and Gray left the two hooting and barking as she continued her duties.

The sunset was creating ribbons of orange and pink across the sky, signaling the onset of a lovely night. Normally, Gray was so busy with never-ending chores that she scarcely had time to notice such things. But she gazed up at the sky, enjoying the colors, her mind eased that they would actually be enjoying a satisfying meal this night. In spite of her caution regarding the mercenary army, they had thus far provided Erith with much appreciated supplies and her resistance to them was beginning to wane. Perhaps she was being too harsh. Perhaps she should be more thankful and less suspicious.

Deep in thought, she wandered from the kitchen yard and into the main bailey. The keep was to her left, a big stone tower that was too cold in both summer and winter. Passing the stables, she kicked a few scrawny chickens out of her way and nearly tripped over a broken piece of some kind of farming tool. Reaching down to pick it up, she propped the piece of wood on a small fence near the stables.

Continuing on, she rounded the keep and ran headlong into several of de Nerra's men. She recognized two of the knights but there was another knight standing with them that she had not met yet. They were a young group, perhaps her age or younger, yet they radiated the aura of seasoned men. All three men bowed graciously to her as she passed, but their interest was apparent. She was uncomfortable with the way they stared at her. Suddenly nervous, she bobbed her head politely and turned for the keep, running headlong into Braxton.

She plowed right into him. He reached out to steady her as she stumbled back. "My apologies, my lady," he said with genuine remorse. "Did I injure you?"

Gray rubbed her nose where she had bashed it against his chest. "Nay, my lord," she said, feeling her nerves and anxious to return to the safety of the keep. "I... I was hoping to find you and thank you for the flour and other provisions that your men

29

brought. It was quite unnecessary, but very generous nonetheless."

Braxton's blue-green eyes fixed on her. "We carry more rations than we can use. If you do not use them, they will rot, so in a sense you are doing us a favor."

She smoothed the hair from her forehead in an edgy gesture. "It was a kind deed, my lord. We should have quite a feast in about an hour."

"We are looking forward to it."

Though his expression was unreadable, the blue-green eyes were intense. Strangely unsettled, not to mention strangely intrigued, Gray dipped in a curtsey and respectfully moved around him.

It wasn't that he frightened her, but he certainly had a disquieting effect on her. There was something in his eyes that was warm and alarming at the same time. Not knowing the man, she did not trust his motives. She'd spent her entire adult life protecting her emotions, first from her domineering mother and then from an abusive husband. She knew of no other way but to continue that inclination. No mere knight, no matter how kind, was going to change that.

As she moved towards the rotted steps leading into the keep, Gray could not help but notice that there were several of Braxton's soldiers taking tools to her steps. She slowed her pace, watching them curiously. Several rotted boards had been pulled off and a two of the men were using a plane on them, shaving off the rotted portion. The others were ripping up the rusted iron nails and replacing them with fresh ones. Curiosity turned to bewilderment. She went to one of the men and peered over his shoulder.

"What are you doing?" she asked.

The soldier looked up at her; he was older, with a sun-kissed face and calloused fingers. "Repairing your stairs, m'lady," he said. "You have several rotted boards. Sooner or later, someone will fall through and hurt themselves. Sir Braxton does not wish it to be you or your daughter."

Gray's mouth fell open in surprise, but she quickly shut it. "So you are fixing my steps?"

"We are repairing what we can for tonight, my lady," the man replied. "Tomorrow we shall go into the woods to seek out strong new wood in which to rebuild the stair case. This entire flight needs to be replaced before someone breaks their neck."

Did they think she could pay them for this work? Clearly, the steps were in bad repair, but it was not for lack of notice. It was for lack of funds to fix them. Panicked, Gray turned on her heel and rushed back to the last place she had seen Braxton. Frantically, she her eyes scanned the area, spying his blond head several feet away. He was standing with his knights. One of the men saw her as she approached and he nudged Braxton. He turned to her just as she came upon them.

"My lady," he greeted her, the warmth still lingering in the blue-green eyes. "How may I be...?"

She cut him off, not intentionally, but it was a rushed gesture. "My lord," she didn't seem to quite know what to say; all she knew was that she had to say it quickly so he could stop his men on the stairs. "Your men are... that is, may I speak you in private, my lord?"

The three knights standing with Braxton immediately excused themselves. Braxton crossed his thick arms, allowing his gaze to move over her luscious blond hair, the sweet shape of her face. She had deliciously delicate features. But he quickly focused on her eyes, a magnificent brownish-gold color, and waited patiently for her to speak. She stood there and fidgeted uncomfortably for several long moments before commencing.

"Your men are... are fixing my steps, my lord," she lowered her voice. "As much as I appreciate the gesture, I am afraid... that is to say, those repairs were something we intended to do when we... well, perhaps before winter sometime we were...."

She was stammering and her cheeks were flushed. Braxton's lips curled into a smile. "You are welcome."

She stopped stammering and stared at him. "What?"

"I said that you are welcome."

Her cheeks flushed a deeper shade of pink. "Of course, it is a most generous gesture, but we cannot... what I mean is that I do not have the means to compensate you for this work."

His smile broadened. "Your generous hospitality this night more than compensates me for the work."

She gazed up at him with eyes that were mesmerizing. "But you have provided the entire meal, my lord," her nervousness was lessening, making way for a tone of wonderment. "All we are doing is providing the means by which to cook it."

"And you are providing your home and your company, of which I am most appreciative." It occurred to him what had her so rattled; she thought he would expect payment for the repair and he hastened to assure her that was not the case. "My lady, you took pity on a host of weary men. Your generosity outweighs any meager chores we could do for you. In fact, before we leave, I intend that we should do much more to thank you for your graciousness."

She was astonished. "But... we would have done the same for any weary traveler. There is no need to rebuild Erith in order to thank me."

He laughed softly, his teeth straight and white. "By the time my men and I are finished, you will not recognize this place."

"But why?"

"I told you why. Because you are kind and hospitable."

Gray wasn't sure what more she could say, but one thing was for certain; he was doing far more than he should. A glance over her shoulder showed that several of Braxton's men were taking a look at the rotten portcullis on the inner wall, gesturing to the working mechanisms and obviously discussing how to remediate it. She took another look around the bailey and realized that his men were spread out everywhere, surveying the decay and already making attempts to repair it. She turned to Braxton, shaking her head slowly.

"You do too much, my lord."

His smile faded, the blue-green orbs gaining in intensity. "I am just getting started."

She gazed into his eyes, wondering why this man should be so kind to her. A great part of her was deeply touched, yet another part of her, the protective part, was still very wary.

"I do not mean to seem ungrateful, my lord," she said quietly. "'Tis simply that guests do not normally work for their hosts to pay for their meal and board. Some people might take it as an insult."

"Do you?"

She lifted her slender shoulders. "Nay. But I am not sure how I can possibly repay you."

His smile returned. "As I said, a good meal and good company is payment enough. It is rare in my line of work that we experience pleasantries and such an event is priceless. We are very glad to do what we can for you to repay such graciousness."

Gray did not know what more to say. She should probably stop him, but she couldn't seem to muster the will. He seemed thoughtful and sincere; it was hard to refute him. He made it sound as if she was the one doing him the favor. Braxton's men were distributed in small groups out all over the fortress, working on various things – the stable roof, the portcullis on the inner wall, and there were several up on the outer wall inspecting the crumbling stone. She stood there a moment, drinking in the activity, allowing herself to feel just the slightest bit touched by his actions. It was an odd, warm feeling that she'd never before experienced.

When she looked back at him, her cheeks were flushed with gratitude. She was not accustomed to someone showing her such kindness and, although she should have still been rightfully suspicious, there was something in his manner that put her at ease.

She hoped that she would not regret it.

CHAPTER THREE

As Gray had planned, the grand hall of Erith was resplendent with light and fresh rushes as it had once been when times were more plentiful. More than the appearance of the hall, it was the mood of it. Standing in the main entrance to the hall and clad in the finest surcoat she owned, a faded yellow silk, Gray stood a moment and absorbed the ghost of the once-great hall; the days when Simon de Montfort and his beloved Eleanor sat at the dais, or when great nobles of the north gathered to feast over a victory greatly won. She could hear their laughter and feel their spirit. It was something she'd not felt in a very long time.

The servants had brought all of the precious fat candles in the keep into the hall so that they would not have to dip into the stores for them. Consequently, the rest of the keep was in blackness. Gray had dressed by firelight from the hearth in the old but clean surcoat that had once belonged to her grandmother. It was sorely out of date but it was the best she had. With her blond hair pulled away from her face and secured with another heirloom comb that had once belonged to the wealthy Grays, she had cleaned up rather well. And old bronze mirror in her room told her so. For a woman who had seen twenty-nine sometimes difficult years, she was as beautiful and youthful as she had ever been.

Brooke was still finishing her dress. It took the girl hours sometimes to dress, a strange occurrence considering they had nowhere to go. It wasn't as if she was fancying herself for a great gala. But Brooke took great pains to brush her hair just so, or put a precious ribbon on a bodice that had seen better days. There wasn't a day that passed that Gray wished she could give her daughter all of the pretty things she longed for. Even though there was no use in wishing for what they did not have, still, it did not prevent her from feeling guilt or sadness for her daughter's plight.

A few of the servants were beginning to bring out the loaves of bread. The rich smell of the baked goods filled the hall and Gray inhaled deeply. As she moved into the room to speak to one of the women about the shortage of wooden cups that would undoubtedly be facing them, Braxton and his men entered the keep. She heard their voices before she saw their faces, and a cluster of powerful men soon came from the entry and spilled into the great hall.

Braxton was the first face she recognized. His blue-green eyes focused on her immediately and, as a good hostess, she went to greet him and his men. Dipping in a graceful curtsy, she smiled timidly.

"Welcome, my lords," she said to Braxton, to the group. "You may take a seat anywhere. The meal will be served shortly."

The men thanked her silently. Gray's gaze moved across the line of men; tall, blond and handsome Sir Dallas, shorter and stocker Sir Graehm, and very tall and sinewy Sir Geoffrey. Slightly behind the knights stood two brown-haired boys, perhaps a year or two older than Brooke. Their eyes were roving about the room, wide-eyed and curious of their surroundings.

The knights excused themselves and the young squires with them, drifting towards the long table and selecting their best spots. Braxton, however, continued to stand in front of Gray. She felt somewhat self-conscious, feeling his heady gaze upon her.

"Where do you sit, my lady?" he asked.

She gestured towards the worn table. "Usually at the end. There is oft much to do and I must be able to move from the table freely."

He lifted an eyebrow. Then he extended his arm, indicating for her to take his elbow. "Tonight you shall sit and enjoy the meal," he said as she hesitantly took his arm. "And I shall sit with you."

His softly uttered words caused her cheeks to flame brilliantly. She had no idea why. He was without his mail and plate armor this night, dressed in a soft linen tunic and leather breeches as he led her over to the table and helped her sit before taking a seat beside her. She stole a glance at him as he poured her a measure of wine into a wooden cup and then took a helping for himself. His face was washed and it looked to her as if he had shaved, for his skin was smooth. It was curious that he had taken time to clean for this meal. As if it meant something.

He lifted the cup in her direction, distracting her from her thoughts. "To our lovely hostess," he said loud enough for his men to hear. "To you, my lady, our thanks for your kindness in offering us food and shelter."

The other three knights around the table took up their cups and drank heartily. The wine was cheap, bitter, but none of them flinched as they sucked it down. In fact, two of them poured themselves more. One of them was Braxton. Gray was suddenly embarrassed at the cheap quality of the wine, but it was all they had to offer.

A few more soldiers filtered into the hall, seasoned-looking men that took up seat in various places around the room. Gray was unused to having soldiers in her keep and she was somewhat nervous watching them mill about. They were wearing weapons. Deep down, she wondered if they weren't going to rob her or seize the castle from under her, but when she gazed back at Braxton, she couldn't honestly believe that. He had been extraordinarily kind to her. But, then again, perhaps that had been his scheme. He was a mercenary, after all. Perhaps he was going to lull her into a false sense of security before snatching the fortress for his own. They were, after all, easy prey.

Her natural suspicion began to grow. More soldiers wandered into the hall and her anxiety took flight. Mayhap she had been stupid about this entire situation, letting her confusion destroy her common sense. Setting her cup down, she excused herself from the table and fled the room.

Braxton sat there a moment, staring at the empty doorway from where Gray had just disappeared. He'd barely said a few words to her and she was running from him. The moment he had met her at the falls of Erith, in spite of the fact that he had saved her daughter, she had been mistrustful of his company. He had reviewed their conversation a few times; he doubted it was something he had said. And since his arrival at Erith, he'd gone out of his way to show her kindness and generosity. In truth, he had no idea what it was about him that frightened her so.

He took a long drink of the unpleasant wine, listening to Dallas and Graehm debate the quality of Hereford leather against Douglas leather. It was a foolish conversation, but Dallas and Graehm seemed to have many foolish conversations. They debated each other on the smallest things to see who had the most knowledge about a particular subject. Geoff usually stayed out of it, content to laugh at the two for their arrogance. Squires Edgar and older brother Norman sat against the wall behind the arguing knights, shoving bread into their mouths.

Braxton usually enjoyed these ridiculous exchanges, but not tonight. Tonight he was in no mood for his men's entertainment. He had been looking forward to Lady Gray's company and was, in truth, disappointed. The servants began to bring out heaping plates of venison, filling the room with its heady smell. He sat back, drank, and watched his men dig into the fare. From the corner of his eye, he caught movement by the door.

Hoping it was the lady returned, he was disappointed to see young Brooke entering the hall in the company of an older woman. Braxton noted the girl, washed and dressed in her worn clothing, but found more curiosity with the older woman. She was fine featured, frail, and he could see the resemblance between Lady Gray and this woman. When the two ladies approached, he stood up politely.

Brooke smiled broadly at him. "My lord," she dipped in a practiced curtsy. "Please meet my grandmother, the Lady Constance Gray de Montfort."

De Montfort. It was the first time Braxton had heard that name within these walls. It confirmed his suspicion that the de Montforts did indeed retain the holding once awarded to their ancestor Simon. Now it belonged to a derelict branch of the family. He bowed his head in greeting.

"My lady," he addressed her. "I am Braxton de Nerra. These

are my men...."

The older woman cut him off before he could introduce her to what she undoubtedly, by her expression, considered rabble.

"De Nerra," she repeated. "Correct me if I am wrong, Sir Knight, but are you of the Anjou de Nerra's?"

Brooke piped up before Braxton could reply. "Anjou? In France?"

Constance nodded coolly, her gaze never leaving Braxton's face. Her entire manner reeked of breeding, of arrogance. "The House of de Nerra is the hereditary family to the Earldom of Anjou."

Brooke's face lit up, looking at Braxton through new eyes. "An earldom?"

Braxton's eyes were steady on the older woman. He never did look at Brooke. "My family is another branch. We do not hold the Earldom of Anjou."

"I see," Constance's amber eyes appraised him. "So you have no connection with Anjou at all?" Before he could answer, she waved her hand as if to wash away the probing tone of her words. "You will forgive me, Sir Knight, but I was raised in a fine house. I am quite familiar with peerage and it is always a pleasure to meet an equal."

Braxton had known the woman all of thirty seconds and already he didn't particularly care for her. "The current earl is my father's second cousin," he replied. "I have never met him, nor have any of my three older brothers."

It was an implication to the old woman not to expect what he thought she might be driving at. An Anjou de Nerra would be a wealthy catch for her granddaughter if, in fact, she was seriously trying to marry the girl off. He could just see by her manner that she was ambitious, vain and haughty. No, he didn't like her in the least.

"You have three older brothers?" Brooke was back in the conversation, oblivious to the odd tension between her grandmother and the knight. "Are they all knights, too?"

Braxton looked at the girl. "Aye, my lady, they are."

Her eyes glistened. "Where? Do they serve great Houses or do they wander around like you do?"

He broke into a grin; she certainly didn't mince words. "My eldest brother remains at my father's house, as he will inherit his rights upon the passing of my father. My other two brothers my father as well, as the sons of Baron Gilderdale."

A servant brought a trencher for both Constance and Brooke. Brooke delved into the venison as if she was starving, while Constance merely picked at it. Braxton was much more interested in watching Brooke, who wasn't particularly mannered. She gobbled and wiped her hands on her surcoat, and somewhere during the conversation had spied Edgar and Norman. Now her attention was torn between Braxton and boys her own age. While Brooke had a sweet innocence about her that was refreshing, the old woman had the countenance of a hawk sighting prey.

"Do you see your father much, my lord?" Brooke asked with a full mouth.

Braxton accepted his own trencher from a nearby servant. "Not too often."

"What of your wife, Sir Knight?" Constance came at him from his other side. "Surely you must see her now and again."

Like a good warrior, the old woman went straight for the jugular. Braxton turned his attention to her as one would attend to an adversary. "I am not married, my lady," he said evenly. "I will never marry."

"Why not?"

"Because I cannot provide my wife with a steady home. I move with my army, constantly. I have no intention of settling in one place."

A light twinkled in Constance's eye. *She's enjoying this*, he thought.

"But surely given the proper circumstance, you would consider it." It was more a statement than a question.

Braxton merely lifted his shoulders. He would not let the old woman get the better of him, no matter what she was driving at.

"It would have to be a tremendously wealthy offer with much to my advantage." He made it clear that Erith did not qualify, nor did a fifteen-year-old bride. "Moreover, I intend to travel to the Continent next year. I have a few contracts that require fulfilling. A wife and a House of my own do not suit my purpose at this time."

Brooke was listening intently to him, chewing loudly. Braxton thought she might have put the grandmother up to this interrogation, but he could see from her expression that she was completely oblivious to what was going on. But Constance was more than aware; she was shrewd. Though Braxton had effectively cut her down, she considered the match over, but not the war. She sipped at her wine, making a face as the liquid slid down her throat.

"Horrid," she hissed. "I do apologize for the quality of the wine, Sir Knight. It is not up to our usual standards."

Braxton didn't say anything. He suspected this wine *was* the usual standard. He looked at Brooke. "Where is your mother? She was here a moment ago but left the hall."

Brooke shrugged, licking her fingers. "I do not know."

"Perhaps you should find her and have her join us."

The young girl dug back into her meal. "She does not usually eat the evening meal."

"Why not?"

"Because there usually is not enough..."

Brooke ended her sentence with a yelp as Constance dug fingernails into the girls' leg. The older woman smiled thinly. "She chooses to supervise the household so that the rest of us may enjoy our meal."

Braxton wasn't an idiot. He thought he knew what Brooke had been prevented from saying and he was equally sure that Constance was either in denial of how bad things were at Erith or simply wanted to cover up the truth. He couldn't tell which. However, neither woman seemed concerned at Gray's absence. It was perfectly normal to them. Irritation bloomed in his chest and he stood up.

40

"Then I shall find her and bade her join us," his voice was low. "As she is the hostess, it is only right she enjoy this bountiful feast."

Constance and Brooke watched him march from the room, curiosity on their faces, but Braxton didn't look at either of them. He was more intent on finding Gray and discovering why she had left so abruptly. He had no idea why her flight should bother him so, but it did.

It was cloyingly dark in the entry hall that led from the keep. To his left was a small room, a solar of some kind he assumed. He peered inside; it was empty but for a chair and a table. He couldn't see much else in the dark. Exiting the keep, he took the repaired stairs down to the bailey, his gaze scanning the yard. It was still for the most part, the ghostly moon creating weak light over the landscape.

Wandering toward the three small fires that his men had started near the southern wall, his eyes continued to scrutinize the area. It didn't take him long to determine that the lady was not out in the yard, so he turned once again for the keep. As he did so, movement on a portion of the wall that was not crumbling caught his attention; a flash of a figure had disappeared into the shadows. Knowing that Erith had no sentries, he switched from feast guest to trained warrior. Until he knew who it was, he would take no chances. He hadn't stayed alive this long by being foolish.

There was an open flight of stairs that led up to a functional part of the wall walk where he had seen the figure. The problem was that he would be exposed the entire time he mounted the steps. He was without his armor, a disadvantage, but his warrior instincts were in action and he mounted the steps anyway, staying close against the wall and keeping himself a low profile target.

At the top of the steps where the landing joined the wall walk, there was an intact tower. Braxton had noted the tower earlier in the day, thinking it strange that it had two floors but no connecting stairs. There was a hole in the second floor, however, indicative that a ladder had once joined the two levels. Silently, with great stealth, he made his way to the tower. He was almost at the doorway when a sword suddenly came flying out at him.

It was a clumsy strike and he easily sidestepped it. In the same motion, he reached out and grabbed the wrist of the hand that held it. He was a split second away from snapping the bones when he heard a decidedly female yelp. Giving a good pull, he heaved his adversary out into the moonlight.

The heavy broadsword clattered to the stone as he found himself gazing at Gray. In the eerie silver light, she had the look of a cornered deer, full of mistrust and panic. His defensive posture immediately turned to curiosity.

"Lady Gray?" his brow furrowed as if he couldn't quite grasp what he was seeing. "What on earth are you doing?"

She opened her mouth to speak but was only able to discharge something that sounded like a whimper. Braxton still had hold of her wrist and she was frightened. But not so frightened that she could not summon her courage.

"I am defending myself," she hissed.

"From whom?"

"You."

His eyebrows flew up. "Me? Why would you feel the need to defend yourself? What have I done?"

She was trying to pull away from him but he would not let her go. "You will not insult my intelligence," she spoke through clenched teeth. "Your men have weapons in my hall, in my bailey. I know what you are planning. I am not as stupid as you would think. You intend to take Erith from me and I will not allow it."

It all came out as a jumble of words. Braxton cocked his head at her. "Take Erith?" he repeated. But he could see by her expression that she was serious and it suddenly explained a good deal about her manners towards him. "Nay, my lady, you are seriously mistaken. My men bear arms because they are soldiers. They would as soon bear daggers as they would wear boots, as both are second nature to them. I assure you that we have no intention of betraying those who would be kind to us."

Gray was still trying to pull her arm free, but his grip was like iron. She began to shake with fear. "Let me go."

He shook his head. "So you can run away again? Nay, my lady, we will clarify this here and now. If that is what you have been thinking since the moment we met, then you are sorely misguided. Though I am a mercenary and not a reputable knight, I am nonetheless an honorable man. I do not command a band of pirates that would steal your fortress."

His voice was soft, soothing. Gray's quivering grew worse and her knees suddenly buckled. Braxton caught her before she could fall, lowering her gently to the stones of the wall walk. He kept a good grip on her, partially to support her, partially because he really did not want her to run away again.

"But... but you have brought weapons into my home," she was struggling to keep her train of thought as a strange buzzing filled her ears. "Your men have swarmed my fortress..."

"Making repairs to repay you for your hospitality." He cut her off without force; it was evident that she had never believed him about that. "I swear it upon my oath as a knight, my lady. I have no intention of seizing your fortress."

"I do not believe you. It is not the truth."

He just stared at her. Then he sighed heavily. "You are correct," he muttered. "It is not the truth. Do you really want to know why we are here?"

She gazed up at him, the pale moonlight emphasizing her ashen pallor. "Tell me."

He met her gaze, his blue-green eyes luminescent in the gray light. "Because earlier today I saw the most beautiful woman I have ever seen," he said quietly. "I came to Erith because I wanted to bask in her presence. I came because of you, my lady, and for no other reason than that. I wanted more than just a fleeting glimpse of you."

Gray stared at him. The swimming in her head was easing, but now her heart was coming to thump strangely.

"Me?"

"You."

She was momentarily stumped. Could it be another untruth? Was he simply trying to divert her from the reality? Looking into his handsome face, she couldn't imagine that he was insincere. But the internal struggle was tremendous.

"How do I know this is not a lie?" she hated sounding so fearful. "How do I know that you are not plotting to gain my fortress even as we speak?"

The corner of his mouth twitched. "I gave you my vow as a knight, my lady. I suppose only time will tell if I was honest or not. When my men and I leave your fortress tomorrow in far better repair than we found it, then perhaps you will trust me, just a little."

She was gradually aware that his grip on her hand had eased and his fingers caressed her flesh gently. The touch was sending jolts of excitement up her arm. "I... I do not know," she spluttered.

His gaze was steady on her, as if trying to read what she was thinking. He finally shook his head. "Who has done such terrible things to you that you would be so suspicious?"

Gray averted her gaze, trying to pull her hand away, but he held her fast. "Nay, my lady, I'll not let you run away. Not this time. I have come to this forsaken place to slake my curiosity of you and I will not leave until I have done so. Who has so horribly mistreated you that you would be so defensive? Tell me his name so that I may seek him out and champion you."

Her eyes riveted back to him again, wide with surprise. She yanked her hand hard, finally pulling free of his grip. But she was still on her buttocks and a quick getaway was unlikely.

"You know not what you ask," she said quietly.

"You are correct; I do not know. But I would ask just the same."

"Why?"

"I told you why."

Frustration blossomed. "Do not toy with me, my lord. If you only think to amuse yourself with my misery, then you may look elsewhere for entertainment. I shall not respond to your attempts to probe me. My life is my own and I do not know you. I will be glad to have you on your way tomorrow if only to be left in peace."

She probably meant it, too. "I am not a clever man, my lady," he did not rise to her irritation. "I have never, nor would I ever, toy with a woman. I have not the patience. What I tell you is the truth. I saw a beautiful lady today and simply wished to know her."

She did not reply. He finally stood up, towering over her as she sat at his feet. Without another word, he turned and descended the stairs along the wall, crossing the dark bailey for the warmth of the keep. Though his body had left her, his mind had not. It was still upon the wall walk, wondering why such a beautiful woman was so embittered and mistrustful. If she did not believe him by now, she never would. He realized he felt a good deal of disappointment about it.

He was just mounting the steps to the keep when movement caught his attention. Glancing over, he could see Gray descending the stairs, clutching the stone walls as she lowered herself one step at a time. She was struggling, that much was clear. She seemed to be particularly weak and not simply because he had startled her by ripping a sword out of her hand. He paused half way up the stairs, watching her labor with every stair. He couldn't just leave her. Slowly, he retraced his steps.

He met her at the bottom of the wall stairs. Gray looked at him, all of the fight gone out of her. Braxton stood there a moment, gazing back at her. He was still trying to figure her out, though he did not completely understand why. He'd never had a woman intrigue him so. Silently, he reached out and scooped her into his arms. She didn't look as if she couldn't walk another step.

Surprisingly, she did not protest. Her arms went around his neck and he could feel her hot breath on his jaw. He knew she was watching him. He was almost to the steps that led back into the keep when he felt her head, soft and sweet, lay down against his shoulder.

"Would... would you mind if we sat by your fire, my lord?" she asked softly.

He paused at the base of the steps and turned around, facing the south wall where three small fires blazed. "Those?"

"Aye."

"Why would you want to sit there when there is a warm hall at the top of these stairs?"

Her head came up, the amber eyes fixed on him. "Because it is full of people. You have asked fair questions, my lord. I would give you answers, but not for all to hear. I... I thought we could speak privately if, indeed, you still seek answers to your questions."

He didn't argue. In fact, his pace picked up as he went over to the first of the three small blazes. He set her on her feet and she weaved dangerously. He reached out to steady her.

"Are you feeling ill?"

She waved him off weakly. "I shall be all right."

"When did you eat last?"

Her head snapped in his direction and he could see the shame in her eyes. "Yesterday," she lied. "I had a large meal. I simply haven't been hungry until now."

He didn't want to dispute her, but Brooke's hint of how her mother went without food because there was not enough to go around rang loudly in his mind. He pulled out the nearest bedroll and put it on the ground under her.

"Sit," he ordered quietly. "I shall go and retrieve your meal."

"Nay, please...."

He was insistent. "I have not yet eaten myself. Sit there and I shall return."

Gray was too weak to argue. She watched him cross the bailey, noting the confidence and power to his stride. He took the steps two at a time and disappeared into the keep. She began to relax, watching the flames as they danced before her. It was hypnotic, easing the strain on her mind. Before she realized it, Braxton was back, a hefty trencher in each hand, a wooden pitcher of the cheap wine hooked into a finger, and wooden cups under both arms.

Gray took the pitcher from him and both cups as he sat beside her. Neither one of them spoke as she poured the wine and accepted her trencher from him. As the fire blazed soothingly into the dark Cumbrian sky, Gray delved into the first real meal she had eaten in days.

Braxton ate silently beside her, watching her from the corner of his eye. He could see that she was famished, stuffing her mouth so full that she could barely chew. The action touched him deeply. Like her daughter, she was starving. There simply wasn't enough for everyone and Gray suffered so that others would not starve. He doubted the grandmother felt the same pangs. He suspected the old woman took what she wanted without regard for anyone else. She looked like the type.

"You were going to answer my questions," he reminded her casually.

Gray swallowed the bite in her mouth, chasing it with a long drink of the bitter wine. "Which question would you have answered?"

His blue-green eyes fixed on her. "Why are you so mistrustful of my actions?"

She met his eyes; the urge to shy away was overwhelming. "I... I really don't know. Perhaps it is because no man has ever been particularly truthful to me. Not my husband or my father." She lifted a hand to suggest he look at their surroundings. "Erith is all I have. I am a lone woman with no army. I must protect myself and my family. It was stupid of me to allow you and your army inside these walls."

"Yet you did. Do you believe me now when I tell you I have no intention of stealing your fortress?"

She shrugged. "I suppose I must."

"I could take Erith at any time and you'd not be able to stop me. You might as well trust me, for you have little choice."

Her silence confirmed what she already knew. Braxton watched her as she averted her focus and looked back to her food.

"What happened to your husband?" he asked, somewhat

47

gently, somewhat seriously.

She picked up another bit of venison and put it to her lips, chewing slowly as she spoke. "He is dead."

"So I was told. But what happened to him?"

Gray couldn't bring herself to look at him. She didn't know why she was about to tell him, but she was. "He was murdered," she whispered. "Over a gambling debt."

"I see." He drew in a long breath, gazing up at the stars over head. "Has he been gone long?"

"Four years."

He looked back at her. "And you have not considered remarrying?"

She met his gaze, then. "Who would have me, my lord?" The strength was returning to her voice. "I have nothing to offer but a broken fortress. No man of standing or decency would want to marry a woman with nothing to offer but poverty."

He lifted an eyebrow. "You underestimate your worth, madam."

She stared at him a long moment before shoving her trencher to the ground and rising on unsteady legs. She had barely turned to walk away before he was up and standing in front of her. She tried to move around him but he blocked her.

"What have I said to make you run away from me again?" he demanded quietly.

Irritated, frustrated, she tried to push through him but he would not budge. She threw both hands out as if to shove him out of the way, but it was like shoving a wall. He was immovable. He grasped her arms and held her fast.

"Answer me," he rumbled. "What did I say?"

The frustration was turning to angry tears. "Let me go."

"Not until you answer me."

She wrestled with him but he only held her tighter. "Let me go, I say."

"Answer me and I shall."

She very nearly exploded. "I told you not to toy with me. Save your sweet words for someone who appreciates empty compliments and stale flattery, for I do not."

His brow furrowed. "Is that it?" He couldn't believe she was upset with him over that. "God's truth, madam, I mean every word. In spite of your broken fortress and destitute situation, you have the beauty of an angel. A wise man would look beyond your situation to see that the true treasure lies with you, not with your lack of a dowry."

She stopped fighting him, looking at him as if he was mad. "How... how can you say such things?" she wanted to know. "Men marry for wealth and status, not beauty."

"I would marry for beauty."

The blue-green eyes were intense on her. Gray suddenly felt warm and confused. The frustration and anger from moments earlier was gone, replaced by a strange sense of euphoria.

"Then you are a unique soul," she was calming, "for most men would not."

His grip on her arms lessened but he did not let go. "They are fools."

Even in the moonlight, he swore he could see a faint blush to her cheeks. It was enchanting. He took the opportunity to gently take her hand, turning her back around towards the fire.

Gray allowed him to sit her back down on the bedroll that served as her chair. He picked up her half-eaten trencher and put it back in her hands. He sat close to her as he reclaimed his own trencher.

"Is the venison to your liking?" he wanted to keep the conversation going but stay away from the heady subjects, of which there were apparently many. "This was a big buck. Sometimes if they are too big and too old, their flesh is tough."

"This is delicious." She chewed slowly, watching him from the corner of her eye. "Did you kill it yourself?"

He took a drink of the nasty wine. "Nay," he shook his head. "I leave the sport to my men, though when I was younger, I was quite a good marksman."

"Surely you still are."

His eyes twinkled. "Perhaps you would like to go hunting with me to see just how good I am, or at least I used to be?"

She fought off a smile. "Nay, I would not. My father considered hunting quite a sport, but I thought it was cruel."

"Cruel but necessary to feed an army."

"Or a fortress."

He lifted his cup to her in agreement. "Was your father a great hunter, then?"

For the first time since they had met, the conversation was flowing freely. No tension, no fears. Braxton was relieved to see that she was finally relaxing around him. It made him feel light hearted as he hadn't felt in years.

"My father had been a great knight, once," she replied. "He was the son of a great knight."

He stared at her a moment. "Simon de Montfort."

She met his gaze. "Aye," she said slowly. "How did you know?"

He poured her more wine. "Because your daughter introduced me to your mother as the Lady Constance de Montfort. Since you said your mother was of the Northumberland Grays, I could only assume de Montfort is her married name. I also happen to know that Erith is a holding of Simon de Montfort, or at least it used to be many years ago. So logically, your father must be a son or descendent of de Montfort."

She nodded. "My father was Simon's sixth child and third son, Richard."

Braxton smiled faintly. Gray gazed back at him, wondering what his reaction would be to her lineage. It was not something she bragged about, being the granddaughter of a publicly disgraced earl. The wine on her empty stomach was loosening her tongue, causing her to speak before she could think through clearly.

"Now that you know my family lines, I do not blame you if you should take back every nice deed you have done for me," she drank of the deep red liquid. "Most people do, you know. Once they discover my grandfather was Simon de Montfort, they smile to my face yet whisper behind my back."

He frowned. "Simon de Montfort was a great man with great

ideas. I have a great deal of respect for his memory."

She snorted. "You speak treason, my lord."

"Perhaps. But I speak the truth."

"Most people do not think that way, especially in these lands where de Montfort held a presence. The king was hard on those who supported my grandfather when the tides finally turned against him. People around here have still not forgotten that."

"True enough. But it is a pity they cannot remember that de Montfort's only true crime was his quest for a better England."

"You know something of my grandfather's history?"

"I know a great deal."

"Then you know that he believed the lesser nobles and common people of England should have a say in the rule of their country. Did you know that there was a time when he had more power than the king? Simon held a parliament of barons to help direct this country on a better path. He did so much good for this country in the short time he was able. But a key ally turned against him because of a silly quarrel and betrayed him to the king at Evesham. It was horrible. My father never recovered from what King Henry did to his father."

Braxton could see her distress. He could only imagine it had been part of her life since the day she was born, the tragic tale of Simon de Montfort. "Be that as it may," he said quietly, "there are those left in England who believe that de Montfort did something great. There are those that believe he has showed us a better way of governing a country."

She smiled, without humor. "Perhaps. But those people were nowhere to be found to support the family Simon left behind."

He wriggled his eyebrows. "Those people conveniently forgot that your noble bloodlines ran deep on both sides of the family," he said softly. "You are the great-granddaughter, niece and cousin of kings. Your grandmother, Eleanor, was King Richard and King John's sister. Your great-grandfather was Henry the Second. Even now, you are a direct relation to Edward Longshanks."

It may have been the truth, but he made her sound more

prestigious than she was.

"For a short time our family was glorified and respected, but when the end came, we became social outcasts," she told him. "When it came time for me to marry, my father had to beg or bribe a suitor for no one wished to be associated with the disgraced de Montforts. I was finally promised to a lesser baron's son, Garber Serroux, after much negotiation. We knew something of his family, but not too much." Her eyes moved across the dark and crumbling fortress. "I suppose you can say the joke was on us. Garber Serroux was as undesirable a marriage prospect as I was only we did not know it at the time. He was a foul, abusive liar with a penchant for gambling. He had no inheritance because he had wagered it all away. Erith did not always look like this; it was still a moderately decent place ten years ago. But my husband sold everything we had to pay his debts, sold off our servants, and when he was drunk, he used our walls as target practice for the trebuchets my grandfather left behind. He left Erith as you see it."

By this time, Braxton expression had darkened. "And then proceeded to get himself murdered for a gambling debt, leaving his family destitute."

"He left us destitute long before that."

The words were softly spoken, but their impact could not have been greater. Braxton had wanted to know the lady, but he had gotten more than he'd bargained for. Though he'd only known her a matter of hours, he could not imagine anyone abusing this gentle, noble and angelic creature. The mere thought made anger burn in his chest.

"I am sorry for your trouble," he said after a moment; he wasn't sure what more he could say. "Life has not been kind to you and I find that grossly unfair. You deserve far better."

Gray took a closer look at him; as always, his manner was honest and sincere. To speak kindly of her grandfather was a rare thing indeed. Be it the wine or the conversation, she was growing more comfortable with him.

"Where are you going when you leave tomorrow?" she asked.

He casually shifted in his seat, moving closer to her. His elbow was brushing against her knee. "I have a contract to fulfill in Kendal."

"What kind of contract?"

It was usual that he did not speak of contract terms with anyone other than the party soliciting his services and it was habit to be evasive with those who did not need to know the details.

"My military services for money, my lady. That is how I make my fortune in life."

She gazed at him seriously. "Do you like being a mercenary?"

"I make a great deal of money fighting other people's battles. The life has done well for me."

"Who are you going to fight a battle for this time?"

He looked at her; she was very close to him now, her sweet face and amber eyes illuminated by the warm blaze. Being this close to her made him feel strangely dizzy. He did not see any harm in telling her one small detail.

"A man named Wenvoe," he said. "He has a fortress a few miles to the northeast of Kendal called Creekmere. It is probably less than a day's ride from Erith."

As Braxton watched, Gray's drunken amber eyes widened to the point where he thought they might pop from her head.

"God's Bones...," she breathed. "What are you to do for him?"

"Why would you ask that? Do you know him?"

She nodded, all of the color gone from her face again. Even in the moonlight, he could see it. "Aye," she said.

"Then what do you know? Why do you look so?"

Her mouth worked as if searching for the correct words. She finally shook her head, unable to do anything more than simply spit it out.

"He is the man who murdered my husband."

CHAPTER FOUR

"He was a gracious guest," Constance told her daughter. "'Tis a fine man who would be so generous to a host. Our stairs are repaired, a new portcullis hung, and the man left food enough for weeks. 'Twas a marvelous bit of luck for us when you crossed his path at the falls of Erith."

Though it was only mid-afternoon, the day had been long already. Gray was positive she hadn't slept a wink the night before. After sitting with Braxton by the fire for hours, she had finally retired in the wee hours of the morn and only then because she was absolutely exhausted. Had she not known any better, she would have suspected that Braxton did not want her to leave at all. Every time she tried to leave, he'd start on another subject and they would become caught up in conversation. They ended up draining two pitchers of wine before the evening was out. But it was the most pleasant evening she could ever remember.

"He was very generous to us," she agreed with her mother's statement. "He seemed like a kind enough man."

"Kind?" Constance snorted. "He was wildly benevolent. No doubt the man respected our station and showed appropriate homage."

Gray didn't reply immediately. She went back to the mending in her lap, an apron of Brooke's that the girl had torn.

"He was simply being pleasant," she said after a moment. "In truth, I do not know if his men even slept with all of the building going on. They were in the forest before dawn selecting trees for the new portcullis, and those rotted stairs were fully rebuilt before mid-morn. They worked like fiends and still had a long march to Kendal when they were finished."

Braxton's army had been gone about an hour. Gray allowed herself to go back to that moment when he bid her farewell, a strange gleam of warmth in his blue-green eyes as he thanked her profusely for her hospitality. It was she, in fact, who should have thrown herself at his feet for what he had done for her and for Erith. He had left the place in far better standing than when he had found it. Frankly, it still puzzled her, no matter how much he had explained his reasoning to her.

"I do hope they visit us again," Constance pulled her familiar tattered shawl about her shoulders. "Perhaps the next time they come, they will gift us with something more useful, like fabric or notions. Would that not be lovely?"

Gray looked up at her mother, a scowl on her face. "What he did for us is quite enough," she said sternly. "I'll not expect another thing from him."

"Do not take that tone with me."

"Someone needs to. Your selfishness is overwhelming."

Constance's thin face tightened. "One of us should be selfish since all you can manage to do is be supplicant and acquiescent of our situation. Someone has to look out for us because you do not have the courage to do so."

Gray stood up. "I do the best I can to keep our family together, which is more than I can say for you. All you do is complain."

"I complain about your lack of courage."

Something very nasty teetered on Gray's lips, but she refrained. Fighting with her mother would not solve their problems. Fact was that Constance believed everything she was saying. Gray would take her mending elsewhere, away from her mother's attitude. Any more time spent with the woman might see them come to blows.

Brooke passed her mother just as Gray was leaving the solar. The young girl paused, watching her mother mount the steps for the upper floors.

"What is wrong with Mother?" she asked.

Constance went over to her granddaughter. "Nothing, my love," she put her arm around the girl's shoulders and pulled her into the room. "So? Did you speak to him as I told you to?"

Distracted from her mother, Brooke nodded. "Aye."

"And your mother did not see you speak to him?"

"Nay. I spoke to him before Mother came to say her farewells."

"And what did he say?"

"That he would return as soon as he could."

"And did you tell him that we very much appreciated his continued generosity?"

"I did. I told him we'd not had new garments in some time and we would appreciate any fabric or clothing he could see fit to gift us the next time he came."

Constance kissed her granddaughter on the forehead. "That is my good girl," she murmured. "He must know that we are very interested in his continued presence here at Erith and if we plan correctly, we should have an offer for your hand very soon." She suddenly paused, looking seriously at Brooke. "You made it clear that you were the object of interest, didn't you?"

Brooke nodded. "I did."

Constance's features took on a shrewd cast. "The knight seems to be very interested in your mother, so we must be clear that you are the one we intend for him."

A shadow of a doubt crossed Brooke's fine features. "But...but if he is fond of mother, perhaps she should marry him."

"Rubbish," Constance snapped softly. "Your mother is not en eligible young maiden."

"But if he likes her..."

"I will hear no more of that. 'Tis you we will match with him."

Though Brooke tried to understand her grandmother, truth was, the woman could be very overbearing at times. Rebelling against her mother was one thing; rebelling against her grandmother was another. Brooke believed her grandmother had her best interests at heart. She believed that Constance wanted her to be rich and happy and well taken care of. It would have never crossed her young mind that it was anything other than pure devotional family love, not some sick, twisted vision of reclaiming something for herself.

"But he does not have a House, grandmother," Brooke said after a moment. "And he is not from a fine family. Did you not say that I must marry someone from a fine family?"

"He is a de Nerra of Anjou, child. Their family is older than the crown of England. And when he marries you, he can make Erith his house and repair the fortress so that there is no finer castle in all of England."

"But he is an old man."

Constance laughed softly. "He is not terribly old. But young or old, he is very wealthy. Just look at all he has done for Erith in the short time he was here. You want a wealthy husband, do you not?"

Brooke agreed, simply because her grandmother had drilled that objective into her head for the past two years.

"But... grandmother," Brooke said as she sauntered into the room, picking at the only chair. She seemed distracted. "What... what do you think mother would say to all of this? I know you said it was a secret, but she will know some time. She will find out. And then what?"

Constance's smile faded. "She must accept it. Your duty is to marry well, Brooke. Your mother knows that. You are of marriageable age and the time to find a husband for you is now."

Brooke faced her grandmother. "Do you think I shall have any more suitors other than Sir Braxton?"

Constance shrugged. "It is possible. I have sent word to a few. But if you do not, we must take advantage of our opportunities."

"You mean the arrival of Sir Braxton?"

"Precisely."

Brooke continued to stare out of the lancet window. She was able to observe the newly hung portcullis on the inner wall. Constance watched her granddaughter's profile, a thousand calculating thoughts running through her mind. She was positive that she knew what was best for the girl, fighting off the knowledge that Gray would undoubtedly become irate when she found out what her mother was doing. It was a miracle she'd not found out yet, considering the planning that Constance had been doing. But no matter. Gray obviously did not have her daughter's best interests at heart.

"Do not worry, darling," she went to her granddaughter,

stroking the silky blond hair. "You shall have a wealthy husband, I promise. But the next time Sir Braxton comes to Erith, we must ensure our position with him. We must make sure that he does the honorable thing."

Brooke looked at her. "What do you mean?"

Constance played with the girl's hair. "There are... ways."

"What ways?"

Constance leaned in close, her lips almost against the girl's ear. "Listen and learn, darling. Your grandmother knows best."

***

Creekmere Castle was a small fortress built in the shape of a triangle. It was partially buried against a heavily forested hill and nicely arranged, as Braxton noticed as his army approached. Baron Wenvoe carried around one hundred fifty men, not a sizable force. In fact, Creekmere seemed like a miniature version of a normal sized castle. Everything about it was small, including its lord.

Neil Wenvoe met Braxton in the bailey of his small, red-stoned fortress. He was short and round, with small eyes and a smelly aura. Braxton left Dallas settling the men and went inside the small keep to conduct business.

He was on edge as he followed the baron into the dark, fragrant structure. He had been on edge ever since leaving Erith, feeling more apprehension with every step of his destrier. It was unusual that he felt such apprehension; he had been a mercenary for twenty-one years and in that time, had learned to keep his apprehension at bay. He knew his anxiety was not because of the job itself. He did not fear battle. His trepidation lay in the unknown details that would soon be made clear to him. Something told him to expect the worst, and for good reason; Cumbria was relatively sparsely populated. How many troublesome neighbors could Wenvoe have? With an unsettled debt with Garber Serroux, a neighbor less than a day's ride to the south, there was good reason to be suspicious.

The keep was three stories, with one room per floor. The baron took Braxton into the great hall, well furnished with fresh rushes, fat tapers, and even a tapestry hung high on the wall. Fine wine, cheese and brown bread were brought out to refresh them. The baron took a seat on the long scrubbed table, motioning for Braxton to sit opposite him.

"I take it your travels were uneventful," Wenvoe said.

"We had no trouble, my lord," Braxton replied.

"Good. Then we may get to business."

So much for the pleasantries, though in Braxton's business, he was used to the lack of social graces. Men did not hire him for his oratory skills

"Your initial missive stated that you had need for my military services, my lord," Braxton said. "You mentioned trouble with a neighbor. I would hear the entire story and what, exactly, you want of me."

Wenvoe nodded. "Trouble indeed," he snorted. "I will tell you my situation and exactly what I need from you. You shall be well paid for your efforts."

"I always am, my lord."

Wenvoe lifted a bushy gray eyebrow at the comment but continued along his line of thought. "I have many friends and allies in Cumbria and elsewhere. Not too long ago, my ally, Edward de Romille of Skipton Castle, sent a missive to me that was of particular concern."

"And what is that?"

"'Twould seem that someone is trying to cheat me out of what is rightfully mine."

"If you would be plain, my lord."

Wenvoe's round face flushed. "Years ago, a former ally borrowed a great deal of money from me. When he could not pay it back, he promised me the hand of his daughter when she became of age in repayment for this debt. Now I am to discover that the family is soliciting marriage offers for this same daughter when the girl, and the fortress, rightfully belong to me. And I would now take what is mine."

Braxton suddenly had a sick feeling in the pit of his stomach. He simply could not believe what he was hearing, though in truth, he was not surprised. The coincidence was nauseating and he knew, before names were even spoken, who the family was. It was all to close, too coincidental. It was like a bad dream.

"And this family, my lord?" he asked steadily.

"Serroux," Wenvoe's expression took on a furious cast. "They are in possession of Erith Castle, to the south about a half day's ride. Garber Serroux was a close ally until he took my money and failed to pay it back. When I discovered his deceit, he promised me his daughter's hand when she came of age, the fortress and his hereditary title of Baron Kentmere in repayment. The fool got himself killed before we could strike the written contract, but of no matter; it was a verbal contact and binding. My majordomo is my witness with that."

Braxton took a long, steadying breath. "How did de Romille come to know that the family was soliciting marriage offers?"

"Because they were sent a missive from Erith. De Romille has two marriageable sons."

"Yet he knew of Serroux's contract with you. How?"

"De Romille is married to my cousin. We have oft spoke of the time when Erith would belong to me. It would strike an unbreakable line of allies between Kendal and Skipton. So when he received the solicitation of marriage, naturally, he knew that I would want to know."

It was a struggle for Braxton not to react. "What do you want me to do?"

Wenvoe's eyebrows rose. "Lay siege to Erith, of course. I am told that they have no army and no defenses, so it should not be a difficult task for you to take the castle."

Braxton stared at him. He fought off the urge to laugh at the irony of the situation. "You have over one hundred men here. Why do you not lay siege yourself? Why send for me?"

"I will send some of my men with you, but your vicious tactics are well known. I heard tale from Carlisle that you led a charge against Grassgarth Castle last year that had your men infiltrating

60

a nearly impenetrable fortress within a few hours after the siege began. You lay siege towers on their sides, bridged the moat, burnt the portcullis and entered. Lord Carlisle said it was the most brilliant strike he had ever seen, hence my reason for contacting you. I would pay handsomely for that brilliance, de Nerra."

Though Braxton had not signed anything, by his sheer presence he was implying that he would take on the task. That is how his sort usually worked. He wasn't sure how he could back out of this. Moreover, Wenvoe had a claim that would hold up. If Serroux had indeed given him a verbal promise, with a witness no less, his claim was quite legitimate. He had every right to seize Erith, and Brooke Serroux, in payment for the debt.

Braxton's mind began to work quickly.

"My lord," he began. "I passed Erith on my way here. It is a broken down castle and nothing more. Certainly not worth all of the expense you are going to pay me to claim it."

"Perhaps not. But the land is worth something. What will be your fee for such a task?"

Braxton regarded him a moment. "How much did Serroux owe you?"

"Why is that of concern?"

"Curiosity, my lord."

Wenvoe shrugged. "He had borrowed twenty thousand gold marks, a handsome some."

"That is a good deal of money."

"Indeed. So you can understand why I would claim my right to Erith."

"I will give you thirty thousand gold marks if you will relinquish your right."

Wenvoe's puny eyes widened. He abruptly straightened, the bench beneath him groaning under his weight. "What's this you say?"

"You heard me. Thirty thousand gold marks and you sell me your rights to Erith."

The baron was clearly astonished. He opened his mouth to

argue, but shut it just as quickly. He gave Braxton a most queer expression.

"What is your interest in Erith, de Nerra? You are a soldier of fortune. You are paid to fight other men's wars. And now you would give me money to forget about mine?"

"My reasons are my own. I will pay back Serroux's debt and then some. Enough so that you should be satisfied."

Wenvoe's wide eyes suddenly narrowed. "But you make no sense. What is Erith to you?"

"Absolutely nothing. But as I said, I passed it on my way to Creekmere. It is a place unworthy of my talents. A child could raze the place. No amount of money could coerce me to shame myself by kicking over a castle made of sand and call it a victory. My skills are worth far more than that."

"Your talents are for sale and if I pay the right price, you will do as I wish."

"Sell me your rights or I'll raze Creekmere."

What had been a fairly pleasant atmosphere of professional bargaining suddenly turned ugly. The mood that swirled between them was dark, moody and ominous. The baron looked at Braxton as if the man had lost his mind.

"You come into my home and threaten me?" he hissed.

"Not a threat, my lord. Consider it a promise of things to come. I will buy Serroux's debt for thirty thousand gold marks, assume your rights to the Serroux heiress, and hear no more about it from you. Are we clear?"

The baron was red in the face. His mouth worked into a thin, angry line. "What about an alliance? You will be my neighbor. Can I expect hostility from you as my neighbor?"

"If you are worried about allegiance, consider me a loyal neighbor." He leaned forward on the table, his blue-green eyes as hard as stone. "And I assure you, baron, that you would much rather have me as a friendly neighbor than a bitter enemy."

"You are giving me little choice."

"I am giving you none at all."

Wenvoe weighed his options. This day had not gone as

planned, but with the acquisition of thirty thousand marks of gold, it had not been entirely unpleasant. He held his furious gaze a moment longer, just to know how displeased he was with de Nerra's threats.

"Pay me my money before daybreak and be gone with you."

"Put your agreement in writing and you shall have your money by within the hour."

Exactly an hour and half later, Braxton and his men were back on the road to Erith. But not before they made a slight detour to Kendal.

***

"Mama!"

In the kitchen yard, Gray heard her daughter calling her. But she was busy churning butter, as the elderly cook had injured her back, and had not the time to stop what she was doing to respond to her child. She called out instead.

"Here, Brooke. In the kitchen!"

Clad in brown broadcloth and the mended apron, Brooke raced around the side of the keep and straight into the kitchen yard. Her blond hair was everywhere, her cheeks flushed with excitement.

"Mama, he's come back. Sir Braxton has come back!"

Gray did come to a halt, then. Puzzled, she wiped the sweat from her brow with the back of her hand before wiping her palms on her apron. It was just shy of sunset; Braxton had been gone a little over a day and already he was back. She felt a strange sense of excitement at her daughter's announcement. But she also wondered why he had returned so soon.

"Where is he?" she asked as the two of them left the kitchen yard.

Brooke was half-trotting, half-walking. "In the bailey. Hurry, Mama. He's brought gifts!"

Gray froze for a moment, staring at her excited daughter. A bit bewildered and more than curious, she resumed following her bouncing child out into the main portion of the bailey.

Braxton and his men were indeed returned. The five massive wagons were being parked against the southern wall while the bulk of the army was already setting up their encampment. Brooke decided her mother wasn't moving quickly enough and raced back to grab her hand, tugging her along. Very shortly, they ran headlong into a big black charger with an equally big knight astride it.

"Sir Braxton," Brooke said excitedly. "Here she is. I found her just as you asked."

Gray looked up, shielding her eyes from the glare of the setting sun. Braxton was astride his destrier, clad in full battle armor. She'd never seen the man with his helm on. In fact, she'd never seen him in full armor. Every time she had been around him, he had been in various stages of dress – mail only, pieces of plate armor, and no armor at all. He didn't seem fanatical about maintaining his plate protection at all times as some knights did. Now, clad as if going to war, he looked imposing, powerful, and frightening. He smiled down at her, his blue-green eyes glowing.

"My lady," he greeted in his soft, deep voice. "This day has you looking well."

She smiled faintly. "And it has you looking as if you are preparing invade a small country," she replied, to which he snorted. "Why have you returned? Has something happened?"

He wriggled his eyebrows in response, dismounting his charger. The two squires were there to take the reins, the older one passing a lingering glance at Brooke. The girl looked back. But the adults were oblivious to the youngsters exchanging glimpses as Braxton focused solely on Gray. In the short time he'd spent away, he'd missed the sight of her.

"Plans have changed," he said vaguely, removing one of his heavy mail gauntlets. "May I be so bold as to ask you to accompany me into your hall?"

Gray nodded while Braxton removed his helm, handed it over to the younger of his squires, and extended an elbow to her. When she looked at him, still puzzled by his swift reappearance, he merely smiled. It loosened her enough to the point where she smiled back. Then she took his arm; it felt solid, reassuring, and safe. She realized she was glad to see him.

Even as he led her up the stairs, there was tremendous activity going on in the bailey. Men were clustered in well organized groups and several of them were offloading wood and other materials out of one of the wagons. That was about all Gray saw before Braxton took her into the keep, yet she could still hear the noise behind her. Once inside, Braxton took her straight into the hall.

Gray recognized Braxton's three knights, lingering near the massive dining table. Servants were bring out pitchers of the nasty wine and trays of dried fruits, as it was the only items of hospitality they had to offer. As she drew close, she noticed that there was a myriad of items strewn over the table; bolts of fine fabric, pins, belts, silks, and a box containing spools and spools of thread. Her mouth popped open with astonishment at the sight while Brooke, having rushed in behind her, began to squeal with delight. Brooke was all over the table, exclaiming about the beauty of the items, as Gray stood there with her mouth hanging open. Braxton stood beside her, watching her astonished face.

"I hope these are to your liking," he said quietly. "I was not sure what women of fine fashion would like, so I asked a merchant in Kendal. He told me that these items were most popular right now."

Before Gray could reply, Braxton turned to Dallas and muttered something. The young knight went over to a pile of fabric at the far end of the table and drew forth a heavy blue brocade cloak lined with luxurious gray fur. He returned with the garment held high as Braxton pointed to it.

"The merchant assured me that this cloak is the warmest one he had," he fingered the gray lining when it came near. "I know it seems foolish purchasing a cloak when the weather has been so warm, but winters this far north can be exceedingly bitter. I was not sure if you had something suitable for the approaching season."

Gray stared at it. It seemed that she was having difficulty speaking. "For… me?" she whispered.

Braxton smiled. "Of course. Unless you do not like it, whereupon I will take it back to the merchant and bring you back something you will like. Or you can keep it and I shall go buy you another one you will like better."

Hesitantly, she reached out to finger the fur. It was some kind of fox, complimenting the beautiful blue fabric. Before she could say anything, Brooke found a cloak for herself in the pile at the end of the table and she hooted with delight. She swung it around her shoulders, delighting in the beauty of it, but couldn't seem to navigate the fasten. Geoff was standing the closest to her and came to the rescue. With the cloak fastened, Brooke put the hood on her head and skipped about the room in delight.

Gray watched her daughter joyfully parade around. It only reminded her that she had never been able to provide her daughter with such comfort. Brooke had never even seen a fur-lined cloak, much less owned one. The sight brought tears to her eyes. She looked at Braxton.

"My lord," her voice was choked. "Your thoughtfulness, as always, is beyond words, but these items must have cost you a fortune. I cannot… that is to say, I could never repay you for these, and all of the hospitality in the world would not do just compensation."

He gazed down at her, the blue-green eyes gleaming. "Standing here with you is enough compensation for a thousand such things." When she struggled to blink away the tears, he tucked her hand into the crook of his elbow. "Walk with me, madam. Please."

Dumbly, she followed him from the hall. Behind them, Brooke was still crowing about her cloak. It made Braxton smile to hear the girl's excitement. He took Gray out of the keep, down the repaired steps, and into the bailey. She kept her head down, struggling not to let loose with an emotional display, as he led her from the fortress and out into the green Cumbrian landscape beyond. The pace was slow, giving her time to compose herself.

"Now," he said quietly. "Before you become angry with me for the gifts I have brought, you should know that I did it for purely selfish reasons."

She looked up at him, her pretty amber eyes glistening with moisture. "Selfish?"

"Aye," he said. "I am hoping to bribe you."

Her expression turned dubious. "Bribe me? For what?"

He came to a halt, facing her in the light of the setting sun. She was an astoundingly gorgeous creature. "Because I want you to allow me to do good things for you, madam."

"I do not understand."

Her hand was still tucked into the crook of his elbow. He took it in his ungloved hand, holding it sweetly. "I have done much in my life that was perhaps not so good. I have killed because men have paid me to kill. I stopped going to confession long ago because the priests said I could never do enough penance to make up for the evils I have done. So I was hoping... nay, I was praying that you would allow me to do good things for you in the hope that it might make up for the wrongs I have done. You look as if you could use good deeds. And I have done many wrongs, madam. Many indeed."

Her tears had stopped. A look of serenity came over her face, illuminated by the glow of the dying sun. "You have been overwhelmingly good to me and my family since we met you, my lord," she said softly. "I cannot imagine you committing horrible deeds. You seem the essence of knightly chivalry, for certainly, you have done more for me in two days than any one person has done for me over a life time."

His smile returned. "It is not something that comes easily to me, I assure you. But it was a strange day when I met you in the trees."

"What do you mean?"

He shrugged. "Simply that I wasn't supposed to be there," he replied. "My men and I were due in Kendal that very day but we veered off track chasing a hefty buck. It was the same buck that we ate that night at Erith. That animal took several arrows and still refused to fall, so we chased it. It didn't fall until right before I heard your screams. And then I followed your cries and found you."

She smiled timidly. "A fortuitous coincidence, my lord."

He shook his head. "'Tis more than that. It was as if… almost as if I was meant to find you there. As if I was meant to save Brooke. I cannot explain it any more than that."

Gray wasn't quite sure how to answer him. Their eyes met and she looked away, smiling bashfully. Never in her life had she met a man who had even said the remotest kind word to her. She did not know how to respond.

"In any case," he continued, enchanted with her dimpled smile. "I do not want you to be angry with me for bringing you gifts. You deserve to be showered in fine things."

She shrugged and resumed their walk at a slower pace. "You are most kind to say so, my lord, but I must be honest when I say that I cannot, in good conscience, accept your gifts. I know that you are trying to do good for me and for my daughter, and believe me when I tell you that it brings me joy as you will never know to see her happy over something as simple as a cloak, but I am not sure that it is entirely proper for me to accept gifts from… well, from a…."

"Stranger?" he finished, watching her nod in mute agreement. "In faith, I am not so sure that I am a stranger. After all, we spent a good deal of time in conversation the other night. We came to know quite a bit about one another."

"True."

"Would you accept gifts from a friend?"

She cast him a glance from the corner of her eye. "I might."

He smiled broadly. "Good. Then I would be honored to call you my friend. And, if God is good to me, perhaps something more in time."

She came to a sudden halt, facing him. All of the warmth was drained from her face. "What more?"

He could see the fear in her eyes again. "My intentions are honorable, my lady, I assure you."

"What do you mean?"

He put his hands on his hips, hoping to lightly diffuse what could build into an unpleasant situation. He could just read the suspicion on her face.

"Can a man not work up the courage to declaring his intentions?" he demanded lightly. "Must I be plain all within the first few days of knowing you? If you must know, then I am a coward. Women frighten me. It is not easy for me to state my intentions right away. I must ease into such a thing. To declare my interest for you all at one time might cause my heart to stop or my brain to freeze. The shock would likely kill me. You would not want that, would you?"

Gray was torn between giggling and the seriousness of the situation. She settled for amazement. "You would... declare your intentions? For me?"

He scowled. "Give me time, you pushy wench."

A grin joined her amazed expression. "But... my lord, we discussed this the other night. I have nothing of value to offer."

"And I am a knight bannerette with no property or standing."

"I am well beyond marriageable age."

He waved her off. "Are you mad? You are young and beautiful and when I gather enough courage, I shall... well, you know...."

She could not believe what she was hearing. The astonishment was more than she could bear. "Nay, I do not know."

Braxton scratched his forehead. In fact, he looked almost nervous. "Must I be plain?"

"I am afraid so."

He gazed down at her, the sweet curves of her face, the delicious manner in which her amber eyes reflected the dying sun. He could look into her eyes and see a daughter with her exquisite face and his blue-green eyes or a strong son with her sensibility and his strength. He could see his unborn children reflecting in the depths of her amber orbs. Before he realized it, his hands were gripping her upper arms and he pulled her against his chest. His face was no more than an inch from hers as he spoke.

"I mean to marry you, madam," he rumbled. "But until that time, I intend to spoil you as you were meant to be spoiled, and to shower you with attention as you were meant to know. Those are my intentions, as plainly spoken as I can make them."

Gray gazed up at him, so completely swept away by his words that, for a moment, she forgot to breathe. There was such power in his grip, such strength in his face. She'd thought so from the moment she first saw him. For the first time in her life, she felt excitement from a man's touch. For the first time in her life, she experienced the first sparks of true joy. It was the most amazing dream she could imagine. So she said the first thing that came to mind.

"Are you drunk?"

Braxton's eyes widened. Then he broke out in laughter so strong that he nearly fell over with the force of it. Gray watched him, a smile on her lips, as he wiped his eyes.

"Aye, madam, I am drunk," he struggled to catch his breath. "I am drunk with your beauty and charm and wit."

She laughed shyly, watching him compose himself. As much as his declaration struck her, she was equally puzzled. "But... even if all you say is true, the fact remains that traveling is part of your vocation. I cannot wander with you. Even if you were to marry me, my place is here, with my daughter."

His laughter was fading. "You worry overly. I would never dream of separating you from your child."

"Does that mean you will live here, with us?"

He could only shake his head. "All I know is that the moment I laid eyes upon you, I knew I had to have you. Beyond that, I have not thought it through. Give me time, madam. I will do what needs to be done, for us both."

It was a vague answer, but not a frightening one. In fact, now that her shock was wearing off, an odd sense of elation was taking hold. Braxton watched her lovely face for a moment before extending his hand to her.

"May I have permission to court you, then?"

She gazed at his open palm before slowly placing her hand within his. "I will consider it."

He brought her fingers to his lips, the first kiss between them sending waves of exhilaration through her body. It was a very sweet, very tender moment, in a life that had known none. But her fingers tasted so sweet that he gave a gentle tug, pulling her up against him once more. He held her close, gazing down into her miraculous eyes and wishing he was without his armor. He so wanted to feel her soft body against his. His lips came down upon hers, tenderly. When he felt her respond, his kiss turned insistent and hot. His tongue gently snaked against her lips, tasting her flesh with all of the satisfaction of a man tasting the ambrosia of Heaven. He forced himself to pull away, knowing he would be lost if he did not.

"Please do," he said huskily.

His passion had left her dazed. She licked her lips, tasting him on her flesh. "What... what if you change your mind?"

"I will not."

They walked back to the fortress without another word between them. They didn't have to.

CHAPTER FIVE

Erith was a fortress under construction.

Three days after making his declaration, Braxton had transformed from a mercenary into a Master Builder. True, all of his men carried varied talents and were well paid for their worth, but now they were focused on building something rather than killing people. And the activity around the dying fortress made quite a site.

Braxton had sent Dallas and Geoff into the nearby town of Levens to recruit workers. They had returned with about thirty men to do a hard day's work at good wages. The next day, those men had brought another fifty men with them looking for work, most of them farmers hoping to earn a decent wage. By the third day, there were nearly two hundred laborers from all over Southern Cumbria working on the fortress; repairing walls, rebuilding the stables, and even building a new structure against the inner wall. Braxton called it the barracks and the men were building it in sturdy stones quarried from a small valley three miles to the east. The area had once been a river bed, long ago, and had tons of stone perfect for building.

Braxton had also put the word out over the countryside that Erith was seeking servants for the domestic chores. He swore to Gray that she would never again have to churn butter or mend an apron. In fact, he made sure that those female servants who could sew were already working on garments made from the fabric he had brought. He wanted to see Gray in something lovely, as she was meant to wear. He seemed to be trying to make up for her difficult life all in just a few days. He couldn't seem to do enough for her fast enough.

As overwhelming as it was, it was also bewildering. Gray struggled to keep her wits about her as Braxton worked to take away all of her troubles. She kept thinking that she was dreaming and that she would soon awaken back to the life she had always known, but so far, each day seemed to improve. There was food aplenty, the fortress was being repaired, and Brooke was the first family member, on the third day, to wear a brand new surcoat with a pretty beaded belt to match. Gray had wept at the sight of it. Braxton had merely smiled.

Through all of the building and sewing and restoration, Constance remained persistently arrogant and existed under a sense of entitlement. As far as she was concerned, Braxton could build Erith into a golden palace and it would be fine with her. She'd not spoken to Gray about it more than to simply voice her approval. Gray, of course, had not mentioned anything about Braxton's intentions to her mother. It would only serve to bring about some manner of disapproval from Constance. Moreover, Gray wanted to see if Braxton still felt the same by week's end. He could very well change his mind after a few days, realizing he'd gotten himself into far more than he'd bargained for. So until then, Gray kept their little secret. But it was a deliriously wonderful one.

Without her usual chores, Gray had very little to do. She had been in her father's solar most of the morning, watching three of her serving women work on surcoats made from emerald brocade and off-white silk. Both were exquisite. She wanted to help but didn't want Braxton to catch her 'working'. He had caught her earlier in the day helping the cook carefully measure brown flour and had given her an earful, however gentle it was. He didn't want her lifting a finger any longer.

The result was boredom. Growing tired of watching women sew, she wandered from the solar and out to the kitchen yard. There were more laborers there, rebuilding the big oven that had partially collapsed a few years before. The cook and her fat daughter huddled near the door to the store room, grunting and hooting like frightened animals. They acknowledged their lady with a panicked gesture in the direction of the oven. Gray assured them that the men were only repairing it, not removing it. The women didn't seem convinced but Gray guaranteed that it was entirely true.

All of the activity at the castle was new and disturbing; the cook and her daughter weren't the only servants she had reassured that morning. All of the occupants of Erith seemed a little edgy. Leaving the wary women in the kitchen yard, Gray meandered out into the stable area. She watched the laborers rebuilding part of the stable before noticing the puny chickens seemed harried by the activity. They were huddling in their coop. Gray went to the chicken coop and noticed there were several eggs inside that had not yet been collected. She reached in and plucked them out.

"What are you doing?"

She whirled around to find Braxton standing behind her. His eyebrows lifted in disapproval. "Well?"

She gestured weakly at the coop. "I was... gathering the eggs."

He frowned at her, though it had no force. "I thought I told you that you are no longer required to do domestic chores," he took a step closer to her, looking down upon her. "The servants will collect the eggs. You are the lady of the castle and these tasks are not for your lovely hands any longer."

She found her tongue. "But, my lord, I am bored senseless. I must do something."

It was difficult for him to maintain his harsh stance with her. "You will call me Braxton in private," he muttered. "And you will do something. You will learn leisurely tasks that fine ladies occupy themselves with."

"What leisurely tasks?"

"Well...," he shrugged. "Knitting, I suppose, or whatever it is fine ladies do with a needle and thread. Don't you know any?"

She gave him an intolerant look. "Whatever tasks I know are necessary ones."

"Then learn some *unnecessary* ones."

She put her hands on her hips. "You cannot place me on a glass pedestal like a fine porcelain doll. I will not break. And I am not one to sit around when there is work to be done."

He lifted an eyebrow at her. Then he reached out, took her hand, and tucked it into the crook of his elbow.

74

"Walk with me, madam."

"Gladly. At least I shall be doing something."

He fought off a grin. "You ungrateful wench. My men and I have been breaking our backs repairing your castle and all you can do is complain because you are bored."

She looked up at him, a grin on her face to melt his heart. When he finally cracked a smile at her, she beamed wide at him. "I simply wish to help, Braxton. Can I not help?"

"Help with what? Can you lift stone or build a roof?"

"Can you?"

He tried to show her how outraged he was by her question, but he only ended up laughing at her. "I could rebuild this entire place myself if necessary. And I have it on good authority that you are about to be spanked if you do not curb this rebellious attitude you are displaying."

She was properly contrite, though it was all an act. "I have no wish to be spanked. But I would like to help."

He came to a halt, sighing with mock frustration. "Very well, then. What do you want to do?"

She lifted a timid eyebrow. "Sew my own dresses?"

His lips curled. "There are servants to do that."

"Please? I enjoy it."

He just shook his head. "You are the most ungrateful woman I have ever had the fortune to come across. Very well, if it pleases you, sew your own clothes." As she grinned triumphantly, he moved closer, caressing the hand he held against his arm. "You are also the most glorious woman I have ever had the fortune to come across. I want to spoil you, madam. Why do you resist?"

Braxton was awakening feelings in her she had never known herself capable of. A look from him could provoke giddiness, a word could provoke elation. Gone were thoughts of self protection, of suspicion. Those feelings had fled days ago. Without even realizing it, she had learned to trust him completely. Not necessarily for the kindness he was doing for her or for Erith, but simply by his manner. If he'd meant to capture her heart, he was well on his way to doing so.

"I am sorry if I seem unappreciative," she replied softly. "I have simply never known anything else but hard work. I feel quite useless sitting around while you hire an army to work on my fortress. I do not want others to think I am taking advantage of your generosity."

"What others?"

She shrugged. "These people are from Levens. They will talk and tell tale of the Lady of Erith sitting idle while an army of mercenaries repairs her keep. Soon all of Cumbria will hear such things."

"Soon all of Cumbria will know that the repair of the fortress was my wedding gift to you," he patted her hand gently; though he desperately wanted to kiss it, he would make no such move. He did not want those who might witness such a thing to believe the lady compromised. "Worry not what others think, madam. You and I know the truth."

She gazed up at him, studying the lines of his handsome face. She hadn't known the man a week and already she felt more comfortable with him than she had with anyone, ever.

"I suppose we do," she agreed softly. She saw the same look in his eyes that she had seen when he had kissed her and, not wanting to make a spectacle for all to see, she backed away. "I shall go now and help the women with my clothes. They're nearly done, you know."

He was reluctant to release her hand. "We shall go into Milnthorpe tomorrow to obtain more fabric. Between you, your mother and your daughter, the fabric is gone."

"We do not need more fabric," she insisted. "What you have provided us is more than generous. We are very grateful."

He winked at her. "You must have a new garment for every day of the week. And I think I shall purchase some jewels for you as well."

Gray just stared at him. "Jewels? What on earth would I do with them?'

"Wear them."

He kissed her hand then, swiftly, hoping that no one would

see. It was a sweet and tender moment, however brief. But he was distracted by someone was calling his name from the direction of the front gates and he turned to see Dallas approach. He discreetly let go of Gray's hand as Dallas walked up.

"My lady," the knight bowed to Gray before focusing on Braxton. "There is a small party approaching from the south, my lord. Shall we send out riders?'

"Indeed," Braxton nodded. "Are their banners evident?"

Dallas shook his head. "They are still too far out."

"Then make haste to identify them. How much time until they are upon us?"

"Less than a half hour, my lord."

"Then be gone."

Dallas excused himself and was gone. Gray tucked strands of blowing hair behind her ear, her expression one of concern.

"What does that mean?" she asked. "Who would be coming to Erith?"

Braxton had many different theories at that moment, most of which he would not verbalize. He remembered Brooke's words to him the day he met her, how her Grandmother had sent invitation to various Houses to vie for the girl's hand. He didn't know what that particular thought popped into his head at the moment, but it did. He'd very nearly forgotten about it. And, as Brooke had told him, Gray apparently knew nothing about it. He just couldn't imagine that she did simply from her obvious attitude.

Though Braxton had seen little of Lady Constance since his arrival, he suspected the time had come for him to better acquaint himself with the self-aggrandizing woman. Though he would love to have Gray all to himself, she came with a daughter whom he was very fond of and a mother he was not. If he was going to declare his intentions to Gray, he would have to declare it to all of them. And part of his declaration would include setting matters straight between himself and the arrogant Lady de Montfort.

"Do not worry yourself," he took her by the elbow and turned her in the direction of the keep. "Go to your sewing now and I shall deal with these visitors."

"Though I appreciate your offer, I am still the Lady of Erith," she said, firmly but politely. "This is still my keep, Braxton. I shall greet our visitors."

He didn't want to argue with her, but if the approaching party had something to do with Lady de Montfort's solicitation, he did not want her to be shocked. The party was less than a half hour off, which gave him little time to figure this out.

"Then wait in the keep until they are upon us," he said. "There is no need for you to wait out here in the sun. Come inside and be comfortable."

That produced the hoped for result; she walked with him into the keep. Once inside, he left her in the solar with the sewing women and excused himself on a weak pretext. What he really intended to do was find Lady de Montfort. A passing servant told him where to find the woman.

***

Braxton figured out where all of the furnishings, beds, linens or other comforts in Erith were kept. Upon entering Lady de Montfort's chamber on the fourth floor of the keep, it looked like a storage room. There were items everywhere. It was rather a shock considering the sparse furnishings of the rest of Erith. It immediately occurred to him that Lady de Montfort refused to give up anything she believed herself entitled to, no matter what matter of poverty her daughter and granddaughter lived in. Though the stuff lining her chamber was worn, it had once been very fine. She needed her possessions to maintain the illusion that poverty had not yet touched her. It made Braxton dislike the lady all the more.

Lady de Montfort sat in a chair near the lancet window, a piece of embroidery in her hand. It wasn't a very nice square of material, old and yellowed, but the work on it was exquisite. Braxton glanced at the piece as the woman laid it in her lap, fighting off building resentment for two reasons; Gray had told him she did not know any leisurely skills, which meant her mother had not seen fit to teach her. Secondly, by the look of the work, it had taken many, many hours to do. This meant that while Gray was blistering her hands with harsh work, her mother was wiling away the hours with dainty hobbies. It was a struggle to keep his rage at bay.

"Sir Braxton," Constance greeted him evenly. "To what do I owe the honor of your visit?"

Braxton stood near the door, keeping a rein on his patience. "You and I have something to discuss, my lady."

Constance lifted her eyebrows. "I cannot imagine what that is, unless you seek my advice on something. What is your wish?"

Haughty till the end, he thought. "I do not seek your advice nor counsel, madam. But I believe we may have a situation arising that could or could not be of your doing."

"What is that?"

He shifted on his big legs, folding muscular arms over his chest. "Brooke has told me that you have sent out solicitations for her hand in marriage, unbeknownst to her mother. Is this true?"

Constance's thin face tightened. "What business is it of yours?"

"More than you know. Did you do this?"

As shrewd as Constance was, Braxton was doubly. But the older woman would not allow herself to be cornered. "This is none of your affair, Sir Braxton. You will kindly leave my chamber."

He lifted an eyebrow. "I am not going anywhere until you answer the question."

So he could not be ordered around. Constance rethought her strategy. "If it is?"

"Then we have a party approaching Erith at this moment who, I suspect, might be coming in response to your offer. If that is the case, your daughter is going to discover the truth."

Constance stood up. "Where is my daughter?"

"In the solar."

The woman grabbed her shawl and swung it over her slender

shoulders, making way for the door. Braxton waited until she had passed him before speaking.

"You do not own the rights to Brooke's hand, my lady."

She paused, hand on the door latch. "Your statement is not only rude, it is insolent."

His blue-green eyes were hard, like blades of sharpened steel. "Perhaps," his voice lowered. "But it is the truth. Listen to me now and understand what I am saying. You do not own the rights to Brooke's hand. I do. I bought them from a man who had acquired them from Garber Serroux in payment for a gambling debt."

He could see from the expression on the woman's face that she was rattled. She instinctively clutched her shawl more tightly about her.

"So you are here to claim Brooke?" For the first time, the confidence was out of her tone. "Why did you just not say so?"

"I am not here to claim Brooke," Braxton clarified. "But she, and Erith, belongs to me."

Constance's expression turned suspicious. "You have no proof of this."

"I have a document signed by Neil Wenvoe that relinquishes his claim to Brooke Serroux and Erith to me for the sum of thirty thousand gold marks. These rights were given to Wenvoe to forgive a debt incurred by Garber Serroux."

Constance attempted to maintain her defensive stance. God knows she did. But Braxton watched all of the fight drain out of her, for the very first time since he had met her. When she realized he would not be withered by her stare, she averted her gaze.

"I see," she murmured. "Does Gray know any of this?"

He felt himself relent, if only just a little. "Nay," he replied. "Though I do mean to tell her."

"When?"

"I am not sure. She is only now learning to trust me. I am afraid that divulging something like this will cause her to think I have had ulterior motives from the beginning."

Constance cast him a long glance. "Have you?"

He shook his head, slowly. "I only acquired these rights three days ago when I went to Wenvoe to fulfill a long-standing contract." He paused, watching the shift of her fine features. "Wenvoe wanted to hire me to lay siege to Erith and claim the rights that Garber had promised him. It seems that Wenvoe was aware you were soliciting offers the girl's hand and he felt compelled to press his claim. So I bought the claim from him."

Constance's amber eyes studied him. "Why did you do this?"

Now it was Braxton's turn to waver in confidence. "Because I could not lay siege to Gray's fortress," he said simply. "In case you have not realized it, I am fond of your daughter, Lady de Montfort. I could not hurt her."

"But now you own her daughter and Erith. What will you do?"

"Give it back to Gray."

Constance reclaimed her chair, a defeated look on her face. It seemed that there was nothing left to fight for. "I would see this document you speak of, knight."

"You shall."

"Then what will you do about the approaching party?"

"That is your problem. I suggest you tell your daughter immediately what you have done."

The older woman's features tightened again. "It is not simply my problem. You own the rights to Brooke, so in essence, you have the final say in determining who she will marry, not Gray. She will not take this well at all. I would suggest we both go tell her what has happened."

He still did not want to tell Gray about the contract from Wenvoe. He felt very strongly that it might ruin the sweet beginnings they were experiencing. But the longer he waited, the harder it would be. With reluctance, he nodded to the older woman's suggestion.

Together, they left the chamber in silence to seek out Gray.

***

For some reason, Gray was nowhere to be found. The women sewing garments in the solar said she had left some time before but they had no knowledge of where she went. While Constance went to check her bedchamber, Braxton went out into the kitchen yard.

There were a few men working on the collapse oven, now almost completely rebuilt. Braxton did not see her anywhere in the kitchen area and moved out towards the stables. There were several laborers working to restore a damaged section and also to build an addition. Additionally, they were framing the stable for several more stalls and a loft. Braxton checked the chicken coop and, on a whim, entered the part of the stables that the men were not working on. It was empty.

He turned to leave and almost ran over Brooke. She was standing behind him, her round face smiling up at him. He reached out to steady her as he bumped into her.

"My lady," he said. "My apologies. I did not see you."

"I know," she replied. "I followed you in here."

"Why?"

"Because I want to talk to you."

"I see," he casually stepped away from her, leaning against the nearest post. "What is so important?"

Brooke took a step towards him, closing the gap he had so carefully established. "Well... it is hard to describe."

"What is hard to describe?"

She tilted her head, looking thoughtful. "Me. And you."

He didn't particularly like the sound of that. "What about me and you?"

She took another step, ending up very close to him. "You do not have to pretend any longer. I can see it in your eyes."

"See what?"

"What you feel for me, of course." She was suddenly pressed against him, her hands on his big arm. "I saw it the first day we met, Braxton. I felt it when you saved my life. Oh, I know you told my grandmother that you had no intention of marrying, but why else would you come back to Erith with gifts? I know it is because you are interested in me."

He moved away from the post, trying to put some distance between him and her. "My lady," he said evenly. "What I told your grandmother is was true. Though I am flattered, I clearly have no intentions towards you."

She was following him. "You do not have to pretend any longer, darling. I would be most pleased to call you husband. I am young and strong and can bear you many strong sons."

Braxton was backing out of the stable. Brooke threw herself forward, her arms wrapped around his neck like a noose.

"You must control yourself," he said sternly, trying to pry her arms off of him. "This is not appropriate behavior for a young woman."

"Kiss me," Brooke begged, making sucking noises with her lips and aiming for his mouth. "Kiss me, my darling. I know you want to."

She was strong for a young girl. Braxton was trying to pull her off of him but he didn't want to hurt her. "Let go, Brooke."

"I will not. You want me. Kiss me!"

Off to his right he heard a strange noise, something that sounded like a gasp. By the time he turned around, Gray was marching up on the two of them with some kind of farm implement in her hand. Braxton's hands were trying to restrain Brooke and he was unable to defend himself when Gray swung the wooden stick at his head.

Stars burst before his vision and he fell onto his back, hovering between consciousness and unconsciousness. Stunned but not senseless, he rolled to his left, away from the second strike that landed very close to him. He could hear Brooke screaming.

"Mama!" she shrieked. "No!"

"You... you beast," Gray swung the wooden implement one last time, missing him by a wide margin. As Braxton struggled to get to his feet, she wielded the pitchfork like a weapon. "Braxton de Nerra, you are a despicable, horrid creature and I want you out of here. Take your gifts and your food and leave my fortress immediately."

His ears were ringing and the world rocked. As his vision cleared, he saw Brooke's fearful face, Gray's angry one, and Constance standing just behind her daughter. For some reason, he found himself focused on the old woman. He did not like the expression on her face. But his attention moved back to Gray.

"My lady," he said. "You are gravely mistaken if you think...."

"Stop it," she hissed at him. "I will hear no more from you. I trusted you and you lied to me."

"What?"

Gray kept the pitchfork between them. "My mother told me what you did." She was suddenly bordering on tears; he could see it in her face. "How could you do that?"

He had no idea what she was talking about, but his gaze moved back to Constance. He has a suspicion that whatever Gray was thinking came from her mother. A dark wave of realization swept him.

"What did I do, Gray?" he asked softly. "What are you talking about?"

Tears welled in her eyes. She looked so very hurt. Behind her, Constance stood cold and silent. Damn the woman; he knew something awful had come from her lips.

"The contract," Gray almost whispered. "My mother told me. Do not try to deny it. That is why you went to Wenvoe, to buy my daughter and my castle."

"I bought the contract because Wenvoe wanted me to lay siege to Erith to claim both the castle and your daughter. I bought it to spare you. Did you not know that your husband had promised him both Brooke and the fortress in payment for his debt to Wenvoe?"

"I did," she said hoarsely. "But Wenvoe promised he had no interest in either. He said he would not hold Brooke or I responsible for Garber's disgrace."

"He had no interest until your mother started sending out invitations to vie for Brooke's hand."

"Do not listen to him, Gray," Constance entered the conversation. "He has been plotting since the beginning. He owns

Brooke, and he owns Erith. He has been sending out solicitations of marriage to sell off your daughter and the castle."

So that's what this was about. The old bitch had turned on him, gaining an upper hand with her lies and deceit. He had underestimated her. Braxton struggled to keep his composure as he faced Constance.

"That, Lady de Montfort, is a lie. You were the one who sent out the solicitations of marriage, not I."

"See how he tries to defend himself?" Constance gripped her daughter's arm. "He is a mercenary, Gray. All he cares about is money. He bought Erith and Brooke for a price. Now he intends to secure a fine return on his investment by selling them both off. Why do you think he is fixing up the fortress? 'Twill make it much more attractive to a future husband."

It was purely amazing how so slight a woman could be so evil. Braxton knew, even as he stared at her, that he was fighting a losing battle. He never knew his heart was capable of breaking, but at the moment, he suspected it was well on its way. He looked at Brooke, cowering beside her mother.

"Lady Brooke," he said steadily. "Perhaps you can straighten this out. Did you not, in fact, tell me that your grandmother was plotting behind your mother's back to marry you off?"

Brooke's eyes widened. She looked at her mother, her grandmother, and visibly shrank. Her head began to wag back and forth.

"I... I did not say," she said.

"The day I met you near the falls of Erith, you did not tell me this?"

"I... I do not remember."

Braxton was not surprised by her denial. He put a hand to his forehead, wiping away the trickle of blood from the crack Gray had given him. He knew he would never be able to convince Gray that both her mother and daughter were lying to her. He did not blame her; they were her family and she had known them a lifetime. She had only known him a few short days. A few short, miraculous days. He could not believe it was all coming to so tragic an end.

The only person who could validate his statement was too afraid to do so. Brooke was only a child, caught up in an adult game. He didn't blame her either. In fact, it was no one's fault but his. He should have told Gray about the situation the moment he had returned to Erith. He should have been the first one to come out with the truth about what had transpired with Wenvoe. But he hadn't; as he'd told Constance, Gray was just learning to trust him. He did not want to ruin that. But his silence, and his conversation with a shrewd old woman, had cost him dearly. He should have been smarter about it.

"Then I would suspect there is nothing more I can say to my defense," he said after a moment. His gaze lingered on Gray; she looked positively miserable. "I will clear out my men before nightfall."

He went to move past the women, giving them a wide birth. Gray called out to him.

"Your gifts and food stores will be brought to the bailey," she said.

He paused, meeting her gaze. "No need, my lady. They were gifts. I do not expect them returned, nor would I want them. They were meant only for you."

With that, he turned and walked away. Gray stood there, pitchfork still in hand, feeling heavy sobs bubbling within her chest. The pitchfork came down and tears spilled onto her cheeks.

"Mama..." Brook began softly.

"Go," Gray threw the wooden implement down and turned away from her daughter and mother. "Just... go. Leave me alone."

Constance took Brooke by the hand and led her off. She had come out on top of the situation and did not feel the need to linger over her victory. The knight had challenged her authority and had lost both the battle and the war as a result. She would never let a low-born knight to get the better of her, no matter how wealthy or powerful. It was over now; she would leave her daughter to deal with it.

Gray listened to their footfalls fade, finally allowing the sobs to come forth. It was the most painful thing she had ever experienced, and she'd experienced many crippling things during her life. This was as bad as she could imagine, mostly because her unprotected emotions were involved. To find Braxton with Brooke in his arms... she closed her eyes to the sight of it, her tears falling on the straw of the stables. Eventually, she sank to her buttocks and wept.

She must have been there quite a while because the sound of footsteps in the straw next to her nearly startled her to death. Looking up, she found herself staring into Braxton's pale face.

"I have something for you," he said before she could open her mouth. He held up a yellowed parchment, rolled and tied with dried gut. "It is the agreement from Wenvoe relinquishing his rights to Brooke and Erith. It is yours now. Keep it safe."

Leaving the parchment in the straw next to her, he turned to walk away. She called after him.

"Sir Braxton," she said. "I would have you read this to me, if it would not be too much trouble."

He paused, turned to look at her, and slowly retraced his steps. There was labored hesitation to his movements, as if it was taking all of his strength to complete them. Crouching down next to her, he sighed before picking up the parchment and unrolling it. His blue-green eyes focused on the scribed lines, written by Wenvoe himself.

"'On this third day of August, in the year of our Lord thirteen hundred and five, let it be known that I, Neil Wenvoe, Baron Killington, Lord of Creekmere Castle, do hereby relinquish my claim to Sir Braxton de Nerra for the Lady Brooke Serroux and her dowry of Erith Castle and the hereditary title of Baron Kentmere for the sum of thirty thousand gold marks in repayment for a debt owed to me by Sir Garber Serroux.'" He lowered the parchment. "That is all it says. Then he gave his seal."

He began to roll it up again but she reached out and took it from him, their hands brushing in the process. It was the most painfully exquisite touch; Braxton had to close his eyes and turn away. He was having a good deal of trouble dealing with all of this at the moment and her proximity was distressing.

Gray's gaze lingered on him a moment before looking at the parchment, looking over the careful words. He didn't know she could read, as taught to her by her father. She had asked him to read the parchment for good reason; to see if he would lie to her. But he had read every word as written.

"Thirty thousand gold marks," she whispered. "You paid thirty thousand gold marks for the rights to my daughter and Erith?"

He simply nodded his head. "Why?" she asked, astonished. "Nothing about this place is worth that kind of money. What would possess you to do such a thing?"

He met her gaze, then. There was hardness in his eyes, a necessary self-protection. "Because I was trying to save you from having your castle razed and your daughter confiscated. If I did not accept this task from Wenvoe, he would find someone that would. This I could not allow. I was trying to do something noble, my lady," the last words were bitter and ironic. "A lot of good it did me."

He stood up abruptly but did not leave. Gray watched him pace around like a caged animal. He wanted to go, she could tell, but he wanted much more to stay. She realized she wanted him to stay, too, in spite of everything.

"Explain to me, my lord, how I could possibly misunderstand all of this," she was begging for an explanation, without her mother hanging over her and her daughter clutching at her. It was just the two of them. "What is the truth of all of this? You have nothing to lose by telling me the verity of the situation now that the damage has been done. Tell me the truth and I shall believe you."

He looked at her and she was struck by the naked emotion in his eyes. "Will you?"

"I said I would."

He took a deep breath, hardly daring to hope. "Then I will swear on my oath as a knight that I will tell you the complete, honest truth. You may believe me if you wish. If you do not, I hold no resentment against you. It would be difficult for you to know the truth living with a viper as you do."

She knew he meant her mother and she was not offended. She knew what the woman was capable of, or at least she thought she did.

"Go on."

He stood in front of her. "Wenvoe had a verbal contract with your late husband. The deal was your daughter and Erith in exchange for the forgiveness of his debt to Wenvoe."

"I know."

"He also said your husband had died before the terms could be put to paper. You said your husband was murdered by Wenvoe. This information is conflicting."

It was her turn to look somewhat less confident. She lowered her gaze. "Since we are telling complete truths, I will tell mine. My husband committed suicide in shame over the bargain he had struck with Wenvoe, the shame of his gambling debts finally catching up to him. The old baron might as well have killed him for all of the humiliation he put Garber through. Somehow it sounds less shameful to say my husband was murdered. There is enough at Erith to be ashamed over without that added trouble hanging over our heads."

He watched the top of her blond head, feeling pity for yet another thing in her life that she had no control over. But it did not deter him from what he must say to her.

"Upon my arrival at Creekmere, I discovered Wenvoe's true plans for me. He had been informed that your mother had sent out offers for Brooke's hand. Given the fact that Brooke was his property, he wanted me to confiscate both Brooke and Erith. He asked me to enforce the terms of his verbal contract with your husband. But I could not do it, Gray. I could not take both your daughter and your castle. So I told Wenvoe that I would buy the contract from him, thereby repaying your husband's debt. When he refused, I threatened to raze Creekmere. So he sold me your daughter, and Erith, for thirty thousand gold marks."

She was gazing up at him quite earnestly. "Was that his asking price?"

"It was my offer. But I would have doubled it without hesitation."

"Why?"

He looked at her as if she was daft. He lifted a big hand, letting it slap helplessly back against his thigh. "Because your happiness is worth all of that and more. How much plainer can I be?"

Gray stood up, unsteadily, tears reforming in her eyes. "You said something earlier. You said that Brooke had told you about my mother's subversive solicitations on her behalf. Is that God's truth, Braxton? Did she really say that to you?"

He nodded. "It is. She told me that your mother said that she was a young woman now and was due a wealthy husband."

Gray blinked and the tears spilled down her cheeks. Braxton's hands ached for want to wipe the tears away but he was afraid to touch her, afraid she would pull away from him.

"I have heard my mother say that before," she sniffed. "But never did I think she would go behind my back. She sent out offers for Brooke's hand, didn't she?"

"That is what Brooke told me and what your mother confessed to when I confronted her."

She blinked again and more tears spilled down her face. Then she dissolved into soft sobs. "Then they both lied to me," she wept. "My mother, most of all, and Brooke because she was afraid. I know how my mother is. She lied to take the blame off herself."

"Your mother does what she must in order to survive."

She wiped at the tears streaming down her face. "It is not a good enough reason to lie to me and to deliberately discredit you," she said. Then she looked at him. "But tell me one more thing."

"Anything."

"Why did I see Brooke in your arms?"

He lifted an eyebrow. "Because she was throwing herself at me. I was attempting to pry her off when you appeared." The blue-green eyes glimmered faintly. "My only interest is in you,

Gray. Do you really think I would show anything other than friendly attention to your daughter?"

She looked at him, seeing the naked honesty in his face. She'd been around enough cheats and fabricators to know when she saw the raw elements of truth. "Nay," she murmured. "I do not."

Braxton didn't know if he felt more relief than anger; relief that she apparently believed him, anger at Constance's tactics. The old bitch did not care who she hurt, not even her own daughter. Poor Gray was on the receiving end of a very unscrupulous woman. He moved towards her to offer some words of comfort but was interrupted by the sudden appearance of Dallas.

The blond knight stood in the stable entry, his eyes fixed on Braxton. "My lord," he said. "The visitors have arrived. They are from the House of Haistethorpe."

"That's in Windermere," Gray muttered as she wiped her nose.

Braxton looked at her a moment before turning back to Dallas. "Did they say why they had come?"

Dallas' gaze moved between the lady and his lord. "At the invitation of the Lady Constance."

Gray's head snapped up. Her face was wet, her eyes furious. "Is that what they said, exactly?" she demanded.

Dallas nodded his head. "Aye, my lady. They asked for the Lady Constance by name."

Braxton dismissed Dallas before Gray could say anymore. She was dangerously close to exploding; he could tell. He stood there a moment, watching her face, waiting.

"What do you want me to do?" he asked softly. "Do you still want me to leave?"

She looked at him, then, and the anger fled from her face. Her lower lip trembled delicately. "Oh, Braxton," she whispered. "I am so sorry. I hit you... I accused you of awful things."

He went to her, pulling her into his warm, powerful embrace. Gray collapsed against him, her soft sobs returning. They clutched at each other, in relief, in sorrow. His hand held her head against his chest, gently stroking her soft blond hair.

"No apologies, sweetheart," he murmured into the top of her head. "All is well again with us."

Her arms were around his torso, holding him tightly. "Please do not leave," she begged softly. "I do not want you to go."

"Then I will not."

"I... I am afraid."

He scowled gently. "I don't believe it. Of what?"

She tilted her head back to look at him. "Of what my mother has done. I have no idea how to deal with these people who believe they are honestly vying for Brooke's hand. She's only fifteen years old, for God's sake. What am I going to do?"

He leaned down and kissed her, tasting the salty tears on her lips. His tongue gently pushed into her mouth, delicately tasting her, acquainting her with the true essence of a delicious kiss. The hand on her head moved to her cheek, her neck, holding her fast as his mouth left her lips and moved across her face. With every suckle, every touch, his want for her was growing. He could not believe how close he had come to losing her.

Gray unwound her arms from around his midsection, raking her fingers through his graying blond hair. His lips were on her throat, savoring the sweet taste of her. But he eventually returned to her mouth, kissing her so deeply that she went limp in his arms. When he finally pulled away and looked at her, it took Gray a moment to come around. Her amber eyes opened slowly.

"You needn't worry," he said huskily. "I will do what must be done. She belongs to me, after all. I have the right to send every one of those hounds away."

Gray smiled faintly. "But not too harshly. We may actually want one of them to return in a few years."

He grinned, kissing her again with lingering sweetness. "Go now," he had to get away from her or risk a complete loss of self control. "Change into one of your new garments. I will entertain your guests until you are ready to speak to them."

"As you say. And, Braxton?"

"Aye?"

"Thank you."

He put his arm around her shoulders, pulling her gently from the stables.

CHAPTER SIX

She was hiding. Or, at least, she thought she was. Whenever Brooke was upset or wanted to be alone, she hid in the storeroom on the bottom floor of the keep. She had a nice little corner tucked away where no one would find her. Until today. Two pairs of eyes were gazing back at her from behind the new barrels of salted pork.

She didn't recognize the eyes, both pairs soft blue and similarly shaped. Startled, and a little miffed at being watched, she stood up and put her hands on her hips. Sir Braxton's squires popped up from the other side of the barrels.

"What are you doing?" Brooke demanded. "Spying on me?"

The older boy spoke in his newly-deep man voice. "Nay, my lady," he assured her quickly. "We were bringing in sacks of pears. We heard a noise and thought it was a mouse."

She scowled. "I do not sound like a mouse."

The boys looked at each other. They had no answer to that. Brooke's angry stance began to fade; living a somewhat isolated life at Erith, she had never had much opportunity to be around children her own age. Now, here were two in her midst and her curiosity overcame her indignation. She'd noticed the boys before, of course, but never this close. And they had never spoken to her.

"What is your name?" she asked the older boy.

"Norman, my lady," he replied. "This is my brother, Edgar."

"You travel with Sir Braxton, do you not?" she asked.

Norman nodded. "We squire for him, my lady."

"How old are you, Norman?"

"I have seen seventeen summers, my lady. I think."

"What do you mean 'you think'?"

He shrugged. "Sir Braxton found me and my brother orphaned on the streets of Oxford. He could only guess that I was five years and Edgar here was three. I suppose I do not know how old I really am."

Brooke forgot all about her rage. She was very curious about the boys. "You were orphans? What happened to your parents?"

Norman shrugged. "I do not know. My earliest recollection is living in a doorway holding my baby brother. Sir Braxton took us in."

"He has been your father?"

"I suppose," Norman replied. "He has taken care of us since we were very young."

Brooke inspected them both closely; they were both brunette, with pale blue eyes, and handsome. At least, she thought so. Except the younger one; he looked rather scrappy. She focused intently on Edgar.

"Does he talk?" she asked.

Edgar's response was to stick his tongue out at her. Then he snarled, making horrible faces at her. Brooke frowned.

"You are a nasty little boy."

Edgar mocked her frown. "I am not a little boy. I am as old as you are, you skinny, ugly girl."

Brooke's mouth popped open with outrage. She went to poke him but he stuck his tongue out at her again and fled. Brooke tore after him in hot pursuit, leaving Norman to follow their trail.

Edgar raced into the kitchen yard, taunting her and dodging when she took a whack at him and missed. He raced on into the stable yard, ignoring his brother's calls to cease. Brooke ran after him, shouting threats. Edgar, much faster and wilier, ran a circle around her as she tried to smack him again. Laughing wickedly, he ran on into the main portion of the bailey where the party of Haistethorpe had just arrived.

Brooke was completely ignorant of the strangers in the ward. In fact, there had been so many strange people about lately that she didn't give it a second thought. But Edgar realized too late that Sir Braxton was standing near the keep, right in his line of sight, and he came to an abrupt halt. Brooke immediately closed the gap and pounced on him.

Edgar howled as Brooke punched him mercilessly. Norman

raced up behind the pair, trying to remove the young lady but not being too successful at it. She was intent on pummeling his brother to death. Edgar rolled over, toppling Brooke onto the ground, which only made her more furious. She pinched and kicked him until he screamed.

Braxton hadn't even said a word to Lord Haistethope before this spectacle erupted. Now he found himself breaking up a fight. Norman saw him approaching and desperately tried to pull Edgar away from Brooke. But Edgar was now angry more than he was afraid of Braxton and took hold of Brooke's hair, pulling sharply. Brooke screamed and took a swing at him, socking him in the jaw. Edgar tumbled off of her, hit the ground, and she jumped on him again.

By the time Braxton reached the brawl, Brooke was on top once again. He shoved Norman out of the way, grabbed Brooke under the arms, and pulled her off of Edgar. But she was a fighter; she continued to kick at him until Braxton growled at her.

"Cease this instant, Lady Brooke," he snapped quietly. "This is behavior most unbecoming a young lady. You shame your mother and the House of Serroux with this wild display."

She yanked herself out of Braxton's grip, turning to him with a scowl much like her mother had when displeased. Braxton had seen the expression before.

"He started it," she said. "He called me ugly and stuck his tongue out at me."

Braxton cast Edgar, now picking himself up off the ground, a long look. "Edgar," he admonished quietly. "I have taught you better than that. Apologize to this young lady."

Only because Braxton told him to did Edgar even consider it. But it was a struggle. "I… I apologize," he mumbled.

"I cannot hear you," Braxton said.

"I apologize," the boy said, louder. He looked between Braxton and the girl. "May I go now, my lord?"

Braxton lifted an eyebrow at him. "You and your brother will go to Sir Dallas, tell him what has happened, and ask for punishment. I will say no more."

With that, Braxton turned away, a tight grip on Brooke's shoulder as he went. Brooke's last look at Edgar showed him making another face at her.

She was going to get even with him.

***

"How dare you believe a stranger over your own mother," Constance hissed. "You have made me ashamed of you."

Gray stood in her mother's chamber in the midst of a tense confrontation. Constance, as usual, denied everything. She was a master of exploitation and deflecting blame. But not this time; Gray would make sure her mother understood just how serious this situation was. And she would tolerate no more of it.

"As you make me ashamed of you," she replied steadily. "My own mother lied to me, manipulated me, and has gone behind my back to involve herself in affairs that clearly do not concern her. Whatever made you think you could assume responsibility for Brooke's betrothal when you knew very well that Wenvoe held her contract?"

"Psh," Constance was fuming. "I will not stand for your questions."

"You will not only stand for my questions, you will answer them. Mother, I demand it or I swear I will banish you from Erith and this family forever."

Constance glared at her. "You will not threaten me."

"It is not a threat, I assure you. You have not only undermined my authority as Brooke's mother, but you took it upon yourself to violate a pact that Garber made. But most of all, you lied about it. You wanted me to think that Braxton had done all of this."

"He still continues to convince you that he is innocent."

"He is." Gray shouted at her mother, and she wasn't the shouting type. But she was sick of her mother's denials. "The House of Haistethorpe is in the bailey. They told Braxton's knights that they were her on *your* invitation, Mother. Not Braxton's, but yours. How can you explain that?"

Constance would not back down. She knew that Haistethorpe's confirmation would blow holes in her denial. So she did the only thing she could do; she tried to turn it around on her daughter.

"What if I did invite them?" she asked haughtily. "What if they are here at my request? You have failed in your duty to provide a wealthy husband for your daughter. Did you think Wenvoe would truly make his claim to her? He's an old man, Gray. He'll be dead in a year or two and the contract will be void. You must think of Brooke, and clearly, you are not. What I did, I did for my granddaughter's sake. She is the last hope this family has of regaining its wealth and honor. *You are failing.*"

Gray just stared at her mother. She would have loved to have called it nonsense, but she knew that Constance believed every word. Some of the fight went out of Gray at that moment. She was so very tired of her mother's interference, her deceptions. It had to end.

"Then you did send out solicitations for her hand."

"What if I did? I had to do something, as you clearly were not."

Gray remained silent for a moment, contemplating her mother's position. She thought long and hard and deep about the women who birthed her, knowing her character, struggling to see some good in her mother. She simply could not. The older the woman became, the worse she became. She began to realize there were choices before her; choices for her, and for Brooke.

"Then I will do my duty now, as Brooke's mother," she said quietly. She looked at Constance. "You have always been vain, petty and deceitful. But your traits have only affected me. Now they are affecting Brooke. I do not want my daughter to grow up thinking that it is acceptable to lie and manipulate. She is growing into a young woman now and I know that you have been filling her head with questionable ideas. I will not let you do it, Mother. I will not let you ruin my daughter. I must protect her."

Constance wasn't following her line of thinking, but she knew it wasn't flattering. "If you consider imparting the ideas of wealth and status into her head, then I would gladly ruin her. Somehow,

I could not ruin you. You did not do as I would have taught you."

Gray smiled thinly. "Nay, I did as father taught. He was a kind, forgiving man and you drove him to his grave with your evil ways. Shame on you."

Constance marched up on Gray and slapped her across the cheek. Stung, Gray reacted by slapping her back. Constance toppled backwards, almost falling to her knees. Gray would never forget the look on her face.

"You ungrateful, insolent bitch," Constance half-wept, half-hissed. "How dare you strike your own mother. May God curse you for your actions."

Gray was at the end of her patience. "And may God curse you for staining this family with your warped ideas and twisted sense of morals. I'll not have you poison my daughter as you tried to poison me. I will not tolerate any more of your interference, Mother. Do you understand me?"

Constance struggled to reclaim her dignity, turning her back on her daughter. "Get out."

"Gladly," Gray said. "But before I go, I will say this. You will stay to your chamber. You will not try to seek my daughter, or me, or anyone else at Erith. I will not see you out of this room, for if I do, I will ask Sir Braxton to send you back to Thirlwall Castle. You were born there. You can die there, too, for all I care."

With a lingering glance at her mother's stiff back, she turned and quit the room. When she reached her chamber on the floor below, she shut the door softly and wept.

CHAPTER SEVEN

Lord Alan Haistethorpe was a tolerant man with a son who was not so tolerant. One look at Brooke Serroux and the Elliott Haistethorpe begged his father to leave for home immediately. But Alan had come this far to examine the prospective bride and would not turn away so easily. Erith Castle was a well-known de Montfort stronghold that Alan remembered from his youth and the idealized memory of it still lingered for him. He did not want his son to pass so easily on a legend.

What he could not figure out yet was where Braxton de Nerra fit in to all of this. He had heard of the mercenary; most people in the north had, for de Nerra had done a lot of fighting for the border barons. He wondered why Erith required the man's services, which put him on his guard.

Braxton was cordial without being overly friendly. He took Alan and Elliott into the great hall and offered them wine out of his own supplies. It was a fine Madera, rich and red and tart. Beyond that, he went so far to explain that the lady of Erith would be joining them shortly, but little else. He was not much of a conversationalist. Alan and Elliott ended up feeling quite unnerved by his presence, made worse by the three knights that wandered in shortly after their arrival. Braxton's men were young, strong and intimidating. They stood in various positions around the room as if waiting for a fight to start.

They had caught a glimpse of Brooke after the scuffle in the yard. She was a pretty little thing. Braxton had sent her to change her clothes and when she reappeared, it was with an older woman with exquisite features. Though the daughter was quite lovely, Lady Gray Serroux was magnificent. Alan, and Elliott's, attention shifted from daughter to mother in a hurry.

Braxton saw their expressions almost as soon as the mood changed. But he was distracted from his thoughts of murdering the pair by Gray's appearance; she was clad in one of her new surcoats, an exquisite emerald garment with delicate lines that emphasized her slender torso and full breasts. In fact, she looked amazing. For a moment, Braxton was actually speechless. He'd never seen anything so lovely, and he'd never seen her in anything other than rags. But he quickly found his tongue as she came upon them. He stood up and held out a hand to her, gently guiding her to a seat.

"My lords, may I present the Lady Gray Serroux, Lady Brooke's mother," he said. "Lady Gray, this is Lord Alan Haistethorpe and his son, Elliott."

Gray smiled at the pair, taking her seat. The men followed suit. "Welcome to Erith, my lords," she greeted. "We are honored by your visit."

"As you honor us with your invitation," Alan said, looking somewhat confused. "Is the Lady Constance indisposed?"

"My mother is unwell this day and unable to greet you," Gray's tone hardened. "With your permission, Sir Braxton has graciously agreed to mediate the negotiations."

Alan and Elliott looked straight at Braxton, who met their gaze emotionlessly. "We were unaware that Sir Braxton had been engaged for his negotiating skills," Alan said. "We thought... well, it is well known that he is a soldier of fortune."

"I am a man of many talents," Braxton said steadily. "Contract negotiation happens to be one of my strengths, as I have brokered many a successful contract for myself. Surely you have no quarrel bartering a betrothal with me."

Alan and Elliott looked at each other. It was clear that neither man knew quite how to react. Alan finally asked the question they were both thinking. "Do you receive a percentage of the dowry for your fee, my lord?"

Braxton's eyes were steely. He let loose a great secret, simply because he wanted to ward off any future complications. And he could see, by the way Elliott had looked at Gray, that there could very well be some.

"I am Lady Gray's betrothed and, as such, will retain wardship of her daughter upon our marriage," he said steadily.

"Negotiating with me is as good as negotiating with the girl's father. Now, shall we get down to business?"

Terms were unable to be reached. One too many glances at Gray Serroux from Elliott Haistethorpe caused Alan to excuse himself with his son while the man still had his head. Within the hour, Alan and Elliott were making haste back to Windermere with harrowing tales of the mercenary Braxton de Nerra and his murderous negotiating skills.

***

Gray had only been to Milnthorpe once in her life. It was a larger berg with an entire long avenue dedicated to merchants. There was also a big stone cathedral and a tournament field at the edge of town by the river that flowed down through the Lyth Valley and dumped into Morecambe Bay.

The party from Erith had left the fortress at dawn. Gray and Brooke were astride two warmblood mares that belonged to Braxton, gentle animals he used to breed with the war horses to produce a sturdy, long-legged offspring which he then sold to the nobility that appreciated fine crossbreds. The morning was soft and bright, and the jaunt along the wide road was at a leisurely pace. For the first time since she could remember, Gray actually felt at ease and without care. She'd never experienced such a feeling, or at least if she had, she could not remember when last. A glance at Brooke showed the young girl to be equally relaxed. Happy for almost the first time in her young life.   It was already starting off a good day.

But the morning had not been without its momentary drama. Before the party left for Milnthorpe, Brooke had apologized to Braxton for lying. The evening prior, Gray and Brooke had had a serious discussion about the rights and wrongs of life. Lying was wrong, even if one was fearful or attempting not to discredit an elder. Gray had also told her daughter that she was to stay away from Constance. Through Brooke had not completely understood why, she nonetheless agreed. Gray secretly wondered how long that would last; Brooke and her grandmother were close. She suspected it would be a bit of a battle.

On the road in the new hours of dawn, the sun was just clearing the horizon. Wrapped in her new cloak with the gray fur, Gray felt like a queen. She was clad in the emerald brocade surcoat but realized when she had dressed that all of her shifts were old and worn. No matter, however; she was grateful for whatever she had and would not complain. So the surcoat went over the worn shift and the new cloak had gone over that. Her blond hair was pulled back at the nape of her neck, wound into a bun that showed off the slender shape of her neck and shoulders. She looked positively elegant.

Braxton rode slightly ahead of her, turning every so often to shoot her a glance. She would merely smile at him. Dallas rode slightly ahead of Brooke while Graehm and Geoff rode behind them. The four knights and two ladies were surrounded by twenty men at arms and one of Braxton's massive wagons that had been brought along to cart back whatever booty that happened to acquire. The rest of the men, and wagons, had been left back at Erith. The rebuild was still in full swing and the remaining soldiers could not be spared.

As Gray and Braxton passed the time exchanging meaningful glances, Brooke was involved in her own silent game. Riding on the wagon seat beside the driver sat Norman and Edgar. Brooke could feel their stares on her back and she would casually turn every so often to see what they were doing. So far this morning, Edgar had stuck his tongue out at her twice. She was keeping track. For every transgression, she was going to punch him twice. He was already racking up quite a bill.

Milnthorpe came into view much faster than Gray had anticipated. She was rather enjoying the ride, watching Braxton's powerful form as he rode in front of her. But soon they had arrived and soon there were crowds of people going about their business all around them. The bustle of the town started well before they actually entered it. It was a busy and bright morning already.

Braxton had been to Milnthorpe a few times and knew the layout. He took the party directly to the Street of Merchants and found an area beside one of the thatched-roof stalls that was roomy enough to park the wagon. Norman and Edgar leaped off the bench, collecting the chargers as the knights dismounted. Braxton dismounted, turned his horse over to a nearby soldier, and went to help Gray.

She smiled at him as he approached, sliding gratefully into his upstretched arms. He lowered her to the ground, his hands lingering on her a moment longer than necessary. He winked at her as he let her go.

"Here we are, my lady," he said, glancing up one side of the street and then down the other. "If I recall correctly, there are several import merchants near the western end of the avenue. They should have fabrics and goods from all over the world."

Gray was essentially along for the ride. Braxton had a definite plan and she would simply follow him. The man was pretending the turmoil of the previous day never happened and she was glad to go along, including the shopping trip he had planned for them before the crisis of yesterday. Taking her hand and tucking into his elbow, he motioned for Dallas to take charge of Brooke. The tall blond knight took the young lady in hand, escorting her after her mother. With Graehm, Edgar, Norman and about ten men at arms in tow, the party moved into the avenue and left the rest the group behind.

Gray's trips into the town of Leven, the nearest village to Erith, had rarely involved anything other than basic needs. But this trip was different and she was a little dazed by all of it; they were going shopping for things they did not need. The concept was mind-boggling. As she soaked up the sights, Braxton paused by an open stall with various fragrant oils displayed. He sniffed the myrrh oil, liked it, and bought it on the spot for a full piece of gold. The merchant wrapped it in a pretty piece of cloth and tied it with a ribbon, handing it over to the knight who, in turn, handed it to an astonished Gray. As they continued their walk,

Gray clutched the oil as if was the most precious gift she had ever received.

The merchant stall he had in mind was a large stall that anchored the entire avenue. The man that owned it wore a strange little cap on his head; Gray would not learn until later that he was a Jew and his shop happened to be the most lucrative shop in Milnthorpe. Entering the dark, cool place, Gray was struck by how packed it was with items. Porcelain, fabric, belts, and phials of secret liquids were strewn all over the place. Awed, she stood by the door for a moment, absorbing the scene, before Braxton gently nudged her inside. She followed him, straight over to the bolts of fabric.

Dallas and Brooke followed them inside while Geoff and Graehm, the men at arms, and Edgar and Norman stood just outside. But the two squires were very curious about the place and strained to catch a look inside. It was a dark and mysterious place inside the wide-mouthed door. Suddenly, Brooke popped out with Dallas on her heels. She almost bumped into Norman, who quickly excused himself. She smiled briefly at Norman but cast Edgar a vicious glare.

"Come, Sir Dallas," she said grandly. "I would like to find a merchant who has spun sugar and treats."

She made sure to show Edgar the coin Braxton had given her, sticking her tongue out at him as Dallas escorted her across the street. Edgar watched her go, angrily. He wanted some spun sugar, too. Norman slapped him lightly on the back of the head and made him go back and stand near the open doorway.

As the men at arms waited patiently and the boys wait, not so patiently, for Braxton and Gray to reemerge, Brooke and Dallas came back from their unknown destination down the Street of Merchants. Brooke was carrying a sack, holding it with her left hand while her right hand burrowed deep inside. She pulled forth a piece of hard candy and popped it in her mouth, making sure that Edgar saw her do it. She came upon the squires where they sat against the wall next to the door.

"Would you like a piece of candy, Norman?" she pulled out a

chunk of gold-colored candy. "It's made from burnt sugar, honey and vanilla. It's delicious."

Norman nodded and held up his hand. Edgar didn't even ask; he knew she would not give him any. Norman broke his piece in two and handed a half to Edgar.

"Why are you giving him some of your candy?" Brooke wanted to know. "He's done nothing to earn it."

Norman shrugged. "He is my brother. I give him whatever I have."

She stuck her lip out in a frown. "You should not give him anything. He does not deserve it."

Edgar chewed the candy, alternately glaring at Brooke and looking at his feet. She looked pointedly at the boy. "If you were nicer to me, I would give you some. But you are a horrid creature."

Edgar didn't say anything; he'd been warned by Dallas against violence involving young ladies and he had promised never to strike one again. But Brooke continued to push him.

"And you are very mean and nasty."

Edgar swallowed the candy. "And you are skinny and ugly!"

She kicked him. He kicked her back. Brooke forgot about the candy in her hand, her new surcoat, and everything else. She leapt over Norman and grabbed Edgar by the hair. The boy howled and tried to get up and run, but she held him fast.

"You apologize, Edgar," Brooke shouted.

Edgar's response was to kick her again, right in the knee. Brooke lost her grip and it was enough for him to pull away. He took off with Brooke on his heels, yelling like a banshee.

Norman was up, racing after the pair. Two of the men at arms broke away from the main body of the group and also made chase. Dallas and Geoff, having been standing in quiet conversation just inside the door, heard the commotion and came out just as Norman and the men at arms took off at a run. They bolted after them, leaving Graehm to wait for Braxton and Lady Gray.

Edgar was fast. He plowed through the crowd on the street,

dashing behind some stalls and coming out on a street on the other side. He could hear Brooke behind him, yelling threats, so he broke right and continued running. Edgar may have been fast, but Brooke was relentless. Edgar left the avenue and crossed a small lot, only to stick his foot in a rabbit hole and twist his ankle. He collapsed in pain as Brooke caught up to him. She jumped on him.

She whacked him on his arms, head and chest. They were open handed slaps, not particularly painful, but loud. Edgar just laid there and moaned about his leg.

"And that's for sticking your tongue out at me!" she told him as she slapped him on the shoulder.

Edgar didn't fight back. His ankle hurt too badly. Brooke gradually became aware of this and slowed her attack just as Norman ran up on them. By the time the big brother arrived, she had stopped completely.

"You are a coward and a faker, Edgar," she scolded him. "You are not hurt in the least. You are just crying because you got beat by a girl."

But Edgar's foot was still in the hole. Both Brooke and Norman turned to see that the foot was indeed lodged. Brooke climbed off of him as Norman tried to remove his brother's foot from the narrow pit. Edgar yelled.

By this time, the men at arms, Geoff and Dallas had arrived. They could see what had happened. Dallas lifted Edgar up gently as Geoff pulled his foot free. Then they sat the boy down on his buttocks so they could take a look at the ankle. Edgar was trying not to cry, furiously wiping at his eyes so no one would see his tears. It hurt terribly and Brooke tried not to look at his face, tried not to feel guilty.

Dallas knelt beside Edgar, running his hands over the joint. The boy flinched. "Well," Dallas said after a moment. "I cannot say if it is broken, but it is certainly sprained. Let's get him up and back to the wagon."

He reached down and lifted the boy in his arms. They began to retrace their steps back in the direction they had come when the sound of trumpets caught their attention. Off to the northwest was the tournament grounds and banners flew high over the lists. There seemed to be a moderate crowd on hand; they could hear the rumble and roar.

"What is that?" Brooke wanted to know.

Dallas, Geoff and Norman came to a halt, gazing off into the distance. "A tournament," Dallas said. "Probably just a local one."

"What does that mean, 'probably just a local one'?" she asked.

"Just that. Only local contenders; no reputable names to speak of," Geoff elaborated. "Matches like that are usually sloppy spectacles. The big matches with reputable knights are the true essence of the sport."

The men started to walk away, but Brooke just stood there, watching the pennants flap in the mild breeze and listening to the ebb and flow of the crowd in the distance.

"Have you been in many tournaments, Sir Geoff?"

Geoff paused. "Aye, my lady."

"Have you won any?"

"One or two. Mostly in the mêlée."

"What's that?"

"When knights see who can out sword-play each other. The combatants are on their feet, not on horseback as they are with the joust. The mêlée is mostly about strength and stamina, whereas the joust is mostly about skill and tactics."

She turned to look at the field in the distance. "What about you, Sir Dallas?"

Dallas was far enough away that he barely heard her, but he politely came to a stop. "I have known a few in my time," he said. "I tend to be more successful in the joust. Geoff wins the mêlée simply because he's so tall. No one can get a good strike at him."

Geoff and Dallas exchanged amused glances as Brooke continued to stare at the distant field. "I want to see this one."

Dallas lifted an eyebrow. "You must ask Sir Braxton and your mother."

"They will let me," she said confidently. Then she turned to look at the knight, with Edgar in his arms. "Edgar wants to see the match, too. Don't you, Edgar?"

She was nodding her head at him as she asked the question. The boy made a face at her and she puckered her lips angrily. "Don't you want to see the tournament? We can sit in the lists and eat custard."

The lure of custard had his attention. Edgar looked at his brother, at Dallas. "I would like to eat custard," he said timidly.

Dallas could see that Lady Brooke would not let the subject rest. It was important he return to Braxton and Lady Gray so that they could take charge of the willful little lady. He turned away from Brooke and the distant tournament field.

"Come along, lady," he said to her. "If you want to visit the tournament, you'll have to ask your mother."

By the time they returned to the Street of Merchants, Braxton and Gray had just come out of the merchant stall where they had been shopping. The men at arms were piling bolts of fabric and other goods onto the wagon as Braxton stood with Graehm, supervising the loading. Hearing the approach of the errant group, he turned to them. By his expression, he did not look pleased.

"What goes on?" he asked as Dallas and Geoff approached. He eyed Edgar, in Dallas' arms. "What happened to him?"

"He injured an ankle running from Lady Brooke," Dallas told him. "I cannot say if it is broken, but he cannot walk on it."

Gray had come out of the merchant stall in time to hear Dallas mention her daughter's unruly behavior. Though Braxton had not told her about the earlier confrontation between Brooke and Edgar, she wasn't surprised to hear of her daughter's actions against the young lad. Brooke could be quite disruptive, and she had been known to be particularly aggressive when challenged. She frowned at her only child.

"Brooke," she scolded. "Why were you chasing him?"

Brooke was torn between self-righteousness and regret. "Because he kicked me."

"You kicked me first," Edgar yelled as Dallas sat him on the wagon bench.

Gray's expression darkened. "You did this to him?" she grabbed her child by the arm. "Tell me the truth."

Brooke's indignant stance was rapidly slipping. "But... Mama, he has been rude and horrid to me. He needed to be punished."

Gray gave her daughter a small shake, silencing her. "Enough. I shall deal with you later."

While Brooke sulked, Gray went over to the young boy with the dark hair and big blue eyes, a victim of her daughter's misbehavior. "Remove his shoe," she told Dallas. "Let me see the ankle."

Dallas obliged and Gray took a close look at the joint. Brooke, hoping to distract her mother's anger, tugged on her arm. "Mama," she said timidly. "There is a tournament happening. May we go watch it? Edgar has said he wants to see it."

Gray's head came up. "Edgar?"

Brooke pointed at the lad. "Him."

Nothing would heal a sprained ankle like entertainment. It just so happened that Brooke would also benefit from Edgar's wish. Not strangely, Gray wasn't buying it.

"Not today," she said. "We have other plans."

"But I do not want to shop," Brooke begged. "I want to watch the tournament. I have never seen one. And it would make Edgar feel better. Please?"

"Nay, Brooke," Gray told her, more forcefully. "We have not the time today. Mayhap another day."

Pouting, Brooke turned away from her mother and folded her arms angrily across her chest. After a moment's indecision, she focused on Braxton. He was standing with Geoff, watching Gray as she gently inspected Edgar's ankle.

"Sir Braxton," Brooke said, mock sweetness in her tone. "Have you ever been in a tournament?"

He looked at her. "Several."

"Did you win?"

He lifted an eyebrow, searching for a correctly worded answer, when Geoff chimed in. "My lady, Sir Braxton is a master on the tournament field," he said. "Since I have known him four years, he has competed six times and has won the joust every time. He has one lost once in the mêlée that I know of, and that was last year. Did you not have a broken shoulder during that bout, my lord?"

Braxton nodded modestly. "Broke it in the joust earlier that day."

Geoff nodded in remembrance. "He should not have even been competing, but honor dictated otherwise."

"Who won the mêlée?" Brooke wanted to know.

Geoff tilted his head in Dallas' direction. "Dallas did."

Brooke was excited with the thought of Braxton and Dallas locked in mortal combat, battling one another to the death before a throng of screaming fanatics. She looked at Dallas, his head bent over Edgar's foot, and then looked back to Braxton.

"Would you please compete in this tournament so that I can see such a fine spectacle?" she asked.

The corner of Braxton's mouth twitched. "I am sure the match cards are full. Moreover, I do not have any of my equipment with me. My joust poles and my banners are back at Erith."

"But you can send one of your men back for those things," she went to him, putting her hand on his arm. "All my life I have wanted to see a tournament, but we never had the time or money. Now we have both. Won't you please take me?"

Gray's head came up from Edgar's ankle. "Brooke," she admonished with a threatening glare. Then her eyes sought out Braxton. "Forgive her, my lord. She is young and silly."

Braxton looked at Gray, so lovely with her hair pulled away from her face, bent over the injured boy. It suddenly occurred to him that he might like for her to witness his skills on the tournament field. He'd never had a lady in the lists cheering him on, at least not one he cared about. A strange sense of pride filled him, and perhaps a stronger sense of egotism. Though he was a warrior, and a mercenary at that, he was also a very skilled knight. Gray had never seen him in action, at least not the kind of action he would have liked her to see. He couldn't take her to the battlefield with him. But he could take her to a tournament.

"So you really want to see a tournament?" he asked Brooke.

She nodded eagerly. "Please? Would you enter?"

Braxton's gaze lingered on the young girl for a long, pregnant moment. "Graehm, send a few men back to Erith for my joust equipment," he spoke to the knight while still looking at Brooke. "Make sure to bring the banners. Dallas, go to the field marshals and see if they have any openings in the match cards."

"Can we all compete?" Dallas asked him, his blue eyes twinkling. "It has been a long time since we've all gone to sport against each other."

Braxton shrugged. "If you are all willing to be crushed by me, then by all means, enter your names," he watched Dallas grin and walk away. Braxton refocused on Brooke. "If the field marshals will allow late entries, we may very well have a tournament for you worth watching."

Brooke clapped her hands in excitement and skipped back over to the merchant stall where she had dropped her sack of candy when she attacked Edgar. Gray, of course, had been listening to the entire conversation; leaving Edgar, she went over to Braxton.

"Braxton," she said quietly. "You do not need to do this to impress my daughter. A tournament is a serious sport. You cannot simply jump in and compete. It takes training and preparation."

He blue-green eyes were soft on her. "No worries, sweetheart," he said softly. "I can joust in my sleep."

"But..." she gestured towards Edgar. "The lad is injured. We must return him to Erith."

"We'll make sure he stays off of the ankle," he told her. "He'll be fine. Besides, he likes a good tournament, too. Your daughter seems convinced it will heal his injury."

She stared at him, realizing he was quite casual about something as serious as a tournament. She furthermore realized that she did not want him to compete. Men in tournaments were often hurt. She did not want him to get hurt.

"Please don't do this," she almost whispered.

He reached up, stroking her jaw tenderly before letting his hand fall back down again. "You needn't worry," he told her gently. "You'll be greatly entertained, I promise."

She did not look at all pleased. He collected her hand, kissed it, and tucked it into the crook of his elbow.

"Shall we go and look at more goods while we are waiting for Dallas?" he asked, attempting to distract her.

She shook her head. "I must tend the boy's ankle. Is there an apothecary around here?"

"What for?"

"Wraps and healing herbs. His ankle is swelling and he is in pain."

"Is it that bad? Boys are fairly resilient."

"It's bad, Braxton. It needs to be wrapped."

He looked around, trying to recall if he had seen a shop during his past visits to this place. "I am not sure where an apothecary might be, but we shall find one."

Leaving Brooke and her candy with Geoff and Norman, Gray and Braxton struck off in search of an apothecary. After asking a few of the merchants where such a place might be, they found their way onto the next avenue where a small medicament shop was wedged in between two larger merchant stalls.

This street was busier than the one they had just left. People bustled all about them, quickly going about their business. Gray almost got run over, twice. The first time was from a busy farmer that crossed her path. The second was a knight on horseback, a big black knight with eyes like obsidian. Though she paid no mind to him, he paid a great mind to her. Fortunately, Braxton did not notice; he was more concerned with getting her out of the traffic.

The apothecary shop was so small that Braxton had to bend over to enter it; once inside, there were odd smells and strange implements all around them. A tiny little man sat behind a cluttered table at the far end of the shop, ignoring them. He either hadn't heard the pair enter or didn't care. As Braxton and Gray made their way toward the old man, a fat white cat jumped into their path. It hissed. Gray shoved the beast away with her foot.

Braxton went straight for the old man. "We are need of healing aids for a young boy's ankle," he said. "Do you have such things?"

The old man blinked up at Braxton, then at Gray standing behind him. He was a frail old soul, with a long yellowed beard and most of his teeth missing. He blinked again.

"What's this you say? You want a young boy?"

Braxton shook his head. "Nay. We are in need of pain medicaments for...."

"Ah!" the old man threw up his hand and turned his back on them, rummaging through a cluttered shelf. "I have something that will help your wife bear a strong young son and crushed root that will take care of her pain in childbirth," he yanked forth a glass phial with dark powder. He thrust it at Braxton. "Pessaries. Guaranteed to produce a son. You place it into your wife before coupling. It will magnify your seed so that a strong lad is produced."

Shocked at the bizarre path the conversation had taken, Braxton looked at Gray. "Is that what I really said?" he muttered to her. "I don't recall asking for pessaries to produce a son."

Gray was struggling not to laugh. After the initial surprise wore off, she found the senile old man absolutely hilarious. "Perhaps you should," she whispered. "Perhaps then we will receive pain medicaments to help a swollen ankle."

He wriggled his eyebrows at her, turning around just as the little man pulled forth another phial containing a clear liquid with dark floaters on the bottom. The old gentleman swirled it around, mesmerized by the drift of the fluid.

"For the pain, my lady," he said. "Boy infants always produce more pain than girl infants. I do not know why. It has always been thus."

Gray struggled not to erupt into giggles. "Perhaps you could provide us with medicines to produce twins. Two male children at once would be most... uh, pleasant."

She had no idea why she asked, only that the entire

conversation, and visit, seemed so absurd. She wanted to see if she could somehow steer the old man towards what they were really seeking. True enough, the old man's face lit up.

"Ah!" he threw up a hand again. "I have just what you need for an aching joint. 'Tis over here, somewhere. It will help with the pain and reduce any swelling."

Gray and Braxton looked at each other. She bit her lip to fight off the laughter while he simply shook his head. He put his arm around her shoulders, pulling her up against him.

"Unbelievable," he muttered, kissing her temple. "It worked."

The old man sold them a solution of willow and ergot, and a viscous cream that was supposed to dull away any aches. It smelled strongly of mint. He also sold Braxton the pessaries and the clear liquid for childbirth because Braxton was sure he could not explain to the man that he did not need such things. He just paid for them and left. By the time they reached the street, Gray was nearly doubled over with laughter.

He grinned at her. "So you think that funny, do you?"

She tried to catch her breath. "Oh, Braxton, that was hilarious. Do you think the old man was hard of hearing or was he just insane?"

"Probably a little of both," Braxton reached out and pulled her to him, stealing a passionate kiss as they passed in an alleyway between the avenues. They paused a moment in the shadows between the buildings, gazing into one another's eyes. "On second thought, I should hang on to these pessaries. I may need them some day."

He meant with her. Her cheeks flushed again, now for an entirely different reason. "Perhaps," was all she would say.

He took her hand again, leading her out into the sunshine of the Street of Merchants. To their left, Brooke was now sitting up on the wagon bench beside Edgar, apparently sharing her candy with him. Braxton lifted an eyebrow at the sight.

"Do you think she poisoned the candy?" he asked quietly.

Gray shrieked softly, giving him a little pinch. "How dare you speak so cruelly of my child. And I would not be surprised if she did."

He winked at her as they came upon the wagon. Edgar had his mouth stuffed with vanilla candy and Brooke was sitting beside him quite innocently. The young boy looked fearful as Gray began to lay out the medicaments on the wagon bed.

"I will need a long strip of cloth, preferable linen," she said to Braxton. "Do you have something that might fit that description?"

He shrugged. "If not, I can find one somewhere."

A half hour later, Edgar's ankle was slathered with the smelly cream and bound tightly in a strip of linen that Geoff had provided from his saddlebag. Just as Gray finished the final tug of the ankle wrap, Brooke caught sight of Dallas' return at the far end of the avenue. She leapt off the wagon and ran to him, dodging customers and merchants as she dashed down the road.

Everyone, including Braxton and Gray, turned to watch as Brooke said something to Dallas and the knight nodded his head. Even though Braxton hadn't heard the words, he had seen the response and presumed what it meant. He began to feel the familiar excitement swell within him.

There would be a bit of sport that afternoon.

CHAPTER EIGHT

The Milnthorpe tournament was only about half full. In a field open to 20 knights, there were twelve competing. The addition of Braxton, Dallas, Geoff and Graehm filled up the cards and bulked up the excitement. The matches were schedule through late morning but in an unusual move, because of Braxton's impressive Patins – or résumé of lineage and bouts – the field marshals had agreed to let Braxton and his men compete against the winners of the morning rounds. There would only be six of them, with four going against Braxton and his knights and the remaining two matched against each other.

Six men at arms and Norman had taken the wagon back to Erith to unload the goods purchased that morning and to collect their knights' equipment, including shields, additional swords, joust poles, pennants and banners, a list of Patins, and additional armor. Norman knew what Braxton and his men would need and ably directed the men at arms to collect and load it back into the wagon. He even brought along two additional chargers, young animals that were still being trained. Not only would it be good to bring them in case one of the other chargers broke down, but Braxton might decide to ride one of them just to give them the experience. It had been over a year since Braxton had competed in a tournament and the men left behind at Erith were disappointed that they did not get to go.

A swift wagon could make the trip between Erith and Milnthorpe in less than an hour. It had taken them less than an hour to return to Erith, the loading had also taken less than an hour, and soon they were back on their way. One of the young chargers was acting up and Norman ended up riding the horse all the way to Milnthorpe.

They met up with Braxton and the others near the southwest end of the tournament area. Braxton's men immediately began unloading equipment and pitched two large tents, both well-made shelters in Braxton's colors of crimson, white, green and gold. The more Gray spent time with the man and saw how he functioned, the more she realized that Braxton de Nerra was no ordinary knight bannerette; he had an entire world that revolved around him, in spite of the fact he was considered a knight without property.

Braxton put Brooke and Edgar up in the wagon to keep them from being run down by the men setting up tents and offloading equipment. Strangely, they had been sitting together eating Brooke's candy since Gray had wrapped the boy's ankle with nary a harsh word between them. Gray stayed with Braxton, watching him direct his men coming to understand a little bit more about the man and his personality. She noticed that he never had to say much; more often than not, he merely pointed or directed with a short word and his men leapt to do his bidding. He wasn't heavy-handed, but he was firm. She liked the way his strong, quiet authority carried. And he always had the right answer for any question.

He caught her staring at him a couple of times, a quizzical look on her face. She would merely smile and he would smile back. As the sun approached its zenith and the little encampment was finally and carefully organized, the knights began to change from the battle armor they had worn for the ride to Milnthorpe into lighter-weight, more pristine protection.

Gray stood in the larger tent, watching curiously as Norman unfastened all of Braxton's heavy, dented armor and began replacing it with nicer-appearing body armor.

"Why are you changing armor?" she asked the inevitable question.

He glanced up from adjusting the hang of the breastplate. "Because this is armor specifically designed for tournaments. It's easier to move in, easier to joust in, yet provides some protection from a blow."

She looked dubious. "I do not understand."

He smiled faintly at her. "The heavier stuff that I wear all of the time is made for battle. It can be restricting, but the

118

protection it provides is worth the difficulty of movement. When you are in close quarters battling to the death, you want something heavy to protect yourself with. When I am up on a charger with a joust pole in my hand, the only protection I need is against my chest, arms and head. The rest of it is superfluous." He held up the lighter weight armor pieces. "See this? It is designed for my right arm and shoulder. See how the section of armor here that fastens to the breast plate is large and circular shaped, like a platter? It's designed to not only protect my right shoulder, which the opposition will be aiming for, but to deflect the blow because it is shaped like bowl. This armor is designed especially for a joust. For the mêlée, I will wear my heavier armor."

She understood, somewhat, watching Norman strap on his leg armor. Braxton stomped his foot, letting the protection settle comfortably on his leg once Norman was finished. Then the lad went to work on the other leg.

"Usually, both Edgar and Norman assist me," Braxton watched the dark-haired lad work quickly. "I am normally dressed far more quickly than any of the other men."

Norman picked up the pace, thinking Braxton was giving him a hint. Gray smiled as she watched the boy's fingers work swiftly over the leather fastens. "I think he is doing a remarkable job," she said.

"He usually does."

When Norman finished with the other leg, Braxton took a couple of good stomps and settled the rest of the armor. He twisted his torso, stretching out and moving his plate protection to a comfortable spot. Norman grabbed Braxton's broadswords, scabbards, and other necessary equipment and made a dash for the charger outside the tent.

Gray stood in the dimness of the tent, watching Braxton fuss with a shoulder strap that was too tight. He glanced up, noticing that she was staring at him again.

"What is it?" he asked.

She shook her head. "Nothing," she cocked her head at him. "I simply haven't seen a man dress for battle in a very long time."

He continued to fidget with the strap. "Your father?"

She nodded. "I remember him going to battle when I was young, though at that point, the wars with Henry had ended. My father was fifteen years old when Simon was killed at Evesham in twelve hundred and sixty five, so he never had the chance to fight alongside his father. He was too young. He went to his grave with that regret."

"What about Garber?"

"Never," she said, her expression changing. It was apparent that when discussing her late husband, there was not much pleasure in it. "Garber was not a knight in spite of being raised that way. I never saw him in a suit of armor, though his father was quite a warrior. Garber was too concerned with his drink and gambling to bother with the anything else."

Braxton had never shown much interest in learning about Garber Serroux other than cursory knowledge. But the closer he drew to Gray, the more he wanted to know about this man she had been married to. He was inherently curious.

"I have only heard the darker side of Garber Serroux," he said, finished adjusting the strap. "Surely the man had some redeeming qualities."

Gray shrugged. "Not particularly. The moment he married me, he began to sell off my father's possessions. They were passed down from my grandfather; furniture, fine weaponry, things like that. He took them all and sold them in London, not telling anyone that they were possessions once having belonged to Simon de Montfort. Then he went and gambled all of the money away on dog races. And that was the beginning of our descent into poverty. He was a drunkard, rude, abusive, lazy and dishonest. I can honestly tell you that he had no redeeming qualities that I was aware of, and I was married to him for fifteen years."

His blue-green eyes were fixed on her. "What do you mean when you say that he was abusive?"

"I mean that he used to like to strike me when he was drunk.

Not always, but sometimes. It depended on what he was drinking. If he was drunk on ale, then he was not so mean. But if it was anything else, he turned quite violent."

Braxton took a step towards her, reaching out to gently stroke her arm. "I am sorry," he said quietly. "You did not deserve that. In fact, you have deserved nothing of what your ties to Garber Serroux brought you."

"It wasn't my ties to Garber. It was my ties to Simon."

He knew that. "You only deserve the greatness of that association, not the unfair shame cast upon it."

He was gentle and sincere. It almost made her forget every bad deed Garber, or her association with the de Montfort name, had ever executed against her. His manner, and time, had eased her dreadful memories a great deal. But it was the first time she had ever heard anyone apologize for the misfortunes of her fate.

"It is of no matter," she said. "He is gone and you are here. That is all that matters to me now."

He didn't take his eyes off her as he stepped close, gazing down into her exquisite face. He didn't want to pull her into an embrace against the hard armor he wore, so he took her hands, bringing them to his lips. He kissed the fingers sweetly, turning her hands over to kiss her palms. It was a tender yet exhilarating gesture that brought a smile to them both.

"And I will be here for some time to come, so you had better become used to my presence," he leaned down and kissed her lips. "Now, I suspect everyone will be waiting for me. Are you ready to be entertained?"

Her gentle, dreamy expression fled. "Braxton, I really wish you would not do this. It frightens me."

He winked at her, kissing her fingers again before letting her hands go. "Not to worry. You'll enjoy this, I promise."

She looked so dubious that he grinned, kissing her lips once, then twice. She tasted so good that he held her face in his hands and kissed her so deeply that his head swam. She was so warm and soft and delicious and with every kiss, he seemed to crave her more and more. She ignited a tingle in his hands and a flame in his heart that only seemed to grow with every touch, every look. He'd never known anything like it. He could only pray she felt the same but he was far too fearful to ask, fearful of the answer. He almost laughed at himself at the thought that he would actually experience fear. Since the moment he met her, he'd never wanted anything more in his life.

"You know," he said after a moment, "you never have given me an answer to my question."

She was still attempting to catch her breath from his ardent kiss. "What question is that?"

"I asked you if I may have your permission to court you. You never have answered me."

A gradual smile spread across her lips. "Isn't that what you have been doing?"

"Aye; but only because I have boldly moved forward in the hope that you would not stop me."

She shook her head slowly. "I will not stop you."

His blue-green eyes glimmered. "Is that an affirmative answer?"

"It is."

He smiled broadly, taking her hand and leading her towards the tent flap. "Then come along, lady," he took her hand, leading towards the tent flap. "Your Intended promises to give you an exciting gift as celebration of your gracious consent."

Gray's smile faded. She doubted it would be exciting. Terrifying was more like it.

***

"Unfortunately, you have arrived at an inopportune time," Constance told the two men standing before her. "My daughter, and Lady Brooke, have gone into Milnthorpe. They shan't return until this evening."

It was a warm day and the dust from the rebuilding of Erith swirled about the bailey. Constance was fearful it would damage the new wine-colored surcoat she wore and she certainly did not want to make a bad impression on the visitors. She had been both surprised and pleased by their arrival not a half hour before.

With Gray and Brooke gone, there had been no one to greet the guests. Constance naturally took the duty, not only because she was the only family member left, but because the visitors most recently arrived at Erith were of such substantial significance that she dare not leave this task to anyone other than herself. She was frankly surprised they had heeded the invitation.

Sir Roger de Clare, cousin to Gilbert of Clare, sixth Earl of Gloucester, stood in the center of Erith's bailey with an expression of dubious curiosity. The depth of the man's significance and relationship to Erith could not be escaped; as the cousin of the man who betrayed Simon de Montfort at Evesham, Roger was an old man who had married late in life. He was propertied but not titled as his cousin had been; he was a glorified, and very wealthy, baron whose seat was Elswick Castle near Blackpool. He had three sons, the eldest of which was almost sixteen years of age. It was this son who had interest in Brooke Serroux and the legacy that was Erith Castle. Being that the lad's cousin had once been Simon de Montfort's best friend and then greatest enemy, the implication of a betrothal to Simon's great-granddaughter could not be overlooked.

Constance knew this. She, more than anyone, understood the importance of lineage and marital ties. When she had sent the original marriage solicitation to Roger, she had not expected an answer. There was too much bitter blood between the de Montforts and the de Clares. But Roger's appearance told her that perhaps it was not so bitter as she had thought. She was tremendously glad that her daughter and the mercenary were away this day. Now, she would be free to do as she must for the survival of the family. To the Devil with this mercenary that was trying to usurp everything she had worked for.

"I know you, Lady Constance," Roger said, his voice quiet and deep. "You and I were acquainted as children, though you were older than I. We would play together at Thirlwall Castle. Do you not recall this?"

Constance nodded. "I do, my lord. It has been many years since we last met."

"Too many," Roger looked her over. Next to him stood a tall, red-haired youth with very bad skin. Roger glanced at his gangly son. "My lady, meet my son, William. He has come today to meet the Lady Brooke."

Constance eyed the young man, awkward and unattractive at sixteen. She nodded to him graciously. "I assure you that Brooke will be most pleasing. Will you not come inside and enjoy some refreshment?"

She led the pair up the newly repaired steps. Roger's keen gaze roved the fortress. "What happened to this place?" he asked. "I can remember when it was a powerful fortress. It looks as if it has seen a great deal of damage."

Constance was afraid he would pick up on the extent of the rebuilding going on; it was truthfully difficult to miss it. But she was thankful that the fortress appeared far better than it had mere days ago. "Erith has seen better days," she agreed "But, if you will notice, we are rebuilding most of the walls with better stone. Some of the materials used to originally build the fortress were not holding up to the test of time. We thought it best to rebuild what was not holding fast. Moreover, we want the young man who inherits this place to have a fine, solid fortress. Would you not agree?"

It sounded like a good explanation, even to her. Roger bought it. "I do," he said as they entered the dark keep. "What of your granddaughter's dowry? Your invitation failed to mention coinage and property."

Constance had to think quickly. She knew this question would come, though she had not expected it so soon. "All in good time, my lord," was the best she could come up with at the moment. "Let us sit and discuss the days of our childhood first. I am eager to learn of your wife; I had heard you had married Anne of Hereford. Is your lady wife well these days?"

"She is dead," Roger evidently did not wish to discuss her. "As

I had heard tale that your only girl child was quite a beauty. Is her daughter also?"

An idea suddenly occurred to Constance. A seedling, growing by the second, took root in her fertile and vicious mind. Her amber eyes glittered at the baron as they took a seat opposite one another at the long table in the hall.

"Both women are quite beautiful, I assure you," she tried to appear casual. "Your wife is dead, did you say? Have you considered remarrying?"

Roger had. Constance was delighted to hear that.

***

The de Nerra knights discovered that there were indeed a couple of noteworthy knights at the small Milnthorpe tournament. When they drew matches, Geoff had drawn Sir Niclas de Aughton, a powerful knight from Northumbria, while Graehm drew Sir Rickard Burton of Somerhill. Burton was a big man with a mean temperament and was known for his violent competitiveness. De Aughton was only slightly less violent, but had the reputation of being extraordinarily cunning and enormously strong. Truth be told, Braxton was mildly disappointed that he hadn't drawn either man in the first round. As good as his knights were, he suspected that if he won his first round, he might be facing one or both opposing knights eventually. It was just a hunch he had.

Braxton had the first match in the new rounds after the afternoon break. He had drawn a knight from Navarre, one Sir Fulk, who looked as if he had eaten far too many pastries in his time. The man was so round that he was barely able to mount his equally fat charger. Braxton took one run against the man, hit him squarely in the chest, and knocked him right off his horse. In less than a few seconds he had won his match and a new roan charger, and the crowd in the lists went mad for his victory.

Gray's relief was palpable. If every match was as easy as this one, perhaps it would not be such a bad day after all. Once

Braxton had unseated the knight, he made a sweeping turn along the lists and thundered past the cheering throng, listening to them scream madly for him. Even Brooke was screaming at the top of her lungs as he cantered in front of their group astride his big black charger. Gray could only sit there and smile, watching him casually acknowledge the crowd as if it meant absolutely nothing at all. When he reached the gate that led from the field, however, he flipped up his visor and his gaze sought out Gray. He lifted a big gloved hand to her.

She waved back, her heart swelling with a feeling she'd never before known. It made her limbs weak and a strange quivering filled her. She couldn't stop smiling. She watched as Norman led Braxton off the field, still astride his beast, and then there was another knight to take his place at the post start. Sir Geoff, astride his big bay stallion, looked every inch as imposing as Braxton had.

The field marshals officiating the event took their places as both competitors signaled their readiness. The crowd hushed to an expectant buzz. As she watched Geoff make a thundering run against the big black knight from Northumbria, she felt Brooke poke her in the arm.

"Mama?" she poked her again. "May Edgar and I have some custard?"

Gray turned to the two faces sitting next to her; lovely Brooke and handsome Edgar. Edgar's ankle was up on the bench in front of them to keep it elevated. Gray was about to reply in the affirmative when she realized that she had no money on her. Braxton had paid for everything. Somewhat embarrassed as to what to say to the children, she was about to give them the generic 'later' answer when she caught sight of a man in armor at the base of the lists. Her amber eyes immediately focused in on Braxton as he made his way towards them from the dusty staging grounds with Norman trailing after him.

His forehead was creased where the helm had rested upon his head and his face was tinged red from having been contained in the sweaty confines of the three-point helmet, but his expression was pleasant. He smiled at Gray when their eyes met, even at a distance.

"Look," Gray distracted Brooke and Edgar by pointing. "Here comes Sir Braxton. Perhaps he would like some custard, too?"

Brooke shot to her feet and began waving madly. "Sir Braxton!" she shouted. "Here we are!"

He lifted his hand in response. As he reached the lists, he stood next to the platform, his eyes only for Gray.

"I thought I'd better come and feed this famished crowd," he said. "Watching a tournament can give one a ravenous appetite."

Gray lifted an eyebrow. "How did you guess?"

He winked at her. "I was a child once myself, believe it or not." He waved a big hand at Brooke. "Come along, young woman. Let us go and find you some custard."

Brooke almost tripped in her haste to leave her seat. "What about Mother? Can she come, too?"

Braxton held out a hand to steady Brooke as she fumbled for the stairs, but his eyes returned to Gray. "I was rather hoping she would."

Gray smiled, a faint pink flush to her cheeks. "I would love to come, but we simply cannot leave Edgar here alone."

The lad looked surprised at the mention of his name. "I can wait by myself, my lady," he stammered.

While Gray looked doubtful, Braxton spoke. "Edgar is indeed quite capable of taking care of himself until we return. Come along, sweet."

Gray stood up and left her seat, descending the steps from the lists right into Braxton's waiting hands. He took her on one elbow and Brooke on the other, feeling prouder than he ever had in his life. It was one thing to be prideful of one's skills and reputation; it was entirely another to be proud of the company one kept. He knew, without a doubt, that he was in the presence of the most beautiful woman in Cumbria and her equally lovely daughter.

"Now that I am the envy of every man here," he said, his blue-green eyes scanning the street and crowds beyond, "let us locate this vendor with custards and fattening tarts."

Brooke giggled girlishly, pulling Braxton along more than she was actually following him. Her pretty new surcoat of soft blue linen looked sweet and elegant. She swished the skirt around with her free hand as they walked, never happier or more carefree in her young life.

"There is a vendor over there with something on his cart," she jabbed her finger over to the left. "There are several people around him. Whatever he has must be good."

Braxton turned in that direction, allowing Brooke to half-pull, half-drag him along. "Then it is as good a place to start as any," he glanced at Gray, looking so lovely with her hair off her slender neck. "And you, my lady? Do you have any preference on sweets and other gluttonous items?"

She met his gaze, feeling the warmth that now sprouted so easily between them. She did so enjoy looking at him. "Whatever my daughter wishes is fine with me," she said, tightening her grip on his arm. "You are most generous to allow her such treats, my lord."

He lifted an eyebrow at her and mouthed *Braxton*. She grinned and nodded her head. "Lady Brooke has behaved herself admirably today in the wake of Edgar's injury," he said. "She deserves a reward."

Brooke's guilt at Edgar's injury returned. She didn't want to incriminate herself and risk not getting custard, so she ignored the comment and continued to pull Braxton and her mother along. Norman was following behind them, a silent reminder to Brooke's bad behavior. She hoped that he would not tell on her, but she could feel his stare against her back. Norman was a big lad; she suspected he could be intimidating if he wanted to be. But she would not let him frighten her. Had Edgar not been so awful, she would not have chased him. It was Edgar's own fault... *wasn't it?*

By the time they reached the vendor, some of the crowd had cleared away and they could get a good look at the vendor's table; dried meats, warm wine, and globs of almond milk pudding nestled in hollow gourds. Brooke immediately went for the pudding and Braxton found himself paying for five of them. Norman inhaled his pudding in three bites. Brooke devoured hers shortly thereafter and Braxton bought her another one. Gray held on to her pudding, and on to Edgar's, fearful that it would vanish if her daughter got a hold of it. Braxton, grinning at the ravenous youngsters, handed his pudding over to Norman. The lad grinned and shoveled it down, although a bit more slowly than the first. Braxton slapped him affectionately on the back of the head.

They were half way across the avenue when Graehm suddenly appeared. In full armor, he made his way straight to Braxton. His expression was wrought with seriousness.

"My lord," he said shortly. "Geoff took a bad hit in his round with de Aughton. The physic is with him now."

Braxton didn't react outwardly, but Gray gasped softly. "What happened?" Braxton asked calmly.

"The pole broke and the jagged edge went right into his neck," Graehm explained. "We carried him off the field and back to the staging area."

Braxton's pace picked up as they continued their way back to the tournament field. "Is it a mortal wound?"

"'Tis possible, my lord. He bleeds a great deal."

Braxton didn't say anymore. He escorted Gray and Brooke back to the lists before continuing on with Norman and Graehm.

As Brooke took Edgar's pudding from her mother and made haste back to her seat, Gray paused as she mounted the steps, watching Braxton and his men stride away. If Geoff was as bad as Graehm said he was, then perhaps she could help. Lord knows, Braxton had already done enough for her and for Erith. Perhaps this was one time she could attempt to return the favor. Gathering her skirt, she bade Brooke and Edgar to wait in the lists as she followed Braxton's trail off across the tournament grounds.

Since she already knew where Braxton's camp was interred, it took her little time to reach it. Several men were milling about, mostly de Nerra men-at-arms. They hovered outside of the smaller of the two tents, speaking in muted tones. Gray acknowledged them as she walked between them, her focus on the tent opening and the dimness beyond. No one stopped her when she peeled back the flap.

She could see someone lying on their back just inside the door; there were at least three bodies hovering over the supine form so she could see little more than booted feet. Braxton, who had been peering over the shoulder of a round, hairy-faced man, looked up when she walked into the tent. His eyes widened at the sight of her and he straightened up.

"Lady Gray," he greeted. "Is something...?"

She cut him off politely. "I came to see if I could help, my lord."

He went to her, his hand on her elbow. "The physic is tending him. Though I thank you for your kindness, I doubt there is anything you can do."

Her amber eyes met his blue-green orbs. There was a spark, a jolt of warmth that passed between them as he touched her. "May I at least see him?" she asked softly.

Braxton could see she only wished to help. He smiled faintly and led her back over to where he had been standing. At their feet lay Geoff, pale and unconscious, with an ugly cluster of splinters sticking out of his neck. The physic and the man's assistant were attempting to pull the splinters free, one at a time, holding a soiled rag up against the gushing wound in an attempt to prevent the man from bleeding to death. They weren't doing a very good job; blood was everywhere.

Gray could see that the knight was going to bleed to death unless they changed their method. She instinctively opened her mouth to speak but quickly thought better of it. She did not want to seem overbearing, yet she could not stand by and watch this man die. Braxton heard her soft gasp.

"What is it?" he asked quietly.

A man's life was at stake. She could not keep silent about it. "They are going about this all wrong," she whispered. "The wound must be stitched closed as they remove the wood. All they are managing to do now is pulling out whatever material is holding back the tide of blood. Soon they will remove it all and everything will drain out, like pulling a cork from a bottle."

Braxton looked over at Dallas, at Graehm. "Remove the physic," he snapped softly. "Lady Gray will tend him."

As the knights not-so-gently pulled the men up, to much protest, Braxton firmly guided Gray to the seat vacated by the physic. She objected for a split second before realizing he was not about to listen to her. He believed what she had told him, having made perfect sense, and was now trusting her with the life of Geoff. She was terrified, uncertain, and pleased all at the same time. The knights had passed the physic and his helper off to the men at arms, who were now practically throwing them from the tent. As she took the seat, she forced away her hesitation and struggled to collect her thoughts.

"I need hot water, needles and gut, and lots of it," she rattled off the list to anyone who would listen. "I also need whiskey and witch hazel. Braxton, do you remember the apothecary we saw this afternoon? He would have these things. More than likely, he would have other things to help heal Sir Geoff. But I need them now. There is no time to waste."

Braxton listened carefully to her demands and nodded shortly, snapping his fingers at Dallas and Graehm. "Dallas, go to the next avenue and find the small apothecary stall near the edge of the street. Get what we need from him." He looked at Graehm. "Hot water, all you can find. And keep it coming." As his men bolted off, he continued to stand over Gray as she gingerly inspected the injury. After several long moments, she shook her head.

"This is bad," she murmured. "I shall have to remove a splinter and stitch the area closed before I remove the next so that the wound will have some chance of healing."

He put his big hand on her shoulder, squeezing gently. "I would be grateful for whatever you could do for him."

She tilted her head back to look at him, his face a few inches from hers. Their eyes met and he could not resist depositing a tender kiss on her sweet lips. He wanted to do so much more but a spasm from Geoff caught his attention. He and Gray looked back at the knight, who was now awake and staring up at them. Braxton wondered if he had caught the kiss, but upon reflection, did not care much if he had.

"D'uberville," he greeted. "You have had a bit of an accident."

Geoff blinked is big blue eyes. "I... I do not remember much," his voice was faint and hoarse. "What happened?"

He was beginning to put his hands up, to feel the area of injury, and Gray quickly grasped both of his hands and held them tight. "Not to worry, Sir Geoff," she said in a gentle, soothing voice. "I will do all that I can to make you as good as new."

Geoff looked at her, a flicker of fear in his eyes. "Is it bad?"

She forced a smile. "I have seen worse. You must rest now and allow me to do this task."

He didn't ask any more questions; he simply closed his eyes. When she was sure that he was dozing and would not try to feel his injury again, Gray let go of his hands and looked at Braxton. There was a mixture of hope and sorrow in her eyes. He put his hand on her shoulder again, giving her another squeeze as his lips found her temple. He kissed her tenderly, twice, before releasing her.

"Do you require anything else?" he asked. "Is there something more I can do?"

She gazed down at the wounded knight, feeling distress at his plight. "Linen to bind the wound. Boiled linen if you can get it."

He left the tent without another word. Gray bent over Geoff, again inspecting the wound but not wanting to start yet without the things she asked for. She waited only a small amount of time before Graehm reappeared with a large iron pot of steaming water. Gray bade him to set it down beside her. The first thing she did was have him pour some of it on her hands to wash them. Then he stood there and hovered, watching Geoff with concerned eyes as Gray wrung out her wet hands.

Braxton returned less than a minute after Graehm's arrival. "My men are setting about to boiling some linen right now," he said. "Is there anything more?"

She shook her head. "I must wait for the other items I asked for before I can begin."

Braxton was about to leave the tent again in search of Dallas when the knight suddenly burst into the tent bearing a wooden box of mysterious items. His face was flushed as if he had been running, and there was little doubt with the speed in which he had returned that he hadn't run.

"I believe that I was able to secure what the lady requested," he said as handed the box over to Braxton.

Braxton peered at the items. "Did you have any trouble finding the apothecary?"

Dallas shook his head, watching as Braxton handed the box to Gray. "Nay," he said. "Although I am not quite sure why I purchased a pungent ointment guaranteed to attract women by the dozens. I did not have time to argue with him so I just paid for it."

Gray laughed softly, looking up at Braxton. He, too, was grinning. Then he shook his head helplessly. "Never mind," he told his knight. "But you are sure you got everything else?"

"I am."

Gray inspected the contents of the box and eventually nodded her head. The first thing she pulled out was an earthenware jug with a heavy plug of cloth shoved into the top of it. She pulled out the plug and smelled it, wrinkling her nose.

"Whiskey," she sniffed. Then she looked at Braxton. "I will need your help in holding him. He'll not like the sting of this, not in the least."

"What are you going to do?"

"Pour it on the wound to cleanse it."

Braxton lifted an eyebrow. "You are not going to have him drink it to dull the pain?"

She shook her head. "In this case, it would do much better on the wound than in his belly. You must trust me."

He did. Graehm took hold of one arm while Dallas took the other arm and threw himself over Geoff's body. Braxton took the legs. When the knights were property braced, Braxton nodded at her.

She had been right. Geoff hadn't liked the sting of the whiskey burn one bit.

CHAPTER NINE

It was dusk in Cumbria, a magical time when the last threads of daylight were woven into the tapestry of the coming night. Gray usually enjoyed the dusk, as there was something innately peaceful in the time before the fall of darkness. But tonight she found no real peace; sitting beside Geoff's sleeping form, she played a waiting game in contest to see who could control the knight's future. If she won the match, he would live. If she lost, then Death would claim him. It was difficult not to be discouraged as time ticked on and the knight remained unconscious.

The tournament had ended some time ago and most of the contestants and fans had already left. A few hung around, mostly to catch a glimpse of Braxton and his men as they milled in and out of the larger of the two crimson tents. Though Braxton had withdrawn from the competition in order to assist Gray with Geoff, Dallas and Graehm had continued at Braxton's insistence. Graehm was unseated in his match by Rickard Burton, who then went up against Dallas for the semi final round. Dallas managed to unseat Burton, causing the man to display a full-blown temper tantrum on the tournament field. The crowd had laughed him right out of the arena.

The final round was between Dallas and Sir Niclas, the same knight who had accidentally driven splinters into Geoff's neck. The match, and the prize, was meant to have been a victory in Geoff's name, but Dallas lost in three very hard-fought glances and the black knight from Northumbria emerged the victor. It had been a bitter defeat to accept, but Dallas had done so graciously. Braxton was just grateful he wasn't down another knight; given de Aughton's reputation, that could have very well been the case.

After stitching up Geoff's neck, Gray had decided it was best not to move him for the night and Braxton had agreed. But they hadn't planned on making a night of it, so Braxton took Dallas with him to procure food for the evening. The men at arms, meanwhile, built a roaring bonfire in the area between the two tents where Brooke, Edgar and Norman now sat. A couple of soldiers set to fashioning a spit, much to Brooke's curiosity. She sat on a stump one of the men had found for her, eating candied pieces of sweet pumpkin that Braxton had purchased for her and watching the activity. She sucked down the pumpkin treat, nearly oblivious to the real reason why they were still in Milnthorpe. In her young mind, this was all a grand adventure and she intended to enjoy every minute.

When the spit was finally ready and the sunset cast gray and purple shadows across the sky, Brooke glanced over to see Edgar glaring at her. Mouth full of pumpkin, she frowned at him.

"Why do you look at me like that, Edgar?" she asked.

He started to open his mouth but Norman smacked him in the head to shut him up. The move only infuriated Brooke.

"Norman, why did you hit him?" she demanded. "Tell me why Edgar is glowering at me. Has my face gone green?"

Norman looked at her; he was a steady young lad, even-tempered, in contrast to his mercurial younger brother. "Your face has not gone green, my lady," he said. "Edgar is simply exhausted. We all are. It has been a trying day."

His calm explanation satisfied her until Edgar grumbled loud enough to be heard. "'Tis her we should be roasting on the pit, the big glutton."

Brooke's eyebrows rose and she leapt to her feet. "What did you say?"

He looked at her, his young face dark. "You heard me."

Norman tried to intervene, but Edgar wouldn't let him. Bad ankle and all, he rolled away from his brother as the youth tried to slap a hand over his mouth.

"You are a big, fat glutton, Brooke Serroux," Edgar shouted, with Norman's hand half-over his mouth. "You ate all of that sweet pumpkin for yourself!"

Brooke's mouth popped open in outrage. "It was mine!"

"You could have shared it. I am hungry, too!"

Brooke's open mouth went into a thin angry line. She rushed Edgar, being prevented from totally destroying him by Norman, who had the unhappy task of being wedged in between the combatants. The older boy was on the receiving end of a few sharp slaps. Norman eventually turned away from Edgar to grasp Brooke around the body, lifting her up and carrying her away from his brother. She screamed and beat on Norman's back.

Inside the larger tent, Gray could not help but hear her daughter's yelling. Geoff hadn't moved so she dared to rise and peek outside to see what was going on. All she saw was Norman carrying her daughter off into the darkness. She sprinted out of the tent and caught up with them.

"Norman," she tried not to sound panicked. "What are you doing?"

Norman immediately set Brooke on the ground, whereupon she bolted back in Edgar's direction. The lad, unable to run, put up his arms as Brooke came down on him with hurling fists. Shocked, Gray ran after her daughter with Norman on her heels. She reached out and pulled her child off of the injured young boy.

"Enough," Gray shouted at her daughter.

Since Gray never shouted, Brooke immediately came to a halt. Her big eyes gazed fearfully into angry amber orbs.

"But... Mama, he...."

Gray shut her down with a harsh shake of the arms. "I said enough," she growled. "I do not know what vendetta you have against this boy, but this is the end of it. Any more violence against him and I shall take a switch to you. Do you hear me? I'll spank you within an inch of your life."

Unbeknownst to Gray, Braxton and Dallas had ridden up behind her. There was a gutted pig strapped across Dallas' horse. Dismounting, Braxton watched curiously as Gray laid into her daughter.

Brooke's eyes welled. "But, Mama, he was so very mean to me. He called me a glutton."

"And so you are," Gray didn't mince words. "You have been

eating since we arrived, begging money from Sir Braxton for your selfish wants. Sir Braxton is not obligated to buy you anything, Brooke. He does it from the kindness of his heart and Lord knows why he indulges you after the way you have treated him, but he does. You are selfish and petty and I am ashamed of you. If your manners were kinder and more gracious, then perhaps this boy would have no cause to insult you. But you deserve every word."

Brooke burst into tears. Gray did not want to comfort her, knowing she must teach her child a lesson. But it was difficult to restrain her motherly instincts as she watched Brooke sob. She let go of her daughter.

"Go and sit down by the fire," she instructed, her tone less harsh. "You will think on what I have said and amend your behavior accordingly."

Weeping, Brooke wandered over to her stump and sat heavily. The mood around the fire was somber as Norman and Edgar tried not to look at her. Braxton, having witnessed the entire event, slowly made his way over to Gray.

"My lady?" he said to catch her attention.

She turned to him, startled. "I am sorry; I did not hear you approach."

He smiled faintly at her. "I know." His eyes moved to his squires, to Brooke. "Is everything all right?"

Gray nodded, sensing he had probably heard some of her tirade. "It will be," she gathered her skirts and moved back in the direction of the large tent. "Sir Geoff has not yet awoken."

Braxton followed her into the tent. Inside, it was eerie and dark but for the soft light given off by one fat taper near the knight's bedside. Geoff was on his back, his neck and left shoulder heavily bandaged, and breathing deeply. Gray resumed her seat beside him, putting her hand on his forehead to feel for a temperature rise.

"He's still cool," she said. "Tomorrow would be the soonest we could expect a change."

He nodded. "Will he be able to travel back to Erith come the dawn?"

She shrugged. "If there is no change, I would think so."

Satisfied, his gaze moved from Geoff to Gray. She looked so lovely and serene and his attention shifted.

"You and Brooke can sleep in the smaller tent tonight," he said. "My knights and I will sleep in here with Geoff."

She looked up at him. "I would prefer to sleep here where I can watch him."

He shrugged. "Then you and Brooke shall have this tent and we will take the smaller one."

"I am sorry. I know it will be crowded."

He waved a hand at her. "That's not it at all. 'Tis simply that the smaller tent is warmer. I thought you would be more comfortable."

She smiled. "You are most thoughtful. Thank you."

He returned her smile, feeling the warmth spark between them again. "You are most welcome."

Their gaze lingered on one another until Braxton moved towards her, crouching down next to her. He was very close, the heat from his big body radiating against her. He looked at her as if he wanted to say something, but no words would come. He couldn't quite articulate the new-found feelings he was experiencing. So he reached out and took her hand instead, bringing it to his lips. She watched him, his face inches from hers.

"Braxton?" she asked softly.

"Hmmm?" he murmured, his lips still against her hand.

"Why are you so good to us?"

He smiled. "Because you deserve it. And because I want to."

She studied his face, trying to detect anything about it that wasn't being totally truthful. "I am sorry that Brooke is so demanding and ungracious."

He shook his head, kissing her fingers at the same time. "She is neither. She is simply a young girl, with all of the wants and dreams and hopes of a young girl. She will settle down soon enough."

"But you spoil her."

He lifted an eyebrow. "You let me worry about that." With one hand, he reached beneath his chest armor and fumbled in the mail. He suddenly drew forth a small wooden box with a ribbon tied around it. The ribbon was a little smashed, but it did not dampen the Gray's thrill when he extended it to her. "Speaking of spoiling, this is for you."

Eyes wide with awe, she timidly took the box. She turned it over in her hands, inspecting it as if she'd never seen such a thing before. "What is it?"

He chuckled. "Open it, you silly wench."

She grinned and pulled at the ribbon. It fell away and she carefully pulled the lid off of the little box. She gasped at the contents before reaching in to pull forth the treasure inside. A beautifully etched thin gold band with a massive pale green stone glistened in the weak light. It was magnificent. She gasped again, in awe, as she inspected it.

"It's... beautiful, simply beautiful," she breathed. "For me?"

He took it from her and collected her left hand, sliding it down over the third finger. It was a little snug, but it fit. Gray held her hand up, staring at the ring as if hardly believing what she was seeing. Braxton's gaze moved between the ring and her astonished face.

"A token of my affection," he said simply.

"When did you get this? I have been with you nearly every moment of the day."

"I bought it when I bought the pig. It would seem that merchants are willing to open their shops, even at night, with the promise of a large sale."

"But this is so beautiful. Surely it must have cost a small fortune. I am not sure I..."

He cut her off. "As my betrothed, you warrant such a thing."

She looked at him, then. "We are betrothed, then? I thought we were merely courting."

He grinned, full-on. "If you think for one minute I am courting without a purpose, think again. I shall marry you before this month is out." He suddenly grasped her arms, pulling her up against his chest as his smile faded. "No one else is worthy of you, madam. You and your head-strong daughter and your broken down fortress deserve everything I can provide for you and more. Do not deny me this honor."

She swallowed hard, feeling his sincerity, finally allowing herself to believe that he was truly genuine in everything he said and did. Until this moment, she'd still held doubt. But no more. She wound her arms around his neck.

"Oh... Braxton," she whispered as her soft lips came down on his.

He pulled her fiercely to him, his kiss hot and lusty and aggressive. In little time she was off the stool, on her knees against him as his mouth ravaged her. With her arms around his neck, there was little she could do other than hang on while he tenderly assaulted her. His passionate mouth moved from her lips to her face, her neck, her shoulders. His lips were hot and moist, stirring the embers of desire in Gray until she was quivering with want. She'd never experienced such passion; in fact, her encounters with Garber had been far and few, usually drunken romps ending in her tears. She had no glorious memories of passion or coupling. But with Braxton, she could only imagine how wondrous it might be.

His mouth moved to the swell of her round breasts and his big hand, very gently, cupped her left breast. She gasped softly and started to pull away, but he held her close and his gentle touch turned more insistent. He fondled her boldly as his lips reclaimed hers, his kiss moving deep. He held her so tightly that he was sure he was squeezing the breath from her because he could hear her gasps and sharp exhales as he had his way with her.

He wanted to taste her flesh in the worst way. He wanted to suckle a rosy nipple until she wept with the pure joy of it. Her breast was soft and round in his hand and he could feel the hard nipple through the fabric. But his kisses slowed as he struggled to regain his control, fully mindful that this was not the time or place for this, no matter how badly he wanted her. When he finally pulled away from her mouth, she drew in a heavy breath as if struggling to breathe. He gazed down into her half-lidded

141

eyes.

"As a man of supreme control, I can tell you that it has taken all of my strength not to continue exploring you," he murmured. "My want for you is more than I can express, sweet. I am sorry if I frighten you with it."

His hand was still on her breast, gently rubbing where moments before he had been passionately fondling her. Gray labored to regain her wits, her hand instinctively closing over his as it held her breast.

"You do not frighten me," she whispered. "I... I have never experienced this level of passion before. It was never this way with Garber. In fact, it would sicken me whenever he touched me. But with you... I love this already, Braxton. I never knew it could be like this."

He smiled at her, his features illuminated by the soft candle light. He kissed her again, tenderly this time, his hand still moving slowly, sensually, over her breast. "It is a promise of things to come, this passion that ignites so easily between us."

"Do you think so?"

He spoke with his lips still against hers. "I know so."

He pulled away to look at her again, her exquisite beauty in the dimness of the tent. But he also pulled away because he was dangerously close to losing control again. Removing his hand from her breast, he straightened her bodice where he had mussed it. Then he helped her back onto the stool at Geoff's bedside before rising.

He was thankful he was in armor, for the mail and pieces of plate concealed a powerful erection. God, he wished he could take her at this moment.

"Now," he said, trying to distract himself. "I shall go and see how they are coming along with the pig. I should probably also see how Lady Brooke is faring after her scolding."

Gray lifted an eyebrow at him. "Do not coddle her, Braxton. She must learn her lesson."

His lips twitched but he bowed his head as if to agree to her wishes. Gray watched him go from the tent, suspecting that he would not. He would fold like a weakling the moment Brooke turned her big, sad eyes to him.

She was right.

An hour later, Braxton had not returned to the tent. With Geoff still unconscious, Gray felt the need to stretch herself, if only for a moment. She rose stiffly and exited the tent only to find her daughter, Braxton and both squires missing. The men at arms tending the fire could only point towards the dark town in response to her query. Since Braxton was with the children, she didn't particularly worry, but she wondered where they could have gone.

The evening was cool but not cold and the stars above were brilliant. Gray wandered away from the encampment, her eyes on the town in search of her daughter and Braxton. The dark tournament field was to her left, the empty lists mere shadows of the excited stands they had been earlier. Wandering aimlessly, and grateful for the opportunity to stretch her legs, she noticed that there were a few tents pitched off to the west of the tournament field.

She could see the triangle-shaped silhouettes and the flicker of the cooking fires. Curious, she wandered in that direction simply because wanted to see their banners and then attempt to deduce which House they were from. Purely idle curiosity. But she did not want to wander too close so after several minutes of pacing, she decided to turn around and head back to Braxton's encampment. Turning on her heel, she almost ran into a massive body standing behind her.

Startled, she yelped and fell back. A big hand reached out to steady her.

"Forgive, my lady," came the deepest voice she had ever heard. "I did not mean to frighten you."

Heart in her throat, she craned her neck back to gaze up into the face that emitted the voice. Surely it was the Devil himself. Eyes the color of obsidian gazed back at her, although it was difficult to deduce much else in the dark. She couldn't see his face clearly. But he was definitely a knight for he still wore his mail and a portion of arm protection was still strapped to his right arm. He was a very big fellow with handsome, rugged features. She took another step away from him.

"You merely startled me, my lord," she said as steadily as she could. "I apologize if I have stepped into your camp. I was... well, I was looking for my daughter but I see that she is not around here."

She walked a wide berth around him; though he did not stop her, his black eyes followed her like a cat tracking a mouse.

"I saw you at the tournament today," he said. "You were sitting in the lists with a young girl who has your same color of hair. Is that the daughter you are looking for?"

She nodded, trying not to be too obvious about making distance between them. "Aye."

"She yells like an alehouse wench."

Gray paused in her attempt to escape and lifted an eyebrow at him. "It was her first tournament. How else should she behave?"

The knight laughed softly. "Exactly as she did. She was all I could hear."

"You were competing, too?"

"I was the victor."

An inkling of recognition came to Gray's eyes. "You are Sir Niclas?"

He bowed gallantly. "At your service, my lady.

"You injured Geoff."

He straightened up, his dark eyes flicking in the direction of Braxton's camp. "It was an accident, I assure you," he said. "How fares the wounded knight?"

Gray regarded him carefully. "We do not know yet," she said after a moment. "We have done all we can. Only time will tell now."

Niclas nodded faintly and his gaze moved to her once again. "Are you d'Uberville's wife?"

"Nay."

"But you travel with Braxton de Nerra's camp?"

The answer was more complicated than that, but she simply

nodded. "Aye."

"Then you must be de Nerra's wife."

She cocked her head. "You ask many questions."

He lifted his big shoulders. "As I said, I saw you in the lists. And, I also saw you in town earlier in the day. If I do not ask questions, how am I to discover anything about you?"

Her brow furrowed. "Why would you want to know anything about me?"

He laughed softly. "Why wouldn't I? Such beauty is rare. Are you married then, my lady?"

"That is none of your affair."

It was Braxton's voice. He suddenly appeared out of the darkness with Brooke, Norman and a limping Edgar behind him. His expression was as hard as iron, the blue-green eyes that could be so soft were like shards of glass. Gray had never seen that expression on his face before. Braxton walked up beside her, sizing up Niclas; though the tournament champion was at least a head taller, Braxton was clearly nothing to be trifled with. He was enormously muscled and powerful.

Niclas knew of de Nerra; almost all fighting men did. Rumors and legends of the mercenary abound in the north. More than that, de Aughton's sworn House was none other than Braxton's own father, Baron Gilderdale. He was surprised Braxton did not know that, or at least, acknowledge it. He'd never met the earl's youngest son before, however, and their first introduction was rather awkward. De Aughton dipped his head in acknowledgement, in respect, though his eyes had lost none of their black glimmer.

"My apologies," he said steadily. "I did not know. I meant no insolence to the lady, or to you."

Braxton just stared at him. Gray could sense the tension and she was uncomfortable. She did not want Braxton getting into an altercation with this knight. She put her hand on his arm.

"I was looking for you and came across Sir Niclas instead," she said evenly. "He has been most kind. Shall we return to camp now?"

Braxton's gaze lingered on Niclas a moment longer before looking at Gray. "I am sorry you had to go looking for me," he took her hand, possessively, and tucked it into the crook of his elbow. "The children were hungry and could not wait for the pig. I got them something to hold them over until sup."

A glance at Brooke, Norman and Edgar showed the three of them eating hunks of brown bread. Brooke had something else in her hand, though Gray could not see what it was. She lifted an eyebrow at Braxton.

"I told you not to coddle her," she said in a low voice. "What did you buy her this time?"

He was defiant and penitent at the same time. "Bread and some kind of candied fruit. I had to pound on four or five stalls before I could find someone who would let us in."

Gray closed her eyes and shook her head. Braxton, not waiting for the rebuke that was sure to come, waved an arm at the children.

"Come along," he told them. "Back to camp."

The three of them scampered past him, although one was limping badly. He started to follow when he heard Gray's soft voice.

"Thank you for not allowing me to come to harm, Sir Niclas," she said. "And congratulations on your victory today."

Niclas thought he had been forgotten and was mildly surprised at the lady's words. "My pleasure, my lady," he said. "And my wishes for recovery to the injured knight."

Braxton did not acknowledge the man as Gray smiled weakly in response. They continued on towards the camp in silence, though Gray kept stealing side-long glances at him. He was distant and cold.

"Are you angry with me?" she asked softly.

He looked at her. "For what?"

"For speaking with that knight?"

He shook his head. "I am to blame. I should have told you where I was going so that you would not go looking for me."

She was on to him. "But you did not tell me so that I would not stop you from spoiling Brooke as I'd asked you not to."

He refused to look at her, but a smile broke through. "That is beside the point. The issue is that it is not safe for you to wander outside of my protection. Men like de Aughton can be less than chivalrous to a lone lady."

"Really?" she turned to look at the spot where they had left Niclas; he was predictably gone. "He did not seem threatening."

"He was not; at least, not at that moment. But he has interest in you."

"Me?" she seemed genuinely puzzled. "Why do you say that?"

He looked at her as if she was a simpleton. "He asked if you were married, Gray. It does not require great intellect to figure out that he was inquiring for his own interest."

She continued to peer at him, studying his expression. It occurred to her that she had never had two men interested in her at one time; at least, not like this. It was an oddly proud and humbling awareness. But something more occurred to her as she gazed at Braxton.

"You are jealous?" It was a statement more than a question.

They had reached the great fire where the pig sizzled and spit over the open flame. He turned to her.

"Call it what you will. You belong to me and I would have every man in England know it."

She smiled at him, her amber eyes reflecting the dancing firelight. "You needn't worry, Braxton," she said quietly. "I wouldn't even dream of looking at another man."

His icy stance broke somewhat. "Is that so?"

"It is."

"Then I have your attention."

"You have all of it and more."

The harsh manner faded completely and his smile broke through. "To be honest, I was not sure. You are a beautiful woman, after all, and I am...."

He didn't finish and she lifted an eyebrow. "You are... what?"

He lifted his big shoulders. "I simply meant that there are better prospects out there than me."

She shook her head. "Not to me there isn't. You are more than I could have dreamed of."

It was a sweet moment. He took her hand and kissed it in full view of the youngsters. Brooke and the boys pretended not to notice, still stuffing their faces with bread, though Brooke was understandably curious. It was the first time she had ever seen her mother smile like that. She was glad her mother was distracted, as it would make her forget that Brooke had, once again, coerced treats from Braxton. Moreover, Braxton seemed to have a way of dealing with her mother that made the woman forget everything else. Even at her young age, Brooke could see that.

Gray and Braxton disappeared into the tent where Geoff lay, leaving the others by the fire. The pig continued to steam and smoke into the night, filling the air with a delicious smell. By the time it was finished, everyone was ravenous and the animal came apart in big pieces. Brooke and Edgar ate until they were sick and Gray found herself tending not only an injured knight but a nauseous daughter.

In the distant camp, obsidian eyes continued to watch the crimson glow of the de Nerra tents as outlined by the great campfire. Pensive thoughts became decisive ones. He'd seen the lady earlier in the day when he'd nearly run her down on the street. He had been struck by her beauty even though she was clearly in the company of a knight he later found out to be Braxton de Nerra.

At the tournament, he had seen her sitting in the stands, a radiant bit of loveliness surrounded by the dregs of society. He would have asked for her favor had de Nerra not hovered around her like an over eager school boy. It was obvious that she was de Nerra's woman, though he could not be sure if they were married. He suspected that they were not. That morsel of information was the one piece he had been looking for. If she wasn't married, then there was still a chance. Even if it did risk the wrath of de Nerra.

Niclas was not an evil man. He was not manipulative or ruthless, at least not in the matters of men and women. But he had always been a man who got what he wanted, and tonight he knew exactly what he wanted.

CHAPTER TEN

"Braxton, do you see the banners? Who do they belong to?"

The morning was soft with dew, bright with new sun. The question came from Gray, seated on the wagon as the party returning from Milnthorpe drew close to Erith. Braxton was on his charger riding beside the wagon, his blue-green eyes riveted to the scraps of blue banner he could see just inside the portcullis. He did not recognize the colors at a distance.

"I do not know," he said. "More suitors for your daughter, I would presume."

Gray didn't like the sound of that, though there could be no other explanation. "What will you do?"

He was very calm, very casual. "Send them away, of course."

Gray didn't say anymore, though her gaze lingered on his strong face. His expression was unreadable. Rightly assuming they could do nothing until they knew who it was, she turned her attention back to Geoff lying in the bed of the wagon.

The injured knight was sleeping again, lulled by the rocking of the wagon. Surprisingly, he had awoken before dawn feeling better and without fever. Gray took it as a good sign and the party packed up for Erith. She wanted to get him back to the fortress and into a proper bed so that he could more readily heal. He's wasn't out of danger by a long shot and she was anxious to return home.

Geoff wasn't alone in the wagon. Edgar and Brooke sat at the very rear, their legs hanging over the back of the flatbed. There had not been a harsh word between then all morning, even when Brooke produced the bag of candied fruits that Braxton had bought for her the night before. She shared it with Edgar, making sure that Braxton and her mother saw her. She even shared it with Norman, who rode beside the wagon astride Geoff's charger. With the children all getting along, it made the ride back to Erith much more pleasant. But Gray kept shooting looks at her daughter, making sure the girl was behaving.

"Leave her alone," Braxton's voice was soft beside Gray.

She turned to him. "What do you mean?"

He looked at her, a smile on his lips. "You know exactly what I mean. She's behaving quite nicely. She needs your trust in her ability to amend her manners, not your constant scrutiny."

She lifted an eyebrow at him, though it was not an unkind gesture. "You know so much about children now, do you? Since when did you become an expert?"

He looked straight ahead. "I know everything," he said seriously.

She laughed. "I believe that you do."

He cast her a sidelong glance, grinning while she laughed at him. The ride back to Erith had been filled with little glances and smiles from them both and Braxton was fairly certain that he'd never in his life experienced such joy. Had anyone suggested to him a week ago that his life would have taken such a dramatic turn, he would have laughed at them. But turn it had.

As they continued to gaze coyly at each other, Erith loomed closer and the sentries on the repaired wall announced the approach of the party. They could hear the shouts echoing as other soldiers took up the call. Braxton broke away from Gray's sweet face and spurred his charger into a canter, loping the big beast under the portcullis and into the ward beyond. He wanted to see for himself who had arrived and he did not want to wait.

The first thing he saw were a few strange soldiers standing in a group near the keep. The horses near them wore blue and white standards. But a glance around the ward showed a heavy concentration of unknown soldiers near the northeast corner of the keep. There were at least a hundred. Uneasiness swept him. Braxton rode up to the small group collected near the keep.

"Who do you serve?" he demanded.

The men looked at him, a mixture of suspicion and defiance on their faces. "Roger de Clare," one of them said. "Who are you?"

Braxton's mood changed instantaneously. He had gone from mildly curiously and confidently unconcerned to deeply uneasy all in one split second. His blue-green eyes swept the keeping, knowing de Clare was somewhere within the walls. Without answering their question, he reined his charger sharply back in the direction he came. He ran into the approaching party just as they approached the portcullis.

He flicked two thick fingers in Dallas and Graehm's direction, motioning for them to attend him. He, in fact, rode straight for Gray, still seated on the wagon bench beside the driver. Her amber eyes studied him expectantly as he and the other two knights rode up beside her.

"Well?" she asked before he could speak. "Who is it?"

Braxton wasn't quite sure how to tell her. There was no easy way. "Roger de Clare," he said. He couldn't help the sharp, helpless sigh that escaped his mouth. "It would see that your mother has called forth the Devil himself, Gray."

She stared at him for a moment as the news, and implication, settled. Then her eyes widened. "De Clare?" she repeated, stunned. "But... he's Gloucester. Gloucester is here?"

Before Braxton could reply, Graehm piped up. "Gloucester is here?" he sounded like a dumbfounded lad.

Braxton gave Graehm an intolerant look. He didn't need one of his knights acting the giddy fool when he had a serious issue on his hands. "Aye, the cousin of the earl is here," he said, somewhat sharply, before returning his attention to Gray. "He's not brought a big party with him and I did not see any knights, but we must handle this very carefully, my lady. You know that. The relationship between the de Montforts and the de Clares is tenuous at best."

She nodded, still astonished at the news. "What shall we do?"

Braxton shook his head, thinking aloud. "Is it possible that your mother sent invitation to Roger de Clare for Brooke's hand? My God, the man has to be beyond sixty years. Moreover, he is already married with children, or at least he used to be married. Is it possible his wife is dead, then?"

He was talking to himself more than he was talking to her. But they should have realized that Brooke would hear them. She was still perched on the wagon bed with her legs hanging over, listening to every word.

"He has male children," Brooke said casually, as if it was nothing at all to be concerned over. "Grandmother said he has many fine sons."

Now that the secret of her grandmother's deeds were out, she was apparently very comfortable discussing what she knew. Gray, Braxton and the two knights were looking at her, a mélange of trepidation and displeasure on their faces. Braxton seemed the least emotional out of the bunch, his expression holding mostly steady.

"Then it must be for one of the sons," he lowered his voice as he spoke to Gray. "But I would be lying if I said his presence did not concern me."

"Why?"

He lifted an eyebrow. "Because your mother has promised suitors Erith along with Brooke's hand. Erith belongs to me and I have the document to prove it. Gloucester might not take the news so easily, especially if he is attempting to mend the ties his cousin destroyed. We do not need Gloucester coming down around our ears." His mind began to work quickly, trying to think of a way out of or around this. His eyes fell on Dallas, the quiet knight. He was young, strong, and powerful, the second son of Baron Lisvane, vassal of the Earl of Cornwall. Though Dallas would not inherit his father's title or baronetcy, he would inherit a small parcel of property from his mother. An idea began to form. Braxton was going to undo what that old woman was trying to do if it was the last thing he ever did.

"Dallas," he motioned to his knight. "A word, please."

Dallas obediently followed him to a resting point several feet away where they paused a moment, chatting quietly astride their snorting chargers. After a few exchanged sentences, Dallas' eyes widened. Though he did not raise his voice or show obvious emotion, it was clear by his expression that he was shocked. Braxton's expression was quite calm as he finished speaking, watching Dallas wrestle with whatever subject was occurring between them. Gray watched curiously as Dallas, still visibly uncomfortable, finally nodded his head. Braxton abruptly reined his horse away from him, emitting a piercing whistle between his teeth. The entire party came to an abrupt halt, wagon and all.

They were almost at the threshold of the main gate. Braxton waved a gloved hand over his head in a circular motion. "Turn the wagon around," he barked to the driver. "We return to Milnthorpe. *Move.*"

Gray held on to the bench so she would not slide off as the wagon abruptly turned around. Then the wagon driver snapped the whip and the horses began to run. The last glimpse she had of Erith as it faded away was of curious soldiers up on the walls, watching their departure.

"Graehm," Braxton's charger was cantering next to the wagon as he shouted his order. "Return to Erith. Collect all of our men and all of our possessions and make haste for Milnthorpe."

Graehm broke away from the party and returned to the fading castle. Dallas, bringing up the rear of the party, shoved a squealing Brooke back onto the wagon bed and slapped closed the door at the rear of the bed where she and Edgar had been hanging their legs out. The wagon was bouncing over the road, rattling heavily, and Brooke and Edgar were bouncing right along with it.

"Braxton," Gray called to him over the noise. "Where are we going? What's wrong?"

He knew she needed an explanation. His mind was working so quickly that he had almost forgotten. But he couldn't stop now; they had to get back to the town as quickly as possible.

"Later," he told her.

Gray watched him spur his horse ahead, charging down the road as if riding to battle. Geoff gave a groan at the bouncing of the wagon and she found her attention turned to him. Even so, her thoughts were still with Braxton and their mad dash back to Milnthorpe.

Something was up. She could feel it.

***

"Are you mad?" Gray demanded. "Have you completely lost whatever good sense God gave you?"

They stood beneath the shade of a mature oak, just Gray and Braxton. On the outskirts of Milnthorpe, the rest of Braxton's army had just caught up to them in the past few moments and had began settling their encampment. The sun was burning bright in the afternoon sky, but Gray wasn't paying any attention to that, or to anything else at the moment. Her focus was solely on the powerful knight with the graying blond hair standing before her.

Braxton was calm in the face of her tirade. In fact, he hadn't expected less. They were away from the rest of the encampment so that no one could hear their emotional exchange. He had brought her to this clearing a-purpose, knowing their conversation had the potential to be explosive.

"Think about it, Gray," he said evenly. "It is the best option unless you want Brooke's future to be marred with uncertainty. You are going to have suitors showing up from now until next year demanding to negotiate for your daughter. But they cannot negotiate for her if she is already married."

Gray knew that; Lord, she knew that. But it didn't help her sense of despair. "But to Dallas?" she shook her head, baffled. "Surely you cannot take marriage so lightly that you would force your knight to marry a young lady without a cent to her name?"

He crossed his thick arms patiently. "I told you that I would supply her dowry. She is most certainly not penniless."

Gray shook her head until tendrils of blond hair escaped from her bun. "I cannot let you do that. You are not responsible for her dowry. And Dallas..."

He interrupted her. "I have a piece of vellum that states I am quite clearly responsible for her. She belongs to me. And since she belongs to me, I will supply her with a suitable dowry."

Gray froze, her amber eyes wide on him. "So you intend to marry my daughter to your knight no matter what I say? Because she belongs to you?"

"Nay," he unwound his arms and went to her, putting his hands on her shoulders. "That is not what I meant and you know it. What I am saying is that I am indeed responsible for her; therefore, I will supply a dowry to make her attractive to a husband. And I am trying to save you and your daughter if you will stop fighting me on this. Would you rather see her married to a de Clare?"

She knew him well enough to know that he wasn't claiming Brooke as some prize to be awarded. Her angry expression wavered. "Nay."

"Haistlethorpe?"

She grimaced. "Nay, not him."

He squeezed her shoulders. "Then you must marry her to someone suitable right away to eliminate the uncertainty that she will end up with men like that. Can you not see the logic, sweet? I am trying to help you. But you must learn to trust me."

She did trust him, but it didn't help her sense of hopelessness and outrage. Still, he was trying to do what he thought was best. Ever since she had met the man, he had been trying to do what was best for her and her daughter and she had resisted him at nearly every turn. She did not want to resist him anymore; she wanted to trust him with complete abandon. He hadn't steered her wrong yet.

"Oh... Braxton," she breathed, the fight suddenly draining out of her. "Must it be like this?"

He nodded his head. "I fear that is the only way to save your daughter from a horrible fate," he pulled her closer, his forehead resting against hers. "Dallas is a chivalrous, gentle knight. I would not entrust your daughter to him if he was not. He will inherit a slight amount of property upon the death of his mother, so he is not completely unsuitable. His father is a wealthy baron."

She was coming to feel so very saddened. "But... he is so much older than she is."

"He is twenty-six years old. There is only eleven years between them, not a tremendous gap. There is more of an age difference between you and I."

"What does he say to all of this? Surely this is not appealing to him."

"He considers it an honor to marry into the House of de Montfort and bear the title of Baron Kentmere. Moreover, a dowry of thirty thousand gold marks is very appealing."

Gray looked at him, shocked. "Is that what you are giving her as a dowry?"

He nodded. "Eventually, Dallas will leave my service and find his path in life. It will be a goodly sum of money to support them."

She went from astonishment to complete, utter devastation over the thought of her daughter leaving her. "He will take my daughter away?"

He fought off a smile, watching tears fill her eyes. "I did not mean it the way it sounds," he shook her gently. "You must get hold of yourself and focus on the issue. Your daughter will marry Dallas, which will end the parade of suitors, and you will marry me."

She wasn't sure she could possibly be more astonished, but she was. "You and I are getting married also?"

He let his grin break through then. "It makes sense. If the priest is performing one marriage, he can perform another. That way, no one can vie for the hand of either Serroux woman." He ran a finger over her cheek, tenderly. "And I have been most anxious to call you wife since the moment I met you."

The tears were still there, but fading. He was so very sincere and sweet. "This all seems like such a dream to me." She dared to lean forward and kiss him softly on the lips. "Never did I imagine my life would turn out as it has. Never did I imagine someone like you."

His response was to pull her into his arms and kiss her with such force that he ended up cutting his own lip with his teeth. Gray responded with equal passion, the caution and reserve that had filled much of her manner since their introduction unabashedly vanished. She was his and she did not care if the entire world knew about it. In fact, she wanted them to know. Braxton pulled her closer, his right hand instinctively finding her breast again. It was like a moth to the flame. She moaned softly as he gently fondled her.

In the midst of their heated kiss, it seemed odd when a loud thud suddenly filled the air and Braxton abruptly released his hold on her. One moment, she was in his arms and in the next, he was lying at her feet in a heap. It all happened so fast that she did not have time to process the event. The next she realized, a man with a club of wood in his hand was standing in front of her. Startled, she looked up into eyes of obsidian.

"So, my lady," said that deep voice again. "We meet once more."

His big gloved hand muffled her scream.

CHAPTER ELEVEN

"Why does he keep looking at me?" Brooke whispered harshly to Edgar.

They were sitting in a pitched tent, watching over a sleeping Geoff until Gray returned. But it had been quite some time and neither Gray nor Braxton had returned. Moreover, Sir Dallas was staring at Brooke from his perch several feet away. He had the strangest look on his face, seemingly lost in thought, as the rest of the camp moved busily around him.

"I do not know," Edgar wasn't particularly interested in Sir Dallas at the moment. "Maybe he does not like you."

Brooke scowled at him. "Why are you so mean to me all of the time?"

Edgar had no good answer. He lifted his skinny shoulders. "I do not know," he fussed with the wrappings on his ankle. "Where is your mother? She was supposed to come back and look at my foot."

Brooke eyed the lad, still lingering on the insult he had dealt her. But she looked around, off in the direction she had last seen her mother heading. "She and Sir Braxton are off somewhere," she sighed. "We'd best wait for them here. I do not think we should go looking for them."

"Why not?"

Brooke gave him a knowing expression, much like her mother's own. "Because they are probably doing something we should not like to interrupt."

"Like what?"

She frowned. "Do you not know anything about the ways of men and women? Sometimes they like to be alone."

Edgar shrugged, fooling with the wrap on his ankle. "I have seen the soldiers grab serving wenches and put their mouths on..."

Brooke held up a sharp hand. "Shhhhh," she hissed. "I do not want to hear that."

"But I have *seen* them."

"I know you have and I do not care. It's... it's unseemly to talk about those things."

"I bet your mother and Sir Braxton are doing the same thing!"

Brooke shrieked. "Do not say such things, you evil boy. I'll slap you, I will!"

Edgar liked the reaction he was getting out of her. She was squirming and the corners of his mouth twitched. "What are you so upset about? I'll wager you don't even know anything about what men and women do."

Brooke scowled and her cheeks turned pink. "I know more than you, Edgar."

"Do not!"

"Do, too!"

Dallas picked that moment to break from his staring stance and move towards the wagon. "Edgar," he snapped softly. "What have I told you about harassing Lady Brooke?"

Edgar looked at Dallas and was immediately quelled, but not entirely. There was still fight left in his expression. "I was not harassing her, my lord. We were... talking."

"What about?"

Both Edgar and Brooke looked mortified. They looked at each other, wide-eyed, and Brooke blurted out: "My mother and Sir Braxton. They've been gone a long time."

Dallas' blue eyes moved in the direction he had last seen the pair wander. He had to admit, they were correct. Braxton and the lady had been gone a long while, but he knew the reason for their disappearance and the contents of the subsequent discussion. He suspected that it had taken longer than expected to convince Lady Gray the course of her daughter's future.

Dallas, in fact, had spent the last hour coming to grips with just that. He'd always hoped to marry, of course, but he'd not thought on it more than that. Braxton's request had been a surprising one. At first, Dallas had been quite shocked. Then his shock had moved to resistance, to contemplation, and finally to resigned acceptance. Though he had not exactly been ordered to marry her, the implication was obvious.

He'd just spent the past several minutes watching Brooke interact with Edgar, observing every movement, every word. She was certainly a pretty thing, like her mother, but she was also very much a spoiled child. Yet he sensed there was something inherently agreeable in her, like a beautiful wild rose bush that needed some pruning and tending for it to fully blossom. He never thought of himself as a gardener, but that was the position he could very well find himself in. If he was successful, he would have a lovely, well-behaved wife. If not, then....

"Should we go look for them, Sir Dallas?"

Brooke's soft voice jolted him from his thoughts. He looked into her luminous blue eyes, the same shape but not the same color as her mother's. "I shall go and look for them," he said after a moment. "You stay here with Edgar."

They watched him walk off towards the east, the tall knight with the damp blond hair. Though he was slender, he had very broad shoulders and muscular arms. He had fought valiantly at the tournament the day before, falling only to a man nearly twice his size. But he had accepted defeat graciously. Brooke had felt rather sorry for him. When Dallas disappeared into the trees, Brooke and Edgar turned their attention back on each other. Edgar reiterated the fact that Brooke knew nothing about men and women. Brooke punched him in the arm and he fell off the wagon.

Dallas was oblivious to the fight going on back in the wagon as he wandered deeper into the trees. His knightly senses were highly attuned to the area around him, not wanting to fall across something indiscreet between the lady and Sir Braxton. He knew very well that his liege had set his sights on the lady. They all knew, and no one blamed him. She was a beauty.

The trees grew denser and more than once a pointy branch caught on his armor. Birds twittered above his head, the waning sunlight filtering through the heavy oak branches. He could see a small clearing up ahead and, oddly, there was something lying in the middle of it. He couldn't quite tell what it was until it suddenly moved. A hand went up; a gloved one. He recognized the glove.

Dallas broke into a run, plowing through the trees and into the clearing. He reached Braxton just about the time the man was trying to push himself up into a seated position.

"Braxton," Dallas grabbed him to steady him. "What happened?"

Braxton had a nasty crack on the back of his head; his scalp was split and there was blood all over his hauberk. Moreover, the world was rocking dangerously and Dallas' voice sounded like it was coming from very far away. He shook his head feebly.

"I do not know," he grunted, then his eyes peeped open. "Where is Gray?"

Dallas looked around, seriously concerned. "I do not see her," he held on to Braxton as the man tried to steady himself. "Did she do this?"

Braxton glared at him as much as he was able. "God, no," he blinked his eyes, trying to focus. "Find her, Dallas. All I know is that the last I saw of her, she was in my arms. And then everything went dark."

"But you are injured..."

"Find her," Braxton barked savagely.

Dallas let go of him and stood up, studying the mashed grass beneath their feet. He whirled around, trying to find a pattern, but the grass was too dry and too mashed to discern much of anything. His fear began to rise.

"I do not see any blood," he said. "Do you suppose she ran off after your attacker?"

Braxton was fighting down the bile in his throat, his senses becoming more oriented and a strong sense of trepidation taking hold. "More than likely whoever hit me took her."

"A wild animal, perhaps?"

"I doubt it. There would be blood all over the place if that was the case. More than likely, it was a man with a weapon."

Dallas could suddenly see a clear path leading off towards the north east into a cluster of trees. "But to ambush you," he paralleled the path, realizing it was indeed something of evidence. "Why would someone hit you on the head and take the lady? It makes no sense."

Braxton was struggling to his knees, seeing where Dallas was heading. Hand on the back of his head, he took a deep breath to settle the spinning world. "Do you see something?" he asked his knight.

Dallas took off at a run, disappearing into the cluster of trees. He yelled something that Braxton could not understand. Braxton struggled to his feet, weaving and stumbling after his knight. By the time Braxton reached him, Dallas was on his knees in some soft dirt behind a massive oak. It was cool and dim and musty in the bramble. Braxton walked up to him as quickly as his shaking legs would allow.

"What is it?" he demanded.

Dallas' blue eyes were focused intently on the marks in the dirt. "Horse shoes," he muttered. "And look; over there. Fresh horse dung. Someone was here, and quite recently. The earth is still damp."

Braxton shook his head, struggling to clear his vision. His head wasn't swimming so much now, but it hurt badly. He knelt opposite Dallas, very careful not to disturb the ground. He realized that only his determination to discover what happened to Gray overrode his terror for the moment. He feared that if he was to lose that focus, he would quickly deteriorate into a blathering fool.

"There are markings on the shoes," he noticed quietly. "Can you make them out?"

Dallas lowered his head so that his nose was almost in the dirt. After a moment, he shook his head. "Nay, my lord," he said. "I see the mark, but I do not recognize it. But look over there," he pointed to footprints a few feet away. "Do you see those? Boots"

Braxton peered closer. "Heavy, well made. See the distinct imprint of the heel? This was someone of means."

"It is a big man," Dallas said what they were both thinking.

They looked at each other and Dallas could see the anguish in his liege's eyes. "Who else would wear footwear like this but a knight or some other man of property?"

Braxton put a hand to his temple, trying to rub away the pain. "I fear that I was being followed and was not even aware," he said with disgust. "God, what is happening to me? I used to be so much more astute. I used to know all, see all. But I did not see this."

"Maybe they were not stalking you at all," Dallas interjected softly. "Maybe they were stalking the lady."

Braxton lifted an eyebrow. "Indeed they were," he said slowly. "And because of my foolishness, they were able to take what they sought. They waited until we were alone. Rather than invite a confrontation that I would very well win, they chose to ambush me and steal her. Bastards."

Dallas could see that he was already beating himself up over the situation. "It was not your fault, my lord," he said steadily. "You could never have anticipated such a thing."

"Maybe not, but I should have." Braxton continued to stare at the imprints, fighting off a clutching sense of horror. He finally motioned to Dallas. "Return to camp and assemble the men. We ride in search of Gray before this trail gets cold."

Dallas nodded and was gone, leaving Braxton on his knees beside the soft earth. He was struggling tremendously against his panic, telling himself that it would serve no purpose. He needed to focus, to find Gray. Moreover, he would have to explain to Brooke that her mother had disappeared and, if for no other reason, had to remain strong for the young lady's sake.

He stood up on weak knees, feeling an odd stinging in his eyes. He rubbed at them, realizing it was tears. He allowed himself a painfully brief moment to feel his emotion, letting the tears fill his eyes. He could not believe this had happened. It was beyond comprehension. What made it even more painful was that he had never seen nor heard anything; as a knight, his life had depended on his senses. But they had failed him at a critical instant for his senses, at that very moment, were consumed with the woman in his arms. He had been blind to all else. But he sought comfort in the fact that there was no blood anywhere, which more than likely meant Gray was still sound and whole. He could only pray that it was true.

"God," he muttered. "Please keep her safe until I can get to her."

Wiping his eyes, he pulled himself together and made his way back to camp.

***

She was not going to go easily.

Gray struggled against a man twice her size, kicking, punching, anything she could manage. But he was still able to get her on to his charger and ride off, tearing through trees and bushes, across streams and through mud to wipe out their trail. He finally managed to get her by the hair, which effectively ensnared her as they rode at break-neck speed into the sunset.

De Aughton was no fool. He had a good grip on her, and for good reason; he did not want her to injure herself in the struggle and he furthermore did not wish for her to escape. At some point, the lady relaxed out of sheer exhaustion and when he relaxed slightly also, a hand came up and nearly gouged his eyes out. It was enough to cause him to lose his grip and topple off the horse, nearly taking her with him. But not quite; Gray stayed mounted and, with actions fed by terror and exhilaration, turned the big bay charger back in the direction they had come. It was a split second decision made in a wink of an eye. She saw the opportunity and she took it.

The horse was exhausted and excited and she kicked it as hard as she could to make distance between herself and de Aughton. She could hear the knight behind her, yelling, but the sounds were growing fainter. The charger was grunting as it galloped, foam flying from its mouth as she urged it down the road. It had been a good hour since she last saw Braxton. She prayed that he was all right after the blow he had received to the head. It was all she could think of.

Gray turned to see if de Aughton was following them; she could not see him back down the road, which would have been likely impossible given the speed the horse was traveling. Still, she was terrified. She had to get away from him and back to Braxton. As the trees sped over her head and the horse grunted loudly, she leaned forward on the beast and showed him the end of the reins now and again. She was, in fact, fortunate the charger was responding to her at all. Most chargers were one-man horses and would only respond to their owners. But this horse was young and apparently not yet fully trained. It was Gray's saving grace.

She followed the road and did not go back into the brush the way the de Aughton had originally taken them. Gray was astute enough to know that they had originally camped on the outskirts of Milnthorpe; when de Aughton had grabbed her, he had headed east into the setting sun. She was now traveling with the nearly-set sun against her back. It would be very dark soon and she did not want to be caught out in the dark. Since the road was so wide, she assumed it would run into Milnthorpe at some point. There would be no other town in this area that would warrant such a well traveled path.

She was right.

Gray passed straight through the heart of Milnthorpe, fully oriented as to where she was. The charger was wet with exhaustion, but she pushed the animal through the town and onto the road heading east. Her heart was thumping against her ribs and she choked back the sobs as the road narrowed into a heavily wooded area that she finally recognized. Just through the trees to the south was the area where Braxton had set up camp. As the charger heaved and snorted, she pushed the animal across a small clearing and through a hedge of trees. Immediately, she saw Braxton's camp and the great fires burning around it. Then the tears came.

She dismounted the exhausted charger and led the beast the rest of the way. Wiping the tears off her cheeks, she entered the main body of the camp and noticed it was oddly vacant. But she heard voices in one of the larger tents and she recognized one of them. It was Brooke.

Dropping the reins, she burst into the tent to find her daughter and Edgar sitting near Sir Geoff's pallet. Brooke was crying. But one look at her mother and the girl shrieked, throwing herself into her mother's open arms. The women came together in a great bustle of sobs and tears.

"Mama!" Brooke wept. "Where did you go? Sir Braxton said you had been taken!"

Gray held her daughter tightly. "I was," she did not want to elaborate further; she was simply glad to be safe. "Where is Braxton?"

Brooke pulled away from her mother, looking her in the eye. "He went out to search for you. They all did."

"And they left you here alone?"

The girl shook her head. "There are a few soldiers about."

Gray took her daughter by the hand and led her out into the cooling evening. A massive fire burned in the middle of the camp, sending sparks into the deep purple sky. Gray moved past the fire, calling for the guards that her daughter said had remained. It wasn't long before two men suddenly showed themselves, having run from the perimeter of the encampment when they heard the distinctly female voice calling.

They were younger men, their eyes wide on the lady. "My lady?" one of them spoke hesitantly. "What are you doing here? Sir Braxton said..."

She interrupted him. "You must find him immediately and tell him that I have returned. How long has he been gone?"

"Not more than an hour, m'lady,' the other man said. "They cannot search much longer in this darkness. I would expect him to return shortly."

"Be that as it may, you will please go and find him and tell him that I have returned," she instructed. "He must know immediately."

The soldiers nodded smartly and were gone. She could hear

them calling to companions in the darkness, letting them know that the lady was in camp. Soon shadows emerged from the trees, men who had been guarding the perimeter that were now back in camp. She counted eight of them. Feeling distinctly more comforted, not to mention suddenly weary, she took Brooke and went back into the larger tent.

Edgar was standing up, his eyes big. Gray looked into the blue orbs and could read a thousand questions in their depths. He was a nice looking young lad, inquisitive and spirited. And she also noticed he had a bruise on his cheek. Suddenly, her abduction adventure seemed far away. She was back where she belonged and she was safe. She wondered at the bruise on Edgar's cheek. She suspected she knew how he got it.

"Edgar," she reached out and touched the hot welt. "What happened?"

Edgar blinked, looking like a child who just got caught raiding the sweets. "I... I fell, my lady."

"Did you have help falling?"

"I do not know what you mean, my lady."

"Aye, you do. Who gave you that bruise?"

He averted his eyes, his brow furrowed. He was struggling to give her an answer but Gray already knew the answer. She looked at Brooke.

"Did you do that?"

Brooke's eyes bulged. "I... I...."

Gray shook her head. "Brooke Serroux, what is the matter with you? I told you to leave him alone. Why did you strike him?"

Brooke looked properly contrite, more panicked than anything else. She did not want to lie, but she certainly did not want to tell her mother the truth. "Because... because he said something rude and nasty and I punished him."

"What did he say?"

Brooke's eyes welled. "Don't make me tell you, Mama. I don't want to tell you."

Gray wondered what had her daughter so upset. But it had been an upsetting night. Perhaps it really didn't matter. She sighed again and shook her head, looking around for the nearest stool.

"No more, Brooke," she told her daughter. "You will leave the punishment to Braxton. If I seen another bruise or welt on this boy, I am going to bruise or welt you. Is that clear?"

Brooke sniffled, wiping her eyes with the back of her hand. "Aye, Mama."

Gray found a stool next to Geoff and sat heavily. "Sit down and I'll hear nothing more from you. We will wait for Braxton to return."

Brooke sat down on the ground next to Edgar. When Gray turned her attention to Geoff to inspect his wound, Edgar stuck his tongue out at Brooke. She pinched him.

***

Braxton briefly inspected the worn bay charger as he thundered into camp. Someone had tethered the animal to a tree. Dallas was ahead of him and had already dismounted, lifting up a hoof to inspect the shoes. As Braxton passed by, he nodded to his liege.

"'Tis the same shoe markings, my lord," he told him.

Braxton didn't say anything, but his gaze lingered on the weary beast. Having been located by one of his soldiers a quarter hour earlier, he had raced like a madman to get back to camp. The lady was back and was apparently unharmed. That was all he could focus on as he dismounted his charger and stormed into the larger tent.

His eyes struggled to acclimate themselves to the weak light. To his right were Brooke and Edgar, sitting on the ground and apparently playing some sort of game between them. He could see sticks laid out in patterns. Looking around, he spied Gray kneeling over Geoff, her lovely face tense in concentration. She must have heard him, or at least sensed him, because she looked up and their eyes met. She bolted to her feet and they came together somewhere at midpoint in the tent.

169

Her arms were wound tightly around his neck, her face buried in his shoulder. Braxton held her so tightly that he was certain he was squeezing the life from her. It was the most amazing, satisfying embrace of his life. Given the horror of the past hour, he could hardly believe she was actually in his arms.

"Sweetheart," he breathed. "What happened?"

She was weeping quietly, trying not to disturb the children too much. They were already watching the reunion with big eyes and she had refrained from showing any emotion in front of them up until this point. She hadn't wanted to frighten them any more than they already were. But the sight of Braxton was enough to dissolve her.

"Are you all right?" she answered his question with a question. "You were hit so very hard and..."

Her hand was moving to the back of his head and he stopped her, taking her hand and kissing it reverently. "I am well enough," he told her. "But what happened? Who took you?"

She wiped at her tears. "De Aughton. He hit you over the head and carried me off."

Braxton didn't know why the news did not surprise him. In fact, he had almost expected to hear that although he was unsure why. All he knew was that he remembered how the man had looked at her the night before. He knew that hungry look.

"Did he hurt you?" he asked softly.

"Nay. But I had to gouge his eyes out to get away."

He lifted an eyebrow. "You gouged his eyes out?"

She nodded. "I do not know where he was taking me, for he never said much at all. We fought for such a long time, Braxton, I cannot even fathom how long. It seemed like days. I relaxed and let him believe that I had given up, but I hadn't. He relaxed, too. When he did, I shoved my fingers into his eyes so hard that he fell right off his charger."

Braxton listened to her with complete, utter amazement. "My God," he breathed. "And then you stole his horse?"

She nodded. "I had to make it back to you. Oh, Braxton, I was so frightened."

"But you are sure you are unharmed?"

"Aye."

He pulled her into his arms again, kissing her forehead, her temple, whispering thanks to God that she was in one piece. She was safe and well, and he allowed those feelings to be his overriding thoughts for the moment. Were he to allow himself to linger on de Aughton, he could very well explode the anger he was trying so hard to bank.

Beyond the relief, beyond the thanks, there was something inside him demanding satisfaction. He could not help it. Niclas de Aughton had made a bold attempt at taking something that belonged to another. Men these days were less likely to do such things as had been the norm in ages past, but it did happen on occasion. Had de Aughton gotten her to a priest to marry her, she would have legally belonged to him and there wouldn't have been anything Braxton could have done about it. Except kill him, which he would have done without question.

He could not have the constant threat of de Aughton hanging over his head. He wanted to find the man and punish him.

"Where did you leave him?" he asked, hoping she wouldn't hear the menace in his voice.

Her face was buried in his neck, burrowing, seeking comfort. "I am not exactly sure. To the west of Milnthorpe, along the main road. I traveled that road for quite some time before coming to Milnthorpe. Then I recognized the town and remembered where you had set up camp."

He snorted softly. "So you took the main road back here?"

"Aye."

He shook his head at the irony. "So that's why I missed you. My men and I set off to find you along every path and trail but the main road. We assumed that whoever took you would not stay to the main highway."

She pulled her face from his neck, looking up at him. "And he did not. He went through trees and fields, and I truthfully have no idea how we ended up where we did. But I just stayed to the road because I did not know what else to do. I figured that if I kept heading east, I would eventually run into a town. I was just fortunate that it was Milnthorpe."

He cupped her face in his big hands, smiling gently at her. He kissed her nose, her lips, listening to Brooke giggle off to his right. He turned around and looked at the girl.

"What's so funny?" he demanded lightly.

Brooke grinned, looking a good deal like her mother as she did. "You kiss my mother the way I have seen women kiss their children."

"Is that so?" he asked. "And how is that?"

Brooke wrinkled her nose. "Little baby pecks. Like you are trying to kiss her to death."

Braxton glanced at Gray and they exchanged grins. He dropped his hands from her and faced Brooke. "I am simply glad to have her back safely, as you should be." When the girl nodded her head, he turned for the tent flap. "Now, I have some things to attend to. Edgar, keep tight watch over the ladies."

The young lad nodded sharply. With a lingering glance at Gray, who had settled herself back at Geoff's side, Braxton exited the tent and found Dallas standing over by the massive fire.

The men huddled together. Now that Dallas was to marry Brooke, their relationship had somehow deepened. There was a kinship forming that did not exist before. Now, they were to become family and Braxton was more comforted, more pleased, than he realized. Dallas would be a fine son-in-law.

"It was de Aughton," he told his knight in a low voice. "Gray said she left him to the west of Milnthorpe somewhere along the road. Since she took his horse, he would have to travel on foot but, I would suspect, his inclination is not to travel back to Milnthorpe. He has to know she would return to me and I would come looking for him."

Dallas nodded. They were joined by Graehm, having just come from inspecting Niclas's big bay charger. "Arnside is a town around five miles to the east of Milnthorpe," Dallas said. "He could have gone there instead."

"Or to any number of little villages to the south," Braxton

countered. "Organize the men into groups of four. Send a group to Arnside, Milnthorpe, and have the rest spread out over the countryside. Leave no stone unturned. I would have them report back to me by late tomorrow, whether or not they find anything. But tell them a bounty will be given to the men that find him. I want this man located and brought back to me."

Dallas nodded smartly and was gone. Braxton watched him march across the dim encampment, fading into the shadows. He turned to Graehm.

"You will find me a priest," his voice was quiet. "Bring the man here posthaste and pay him well for his trouble."

Graehm blanched. "Is Geoff...?"

Braxton cut him off. "No, not for last rites. For a marriage. Actually, two."

Graehm's eyebrows lifted slightly but he obeyed, disappearing into the darkness to collect his charger. With his men on the move, Braxton went back to the tent and stuck his head in through the door.

"Gray," he called softly. "A word, please."

She rose from her position next to Geoff and obediently went to him. He pulled her gently outside, under the blanket of stars that spread across the sky. It was a lovely night in spite of everything that had gone on. He crossed his big arms, facing her as the firelight flickered off his features.

"Surely you understand that with de Aughton's threat, the event of marriage is even more important than ever," he said quietly. "I have sent Graehm to find a priest. Before this night is out, your daughter will be married to Dallas and you shall be married to me."

There was no longer any hesitation or reluctance in Gray's expression. She had learned to trust Braxton completely. "Then I must tell my daughter she is to be a bride," she said softly.

He nodded. "Would you like for me to tell her?"

Gray shook her head. "Thank you, but no. This is something I must do."

He gave her a wink, a supportive gesture, and followed her

173

back into the tent. While he took up station next to Geoff, Gray took Brooke out into the night to tell her of her future. He was not surprised, moments later, to hear the young girl weep.

CHAPTER TWELVE

"He must have turned back for Milnthorpe," Constance said. "There could be no other explanation, my lord. When your men told him who had come to Erith, naturally, he would do everything possible to keep my daughter and granddaughter from you. He has claimed them as his possessions, I tell you."

Roger sat in the great hall of Erith. The fire in the heart spit and smoked, filling the room with silver haze. It was sunset, the end of a long day. He had been informed some time earlier that a party had approached and a man had entered the bailey, demanding to know who bore the colors of the blue and white standard. Then the man and his party had turned away from Erith and made haste in the direction they had come. Only curiosity, rumors, and an eventual conversation with Lady Constance had made sense of the visitor. It had not been a pleasing realization.

Roger eyed the Lady de Montfort seated across from him, toying with his wooden cup of cheap wine as he did so. There were a great many things on his mind.

"Braxton de Nerra," he rolled the name off his tongue. "You failed to inform me when I arrived that he was involved with this."

"His involvement is purely by sheer aggressiveness, I assure you," Constance said. "We offered him shelter a week ago and he's not left since. He sticks to my daughter like a disease and has taken control of Brooke. We've been unable to rid ourselves of him. Even now, he parades them around the countryside against their will."

"Is it your daughter's pleasure that he stays? Perhaps she is considering marriage to him."

"She is not," Constance said flatly. "My lord, I beseech you. I very much need your help if I am to save my daughter and granddaughter from that mercenary. For your aid, I assure you

175

that your son will marry Brooke and you shall have my daughter if you deem her suitable. Will you not help me, please?"

Roger sighed, turning his attention back to his cup as he spun it in slow circles. "Did you know that de Nerra's father is Baron Gilderdale?"

It was evident from her expression that she had not known. She did not want to come across looking like a fool. "He said he was distantly related to Anjou."

"And he is. But he is also the son of Thomas de Nerra, fourth Baron Gilderdale. And Gilderdale is a massive war machine as I am sure you know. Anyone in Northumberland knows of Gilderdale's military might. Where do you think Braxton achieved his connections and knowledge? He is bred from a long line of warriors. The entire family is full of blood thirsty fiends. The Scots do not even like to go against them but God knows, they have. And they have lost."

Constance was still trying to recover her shock, fighting off the uncertainty now that she was not in charge of the conversation. "Do you fear that he will call upon his father if you move against him?"

"He could. Certainly it would be a risk."

William de Clare sat silently next to his father, watching the man fiddle with the utensils. William may have looked like a pimp-faced lad, but in truth, he was even-tempered and wise as his mother had been. While most de Clare men were warriors with a mean streak, William did not possess this trait. True, he was training as a knight, and a very good one, but he was not mean by character. He was the opposite.

"Father," the lad said. "If Lady de Montfort is asking for our help, perhaps we should. There is no telling what peril Lady Gray and Lady Brooke might be in. Even if Gilderdale does support Braxton, they cannot defeat the House of de Clare. We are greater in number than they are."

"I'll not start a war with someone I have no quarrel with," Roger said with irritation. Then he slowed himself; he was beginning to sound like a coward. "De Nerra's reputation is well known. He's as ruthless as they come. Obviously, the man saw a fortress without a man to run it and has taken advantage of the situation. He's a mercenary. He only sees the value of this acquisition."

William watched his father closely. "Then we will help?"

Roger pursed his lips, looking at Constance and watching her anxious features. It was apparent that he was still weighing his options, struggling not to show his reluctance and trying to see the larger picture in all of this. He did not want to provoke Gilderdale, but there was something valuable at the end of all of this. Perhaps the risk would be worth it. When he spoke, it was to Constance alone. "If I do lend aid, have I your vow that Lady Brooke shall wed my son and Lady Gray shall wed me?"

"Of course, my lord," Constance agreed.

"And Erith shall become William's holding?"

"Indeed it shall."

That was enough for Roger. He had just acquired a castle for his youngest son and a wife for himself. He was anxious to have more sons to carry on the de Clare name; there was no guarantee the three he had would survive to perpetuate the family. One had to plan for all possibilities of the future and Lady Constance's suggestion of marriage to her widowed daughter had been an attractive one. Unexpected, but attractive nonetheless.

"Then we shall send for more troops to reinforce Erith as we search for de Nerra and his bunch," he abruptly stood up, startling William. He reached down and yanked his son to his feet. "Go tell the captain of the guard to send a rider home to Bronllys Castle to assemble two hundred of our men. Send to Caerphilly Castle for five hundred more. If we are going against de Nerra, then I would be prepared. The men will proceed to Erith immediately for further orders."

"Thank you, my lord," Constance said sincerely, perhaps a bit dramatically. "I am sure my daughter will thank you as well when she is free of this menace."

Roger lifted an eyebrow at the woman. For some reason, he was coming not to like her. He couldn't quite put his finger on it, but there was something untrustworthy and intolerable about her. He hoped he hadn't just consigned himself to a nasty fight against Gilderdale.

"We shall see," was all he said.

When the men had left the hall and she was all alone with the dim flicker of the hearth, Constance sat at the table and smiled. De Nerra might have been able to defeat her in her attempt to rid him from Erith, but he would not defeat Gloucester. Roger de Clare would squash him and the de Montforts would once again be in favor with a political marriage. And Constance would return to the life of luxury she deserved.

Her smile grew.

***

To the south of Milnthorpe near an ancient mound built by the Saxon forefathers, Graehm located a small church. It was a dark and boxy structure with few windows. Vespers had ended and the two priests that lived at the church were locking up for the night. It seemed they weren't very interested in Graehm at first; in fact, they seemed rather fearful of him and his purpose. But the promise of a sizable donation to their cause was enough to prompt the older priest to ride with Graehm back to Braxton's encampment. Even though the man loaded himself onto the oldest mule Graehm had ever seen, they were still able to return to Braxton's camp within an hour.

Once arrived, there was little time for introductions or niceties. Although it wasn't exactly how Gray would have planned a wedding, and it certainly wasn't how she would have planned a wedding for her daughter, it really didn't seem to matter. She stood next to Braxton as Brooke stood next to Dallas, her daughter still sobbing intermittently as the priest said the mass. The ceremony itself was short, to the point, and before Gray realized it, both she and her daughter were married women. Even when Braxton kissed her lips, her cheeks, and both her hands, it did not seem real. Even so, she knew in her heart it was the best thing she had ever done. She felt content, and she felt at peace.

Brooke, however, was a completely different story. She was terrified of the tall blond knight eleven years her senior who was now her husband. He had hardly said a word to her but had shown an inordinate amount of courtesy and patience. When the priest blessed their union, he leaned down and, very properly, kissed her cheek. He came away with tears on his lips.

Graehm, Norman and Edgar had witnessed the ceremony. The priest scribed marriage certificates on pieces of vellum he brought with him and had each man sign their name. In Norman and Edgar's case, writing their name was the only thing they knew, as neither of them had acquired the skills of reading or writing. Then the priest sanded the documents and handed them over to the respective grooms, whereupon Braxton paid the man more money than he had earned the entire previous year. It was a tidy sum.

And with that, Lady Gray de Montfort Serroux became the Lady Gray de Montfort Serroux de Nerra, and her daughter became the Lady Brooke Serroux Aston.

It was nearly midnight by the time everything was said and done. The priest would spend the night with them because traveling the roads in the dark was not safe, even for armed men. They gave him a bedroll and plied him with food and drink. Braxton's men were spread out and several campfires burned throughout the dark, eerie oaks. Gray stood with her arms around her daughter, comforting her as they watched Dallas and Norman pitch another tent under the half-moon sky.

Braxton had walked the perimeter to make sure the posts were set for the night. He couldn't remember ever feeling lighter of heart. For the first time in his life, he was actually happy. When he returned, it was to stand behind his new wife and daughter, watching as Gray gently stroked her daughter's arms, whispering soft words to the girl. He felt rather guilty, knowing Brooke was frightened and upset by the turn of the day's events. But it had been in her best interest. And he knew Dallas, and the man's character, better than she did. She had nothing to fear.

He moved from behind them and stood alongside. He cast a sidelong glance at Brooke, intermittently sobbing with her head on her mother's shoulder.

"Brooke," he said quietly. "May I express my pleasure at becoming your father?"

Both Gray and Brooke looked over at him; Gray was smiling faintly and Brooke was hiccupping with a finger in between her teeth. She blinked her luminous brown eyes at him.

"T-thank you," she replied only after her mother gave her an encouraging squeeze.

Braxton smiled at her. "May I tell you something?" She nodded and he continued. "I realize this night has been upsetting and surprising to you. I know you were not prepared for this. But you must realize that Dallas was not prepared, either. This is as much a life change to him as it is to you. And I promise you that I would have never suggested this to either of you if I did not, for one moment, believe it was the right thing to do. Do you believe that?"

Brooke's sniffles were fading and she removed the finger from her mouth to wipe the tears from her eyes. "A-aye," she said quietly.

"Good." He reached out and pushed a stray lock of hair out of her eyes, tucking it behind her ear. It was a gentle, fatherly gesture. "Dallas is a very fine man. I have known him many years and he has never once shown me that he is anything other than chivalrous, kind and wise. If you searched your entire life for such a man, you could not have found a better one. I know he will make a fine husband and you must give him that chance. Will you do this?"

Brooke slowly lifted her head from her mother's shoulder, her gaze moving to the tall man tying off the last of the tent lines. She sniffled again, but it was only remnants. Her tears, for the most part, were gone.

"Aye," she said, her eyes still on him. "But... but I do not even know him."

"Nor he, you. All he knows of you is a scrapper who fights with boys. Now show him a wife he would be proud to have."

She looked at him, her big eyes blinking thoughtfully. "How do I do that?"

Braxton's smile broadened. "Ask your mother. She is far more knowledgeable in these areas than I."

Brooke turned to her mother, who wriggled her eyebrows in response. "I am not sure if I am more knowledgeable, but I have had some experience. All I can tell you is to be kind, patient and obedient. The rest you must learn on your own." She gave her daughter a squeeze. "I like Dallas. I believe he will be a fine husband for you."

By this time, Dallas had finished the tent and was half way over to them. Brooke saw him coming and her eyes widened. But she admirably controlled herself and settled down as he came upon them. It would seem that Braxton's words had some impact on her.

"Norman and Edgar are going to bed with Graehm tonight, my lord," Dallas said to Braxton. "Lady Brooke and I shall have the smaller tent while you and your lady wife share the larger one."

Braxton nodded his acknowledgement, thinking it would perhaps not be much of a wedding night with Geoff a few feet away. But he said nothing to that effect; impatient as a bridegroom though he may feel, he was well aware of the logistics of their sleeping arrangements.

"It has been a long day," he said. "I would suggest that we all retire and take what sleep we can. We will leave for Erith before dawn."

He took a step back in the direction of the larger tent, noticing that Gray hadn't moved. She was still standing with her arm around her daughter. Dallas was standing there, looking between Brooke and her mother, and the mood was becoming awkward. Though not unfeeling, Braxton could see Gray's reluctance and he understood. Yet he would do what needed to be done; moving to the women, he took Gray's hand and gently pulled her away from her child.

"Let us retire, Lady de Nerra." God, how he loved using that title for the first time. "I am sure Brooke is exhausted and wishes to sleep. Bid her a good night and we shall see her on the morrow."

In control for most of the evening, Gray suddenly looked as if she was about to burst into tears. She reluctantly let Braxton lead her away, her gaze lingering on her daughter as the distance between them grew. Brooke just stood there with her head down, looking at her feet. When Gray and Braxton finally disappeared into the tent, Dallas spoke.

"You must be very tired," he said in a quiet, deep voice.

She nodded, still looking at her feet. "I... I am, a little."

"Perhaps we should retire."

Woodenly, she headed for the tent. Dallas followed. He reached over her head to shove the flap out of the way and she froze when she entered; Norman and Edgar were finishing laying out the bedrolls. An oil lamp sat on the ground, burning brightly in the black of the tent. The boys looked up at her, uncomfortable emotions in their eyes as they gazed at her, but just as quickly lowered their heads and vacated the tent. Brooke swallowed hard as the shelter cleared, leaving her standing there with Dallas, still in the doorway.

"My lady?" Dallas urged her gently inside.

Brooke took a few strained steps into the tent, startled when Dallas let the tent flap fall shut. He was quiet as he removed pieces of his armor, down to his hauberk. She just stood there, unmoving and uncertain. Then he turned to her.

"My lady," he said. "Would you be so good as to help me?"

She eyed him with hesitation but obediently went to him. "What would you have me do, my lord?"

He bent over and extended his arms to her. "Pull on the mail."

She grabbed hold, timidly at first, but then got a good grip on it and yanked. She almost pulled his head off and he pitched forward against her. He grabbed her so he would not topple her over, still restrained by his half-removed hauberk. Brooke took hold again and pulled and pulled. Because he was sweaty, the mail seemed to want to stick to him and to his padded shirt beneath. She only managed to remove one arm and was still struggling with the other when she heard a low rumble.

She paused, wondering where the sound was coming from. It took her a moment to realize that Dallas was laughing.

Brooke dipped her head so she could look him in the face; because of the placement of the hauberk, he couldn't lift his head. "What's so funny?"

He was giggling like a fool. "I am not sure," he gasped. "But the more you pull, the more twisted I become."

In spite of herself, Brooke grinned and gave another yank. The hauberk got stuck around his ears, covering his face. Dallas only laughed harder and Brooke's grin broadened.

"What should I do?" she demanded. "You are stuck."

He snorted and snickered. "Just keep pulling," he told her.

She did. Eventually, the piece came off, but not before it almost ripped his ears off. Brooke fell back with the weight of it when it finally came free, falling on her arse as she did so. But it was very humorous. When she fell on the ground, she laughed uproariously. Dallas stood there with his hands on his hips, looking down at her.

"You are going to have to become much more adept at helping me dress or I shall have my ears ripped off every time," he scolded with a grin on his face.

She shrugged, trying to get back up. He pulled on her arm and set her on her feet.

"This is my first experience with removing armor," she told him.

"I can tell."

She tossed the hauberk back at him and he deftly caught it. "I haven't had years of practice like you have."

Laughter fading, he threw the hauberk to the ground with the rest of his armor. "You will from now on, I promise."

He went about removing what was left of his leg armor. Levity waning, Brooke felt her trepidation rise once again as she watched him. She had many questions and many fears, and she knew that he was the only one who could satisfy them. She summoned her courage.

"Sir Dallas?"

He looked at her. "I am your husband, my lady. You do not have to address me as 'Sir'."

She cocked her head. "And I am your wife. You do not have to address me as 'my lady'."

The corners of his mouth twitched. "True enough."

"But it seems strange to call each other by our names so informally, doesn't it? We hardly know each other."

His smile grew. "It does indeed. We will do whatever you are comfortable with."

It was a kind statement. Brooke was comforted by it somewhat. He didn't seem pushy or assertive of his new role. Her courage grew.

"Maybe we should talk and get to know one another," she suggested.

He sat down on one of the bedrolls. Without his armor and clad only in his breeches and padded linen undershirt, he appeared far less imposing. He gazed up at Brooke and she studied him as if just seeing him for the first time; he had a nice, square jaw and a handsome face. His eyes were deep blue, like a lake on a warm summer day, and his long blond hair dusted the tops of his shoulders. It was very attractive hair, she thought to herself. *He* was attractive.

"An excellent suggestion," he said. "What would you like to know?"

The focus was back on her. Hesitantly, she sat opposite him on the other bedroll. "Well," she said slowly. "Where were you born?"

"At my family's home in Cornwall," he said. "My father is Baron Lisvane, a title he inherited from his father."

"Do you have any brothers or sisters?"

"I have an older brother. His name is Ferris."

"Is he a knight?"

"Aye, and a good one."

She thought of more questions. "Where did you learn to become a knight?"

"At Okehampton Castle in Dorset. I spent twelve years there before receiving my spurs. Then I swore allegiance to Sir Braxton and have been with him ever since."

She cocked her head. "Why did you not swear allegiance to a big house or to the king? Why do you serve Sir Braxton as a soldier of fortune?"

He smiled faintly. "Because I must make my own fortune, my lady. My brother will inherit my father's lands and title upon his death. What I am to inherit comes from my mother's side and it is not a tremendous amount. I must therefore make my own way. Sir Braxton has provided me with that opportunity."

"Oh." She nodded in understanding, having run out of questions for the moment. But she did think of one more. "Then why did you agree to marry me? I don't have anything of value to offer you. Shouldn't you have married for money?"

Dallas held an even expression; he didn't want to tell her the truth, that Braxton had very nearly forced him into the marriage with promise of a very large dowry, Erith Castle and the Kentmere title. He didn't think that would be a very good way to start off their marriage, though it was the truth. Judging from her youth and immaturity, he didn't think she would take it very well.

"I think that you do," he said ambiguously. "You come from a fine family and I think this will be an agreeable marriage for us both."

He shifted on the bedroll and she leapt to her feet, her eyes wide with fright. Dallas had no idea what had startled her until he realized he had inadvertently moved closer to her.

"Sorry," he moved back to his original position. "I did not mean to frighten you."

"You did not," she lied, but looking in his eyes, she realized that he was very aware of her fright. "'Tis just that I..."

He patted the bedroll beside him. "Come, lady wife. You must get some sleep. We have an early day ahead of us."

She stood there, watching him remove his boots. Her face

began to flush as the moment she had been dreading was fast approaching. She felt embarrassed, terrified, and curious all at the same time. But Dallas lay back on his bedroll, quite primly, and folded his hands across his chest. He looked up at her.

"Is something wrong?" he asked. "Do you require something?"

She stood there and twisted her hands. "Nothing is wrong," she lied for the second time, very timidly kneeling down on the bedroll. Though he was at least an arm's length away from her, he might as well have been lying on top of her for all of the dread she was feeling. But she managed to lie down, fully clothed, and pulled part of a blanket on top of her. Dallas suddenly sat up and flipped the rest of the blanket on top of her, covering her feet. Brooke yelped with fright, preparing to leap up again, but Dallas put his hands on her and shoved her back down.

"You'll never get any sleep if you keep jumping up every time I move," his voice was low. When she opened her mouth to protest, he cut her off. "Listen to me and be done with this foolishness. I have no intention of claiming my husbandly rights tonight, so you can rest your mind. Now, will you go to sleep?"

She gazed up at him, the blanket pulled up around her neck. "You… you do not want to…?"

He shook his head. "If I did, I would have to take it by force and that is not the manner in which I wish to start out this marriage."

She was calming with amazing speed. "But… but it is your right. My mother said I should be obedient and do what you tell me."

He almost laughed. "And do you plan to listen to her?"

She nodded emphatically but when he lifted an eyebrow at her, her enthusiasm waned. "I will listen to you but I would like for you to listen to me, too."

"Very well," he propped himself up on an elbow, gazing down into her sweet face. "What would you like to say?"

She blinked; what *did* she want to say? "I.. I should like to say that Sir Braxton and my mother tell me you are a fine man and that I am thankful that you are a fine man and do you at least want to kiss me?"

It all came out as one rapid-fire sentence. He couldn't help it; he burst into laughter. Brooke sat up, frowning.

"Why are you laughing at me?" she demanded.

His blue eyes twinkled. "Because I find you humorous," his laughter faded. "And very pretty."

Her cheeks flushed. "Oh."

She looked uncertain again and lay back down. Dallas watched her for a moment as she pulled the blanket up to her neck again. Then he leaned over her, very close to her face. He was surprised she didn't bolt again.

"Yes, I would at least like to kiss my wife on the eve of our wedding," his voice was low and deep. "May I have your permission?"

Brooke's heart was thumping wildly against her ribs as she gazed up into his strong face. She was positive he could hear it. Maybe having him close wasn't such a horrible idea.

"Aye," she managed to stammer.

Dallas lowered his lips to hers, slowly as not to startle her. When their mouths touched, it was a magical moment. She was soft and warm and sweet. He kissed her gently, his lips gently suckling hers. He kissed her longer than he had intended simply because she was so delicious. He pulled away before he lost his control, his deep blue eyes lingering on her.

"Good night, Lady Aston."

Brooke's head was swimming. She was stunned, overwhelmed.

"Good night."

Dallas blew out the light. Brooke lay there for an indeterminate amount of time, listening to the sounds of the night outside the tent, feeling strangely warm and safe. She'd never felt anything like it. Suddenly, Dallas' hand was on her arm, a gentle yet inherently protective gesture. He had a big hand, strong and warm. She liked it.

Brooke fell asleep with her fingers touching his.

***

"Gray," Braxton's voice was a soft growl. "Come lay down, love. Come away from the door."

But Gray couldn't. She was standing in the tent flap of the larger tent, her eyes on the small tent in the distance. Her amber eyes were full of unshed tears when she finally managed to pull herself away.

"She's so young," she said as she made her way over to the pallet that Braxton had fashioned for them. It was about as far away from Geoff as they could get without actually leaving the tent. "I am afraid that she will...."

"How old were you when you married Garber?"

She eyed him. "Fourteen years old."

"And your daughter is fifteen years old. She is no longer a child."

"But she is still very young."

Braxton reached out and grabbed her when she came close enough. He pulled her onto his lap as he sat on the pallet and his big arms went around her.

"You worry overly," he told her, nuzzling her shoulder. "Dallas will not be unkind. Besides, she is his wife now. You must not interfere."

She gazed at him, the blue-green eyes that were now the center of her world. She smiled weakly, wrapping her arms around his neck and rubbing her nose against his.

"I have every right to interfere," she told him lightly. "I am his wife's mother, after all. And you are his liege."

He groaned. "God, you are not going to be meddlesome, are you?"

She laughed softly. "Perhaps on occasion."

He grinned and kissed her. She tasted so good that he kissed her again. The spark that ignited so readily between them burst into flame and his mouth claimed her firmly, his tongue probing the tender places of her mouth.

"Dallas isn't the only man with a new wife," he murmured, his mouth still on hers. "I have one, too."

His hand was on her breast again, the powerful warmth firm against her body. She could feel his heat through her bodice.

"Is that so?" she whispered as his mouth moved across her jaw. "And what do you intend to do with her?"

Braxton's response was to latch on to her neck, half-biting, half-suckling. It was enough to drive her mad, a soft moan escaping her lips. They fell back on the pallet, his arms around her, his mouth on her neck.

Acutely aware of Geoff's presence, Braxton pulled the blanket up over them both just in case the man should awaken. At least he wouldn't see much. Braxton's mouth returned to her lips and he kissed her with ferocious intensity, each suckle or stroke of the tongue giving way to stronger passion. His big hands pulled at the top of her shift, pulling down the surcoat and fabric until the rise of her breasts was evident. Beyond that, he had to unfasten the back of it. In a flash, he rolled onto his back and Gray ended up straddled on top of him.

He stopped kissing her long enough for their eyes to meet. With a glance at Geoff, Gray reached behind her and unfastened the back of the surcoat. She pulled it off with Braxton's assistance, baring her breasts slowly and modestly. When her firm, round globes were revealed in the weak light, Braxton reached up to touch them ever so gently. He was reverent and adoring. Then he pulled her down to him, his mouth seeking a rosy nipple.

Gray gasped when he suckled her, gently at first, and then with more force. Painful jolts of excitement ran throughout her body and she had to make a conscious effort not to make any noise. But her ragged breathing told Braxton how much she liked it, the hands in his hair encouraging him on. She held him to her breasts as he nursed between them, his tongue lapping at her soft flesh.

Gray removed his padded shirt, leaving his broad chest bare. The moment was not lost on either of them; Braxton's mouth moved back to her lips and their naked flesh touched for the first time, her chest to his. It was a wildly erotic moment, full of magic. But they knew, instinctively, the best was yet to come.

Somehow, she managed to remove herself from both the shift and surcoat and Braxton's breeches were off and laying somewhere next to them. Completely nude, the touch of their heated bodied against each other was dizzying. Gray was lost in a haze of desire, feeling Braxton's hands all over her, his mouth in tender places. When he rolled her over onto her back and began to kiss her belly, she put a hand in her mouth to keep from screaming. It was the most amazing thing she had ever experienced.

Braxton moved lower still, his mouth now on the mound of dark curls. Gray's legs instinctively parted for him and he settled his big body in between them, his mouth loving her most private core. Both hands went into Gray's mouth as she literally bit off the screams of passion bubbling up her throat. His tongue was wicked, his mouth hot, and she had never before experienced anything so intimate or powerful. Every lap of the tongue and she was ready to scream.

But she was quickly reaching her climax; Braxton could feel her body beginning to twitch. Lifting himself up, he gazed into her eyes, his fingers on her lips. He was so overwhelmed that he couldn't even speak. All he wanted to do was look and touch and feel. Gray gazed back at him, trusting, passionate, as he put his massive manhood at her threshold. She could feel it lingering there, hot and pushing against her. She wanted him so badly that her limbs ached. With the prelude of a deep kiss, Braxton drove deep into her slick folds.

Gray's knees came up, her body arching into his thrust. Braxton was the one who groaned this time, biting his lip to keep quiet. She was tight and hot and he withdrew, thrusting hard once again and seating himself fully. Gray's pelvis rocked up against him and he lost his control then, feeling the animal instinct to mate with this woman. He thrusts were measured, deep, pelvis against pelvis as they matched each other move for move. Sweat began to glisten. Braxton lifted himself up on his arms just so he could watch her magnificent body in the weak light. It was an awesome sight.

His thrusts grew deep, harder, as he felt his release approach. He fell back on top of her, gathering her against him, his face buried in the crook of her neck. He could hear someone whispering sweet words to her and he realized it was him. He was telling her of his desire for her, since the moment they met. She was weeping with joy.

My wife. He whispered the words, thrusting deliberately with each syllable. *My wife*. He thrust hard again, feeling his climax come. *My wife*. He said it through gritted teeth, feeling Gray's body tighten in response, a volcanic climax throbbing through her slick walls. But she never uttered a sound; when he opened his eyes, her hands were in her mouth. She had bitten down so hard that she had left big red welts, evidence of the staggering sensations he had provoked within her.

His movements slowed to a stop, but his arms remained around her, holding her so tightly that he squeezed the air from her. But Gray didn't care; she was in a stupor, a haze of satisfaction such as she had never known. Braxton was all around her, his body still embedded within her. She never wanted to move from this state. She could hardly believe he belonged to her, and she to him. The hands came out of her mouth and wound around his neck, holding him as tightly as he was holding her. In this position, they fell into a deep, sated, dreamless sleep. It was a night to remember.

On the opposite side of the tent, Geoff lay there with his eyes wide open, staring at the ceiling and beads of sweat on his forehead. The night had been an evening for him to remember, too.

CHAPTER THIRTEEN

The morning broke heavy with mist. The fires from the previous night had burned into low, smoking embers that, by dawn, were being re-stoked by the soldiers.

Braxton left Gray sleeping soundly, having dressed with extreme quiet before quitting the tent. He emerged into the cold gray dawn to find Dallas standing near the larger of the fires. Smoke was heavy in the mist, clinging, as he approached his knight, now his son-in-law.

Dallas nodded as their eyes met. "My lord," he greeted. "How does your lady wife fare this morning?"

Braxton eyed Dallas, a smile lurking on his lips as he recounted the night's unbelievable passion. "Well enough," he said. "Though she was terribly worried about her daughter last night. I trust all went well?"

Dallas' demeanor moved from that of a professional soldier to one of a new bride groom. He lifted his eyebrows. "She stopped crying, if that's what you mean," he said. "I believe she slept well. She is still asleep."

Braxton nodded his head as if that was enough answer to his question. But it wasn't. "Everything... went well?"

Dallas knew what he meant. He looked at Braxton, a slightly confused expression on his features. "It seems rather strange now that you and I are related."

"Aye, it does. In private, you will call me Braxton, as befitting my daughter's husband. There is no need to be so formal."

Dallas seemed rather pleased at the prospect, though it was still a bit odd to him. "As you wish," he said. After a moment, he answered the original question. "I did not bed her if that's what you are asking. She would not have taken that well at all. That is something that will come with time."

Braxton drew in a deep breath. "You would be correct had you the luxury of time," he looked pointedly at him. "But you do not.

192

Suitors will be coming from now until Martinmas and you must consummate your marriage so there will never be any chance of an annulment or any other breach of contract. You married Brooke for a reason. Do I make myself clear?"

Dallas met his gaze, finally lifting his eyebrows in surrender. "You are right, of course," he said. "But last night... that was not the night to do it."

"It doesn't matter. For her sake, you must do as you must. She will understand when she grows older."

He nodded reluctantly. "As you say."

"Before we leave for Erith, Dallas."

"Aye."

Silence settled between them like the fog, heavy and pensive. They stood and watched a couple of soldiers tease the embers into a roaring blaze and put water wine on to boil. Other soldiers were breaking down the camp and loading the wagons. Graehm approached from a cluster of trees to tell them that the men searching for de Aughton had returned empty handed. They had searched as far as Redmayne, several miles to the south, but had been unable to track the man. The knowledge made Braxton uneasy.

"He could not have simply disappeared," he said. "He must be somewhere."

"If he is, he is well hidden," Graehm said. "We had some of our best trackers looking for him."

Braxton's blue-green eyes took on a distant look as his mind moved to the knight that had so boldly gone after Gray. "That may be, but they did not look in the right place."

"What are you suggesting?"

He was silent a moment, contemplating. "If it were me, and knowing that I would be tracked, I would not try to run unless I had a very fast horse. And de Aughton was horseless. Moreover, we have all of his possessions with us – the saddlebags on his charger were filled with his money, clothes, and other items. He literally has nothing with him but the clothes on his back. So perhaps he's not run. Perhaps rather than move away from us, he's moved closer. Would you not want to recover what was rightfully yours?"

Graehm wasn't following him, but Dallas was. "Do you think he's watching us even now?" he asked.

"Perhaps," Braxton shrugged. "Where is his horse and possessions?"

"The charger is tethered with the others and his possessions are with Graehm."

Braxton nodded faintly, his mind still working on the possible whereabouts of the vanished knight. "As far as I know, the men did not search the vicinity of this camp. They spread out and started looking once they reached Milnthorpe. If De Aughton is watching us even now, it would be a very clever posture. He knows we would be looking elsewhere for him, not in our midst."

Graehm looked stricken as it all suddenly made sense. "We should put an extra watch on his charger."

"And on his possessions."

Dallas suddenly broke away from them and marched for his tent. Braxton and Graehm watched him go. "Where are you going?" Braxton asked.

Dallas kept walking. He looked over his shoulder. "To rouse my wife and put her under my protection."

Braxton had to agree with him. He, too, moved back for the larger tent where Gray was still sleeping. She was the target, after all, and with this latest development he was uncomfortable leaving her alone, even just a few feet away from him. He pushed back the tent flap, his eyes focusing on his new wife.

She was fully dressed, rolling up their pallet. When the flap moved, she looked up and her gaze locked with Braxton's. His heart softened at the sight of her and he smiled broadly.

"Good morning, Lady de Nerra," he went to her, putting his arms around her when she stood up to greet him. "Did you sleep well?"

She kissed him in greeting. "Better than I ever have," she said softly, gazing into his eyes intently. "I do love sleeping in your arms."

"And I love having you in them."

She grinned and kissed him again. He responded with passion, with force, his mouth and tongue titillating hers. She pulled her lips away just to catch a breath, embracing him tightly.

"Oh, Braxton, how I do adore you," she murmured.

He pulled back to look at her. His expression suggested disbelief and elation. After a moment, he cupped her face in his hands, the blue-green eyes glimmering.

"I adored you the moment I saw you wandering the Falls of Erith," he told her as if she should have already known such a thing. "That adoration has turned into love and it grows stronger by the day."

She was speechless, breathless. "You love me?"

His brow furrowed, but there was a smile on his face. "My God, woman, how could you think anything else?"

"Because... because you have never told me until now."

He gently squeezed the face between his hands and kissed her on the end of her pert nose. "You are right. It is my most grievous mistake. I just thought you would know."

"Then tell me again."

His smile broadened. "I love you madly."

She threw her arms around his neck, squeezing tightly. "And I love you also."

It was a pivotal moment in a morning, and a night, that had been full of them. Braxton was so happy that he was nearly delirious, thoughts of Niclas de Aughton being pushed from his mind for the moment. With Gray finally his wife, how could there be a horrible thing in all the world? He spun her around, listening to her squeal. In spite of the warm moment, however, he did remember that he had come for a reason. He forced himself to focus whether or not he wanted to.

"I did come with a purpose," he took his arms off her, reluctantly. "We were unable to find de Aughton last night and I am uneasy with him on the loose. We need to return to Erith immediately."

She looked slightly fearful before nodding. "Of course, Braxton.

195

I was already packing up."

He looked over at Geoff. "And we need to return Geoff to a decent room and warm bed," he wandered over to his knight, realizing the man was awake and looking at him. Somewhat surprised, he knelt down beside him. "D'uberville, how long have you been awake?"

Geoff was moving and speaking slowly. "I am not entirely sure, my lord. Before you came into the tent, at least."

So Geoff heard everything. He felt a flash of embarrassment, an instinctive reaction to revealing his most personal thoughts in front of a subordinate. No matter, though. She was his wife and they all knew he was mad about her.

"How do you feel?" he asked.

Geoff gingerly moved his arms, twisted his spine a little. "Sore."

By this time, Gray was leaning over Braxton's shoulder. She smiled down at her charge. "At least you have had no fever," she said. "We are very grateful for that."

Geoff's green eyes focused on her, remembering the sounds of passion from her the night before and struggling not to let his thoughts show. "I owe everything to your skill, my lady."

Her smile broadened in thanks and she switched places with Braxton so that she could take a look at Geoff's bandage. Braxton left her alone with Geoff, going outside to find a couple of soldiers to start disassembling the tent. He ran right into Norman and Edgar, who had been out in the trees collecting more firewood.

He instructed the boys to stick with Lady de Nerra and help her however needed. Dropping the wood, the boys obediently went into the large tent to assist in the packing process. Braxton watched them disappear into the tent, his mind moving from his wife to de Aughton. He debated whether or not to personally make a sweep of the area; the more he thought on the knight's movements, the more convinced he became that the man was somehow near them. It made sense. Part of him wanted to make a search, but most of him wanted to remain with Gray for her protection. He could not take the chance of de Aughton circumventing him somehow.

And that's when he heard the scream.

Braxton bolted back into the tent in time to see de Aughton, as big as life, with his arms around Gray. Edgar had the man by the ankle while Norman rolled on his back several feet away; a bloodied face indicated a strike from de Aughton. Geoff, injured though he might be, was on his hands and knees, having rolled from his position on his back to his saddlebags several feet away. He had a sword in his hand but Braxton snatched it from him, all fury and fire and lightning-fast movements as he went after de Aughton. But the moment he brought the broadsword up for a strike that would clearly behead, de Aughton flicked a dirk against Gray's neck.

"Another step and she dies," Niclas growled. When fury and panic twitched through Braxton's poised body, de Aughton jabbed the tip of the dirk into her neck and she gasped. "Another step and I drive this through."

The broadsword in Braxton's hand clattered to the ground. He stood several feet away, his face trembling with the level of emotion surging through his vein and the blue-green eyes fixed on de Aughton's face. They were probing, furious, and finally pleading. After a moment, he sighed heavily.

"I had heard, by reputation, that you were an honorable knight," he said in low, even voice. "I can see that those words were untrue. No honorable man would do what you are doing."

Niclas had calmed a great deal since his initial burst of threats. He moved the dirk away from Gray's neck and she closed her eyes in relief, tears coursing down her cheeks. She was frightened but unharmed. Braxton didn't dare look at her for fear of losing control. And he had to stay in control; too many lives depended on it.

"These are brutal times, my lord," Niclas finally said. "One must often take what does not come easily."

"So you would take my wife?"

Niclas's dark brow furrowed slightly. "So she is your wife? That was not made clear to me."

Braxton nodded, looking at Gray's face for the first time. It was wet with tears and he felt his heart lurch. His gaze was fixed on her as if he could not tear it away and his heart was beginning to squeeze. "Give her back to me, de Aughton, and I shall let you go in peace. There is no harm done for the moment unless you consider scaring her half to death a crime."

Niclas lowered the dirk completely; it hung at his side but he still had Gray's neck in the crook of his elbow. One good squeeze and he could snap it. The obsidian eyes looked at the top of her blond head, a queer expression crossing his face.

"I have never been denied what I have wanted," he muttered. "A victory, a horse, a woman... I have always gotten what I wanted."

"Not this time. By the laws of England and God, she is my wife and belongs to me. And I want her back more than you want to take her."

More uncertainty crossed Niclas's features. After a small eternity, it was he who sighed heavily. "And she wants to stay with you, I would imagine, which is why she nearly put my eyes out."

"Exactly. Even if you were to take her, she would not be a content captive. She would escape you, or I would find her. Either way, we would be united again and you would either be dead or alone. Think about what you are doing, man. This is not the way to achieve your wants."

Niclas just stood there. The dirk in his hand came up again, half way to Gray's neck, as he toyed with the blade in a bizarrely thoughtful manner. By this time, Norman was up, his nose bloodied, standing by Braxton's side and Edgar was over with Geoff. The injured knight was in bad shape as the young lad helped him back onto his pallet. Niclas caught the movement, remembering the knight he had injured in a fair joust. An odd sense of guilt, of disorientation, washed over him and he lowered the dirk to his side again.

The tension in the tent was unbearable. Braxton kept waiting for Niclas to bring the dirk up again and somehow threaten his wife. But the knight suddenly dropped his arm from Gray's neck and she lurched forward, falling into Braxton's waiting arms. He held her tightly. Niclas watched the interaction, the genuine affection to it, and it tugged at him. He would have liked to have had that, too.

"I thought she was simply a woman who traveled with your army," Niclas's voice was low, laced with acceptance. "I did not know she was your wife, de Nerra. I swear it. I thought she was a camp whore."

Braxton's eyes flashed. "Are you blind as well as daft? Does she look like a whore?"

Niclas shook his head, the corners of his mouth twitching. "Nay, she does not, which is why I wanted her. But when I asked her if she was your wife, she did not answer me."

"Probably because she wasn't at the time. But she is now and I have the witnesses and document to prove it."

Niclas's obsidian eyes widened briefly. Then he broke down into snorts. "Are you saying that somewhere within the past day, you married this woman?"

"Had you taken her to a priest first, it would be another story."

Niclas shook his head with the irony of the situation. Then he looked at Braxton. "Fair enough, de Nerra. You won the prize." He looked at Gray. "My lady, I am sorry to have harassed you. I saw you as something to be plucked for the taking, but I was wrong."

Gray was still very frightened and very upset. Jerking herself from Braxton's arms, she marched up to de Aughton, who was a good deal taller than she was, and swung at him with a balled fist. She caught him right in the nose. It was a surprising action for a normally very docile lady.

"That is for scaring the wits from me, you big dolt," she squared off against him. "And the next time you fancy a lady, you would do far better to behave like a gentleman than a mindless beast."

Niclas stood there with his hand on his nose; there was a smear of blood on his fingers. "You are correct, of course. And may I say that you pack a mighty wallop, Lady de Nerra."

She thrust her chin up at him. "Get out. Get out before I gouge your eyes again. And this time I will not miss my mark."

Braxton, fighting off a grin, put his hands on her shoulders and pulled her back from the enormous knight. He did not want her provoking de Aughton, although the man deserved worse than what he got. He passed her off to Norman, who put himself between the lady and the offending knight. Sweet, young Norman on the brink of manhood was fully prepared to protect the lady with his life.

"I will give you back your charger and your possessions and you may be on your way," he said with more benevolence than he felt. "But I do not want to see you again, de Aughton. Not ever."

Niclas nodded briefly. "That may be difficult, my lord, should you ever return to your father's castle."

Braxton's expression didn't change, but Gray looked confused. "His father's castle?" she blurted. "Why do you say that?"

Niclas fixed on her, the obsidian eyes twinkling with misplaced mirth. "Because your husband's father is Baron Gilderdale. I serve Gilderdale."

Gray's eyes widened. She looked to Braxton for confirmation but Braxton was fixed on Niclas. "You are my father's knight?" he asked steadily.

"I have served him for four years, my lord."

Braxton's lips pressed into an ironic line. Lowering his gaze, he shook his head and began to wander around, looking for a place to sit. He settled on a three legged stool next to Geoff. His expression was infused with disbelief, sarcasm, and some disappointment. Gray watched him closely, not wanting to speak for she was not sure what to say. It was clear that he did not seem pleased.

"And how is my father?" Braxton asked, almost wearily.

"Well enough, my lord," Niclas replied. "As is your brother, Sir Robert, although he has a disease of the joints that has shortened his days as a knight. He is in pain a good deal of the time and can no longer ride his charger because his fingers are so gnarled that he cannot handle the reins."

Braxton thought on the oldest brother he'd not seen in ten years. "I miss my brother," he finally muttered. His gaze fixed intently on Niclas. "What are you doing so far away from Black Fell? And why did you not compete in the name of Gilderdale?"

Niclas's dark eyebrows lifted. "Your father sent me on a mission to Manchester. Once delivering the missive and goods to the earl, my time was my own for a short while. Gilderdale is a land of peace these days and I was taking the long route home. It has been a long time since I have done any traveling. So I passed through Milnthorpe, saw there was a tournament, and added my name. It was safer not to compete as Gilderdale; when I do that, everyone immediately has double the reason to try and unseat me."

Braxton nodded in understanding, but Gray did not understand at all. She entered the conversation as much as she dared. "I do not understand," she said timidly. "Who is Gilderdale? Why does that increase your chances of an opponent attempting to unseat you?"

Braxton reached over and took her hand, toying gently with her fingers. "Have you never heard of Gilderdale?"

"Nay. Should I?"

Braxton smiled wryly. "If you are a knight, aye. But since you are not, I will enlighten you. Gilderdale is in Northumberland, near the borders. You could say that we are Northumberland's war machine. The Earl of Northumberland calls upon my father to quell uprisings, settle disputes, curb unruly Scots. Anything that involves quick, violent action, Gilderdale answers the call. Gilderdale is Northumberland's avenging angel."

Gray mulled over that bit of information. She was not surprised that Braxton came from a warring family; it would explain why he had chosen the life he had. He knew of no other way. "I see," she said. "Gilderdale is great, then?"

"The greatest, Lady de Nerra," Niclas replied before Braxton could. Even in defeat for the lady's affections, he was still competing for her attention, unconscious as it may be. "Sir Thomas de Nerra is the fourth earl in a long line of great warring noblemen. Each of his four sons has also chosen the warring way and, as rumor would have it, the power and skill has increased with each successive son."

Gray's amber eyes were fixed on the big black knight. "What does that mean?"

"It means that your husband, as the youngest son, is the greatest of the line."

She looked at Braxton, a glimmer in her eyes. "I would agree with that."

Braxton smiled modestly. "You must agree, as my wife. But know that my other brothers are quite formidable. I am not sure that Niclas's assessment is fair."

"You are too humble, my lord," Niclas broke into their conversation. "I saw you in the joust yesterday. Your talent is astounding."

Braxton didn't reply; he was not about to thank a lesser knight for a compliment, especially in light of the evening's events. Better the man realize that he was indeed superior so he would not try anything so foolish again.

To their left, Geoff suddenly let out a groan when he shifted on his pallet and inadvertently caused himself some agony. Conversation and fright forgotten, Gray immediately went to the knight, remembering his rough handling during the course of the earlier crisis. She knelt beside him, full of concern, to check the bandages on his neck.

"Geoff," she murmured. "I am so sorry I forgot about you. How brave you were to try and protect me."

Geoff was deathly pale; it was evident he was struggling, a miracle he had stayed silent this long. "As any man would have done, my lady," he said faintly. "But I fear I may have re-injured something. My left arm is numb."

Gray knew that could not be a good sign. She felt horribly guilty that her first thoughts had not been of him when Niclas had released her, for she had clearly seen Geoff's valiant attempt to aid her. She checked wound; the stitches had held, but there was some additional bleeding with his movement. Nothing looked terribly out of order. As Braxton, and even Niclas, stood in various positions behind her, she re-secured the bandages and looked up at her husband.

"He cannot be moved for quite some time," she said firmly. "Tonight's events may have caused more damage to him. I will not risk him in a wagon, on an open road, even to take him to safety. He must stay still and rest."

Braxton's face was grim. "How long?"

"A few days, at least."

He didn't hesitate. "As you say. What more do you need in order to help him?"

She sighed, looking back at the ashen young knight. After a moment, she rose to her feet and faced Braxton so that Geoff could not overhear her.

"I fear his condition is beyond my skills," she said softly. "I would feel more comfortable if a reputable surgeon examined him. He very well may have re-injured himself attempting to defend me."

Niclas heard her. "I will ride to Grange-over-Sands," he said, already moving for the door. "It is a large town. Surely there will be a surgeon of reputation to examine him. I will bring him back as soon as I am able."

Both Braxton and Gray looked at him, varied degrees of surprise in their expressions.

"This is not your trouble," Braxton told him. "I believe you were going to leave, anyway."

Gray put her hand on Braxton in preparation for defending Niclas's actions, but the knight beat her to it.

"This entire folly with d'Uberville is my fault," he said. "As an honorable man, I would right my wrong. I know that you do not believe me to be the honorable type, my lord, but I would consider it a privilege to prove you wrong."

Under normal circumstances, Braxton would have rejected the request. But Niclas was trying to make amends and Gray's hand on his arm told him that he should allow such an attempt. If the man left and never returned, it was of little consequence other than Geoff would have to wait longer to be examined by a surgeon. But if the man did as he said he would, then it was a statement of his word. It would aid in restitution for his earlier behavior. As Braxton was preparing to reply, the tent flap moved and Dallas entered the tent.

The knight was in full battle armor, broadsword in hand and smaller weapons slung and secured about his body. His visor was up, his pale blue eyes scrutinizing the tent and its occupants. At the sight of de Aughton, he was inclined to raise his sword and go on the offensive, but he could see that no one in the tent seemed particularly upset. Puzzled, he nonetheless remained in a defensive posture.

"Is everything well, my lord?" he asked in an authoritative voice that Gray had never heard from him before. "I was told there were sounds of trouble here."

Braxton's eyes were on Niclas. "No trouble," he said. "De Aughton was just leaving."

Dallas moved away from the tent flap, his armored body between Geoff, Gray and Braxton. He watched de Aughton with the expression of one sighting prey. "Then leave, de Aughton," he said to the big black knight.

Niclas put up his hands to show he was no threat. "I shall, as soon as my horse and possessions are returned to me," he said, glancing at Braxton. "I can hardly walk to Grange-on-Sands, my lord."

Braxton nodded at Dallas, who had focused on him for an affirmation. "Give him back his property," he said. "He is riding for a surgeon for Geoff."

Dallas instantly dropped his sword and quit the tent. They could hear him shouting orders outside, rousing the men and having Niclas's property brought forth. Listening to the shouts outside, Niclas's gaze lingered on Braxton a moment. It seemed that he wanted to say something more but ultimately held his tongue.

"I shall take my leave, my lord," he dipped his head. Then his gaze moved to Gray. "My lady, I shall return as soon as I can."

With that, the big black knight left the tent. Braxton and Gray stood there a moment as if still trying to absorb the events of the morning. After a small eternity of digesting their shock, they finally turned to each other. Blue-green fixed on amber and Braxton stroked his wife's cheek. She smiled weakly in return.

"Are you really all right?" he asked softly.

She nodded, winding her arms around him just to draw strength from his embrace. "I am fine, truly," she sighed as his arms tightened around her. "But it was rather frightening."

"No doubt," he murmured. "Will you be all right if I leave you a moment?"

"Of course. I am not a weakling."

He laughed softly. "God's Bones, you are most certainly not. I must speak with Dallas a moment."

Dallas was standing outside, several feet away, with Brooke standing beside him. They were both watching something in the distance. As Braxton marched up on them, he noticed that they were watching Graehm issue de Aughton his possessions and horse. Brooke, her fair young face anxious, fixed on Braxton.

"Is my mother all right?" she demanded. "What happened?"

Braxton held up a hand. "She is well enough."

"But what happened?"

"Sir Niclas paid us a visit, Lady Aston. Now he is riding for a surgeon for Sir Geoff."

Brooke's pretty face darkened with confusion, with concern. "But... but a soldier told us he heard suspicious sounds coming from your tent and then Dallas dressed in his armor and ran over there with his sword and... are you sure my mother is all right?"

"Go and see for yourself."

She did, without hesitation. As she bolted into the distant tent that contained her mother, Braxton turned to Dallas.

"What took you so long to come?" he asked quietly. "Gray was in peril for several moments until I diffused the situation. Where were you?"

Dallas shook his head. "In my tent, with Brooke. We are far enough away that I did not hear anything until a soldier came to me and said he had heard strange sounds coming from your tent. I wasn't sure the strange sounds he heard were indicative of trouble, if you understand my meaning, so I took my time to investigate. But when I approached your tent and heard a strange voice, I suspected the worst and made haste to retrieve my armor and weapon."

Braxton nodded, satisfied. "As I would have more than likely followed the same path of logic."

"Your wife is uninjured?"

"Just frightened. And speaking of wives, have you carried out your obligation yet?"

Dallas wriggled his eyebrows. "I was preparing to broach the subject when I was interrupted by the soldier."

"Then resume your plans. I will keep her mother away from your tent for the time being."

Dallas sighed heavily. "Nothing like the screams of a child to incite the mother."

"Exactly."

They broke from their stance and walked back to the larger tent. As they were preparing to enter, Norman and Edgar exited, moving quickly out of the way. Braxton grabbed Norman by the arm, forcing the lad to stop so he could take a good look at his face. Dallas peered at the swollen nose over Braxton's shoulder.

"You took a good hit," Braxton said to the young man. "Is it broken?"

Norman's eyes were already becoming dark-ringed as his nose swelled. "Lady de Nerra already looked at it and says she does not believe so."

Dallas lifted his eyebrows, looking at Braxton. "Young Norman went on the offensive against de Aughton?"

"Indeed."

"Most impressive."

Dallas slapped the boy lightly on the head and continued past him, into the tent. Braxton lingered with the boy a moment longer, inspecting his face as if suddenly seeing something more mature in the youth. The lad was sixteen or seventeen years, after all. He was becoming a man. He let go of his arm with a satisfied nod.

"Most impressive indeed," he said. "Norman, you and I will speak later on your training. Perhaps it is time you moved past the duties of a squire. Perhaps it is time for you to learn to serve as a warrior."

Norman watched Braxton disappear into the tent. There was a somewhat dazed expression on his face. A few feet away, Edgar was struggling to light a cooking fire, scowling at his brother. He thought he had been rather brave, too, although he hadn't gotten bloodied for his efforts.

"Maybe next time I'll get an arm cut off," Edgar sniffed. "Then Sir Braxton will appreciate my valor, too."

Norman pursed his lips at his brother; leave it to Edgar to ruin a proud moment. "Don't be such an idiot," he said.

Edgar just made a face at him as he continued to try and light the stubborn fire. Norman watched for a minute or so before shoving his brother aside, adjusting the kindling, and lighting the blaze on the first try. Edgar's spirits sank lower.

"Show off!" he yelled.

CHAPTER FOURTEEN

Both Gray and Brooke were bent over Geoff when their husbands arrived. Geoff was starting to cough up blood, never a good sign, and Gray was struggling to figure out where the bleeding was coming from. Braxton and Dallas watched with mounting concern as Geoff continued to spit up bright red blood. Braxton finally knelt beside his wife, his gaze fixed on his knight.

"De Aughton should be back before noon, Geoff," he said quietly. "Lady de Nerra will do all she can until then. You must hold on."

Geoff was conscious and miserable. He nodded his head, his eyes closed. "I would not want to despoil her efforts, my lord."

Gray passed a sidelong glance at Braxton, letting him know that she was very concerned for the young knight. Brooke was mostly hovering aimlessly, not knowing what to do but wanting to help her mother just the same. When Geoff coughed up more blood and splattered it on her arm, she nearly had heart failure. Having never been exposed to battle or blood on a serious level, she was unused to the reality of gore.

But she made a brave attempt to wipe it off of Geoff's mouth, mostly smearing red streaks down his chin. Then she wiped furiously at the blood on her arm, feeling nauseous at the sight. Above her concern for the knight, Gray noticed her daughter's pale pallor.

"Dallas," she said softly. "Would you mind taking Brooke to finish packing? Braxton would like to be on the road to Erith before noon and I am sure my daughter has yet to make preparation."

It was just an excuse to remove Brooke from the tent but Dallas took it. He was deeply concerned for his friend's health but reckoned there was nothing he could do about it. Moreover, he still had a directive from Braxton that he had yet to fulfill. If ever there was a time to complete his objective and make Brooke his wife in every sense of the word, the time was now while everyone was distracted. He grasped his young wife by the arm and gently escorted her from the tent.

The day was beginning to warm outside. The grass was cool, the trees green, and nary a cloud in the sky now that the morning mist had burned away. Dallas silently led Brooke over to their tent, holding back the flap as she went inside. He followed her and secured the ties that held closed the flap.

Reluctantly, he eyed her as she went straight for the pile of clothes on the ground that she had created when she had to dig through her satchel for something on the bottom. She began to wad up her meager possessions and shove them back inside. He moved up behind her.

"We shall make a shopping trip into town in the next few days to acquire more material for you," he said quietly.

She looked up at him. "What for?"

"For clothing. I would like my wife to be well dressed."

She looked down at what she was wearing; it was a surcoat made from a wool tartan fabric that Braxton had brought them. She had three new surcoats; she'd never had three new of anything in her entire life.

"But I already have this," she told Dallas. "Do I need more clothing?"

The corners of his mouth twitched with a smile as he crouched beside her. "Wouldn't you like some?"

She was gazing at him quite openly, her innocence obvious. "I do not know. I already have some new dresses that my mother made me. I am not sure I need more. She told me I was being selfish and petty, after all. If I have more new clothing, she will think I badgered you into it."

He did laugh, then. "She will know the truth when I tell her I insisted. " His smile faded as he gazed into her big blue eyes. "As I said, I should like my lovely wife to be well dressed. It is a direct reflection on my ability to provide for you as a husband."

She flushed around the ears at his compliment. Then she shrugged weakly. "If you think it is the right thing to do."

"I do."

She didn't have anything more to say to that. Cheeks still warm, she returned to her packing as Dallas stood up and began removing pieces of armor. She could hear him setting the pieces down carefully. But she was focused on shoving the last of her possessions into her satchel and he startled her when he suddenly sat heavily on the bedroll next to her.

"Brooke?"

She looked at him, her fingers pausing as she tied up her bag. "Aye?"

For the first time since she had known him, Dallas looked uncomfortable. He sighed heavily, reaching out to take one of the hands that were lingering on the bag. He stared at her hand a moment and Brooke's heart thumped loudly against her ribs at the warmth of his touch. Since last night, the sight or sound of him made her heart do strange things. His touch only increased the effect.

"I have debated how to deal with this situation and I have considered keeping it from you and simply doing as I see best," he began. "But I feel strongly that if this marriage is to have any chance of surviving, we must be honest with one another. Do you agree?"

Brooke gazed at him. "I... I suppose so."

"Good," he said, wondering if he should, indeed, be open with her. She was so very young. "You are aware that you and I were married for a reason, correct?"

She nodded slowly. "Aye."

"And that reason was to not only provide you with a suitable husband, but to prevent your grandmother from awarding you to the highest bidder. Are you with me so far?"

She nodded again, curiously, and he continued. "Even though we are married, this union will not be truly binding until we consummate it. I should have done it last night but I felt strongly that it was not the right time. However, with our party returning to Castle Erith, I cannot delay. We already know that de Clare is at Erith at your grandmother's invitation. We must make sure that our marriage is secure."

By this time, she was looking at him fearfully. "Then we... we must...."

He nodded faintly, looking into her wide blue eyes. "Aye, we must. And I swear to you that I will be as gentle as possible. But it must be done."

Brooke blinked, averting her gaze as she thought about what was to come. She was naturally frightened, but she was also naturally curious. Last night, she had slept next to Dallas and had felt such comfort and security as she had never known. She was coming to feel comfortable with him as much as their short marriage would allow, but he was still a stranger. Hesitantly, she met his gaze again.

"My mother has explained to me the way of men and women," she said quietly. "And I have seen animals couple. We had a dog once that had a litter of puppies twice a year. Every time I saw her, she was being mounted by another dog. But as for people coupling...."

He smiled at her innocence; he couldn't help it. "It is different than dogs."

She saw his grin and thought he was laughing at her. "I know that," she snapped softly, immediately cooling when she realized that he was not mocking her. Dallas didn't seem the type. "But... but I have never even had a suitor and the first time a man kissed me was last night when you did. I do not know what to do. What if I do the wrong thing? You will be sorry that you married me."

His smile grew; fortunately, he had not taken offense to her snappish reply. "I would never be sorry, Brooke. And you cannot possibly do the wrong thing. Just listen to what I tell you and I promise you will gain some enjoyment from it."

She regarded him carefully. "You have done this before."

He cleared his throat and averted his gaze a moment, shifting his seat. "I have."

"With whom?"

He lifted an eyebrow at her. "It does not matter. Suffice it to say that I believe I can navigate my way through this."

She cocked her head. "But why is it expected that I am a virgin and acceptable that you are not?"

His gaze was steady on her. "Because one of us must know something or both of us will be making fools of ourselves. Therefore, in preparation of this moment, I have had to learn so that I can teach you."

She cast him a long glance, suggesting that she thought his answer was ridiculous. Then she actually laughed. "You are good at thinking of answers that make sense. But I know it is a preposterous answer you give me."

"Why?"

"Because it is," she insisted. "I want to know why I must remain pure, yet you did not have the courtesy to remain pure for me. Well?"

She was a spitfire, spoiled and selfish, but she was also intelligent and quite pretty. He reached out and grasped her face gently with one hand.

"If it is any consolation to you, no one has marked my heart," he said quietly, watching her fire cool. "That, my lady, I have indeed saved for my wife. For you."

Her fire banked completely and she took on the wide-eyed innocent look again. "How do you know?"

"How do I know what?"

"That you will give me your heart?"

He wriggled his eyebrows and dropped his hand. But he was smiling. "I do not, for certain. But I can hope."

Brooke simply nodded. There wasn't much more to say on the subject. Now the reality of what they must do began to weigh heavily on her and her cheeks began to grow warm again. She kept her head down, looking at her bag. Without another word, Dallas reached over and put a hand on her neck, pulling her to him. He very gently kissed her cheek.

"Trust me, Brooke," he murmured against her flesh. "I promise I will be gentle."

She had no choice but to comply, her eyes closing as he kissed her cheek again. His mouth moved across her face, to her chin, before finally claiming her lips.

It was as he had remembered it the night before; she was sweet and warm and soft. Although he was performing a duty, it quickly became a genuine want. He knew he must go slowly with her, but he found that the feel and smell of her ignited a flame deep within him. Before he realized it, both arms were around her slender body and he was pulling her onto the pallet beside him.

Brooke's heart was thumping so loudly that she was positive he could hear it. His mouth was warm and gentle, his touch strong and tender. Having never experienced an embrace of any kind, the newness was disorienting. But the disorientation quickly evaporated in favor of giddy warmth that bloomed deep in her belly. When his mouth clamped down over hers, the warmth grew in size and breadth and spread through her torso. Hesitantly, her arms went around his neck. It was all the encouragement Dallas needed to pull her fiercely against him.

Brooke was lost in a haze of passion and curiosity. She was aware when he laid her back on the pallet, aware when his tongue licked at her lips. Not knowing how to respond, she opened her mouth to ask him for instructions and his tongue snaked inside her pink orafice. Momentarily shocked, she very quickly realized she liked it. His kiss was bold, intimate, heated. Aye, she liked it very much.

Dallas unwound one of his arms. His hand drifted over her belly, touching her arm, shoulder, her hair. Then it moved down her chest, finally coming to rest on a pert breast. He gently squeezed and she yelped.

"What are you doing?" she demanded breathlessly.

He was fairly breathless himself. "Touching you."

Her eyes were wide on him. "But... you are putting your hand on my...."

He squeezed her gently again, watching her mouth pop open in outrage and, possibly, some semblance of pleasure. He laughed softly and caressed her breast again.

"I am your husband," he whispered. "I may touch you

213

anywhere I please. Does this disturb you?"

She wasn't sure. "But... but what if I don't want you to?"

"Then I will stop. Do you want me to stop?"

Her cheeks flushed and she tried to avert her gaze, but he was so close that she could not reasonably look away from him. "I... I suppose not."

He squeezed her again, feeling a hard nipple against his palm. His mouth descended on her once again as he spoke. "Good."

Brooke lay there with her eyes open, responding to his bold kiss and evaluating the feel of his hand against her breast. It was shocking and new, but the more he caressed and teased, the more she liked it. Her young body began to twitch with pleasure and she was not even aware. But Dallas was acutely aware; he'd never been more aware of anything in his life.

He abruptly sat up, pulling her with him. His arms were around her, untying the stays on her back.   Brooke didn't protest but she didn't help either; she wasn't entirely sure what to do. When he pulled the surcoat over her head, she sat dumbly as he had her lift her arms and yanked the shift off as well. Clad only in her pantalets, she crossed her arms over her bare chest as Dallas quickly removed his tunic.

He turned back around to see her trying to cover herself with great embarrassment. In fact, she was trying not to cry. He put his arms around her and lay back down on the pallet, covering up her nakedness with his big body.

"You are so beautiful," he murmured, his lips against her temple. "You do not need to be embarrassed."

She sniffled, trying hard to stifle the tears. "I am not," she lied.

He smiled, kissing her again. Very gently, he unwound her arms from her breasts. She was small-breasted, but they were pert and perfect. His big hand covered one completely and then some, but it did not take away from his pleasure. In fact, he was wildly aroused by them.

Brooke felt his hot hand close over her breast and she shuddered, her embarrassment quickly fading as he gently touched her. He was very careful with her and his patience helped immensely. He continued to knead and caress, his lips against her forehead, allowing her to become accustomed to his touch. Brooke concentrated on the encounter, gradually relaxing enough so that he was able to shift his body. When he put his heated mouth on her hard nipple, she gasped again.

"What are you doing?"

His reply was to suck harder and she gasped and groaned, twitching beneath him. His mouth on her body was causing lightning to course through her limbs, heat that she could not control. Though she was young and innocent, her body was all woman. Hormones and desires raged. As Brooke lay panting beneath Dallas, he deftly removed her pantalets and settled himself between her legs.

She lifted her head to watch him as he lay between her legs. His mouth was still on her breast, his hands around her waist. Brooke's heart was pumping so hard that she felt faint. She lay her head back down, staring at the tent ceiling and experiencing every new sensation that Dallas brought upon her. She liked his mouth on her and she liked his big hands on her slender body. She liked everything about this so far. But when he lowered his breeches and put his manhood against her virginal lips, she grew worried all over again.

He was back in her face, his big body lying on top of her. He wasn't heavy, but the intimacy was overwhelming. She began to tear up again and he kissed her eyes tenderly.

"No tears, sweetheart," he said softly. "Relax and accept me. It will make things easier."

"But I am afraid."

"I know," he kissed her again. "But you must trust me. I would never intentionally hurt you."

She began to sob softly and he kissed her strongly at the same time he thrust into her. She yelped at the first thrust, gasping slightly at the second. By the third and final thrust, her tears had faded and she simply groaned. She could hear Dallas breathing heavily, his lips on her cheek. When he withdrew completely, she felt a distinct sense of relief. But he was suddenly thrusting into

215

her again and she sucked in her breath sharply as he began to move deep within her.

There was no real pain, only a sense of fullness. Within the first several thrusts, she forgot her fear and embarrassment completely. Whatever he was doing sent wild sensations throughout her body, sensations that caused her to writhe and spasm. She was vaguely aware of her arms around his neck, holding on to him as he beat a sensual rhythm against her hips. Somewhere in the movement, she began to move with him. It felt better when she did. Some exquisite sensation was blossoming in her loins and she liked the sparks she felt when she ground her pelvis against his. When she figured out that the more she rubbed against him, the more sparks flew, she began to grind her hips madly against his body.

Dallas had one arm round her, one hand on her left breast. Brooke was concentrating on making sparks fly as she rubbed herself against him in rhythm to his thrusting. Suddenly, her entire body tightened and a burst sensation rippled through her loins. It was the most amazing thing she had ever experienced. As she gasped with her first climax, Dallas released himself deep within her beckoning body. Brooke felt him shudder. But he continued to move, continued to touch her, not wanting the experience to end. Truth be told, Brooke didn't want it to end, either.

What had started out as a totally fearful concept had become the most miraculous experience of her young life. Brooke laid there, her arms around her husband, staring up at the ceiling and struggling to absorb what had just happened. She could not seem to wrap her mind around it. All she knew was that it was nothing as she had feared.

"Are you well?" Dallas' soft question filled the air.

Her gaze moved to his handsome face as he loomed over her. *He has such nice eyes,* she thought. "Aye," she replied.

"I did not hurt you?"

She shook her head. "Nay."

"Good."

He gazed at her, his eyes drifting over the delicate shape of her eyes and the way her blond hair brushed across her face. He would have liked to have lain with her all day but he knew that time was growing short. They had accomplished their task, which had turned out to be far less of a task and far more of a pleasure. He pushed a stray lock of hair from her eyes.

"We should get dressed and finish packing."

He started to move but she tightened her arms and legs about him; he was still embedded in her. "Do we have to?"

He looked at her, surprised. Then he burst out in soft laughter. "You would rather stay here?"

Her cheeks flushed scarlet and she unwound her arms, her legs. He could see that he had offended her and his grip on her tightened as she tried to squirm away from him.

"Lady Aston," he murmured against her flushed, angry cheek. "I would give all that I have to remain here with you for the day. But I fear your step father and mother will become impatience awaiting us."

She eyed him, somewhat appeased. "You will stop laughing at me every time I ask a question."

He shook his head, his lips nuzzling her jaw line. "It was laughter of pleasure, I assure you. I am pleased that you thought so much of our experience that you would not want to end it."

Her anger fled in lieu of shy eagerness. "Can we do it again sometime? I mean, if you wish it?"

His eyebrows drew together in feigned outrage. "Good lord, lass, I will wish it every day for the rest of my life. Sometimes more than once a day. Was it that good for you?"

She nodded once, too embarrassed to elaborate. He laughed softly again and kissed her on the cheek. "Very well, Lady Aston. We will do it as much as you wish, whenever you wish. I will not protest in the least."

She refused to look at him, making a face when his laughter grew stronger. Withdrawing himself from her tight little body, he made sure to kiss her face, both breasts, her belly, and the inside of her right thigh as he pushed himself off of her. There was a slight amount of blood on her skin but certainly nothing shattering. He didn't mention it to Brooke, however; he simply collected her pantalets and shift for her. She took them in silence, pulling her clothing on swiftly while he pulled on his own clothing. By the time she had her shift and shoes on, he had on most of his mail. The entire time, they had dressed in silence. When their eyes finally met, they smiled at each other warmly. Brooke flushed to the roots of her hair.

"Do you need any help to finish packing up?" he asked.

She shook her head. He collected his armor from where he had set it down, took her chin in one hand, and kissed her on the cheek.

"I shall be outside if you need me," he said quietly. "I will send Norman and Edgar to finish packing my things."

"I can do it for you," she said eagerly. "I mean, shouldn't I? As your wife?"

He smiled faintly. "Of course you should. How stupid of me."

She returned his smile, looking rather pleased, and he winked at her as he quit the tent.

Brooke stood there for several long moments after he had gone, reflecting on the past several minutes. Warmth filled her, making her limbs soft and mushy. She truly didn't know if she could even walk, but walk she did. She had to. She had to pack her husband's things so that they could return to Erith.

Her husband. Every time she thought of Dallas, she couldn't help the smile that spread across her face.

True to his word, d'Aughton returned by mid-day with a surgeon from Grange-on-Sands. The physic was a fairly young man, driving an old cart pulled by an old donkey. Even though in years, the man was not over thirty, he walked, acted and looked like someone much older. In his dirty gray robes and mussy brown hair, he pulled his donkey to a halt and looked curiously around the camp.

Graehm and Dallas helped the physic secure his beast and collect his bags while Niclas remained standing next to his charger. Although he had fulfilled his promise, he wasn't sure if he was welcome.

"How is d'Uberville?" he asked Dallas.

Dallas handed the bag he had collected to Graehm and instructed the man to take the physic to Geoff immediately. He waited until the two men were out of earshot before turning to the big black knight.

"Worse," he said evenly. "His attempt to defend the lady from your abduction attempt worsened his injuries. He's been coughing up blood all morning."

Niclas didn't show the guilt he was feeling. He remained quite unemotional. "I am sorry for that, then. But this physician comes highly recommended. He should be able to help."

Dallas didn't reply; his gaze lingered on the man a moment before turning back to camp. Niclas watched him walk away, knowing there was no longer any reason for him to be here. He had completed his task.

Consigning d'Uberville to his fate, he turned his steed for home.

***

On the road for the past hour, the mercenary army traveling back to Erith was moving slowly for Geoff's sake; the physic that de Aughton had brought from Sands-on-Grange had recommended a very slow pace and Braxton took the man at his word. Gray sat on the wagon bed beside Geoff, monitoring his condition; the knight had responded to the surgeon's treatment enough so that he was somewhat stable and it had been decided to move him back to Erith for a measure of permanent shelter and protection.

Gray sat beside the knight diligently, watching every move and listening carefully to every sound. She was sorry they hadn't brought the physic with them, fearful that she wouldn't be skilled enough to aid Geoff is something went horribly wrong. Oddly, Braxton didn't travel with a surgeon and most of his men were surgeons unto themselves; they could all stitch wounds and repair broken bones to a certain degree, including Braxton himself. So Gray was, essentially, on her own.

Braxton rode beside the wagon, just a few feet from her. He was in full armor, his visor lowered, but every so often his helmed head would turn to her and she would catch his movement, turning to smile at him. She could not see his face beneath the visor but knew he was smiling back. It made her warm and giddy inside, but truth be told, it all still seemed like a dream. In a few short days she had met and married a man whom was very quickly becoming everything to her and at her age, she never imagined she would be so fortunate. But fortunate she was and she was deeply thankful.

Another figure capturing her attention had been her daughter. The young woman rode on the rear of the wagon bed along with Edgar but there had, remarkably, been no harsh words between them. In fact, Brooke seemed very distracted when she realized that it was more than likely because Dallas was riding a few feet behind her. He, too, was in full armor with his shield slung and his visor lowered. Gray couldn't see his face. Having not talked to her daughter since last night, she had no idea what had transpired between the newlyweds. Focusing on Braxton, she motioned him near her.

"Braxton, look at Brooke," Gray said softly. "Does she look upset to you?"

Braxton's helmed head turned in the young lady's direction. "I cannot see her face. Why? Is she upset?"

Gray shrugged. "I do not know," she said quietly. "She has barely said a word to me all morning. Have you spoken with Dallas?"

"Not since this morning."

"Do you suppose things are not well between them?"

"If things are not, you must let them work it out."

She sighed, turning to face forward. "I was not attempting to interfere. But Brooke is my daughter and...."

"And Dallas is her husband," Braxton cut her off. He flipped up his visor and looked at her, although not unkind. "You have your own husband to worry over, my lady. That is where your focus should be."

She fought off a grin. "Is that so? And when has my focus not been completely and utterly upon you, my lord?"

He smiled at her. "Never. You are my devoted angel."

She smiled shyly, a gesture that enchanted him. Then her smile faded as her amber gaze fell on the road ahead. "What do you intend to do if de Clare is still at Erith?"

His own smile faded and he too turned his attention forward. "Offer them the hospitality of Erith, of course," he said evenly. "But it is now Dallas' keep; that is his decision."

She gazed at him, his strong profile through the limited view of the visor. "Braxton, I am afraid."

"Of what?"

"Of these Houses that my mother has invited to vie for Brooke's hand. What if they become enraged because she has already married? Erith cannot withstand a siege. There is nothing to hold back the enemy."

He looked at her, then. "You forget that you have the army of Braxton de Nerra within your walls. Only a fool would knowingly attack me."

"But you have less than two hundred men. De Clare, and others, have hundreds."

"One of my men is worth ten of someone else's. Do you have so little faith in me?"

"Of course not," she said softly, putting a hand on his armored arm. "I did not mean to insult you. I know your reputation is great."

He grunted. "Great indeed. If anyone should be afraid, it should be de Clare." With that, he turned his head and emitted a shrill whistle from between his teeth. Dallas spurred his charger forward, kicking up rocks and dirt as he did so. One rock flipped up and hit Brooke on the face, just below her left eye. She screamed and threw her hand over her cheek.

The sound brought everyone running. Gray was already climbing from the wagon bench back into the bed in an attempt to reach her daughter. Dallas, having reined his horse around at the sound of his wife's cry, was joined by Braxton. Everyone was racing to her side. Brooke sat on the open wagon bed and wept.

Gray was the first to reach her. "Let me see, sweetheart."

She peeled her daughter's hand away from her face to find a bloody cut underneath. Brooke continued to weep as Gray looked around for something to wipe the blood away with, taking an offered strip of boiled cloth from the wagon driver as he yanked it from one of the bags at his feet.

"There now, love," she smiled as she put the cloth over the cut to stop the bleeding. "It's not bad. What happened?"

Brooke's luminous blue eyes were shedding rivers of tears. "The horse kicked up a rock."

"What horse?"

"Dallas'."

Dallas was off his charger, walking beside Brooke as the wagon plodded along. He flipped up his visor, gazing at Brooke's face with great concern. Holding the reins in one hand, he put the other on her knee.

"I am so sorry, Brooke," he said softly. "It was an accident."

Gray watched the young knight interact with her daughter, surprised at the emotion in his voice. She had not expected it. She was even more surprised when Brooke stopped crying immediately and smiled at him. It was just like magic.

"I am all right," she assured him in a tone her mother had never heard her use before. "I know you did not mean it. I... I think I was startled more than anything. It will heal."

Dallas smiled back at her, patting her knee before looking to Gray. "Is it bad?"

Gray was still lingering on the exchange between her daughter and Dallas. It took her a moment to realize he had asked her a question.

"Nay," she forced herself to shift her focus back to the cut. "It doesn't look like she'll need stitches. She will mend."

"Good. I do not want anything to mar that lovely face." Dallas looked back to his wife and gave her a bold wink. Brooke smiled broadly. Gray was astonished at them both.

"Dallas," Braxton was still astride his charger, plodding alongside the wagon. "A word, please."

Dallas tore his gaze from Brooke and swiftly mounted. Together, they spurred their chargers to the head of the column so that their conversation would not be overheard. Gray cast a glance at her husband as he cantered off before returning her attention to her daughter. Even as she tended the cut, her mind was on the exchange between Brooke and her new husband. Being a mother, and a very concerned one, she could not help her curiosity.

"Is all well, Brooke?" she asked softly.

Brooke could see Dallas in her peripheral vision. She kept trying to turn her head to watch him as her mother cleaned the cut. "Aye, Mama," she said, still trying to catch a glimpse of her husband. "Everything is fine."

Gray's movements slowed as she fixed her daughter in the eye. "Are you sure? He was... kind? You are not injured?"

Brooke knew what her mother was speaking of and she flushed violently, averting her gaze. "Everything is fine, Mama. Truly."

Gray sighed faintly and resumed cleaning the wound. She wasn't going to press if Brooke did not want to speak of it. As long as Brooke said she was fine, she would ask no further. Still, it was difficult to fathom that her little girl was now a married woman. She wasn't used to the idea.

Up at the front of the column, Braxton was amused to notice that Dallas seemed unfocused also. He kept looking back over his shoulder. Braxton finally cleared his throat loudly.

"She is a lovely girl," he commented casually.

Dallas apparently hadn't realized how distracted he had appeared. He faced forward, pretending to focus on the road ahead. "What did you wish to speak of?"

Braxton fought off a smile. "Your wife. Did you do your duty?"

"I did."

"Completely? So it can never be questioned that the marriage was consummated?"

Dallas looked at him, then. "I performed as a husband. And she performed as a wife."

Braxton could see he was being truthful. He would not press further. "Excellent," his gaze moved forward again. "Now we have a bit of a situation on our hands; Erith is now your keep. The de Clares were guests there last we saw. What is your wish as far as they are concerned? Will you continue to show them hospitality or will you order them to leave?"

Dallas fell into contemplative silence. "I have no reason to order them away if they have come peacefully," he said after a moment. "Of course, I would know the reason for their visit. If they have come to seek Brooke's hand, however, I will throw them out on their arse."

Braxton looked at him; Dallas was usually quite calm, even in the heat of battle. It was a powerful quality in a powerful man. To hear him speak with such force was completely uncharacteristic. Braxton fought off a grin, suspecting that the lovely Lady Brooke had somehow left a mark on the dedicated young knight.

"As you wish," he replied. "But we must be mindful of their numbers. They are, after all, Gloucester, and Erith is in no condition to withstand a siege. Whatever you decide to do, it must be done with great foresight."

Dallas nodded, thinking of the broken down fortress that was now his. Strange how the castle now seemed so magnificent to him and he felt quite naturally protective of it.

"I will tell you what else I wish," he went on. "I wish for Lady Constance sent back to wherever she came from. I do not want that old witch within my walls or near my wife. She is a snake."

"You are speaking of my wife's mother and your wife's grandmother," Braxton reminded him. "You must be very careful how you approach this."

"Do you disagree?"

"Hell no. But you must be very careful when throwing her bodily from the keep. You do not want to appear cruel or controlling. More than that, the old woman is of the Northumberland Grays. It would do Erith absolutely no good to offend the whole of Northumberland."

Dallas looked at him, a twinkle in his eye. "Will your father not ride to our aide?"

"My father will be leading the attack against us."

"Marvelous," Dallas snorted ironically. "A most twisted predicament we find ourselves in."

Braxton could only lift his eyebrows in agreement, his gaze moving back over the scenery around them. It was lush and quiet. Erith was only a few miles to the north. They would be arriving soon and his trepidation sparked.

"If I can make a suggestion, Dallas," he ventured.

"Of course, my lord."

"Do not address me so formally in moments like this."

"Of course, father."

Braxton's head snapped up, seeing Dallas silently laughing at him. He smirked. "Whelp," he muttered insultingly. But he grew serious. "I would suggest you send word ahead to Erith announcing not only your marriage to Lady Brooke, but your impending arrival as the new lord of Erith. If de Clare is still there, they must know immediately. And be forewarned."

"Do you believe that entirely wise? It might give them time to build up a righteous rage."

"Indeed it will. But I would rather meet that rage head-on than wait until we are at Erith and trapped by the de Clare army within her crumbling walls."

Dallas turned his head, lifting a gloved hand in Graehm's direction. The stocky knight was almost to the rear of the column but caught the gesture and spurred his charger forward. He met up with Braxton and Dallas at their position near the front.

"Aye?" he answered Dallas.

"Send word ahead to Erith announcing the marriage of the

Lady Brooke Serroux to Sir Dallas Aston."

"Very good," Graehm saluted sharply, grinning. His gaze moved to Braxton. "And you, my lord? Am I to announce your marriage to Lady Gray?"

Braxton's focus was on the road ahead as if he could see Erith in the distance. He began to seriously wonder what lay in wait for them. With Constance's treachery, he could only imagine. And he knew she would not take the announcement of the marriages well. But he didn't care.

"Absolutely," he said. "You will let the world know that Braxton de Nerra has taken a bride."

Graehm was gone. Braxton glanced over his shoulder at Dallas to notice that the young knight was staring at him. They gazed at each other a moment, a thousand words of curiosity and foreboding filling their air. Braxton faced forward again.

"Put the wagons and the ladies to the rear," he said quietly. "Put the men on alert. Knights with shields slung."

Dallas moved swiftly to carry out the order. The last glimpse that Braxton had of his wife was as the wagon made a sweeping turn for the rear of the column.

His visor went down and his shield went over his left knee.

CHAPTER FIFTEEN

Gloucester didn't simply release a barrage. He released chaos.

As soon as Braxton's army neared the outer perimeter of Erith, the three hundred men that Roger de Clare had brought with him attacked from the woods. The fortress was hardly manned, being that it provided no protection whatsoever. Roger had wisely sent his men into the cover of the trees to attack de Nerra's army.

The first volley of arrows struck the men at the front of Braxton's column. He lost four men right away, pierced through their bodies and heads with Gloucester arrows. Braxton himself was hit, but only in the wrist. The arrow didn't even lodge itself; it simply pierced him and fell away. Knowing they had walked right into an ambush, Braxton did the only thing he could. He called a retreat.

But there were de Clare men lining the woods for several hundred yards. Even in retreat, they found themselves in a full-scale battle as Roger's army almost completely encircled them. Braxton's heart was in his throat as he thundered his way to the rear of the column where Gray and Brooke were; he found them laying in the wagon next to Geoff, being shielded from the arrows and fighting by none other than Norman and Edgar. When the soldier driving the wagon was hit with an arrow to the neck, Braxton leapt from his charger and took the reins himself.

The wagon barreled back down the road as fast as the horses would go. His only thought at the moment was to get the women to safety. Gradually, the fighting fell away from them and they were alone, tearing down the road towards Milnthorpe. He could hear Brooke weeping softly in the bed of the wagon but he did not stop; he continued for another mile at least, far enough away so that he was sure they were clear of the fighting. But he did not trust Gloucester not to follow him. He drove the wagon off the road, across a small brook, and continued into a heavy thicket.

By this time, Gray had lifted her head. Realizing there was no longer a war going on over her head, she climbed onto the wagon bench beside her husband and held on for dear life as he drove a crazy path through the foliage. Braxton felt her presence but didn't look at her; he could not afford the diversion. His primary focus was to get them to safety.

They finally reached a cool, grassy area imbedded in a cluster of white birch trees and Braxton pulled the wagon to an unsteady halt. It was silent but for the singing of the birds overhead. As Gray turned to Braxton, the thunder of hooves behind them startled everyone. They turned to see Braxton's charger rushing up behind them, riderless. The horse had followed his master all the way from the battle, very well trained to stay with his lord.

When they saw it was only the destrier, everyone emitted varied sighs of relief. Braxton's gaze lingered on Gray a moment, just to see for himself that she was all right. She smiled wanly. He patted her cheek, bailed from the wagon, and went straight to the team of horses. Gray watched him unfasten the tack.

"What are you doing?" she asked.

Braxton uncoupled the team as Norman and Edgar ran up. The boys began unstrapping the leather connecting the animals.

"I must return," he told her.

"But why are you unhitching the horses?"

"Norman and Edgar return with me."

Gray didn't say anything, but her wide-eyed expression conveyed much. Braxton couldn't linger on her fear, however; she was safe and that was all that concerned him. He had a job to do.

When he had helped the boys as much as he was able, he went to the wagon and motioned Gray down off the bench. She slid into his waiting hands and he put his arm around her shoulders as he led her back towards his now-grazing charger. She laid her head on his shoulder, clinging to him.

"I will go back and fight off de Clare, but I wanted you safe," he explained, trying to alleviate her fears. "It should not take long. Skirmishes like this usually don't. But you will say here until I come for you. Is that clear?"

They had reached the charger and now faced each other. "Aye," Gray nodded, dread in her eyes. "Please be careful, Braxton. Nothing about Erith is worth dying for."

He smiled at her. "It is Dallas' fortress now. He might have something different to say about that."

She rolled her eyes miserably. "Do not be glib," she begged. "I am serious. I would rather have you safe and whole than any piece of that old fortress. It has only brought me misery. But to lose you would...."

He kissed her swiftly once, twice, then slanted his lips over hers hungrily. "You will not lose me," he whispered against her mouth. "I will return."

Norman and Edgar were already mounted, riding up beside him. Braxton kissed her one last time and vaulted onto his charger, gathering the reins.

"Stay here," he ordered softly. "Make a fire and shelter, and anything else to keep you comfortable until my return."

Gray was trying not to cry. "When will you be back?"

"Hopefully before nightfall."

Brooke wandered up beside her mother, her lovely face pale and tear-streaked. Gray put her arm around her daughter to comfort her.

"Dallas," Brooke sniffled. "You will make sure he is all right, too?"

Braxton smiled at the young woman. "Dallas is a fine knight, Lady Aston. He can take care of himself."

Seeing that Gray was distracted comforting her daughter, Braxton spurred his horse back through the trees. Norman and Edgar followed close behind. In little time, they were back on the road and heading back into the heat of battle.

The skirmish was still going when Braxton and the boys returned. Braxton plunged right into the fighting, wielding his

sword against the heavily-armed de Clare men. Norman and
Edgar stayed to the outskirts as they usually did, dragging the
wounded out of the fighting and trying not to become one of the
casualties themselves. It was close-quarters fighting now that
the archers had been called off for fear of hitting their own men.

Dallas and Graehm were in the thick of it; Dallas was still on
horseback, fighting more fiercely than Braxton had ever seen
him. Perhaps it was because now he was fighting for something
that belonged to him and there was a measure of anger in his
movements. He had a customized broadsword with a serrated
edge that could slice a man's head clean from his body. Braxton
saw a few headless corpses around, knowing that Dallas had
been hard at work.

Braxton's men may have been outnumbered, but the de Clare
men were clearly suffering. Braxton's fighting force was well-
seasoned and well-trained; hence, they were the better army. De
Clare's band of not-so-skilled men was taking a beating. Braxton
personally dispatched several without raising a sweat and his
thoughts began to turn to de Clare himself. Leaving Graehm in
charge of the skirmish force, he collected Dallas and a few
soldiers and fought his way towards the keep. There seemed to
be less men the closer they drew to Erith, as the bulk of the army
was out on the road.

Braxton and Dallas charged into the dilapidated bailey of Erith
and were met with little resistance. On high alert, they
dismounted their chargers and made way for the keep. Dallas
was slightly in front of Braxton, his sword leveled defensively
while Braxton walked with his sword lowered. He was cool but
cautious. As soon as they mounted the top step and prepared to
enter the keep, a body suddenly came flying out at them.

Dallas struck the figure down in one deadly thrust; it was a
purely reflexive move on his part. He had seen the body, seen the
weapon, and had responded. Braxton was right on his heels,
preparing for an all-out assault of more warriors, but there was
none. Lying dead at their feet was a lone boy, no more than
Edgar's age. They heard a cry coming from inside.

"William!" a man screamed, coming to the doorway. His eyes bugged at the youth lying on the top landing. "You killed my son! You killed him!"

Dallas sword was still raised, red with the young man's blood. "He charged me with a weapon. I had no choice."

"But he has no armor, no protection," the older man was coming apart, falling to his knees beside the dead boy. "Could you not see that?"

Dallas was not swayed; his face remained hard. "Then he should not have been using a weapon is he was unprepared to die for his actions. I was defending myself."

The man dissolved; spittle dripped from his lips as he lingered over the lad. "William," he wept painfully. "My boy is dead. He's *dead*!"

Braxton stepped forward. "Who are you?"

The man seemed not to hear him. He wept with agony over the boy, shaking him in an attempt to rouse him. "William, lad, get up," he sobbed. "Get up and embrace me."

Braxton was unmoved. "You will answer my question. Who are you? And who is this boy that attacked us?"

The man's head snapped up, his eyes mad with grief. "I am Roger de Clare," he snapped savagely. "And this is my son William that you have murdered."

Braxton felt the impact of the words, realizing all of the implications they held; he didn't dare look at Dallas. "I am Braxton de Nerra," he said evenly. "Your son attacked us. We were defending ourselves."

"William was defending his holding!" de Clare barked. "You have no right to be here! It belongs to him!"

"It belongs to me, my lord," Dallas said. "I married the Lady Brooke and the holding is mine. You and your son are trespassing."

Braxton looked at Dallas, then. He was somewhat surprised with the word 'trespassing', true though it might be. Roger, too, focused on the tall young knight, his expression wavering between outrage and agony.

"You are lying," Roger hissed.

"I have the document and witnesses to prove it."

Roger struggled to stand. "But William was promised the Lady Brooke's hand and this holding. You stole it!"

"Who promised it to you?"

"Lady de Montfort, of course."

"My wife's grandmother had no authority to do so," Dallas replied. "This castle belongs to my wife's mother, the Lady Gray, who pledged both her daughter and the holding to me. It is therefore legally and morally mine. You have no claim. You never did."

Dallas sounded very matter of fact. Roger stood on unsteady legs, glaring at the young knight. "Lady de Montfort is the lady of this keep, for it was her husband's holding," he snarled. "She has every right to broker it."

Dallas shook his head. "The castle was Lady Gray's dowry upon her marriage to Garber Serroux. It was her husband's to do with as he pleased. Having used the keep to pay a gambling debt to Baron Wenvoe, Sir Braxton then purchased the rights to Erith from the old baron. Technically, it is Sir Braxton's holding. But he returned it to the Serroux family and it became my holding when I married Brooke. Is any of this clear to you yet, my lord? Understand that Erith was never yours. Lady Constance had no right."

Roger began to shake. With clawed hands, he reached out towards Dallas, his mind filled with madness. "I will kill you!"

Dallas deftly side-stepped the old man, who tripped over his son's supine body and tumbled forward. Because Dallas was not there to prevent his fall, he plunged over the side of the landing and to the bailey two stories below. Shocked, Dallas and Braxton could do nothing more than watch the man crash on his head. He was dead upon impact.

They stood atop the landing, staring at the body below them. After long moments of silent dread, Braxton looked at Dallas.

"I fear," he said quietly, "that we are in for a good deal of trouble."

***

"None of this would have happened had it not been for you," Gray's voice was icy. "I want you out. I do not care where you go, but I order you from Erith. I never want to see you again."

Constance sat in her fine bedchamber, facing the window. She refused to look at her daughter, who was visible upset. After the events of the last several hours, the tension between mother and daughter was at splitting capacity. But Constance chose to ignore it.

"I will not leave and you cannot force me," she said firmly.

"I will have Braxton bodily remove you, Mother," Gray was in no mood for her mother's arrogance. "You have schemed your last scheme. Now see what you have done to us with your treachery and selfishness. De Clare's brother will return and destroy us, and it is all your doing."

The old woman turned to her, eyes flashing. "You will not speak to me like that. I will not tolerate your insolence."

"Your behavior dictates mine. You are to be treated accordingly."

"What is that supposed to mean?"

Gray's amber eyes blinked slowly, with exhaustion. It was slightly after the nooning meal in a day that had seen far too many shocking events in it already. But it was about to see one more.

"It means that you are treacherous, deceitful and horrid. It means that I am embarrassed to call you my mother. It means that after this day, you will be dead to me."

Constance's thin face tightened; she approached her daughter with fury in her manner. "You impudent girl. What gives you the right to judge me? I was doing what I had to do in order to preserve this family. You would see us die away without lifting a finger. You are weak; *weak!* I am ashamed I birthed such a creature!"

Gray watched her mother's features as she spoke; the old

233

woman believed everything she said. She simply didn't understand. In the world of the Northumberland Grays, what she had done was perfectly acceptable behavior and Gray knew there was no use in continuing the conversation.

"You have one hour to pack," she said, moving for the door. "If you pack nothing, you take nothing. But mark my words, Mother; you shall be removed from this place and I do not want to see you again. Is that clear?"

Constance was quivering with rage. "You cannot banish me. This is my home. I forbid it."

Gray wasn't going to get into a verbal altercation with her mother any more than she already was. She'd made her position clear. When she put her hand on the latch to open the door, she was hit in the ear with something hard and heavy. Stunned, she put her hand to her head, drawing away blood. At her feet lay the iron candle holder that had done the damage. She looked to her mother in horror.

"Why did you do that?" she demanded.

Constance would not cower. She lifted her chin defiantly in a gesture that was very reminiscent of her sometimes-rebellious granddaughter. "You are an evil child, Gray. You deserve to be punished for every evil thing you have ever done to me. Have you no respect for your mother? How dare you order me from my own keep. And you are raising Brooke to be just like you. She is as evil and disobedient as you are. If given the chance, I would take her from you and raise her as she should be raised."

Gray's horrified expression turned to one of threat. "And just how should that be?"

Constance's eyes blazed with a deeper madness. "Like *me*."

Gray's control snapped; she had always kept her composure with her mother, no matter how the woman had behaved. She was her mother, after all. But in that statement, every thread of respect vanished. The woman was vicious and evil. If she would harm her daughter, then there was no knowing what she would do to someone else. Gray could not allow her to get her hands on Brooke. She simply couldn't take it any longer and momentary insanity filled her.

She rushed to her mother and grabbed the woman by the hair. Gray was taller and stronger than her mother and used that to her advantage; as tears streamed down her face, she yanked the screaming woman to the door and threw it open.

The entire keep suddenly came alive to the screaming of Constance and the cursing of Gray. Gray pulled her mother down the narrow spiral stairs, almost tripping but managing to keep her balance. She was mad with grief, with fury, as she continued to pull the woman down the second flight of stairs to the main living level.

Servants came rushing out to see what the matter was, dumbfounded to see Gray towing her mother brutally by the hair. But no one moved to intercede; they all knew that Lady Constance had punishment coming to her. For the years of harassment and cruelty to her daughter, for the evils she had sewn during that time. In fact, there wasn't one witness that did not approve of what they saw. They saw justice.

Gray was sobbing and cursing as she pulled her mother outside. She yanked the woman down the first two steps but Constance grabbed hold of the banister, holding herself firm. Gray took hold of a bird-like arm and gave another pull, managing to move the woman another two steps down the flight. But Constance took hold of the railing with another hand, holding fast as Gray pulled. There was much screaming going on, and some blood. It was the screaming that attracted Braxton.

On the outer wall with Dallas, he had been consulting with his men as to the fastest and most complete way to reinforce the crumbled sections before Gloucester undoubtedly came down around their ears. De Clare's army had left a few hours before with their dead liege and his dead son as somber cargo and Braxton had no doubt that they would return in force to avenge the deaths. He wanted to be ready. But the screaming distracted him, especially when one of his soldiers, with a better vantage point, told him what was transpiring.

He bolted off the wall with Dallas close behind. By the time they reached the keep, they could see Gray with a vicious grip on Constance. Shocked, Braxton ran the breadth of the bailey towards the stairs, watching his wife practically yank her mother's hair from her scalp. As he approached the steps, Brooke suddenly emerged from the keep and began screaming. Her crying granddaughter was enough of a distraction that Constance lost her grip on the rail, tumbling back into Gray. Gray lost her balance. Before Braxton could reach them, he watched with horror as his wife and mother-in-law tumbled down the newly repaired steps.

They landed in a heap about the time Braxton got to them. He felt to his knees, shoving the old woman off of his wife.

"Gray, sweetheart," Braxton's voice was shaking as he tried to assess any visible injuries. "Are you hurt? Speak to me, sweet; where do you hurt?"

Gray was staring up at the sky, her expression void. She swallowed hard, her eyes slowly blinking. "Braxton?" she whispered feebly.

"I am here, sweet," he moved so she could see him, his face very close to hers. "Where are you hurt?"

She swallowed again and closed her eyes. "My mother," she murmured. "Remove her from Erith. Remove her before I kill her."

He cast a glance at the disheveled, and unharmed, old woman now in Dallas' grasp. "I will," his told her, his eyes finding Dallas. "Go and get a physic. Hurry!"

Dallas pulled Constance with him as he stood up. His attention found Graehm, having just run upon the group. "Find a physic," he ordered sharply. "Ride to Milnthorpe or Leven. Go!"

Graehm bolted off in the direction he had just come. By this time, Brooke was at the bottom of the steps, weeping loudly at the sight of her mother lying on the ground. Dallas shoved the old woman at a couple of soldiers for safe keeping and went to his wife. He put his arms around her as they both gazed down at Gray.

"Mama?" Brooke wept, trying to move closer but being

prevented by Dallas. "Mama, are you all right?"

Gray lay there, breathing heavily and not moving. Braxton realized he was as close to tears as he had ever been in his life. He touched her face, her arms, not wanting to move her but wanting to do something. He felt so helpless.

"Gray," he murmured, bending down to kiss her forehead. "Can you tell me where you hurt? Please, sweetheart. Where do you hurt?"

Gray's eyes lolled open, the magnificent amber orbs glazed with shock. She took a deep breath and shifted slightly, her right leg coming up to bend at the knee. Then she moved again; her arms and torso flexed. She lifted her hands to Braxton and he grasped them tightly.

"I... I think I am all right," she whispered. "Just... stunned. Help me to sit up, please."

Braxton was shaking like a leaf. He helped her to sit, very carefully, making sure to support her back as she tried to catch her balance. She blinked, putting a hand to her head. Braxton was deeply relieved to see that she was at least able to sit.

"How do you feel?" he asked.

She put her hand to the bloodied side of her head. "A little weak, but I believe I am all right."

"Are you sure?"

"I think so."

Braxton was so relieved that he nearly collapsed with it. But her bloodied head had his attention and he fingered her silken blond hair, looking for the wound.

"You have hurt your head," he said. "The physic may need to put a few stitches in your scalp."

Gray shook her head. "The fall did not do that," she said quietly. "My mother did."

Braxton's gaze flew to the old woman, now trapped between two seasoned soldiers. His nostrils flared, indicative of his level of emotion, and the blue-green eyes blazed.

"She hurt you?" he asked his wife.

Gray looked over at her mother; she was finished protecting

the woman. "Aye."

"Is that why you were fighting with her?"

"I was bodily removing her from Erith. She did not want to go."

Braxton stood up and snapped his fingers at the soldiers, who immediately grabbed Constance and began dragging her across the bailey. The old woman began to scream again, howling an unearthly sound. Brooke's loud crying resumed as she watched her grandmother's removal.

"Where is she going?" she begged. "What are you doing with her?"

Gray was attempting to stand with Braxton's strong assistance. "She is banished from Erith," Gray told her daughter as firmly as she could manage. "Because of her, we are facing more peril that we can possibly fend off. Everything horrible that has happened is a direct result of her actions. I will tolerate her no longer, Brooke. I will not allow her to continue to harm us. To harm you."

Brooke was weeping softly against Dallas' chest. He was trying his best to comfort her. Gray was steadier now, leaning heavily against Braxton. Slowly, the two of them began to walk back to the steps that had almost claimed Gray's life. They passed close to Brooke and Dallas as they did so, one glance at her mother propelled Brooke from Dallas' arms and into Gray's. She wept dramatically against her mother as Braxton support them both.

Dallas met his father-in-law's gaze over the two blond heads. "What do we do with Lady Constance?"

Braxton was very close to giving a brutal order but he kept himself in check. He had more important things to contend with.

"Give her a few coins and have her escorted into Milnthorpe. Pay for a few days of lodging for her. But beyond that, she gets nothing. My patience with her is at an end for what she has done. Tell her that I will throw her in the vault if she ever shows her face here again."

Dallas was pleased with the order but did not show it. Leaving his wife clinging to her mother, he went to give the command that would send Constance from Erith forever.

Or so he hoped.

Up in Gray's poorly furnished chamber, Braxton inspected her from head to toe for any injuries related to the fall. She had perked up a great deal, now seemingly just exhausted more than anything else. Satisfied that she was moderately intact, Braxton proceeded to put three neat stitches in her ear. Since Gray was feeling better, he called off the hunt for a local physic and decided to take care of her himself. Brooke sat with Gray the entire time; she even helped the Braxton when the man put the small stitches in her mother's skin, a big step for the normally squeamish young lady. When the stitches were in, he gave her a brewed willow bark potion for her throbbing headache.

"Are you hungry, Mama?" Brooke asked as she put away the bowl that Braxton had used. "The cook made some wonderful bread with the last of Braxton's white flour."

Gray was lying on her small, sparse bed and immediately tried to rise. "I will attend the meal downstairs. No need to cater to me, for I am well enough."

Braxton sat on a stool next to the bed, eyeing his wife as she tried to stand. "The physic said you should rest," he told her. "Perhaps you and I could take our meal in our chamber tonight."

Gray gave him a blank expression. "But who will see to the meal? I must go down and...."

He stood up, putting his hands on her gently. "You have a grown daughter who is now lady of this keep. She will see to the meal."

Gray turned astonished eyes to Brooke. Brooke, in fact, looked rather surprised by Braxton's suggestion. But in the same breath, she was aware that her new father was correct. In the face of her mother's reluctance, Brooke summoned her courage.

"Aye, Mama, I will see to it," she said eagerly. "I will go right now."

"But...."

"I will do a good job. You'll see."

Gray watched Brooke bolt from the room, much to Braxton's amusement. Then she looked at her husband in shock; her daughter was indeed growing up and she wasn't so sure she liked it. Braxton put his arms around his wife, careful of her bumps and bruises.

"You see?" he murmured into her temple. "She is capable of the duty. Have some faith in her."

Gray was torn between doubt and agreement. "I do," she said, though she wasn't sure she meant it. "But she has never supervised a full meal before."

"Yet you have taught her what you know."

"I have tried."

"Then there is always a first time for everything."

Gray was forced to agree with him. Either Brooke would succeed or she would fail. But she must be given the chance.

Brooke never gave failure another thought. She bound down the stairs to the great hall, nearly plowing into Graehm as he went to tend Geoff. The red-haired knight was stuffed into an inconspicuous corner of the great hall and Brooke went over to him, peering over the Graehm's shoulder as the man checked his bandages.

"I am supervising the meal tonight, Sir Geoff," she said, sounding rather proud of herself. "Is there anything special you would like to eat?"

Geoff was pale but lucid. He looked up at Brooke as much as his restrictive bandages would allow. "Nothing comes to mind, Lady Aston."

She smiled at his use of her title and Graehm interrupted. "The physic in Milnthorpe said he is to eat soft foods, my lady," he instructed. "Soup or porridge only."

"But he may want something else."

"Nothing else for him. Soup or porridge *only*."

Brooke made a face, causing Geoff to smile weakly. She stuck her tongue out at the back of Graehm's head even as she answered affirmatively.

"As you say," she turned back for the kitchens.

Somehow, she felt different this night. Usually, she was in the kitchens helping the cook while her mother was doing everything else. But tonight, she was actually doing the managing. She went into the kitchens and told the cook that Geoff must only have soft foods; the cook barked like a dog in response. Brooke was used to the strange behavior. Then she walked around the kitchens like an inspector, noting what food was being prepared and how they were doing it. She missed nothing and was feeling quite important.

Edgar and Norman entered the kitchens through the open back door. They had sacks of grain in their arms, looking for a place to drop them. Norman spied Brooke first, standing across the kitchen by the great hearth.

"Where would you have us put this, Lady Aston?" he asked her.

Brooke went over to them. "What is it that you have?"

"White milled flour," Norman told her. "Sir Braxton and the knights like white bread. They will wish it for their meal."

Brooke looked thoughtful. "Why not put it here, by this cutting table. Prop it up so that it is out of the way."

Norman looked at the table shoved up against the stone wall. "If I can make a suggestion, my lady, perhaps we should put the sack on the top of the table so that they are off the floor."

"Why?"

"So the mice can't get at them," Edgar said as if she was the stupidest creature on the face of the earth.

Norman cast his brother a quelling glance. "The mice like the flour," he said nicely, hoping Brooke would not react to his brother. "We should put it somewhere off the floor."

Brooke was still eyeing Edgar. "Very well," she told Norman. "Put them somewhere safe."

Norman heaved the sack onto the table top, helping Edgar do the same. Brooke was still glaring at the younger boy, watching him follow his brother from the room. She called to him before they could reach the door.

"Edgar," she called.

Both boys came to a halt; Norman's expression was wary while Edgar's was downright hostile.

"Aye, Lady Aston?" Edgar emphasized 'lady'.

Brooke approached. "You cannot be disrespectful to me any longer," she came to a halt in front of the younger brother. "My husband would be most displeased if he knew how mean you were to me."

Edgar's face turned red. "I wasn't mean to you."

She put her hands on her hips. "You will address me as Lady Aston. That's my name."

His cheeks grew redder. "*Lady* Aston," he repeated.

Brooke studied him closely for any sign of insubordination. "You are indeed very mean to me. I have no idea why you treat me so badly. I have only been nice to you and have even shared my treats with you."

Norman looked away and rolled his eyes. Brooke was taunting Edgar; he could see it and he had to do something before Edgar exploded and Sir Dallas came down on both of them. He turned back to the pair.

"Lady Aston," he addressed her correctly. "We have work to do, if you don't mind. I would beg your leave."

Brooke's gaze lingered on Edgar a moment longer before looking to Norman. "You may go, Norman. But I want Edgar to stay here and help the cooks."

"What?" both boys blurted. Then Norman spoke quickly. "My lady, Edgar has a good deal of work awaiting him in the stables. It is his duty to feed and water the chargers."

Brooke's stubborn streak took hold. "I need him here to help in the kitchens. You can handle the chargers by yourself, Norman. As lady of the keep, I demand it."

Norman didn't know what to say. God help them, she *was* the lady of the keep. He looked at his brother, still red in the face. He did not want to think on what would happen were he not there to act as a buffer between Brooke and Edgar.

"Edgar is not a kitchen servant, my lady," he said, hoping she

242

would see his point. "He'll probably burn the keep down if you try to force him. He wouldn't know what to do."

"But I wish it. We need the help. Go away now, Norman."

He sighed reluctantly. "Very well, Lady Aston."

Brooke watched Norman walk away. She looked back to Edgar, who had his head down. A fiendish sense of pleasure swept her to think that he was now in her power.

"Come along, Edgar," she said, turning back into the kitchens. "You have much work to do."

"Like what?" Edgar blurted. "I am not a kitchen servant. I would not know the first thing about working in a kitchen."

She frowned at him. "You are going to learn."

"Why?"

"Because I said so."

Edgar came to a halt, glaring hatefully at Brooke. "You cannot order me around. I serve Sir Braxton. In fact, I do not have to listen to you at all."

Brooke's mouth pressed into an angry flat line. "You do too have to listen to me. I am the Lady of Erith. My husband is Sir Dallas and if you do not do as I tell you, then I will tell him that you are insubordinate and need to be whipped."

Edgar shook his fist at her. "Go ahead. You are nothing but a skinny, ugly girl that Sir Dallas was forced to marry. I'll bet he hates you already!"

Brooke's mouth popped open in outrage. "How dare you say that to me!"

"It's true! Just look at him and see how much he hates being married to you!"

Brooke charged him; it was inevitable. Edgar dodged out of the way and she smacked into the cutting table, bruising her wrist. But she would not let Edgar get away. As he barreled out of the kitchen, she barreled out right on his heels.

Edgar was well acquainted with running from Brooke. He'd been making a career out of it over the past few days. His ankle was sore from his fall in Milnthorpe but worked well enough. He would make sure to step in no more rabbit holes.

Edgar tore a wild path out of the kitchen yards and out towards the stables. His arms and legs were pumping so fast that they were in danger of getting all tangled up. Brooke screeched after him, her skirts hiked up around her knees as she ran. Edgar looked over his shoulder to see that she was gaining ground and he ran faster. Out into the main ward he ran, flying like the wind with Brooke hot on his tail. He roared through the destroyed entry as some of Braxton's men were working on the crumbling portcullis, heading out to the road beyond. Brooke roared after him.

The men working on the crumbling wall and destroyed gate watched curiously. Braxton, his head bent over a section of the wall that was particularly shattered, heard the distant hollering and looked up just in time to see Edgar shoot from the ward and out onto the road with Brooke right behind him. He shook his head and sighed heavily.

"Dallas," he called.

Dallas' dusty blond head suddenly popped up from a mound of rubble; he had been inspecting the foundation of this particular section of wall. He looked at Braxton, who pointed to the two running figures moving down the road. Dallas' eyes widened briefly before he muttered a curse. Then he leapt from the hole he had been standing in and bellowed for a mount.

Someone brought about a horse just as Norman ran past. Dallas vaulted onto the animal's bare back.

"Norman," he shouted as he gathered the reins. "What is going on?"

Norman paused long enough to look at the knight. "Last I heard, Lady Brooke was ordering Edgar to work in the kitchens. He must have disobeyed her."

Dallas cursed again and spurred the horse after his wife. Norman, without a horse, was much slower. Galloping down the road, Dallas caught up to Brooke about a half mile from the castle. She was still running as fast as she could. Edgar, however, had slowed considerably. Dallas reached his wife about the time she was nearly on Edgar. He grabbed her by an arm.

"Stop," he shouted, sliding from the horse before it even came to a halt. He had Brooke with both hands. "What in the world are you doing?"

Brooke's pretty face was flushed and she was panting heavily. "He... he called me ugly and skinny. He must be punished!"

Dallas still had hold of his wife as he turned to Edgar, now lying in an exhausted heap in the grass several feet away. "Edgar!" he bellowed.

The lad shot to his feet and weaved a weary path back towards the knight. He, too, was flushed and panting. "My lord?"

Dallas' expression was hard. "Did you call my wife ugly and skinny?"

Edgar's weary expression was replaced by a fearful one. "I...I...."

"Speak up, boy."

Edgar's gaze moved between Dallas and Brooke. He finally lowered his head. "Aye, my lord, I did."

"He said that you were miserable because you had married me," Brooke wanted to get Edgar in trouble. But half way through her statement, she burst into tears. "He said you hated me."

Dallas looked at his wife with some concern before turning back to Edgar. "Is this true?"

"Aye, my lord," Edgar mumbled.

"I see," Dallas' eyes narrowed. "Have you anything to say in your defense before I dispense your punishment?"

Edgar was still looking at the ground. "She... she wanted to make me a kitchen servant, my lord, even though I had to tend to the chargers. That is my job. She told me that she was the Lady of Erith now and I had to do what she said. But Sir Braxton is my liege. I only do what Sir Braxton tells me."

Dallas looked at Brooke, wiping tears off her cheeks. "Did you order him to tend the kitchens?"

After a brief hesitation, she nodded. Dallas' grip loosened and he let her go, his attention moving back and forth between his wife and the young squire. He sighed heavily and scratched his dusty head.

"I am not entirely sure why you two seem so intent on harassing each other, but it is going to stop here and now," his voice was low, threatening. "Brooke, Edgar is indeed Braxton's squire and you may not order him about. He answers to Braxton alone. Is that clear?"

Rebuked, she kept her gaze averted but nodded her head. Dallas looked at Edgar. "And you," he addressed him. "I will hear of no more insults dealt to Lady Aston. She is my wife and your words are slanderous. She is neither skinny nor even remotely ugly, and as for my being unhappy that I married her, I will tell you now that I am quite satisfied. If I hear of you calling her any more names or harassing her in any way, I will blister your backside. Is that understood?"

Edgar's head was also still lowered but he nodded firmly. Dallas put his hands on his hips. "Now go," he ordered quietly. "Take this horse with you. Tend all of the chargers and when you are done, you can clean out their stalls and make sure they have fresh bedding. Then you can clean my armor and Sir Braxton's armor until it shines. I want to see my face in it come morning."

"Aye, my lord."

Edgar fled back towards the castle under Norman's silent escort. Dallas and Brooke were left standing alone, Brooke wiping at the remainder of her tears as Dallas turned his attention to her. His expression softened.

"You will leave Edgar alone," he said quietly. "No more fighting with him. It is beneath you."

She nodded, wiping daintily at her nose. Dallas took pity on her and took her hand, gently tucking it into the crook of his elbow as they began their walk back to the castle. Brooke remained silent but for an occasional sniffle.

"Did you hear what I told him?" Dallas asked quietly.

She looked at him, her expression guarded. "What do you mean?"

He met her gaze. "That I am satisfied with this marriage."

She hiccupped. "Are you really?"

His lips twitched with a smile. "I am. So do not let his words upset you so. He couldn't be more wrong."

She smiled timidly. "Are you sure?"

Dallas returned her smile and took her in his arms, gazing down into her lovely young face. His eyes were intense as he studied her, thinking her to be a beautiful creature indeed. His soft kiss was met by a powerful response as Brooke threw her arms around his neck. He reacted by squeezing her so hard that she gasped. He laughed low in his throat.

"I hope this means that you are growing to like my kiss," he said as he released her.

She nodded, breathless. "Do it again."

He did, with pleasure. When Braxton looked out to the road to see what was keeping Dallas, he saw the passionate embrace in the distance. With a grin, he turned back to the crumbling wall.

CHAPTER SIXTEEN

Unfortunately for Constance, she had spent most of the money Braxton had given her for food and lodgings in the town of Levens. The town was small but had several well known inns, and Constance set herself up in the finest tavern in town, the Dixon Arms, and lived like a queen until she realized that she was very nearly out of coin.

Her plan had always been to return to the seat of the mighty Grays with a grand story of abduction and exile. It was not in her nature to admit the truth; in fact, the truth had long since become amalgamated with the fiction created in her mind into a story that she was truly coming to believe herself. In her mind, Braxton had taken over Erith and forced Gray into marriage. Worse, he had forced Brooke into an unsuitable marriage with one of his knights. Then, he had exiled Constance, the last line of defense between her daughter and granddaughter and the mercenaries knights. Constance considered herself the victim in all of this.

The other details were conveniently forgotten, those that pointed out Constance's foul actions. In her mind, she could do no wrong. She did what she had to do, in all things. And a mercenary knight bannerette was not going to best generations of breeding and intelligence. She was going to punish the knight and emerge the victor no matter what the cost.

So she hired two men to take her to Thirlwall Castle, the Gray stronghold in Northumbria where she had been born. It was at least a four day ride from Levens. Unfortunately, she had agreed to pay the men by the day and by the third day, her funds had run out and they left her in the small town of Rosehill, just to the east of Carlisle. On a very expensive palfrey that she had purchased in Levens, Constance was forced to travel the last fourteen miles alone, arriving at Thirlwall Castle just after sunset on the fourth day.

Thirlwell was a small castle with an all-inclusive keep that contained stables on the bottom floor and the hall, kitchens and bed chambers above. The castle itself was heavily fortified with soldiers, being so close to the Scots border, but the only remains of Constance's family were a distant nephew and his son.

Nonetheless, they were family and they listened to Constance's tale with great concern. She came across as intelligent and victimized, not a conniving shrew who would stop at nothing to obtain a victory. And she made sure to throw Braxton de Nerra's name into the story at every opportunity. She wanted the name ingrained into their brains as a man of great evil. She wanted Braxton to pay.

Her nephew immediately sent word to the Earl of Northumberland, Yves de Vesci, asking that men be sent to Erith Castle to save Lady Constance's daughter and granddaughter from the wicked mercenary de Nerra. De Vesci, recognizing the de Nerra name as the Lords of Gilderdale, his vassals, sent word to Thomas de Nerra forthwith to seek out his son and rescue Lady Constance's family. And with that, victory, for Constance, was guaranteed. She would finally have the last word.

But her assured victory was not to be. Weary from travel and stress, Constance went to bed that night with dreams of success over Braxton de Nerra on her mind. But those dreams soon faded and she began to dream of a great knife stabbing her in the chest. The pain was tremendous and in her dreams, she struggled to get away from the knife but it remained firmly lodged in her sternum, creating waves of anguish. And that was the last thing she remembered, for one of the servants found her stiff and cold in the morning, having died sometime during the night in her sleep.

She was buried the next day in the vault of her ancestors, finally, as she had always asserted and demanded, among her own blue-blooded peerage.

The peerage of the dead.

***

Black Fell Castle, Northumberland

"My son would not have kidnapped women and absconded with a fortress," the man who spoke the words used a deadly tone. "Who spreads these lies?"

A knight bearing the red and blue shield of the Earls of Northumberland stood in the great hall of Black Fell Castle, delivering a message from his liege, Yves de Vesci. He tried not to appear nervous but, truth be told, everyone was always a bit apprehensive upon entering Black Fell. The place was full of the dark ambiance that is given to those whose life and vocation is geared towards battle.

Sir Thomas de Nerra came from a long line of aggressive soldiers; powerful but not brutal, brave but not reckless. Still, the man was more of a warrior than most, seasoned and bred along with the rest of the Lords of Gilderdale. The sons that stood with him were of the same mold; powerful, cunning, calculating and cold.

But the messenger held his ground. "My liege has received this information from Thirlwall Castle, seat of Sir Edmund Gray."

"And how would he know this?"

"Because his father's sister, the Lady Constance Gray de Montfort, has returned to Thirlwall with this information. Sir Edmund is most concerned for his cousin and her family."

Thomas de Nerra gazed at the man with calculating blue-green eyes. Most of his sons resembled him to fault, the exception being his eldest, Robert. Robert had the dark of his mother. Even now, Robert stood beside his father, his blue-green eyes hard as he listened to the tale involving his youngest brother. Before his father could reply, he interjected his thoughts.

"There must be a logical explanation for what Lady de Montfort has said," he replied firmly. "My brother is not the sort to go around confiscating castles and abducting women."

The messenger's eyes flicked to him. "Be that as it may, the earl is concerned enough that he asks you to ride to Erith Castle and remove your son. This he demands on behalf of the Grays of Northumberland."

"God's Beard," the second eldest brother, a big man with graying blond hair named Davis, cursed lowly. "Braxton is a grown man and, I might add, a powerful knight in his own right. Do you think we can simply march to Erith and scold him like a child? That is ridiculous."

Robert shook his head in agreement, glaring at the messenger as he turned away. Not to be left out, the third de Nerra son, Steven, made his presence known. He was a massive, hairy beast of a man with shaggy gray hair and hands the size of trenchers. He was also the most volatile, which is why Davis grabbed the man before he could throw the messenger into a head lock.

"Braxton would not do what your lord fears," he snarled. "He is a man of honor."

"He is a well-known mercenary," the messenger unwisely countered. "He will do what is necessary if there is profit involved. Lord de Vesci is simply concerned for the safety of Lady Constance's daughter and all of you, as vassals of de Vesci, are obliged to obey his command."

There was truth in the statement that none of them could refute. Thomas sighed heavily, thoughtfully, averting his gaze as he scratched his neck and generally fidgeted about as his sons grumbled and postured. He rose from the bench upon which he was seated, stretching his muscled legs and thinking of the son he'd not seen in years. He hadn't even heard of him in nearly as long until one of his knights, Niclas de Aughton, returned from mission to Gloucester. He had run across Braxton and his army and told quite a different tale than the one being carried by de Vesci's knight. Thomas sent a soldier for de Aughton before returning his attention to the messenger.

"One of my knights has recently seen Braxton," he said. "I have sent for him and we shall clear this up once and for all."

The messenger didn't say any more; he was only the messenger, after all, and not qualified to argue the point. So he stood politely while de Nerra's sons conferred between them, big men with big reputations. They were growing older now and their own sons were beginning to take on the family mantle; Robert had two boys while Steven had one, young men that were even now outside with the army. Thomas went back to the bench and lowered his body heavily, sitting near the fire because his joints ached.

The messenger's gaze moved from the whispering sons to the pensive father, brushing over the features of the massive two-story hall that smelled like dogs and men. He'd never actually been to Black Fell Castle but he could see why it was considered a foreboding stronghold; it reeked of war. He could feel it, and see it, everywhere. It was a dark place of stone, smoke and power.

De Aughton wasn't long in coming. The big black knight with eyes of obsidian entered the smoky great hall from the bailey outside, approaching Thomas with pounding steps. Before Thomas could speak, Steven leapt out to intercept him.

"This fool has come to tell us that Braxton has taken Erith Castle hostage," he barked. "You have recently seen my brother. Is this true?"

Niclas had to step aside or risk being run over by Steven in the man's anger. His dark brow furrowed as he looked from the enraged de Nerra brothers to the de Vesci messenger several feet away. Puzzled, he focused on the messenger.

"Who told you this?" he demanded.

The messenger was outnumbered but he held his ground. Each successive man at Black Fell seemed to be bigger and angrier than the last. "Lady Constance Gray de Montfort," he replied evenly. "She has come to my lord de Vesci for assistance. She claims that Braxton de Nerra has confiscated Erith and is holding her daughter, the Lady Gray, hostage."

Niclas stared at the man a moment, pondering his words, before clearing his throat softly. He turned to Thomas and the de Nerra brothers who were clearly looking for an answer. "Braxton de Nerra is married to the Lady Gray," he explained. "If she is a hostage, she is the most willing hostage I have ever seen."

Thomas bolted off the bench, his blue-green eyes wide.

"What's this you say?" he barked. "Braxton has taken a wife?"

Niclas nodded, a faint smile coming to his lips. "The most beautiful woman I have ever seen. In fact, I...," he caught himself before he could finish the story, which would not go well in his favor. "Suffice it to say that he has married her and when last I saw them, they were very happy."

Robert was grinning like a fool while Davis and Steven simply appeared stunned. Only Thomas seemed capable of speaking in light of this shocking news. "Why did you not tell me my son had taken a wife before now?" he demanded.

"Because it was not my place, my lord. That news should come from your son."

Thomas growled and made a face, but he understood. He waved his hands dramatically. "But what about Erith Castle?" he persisted.

Niclas shook his head. "I do not know anything about Erith Castle, my lord."

"Nothing at all? Braxton did not mention it to you?"

"Nay, my lord. It was never discussed."

Thomas' gaze lingered on the big knight a moment longer before turning to his sons. They all gazed back at him with varied degrees of confusion and delight. Thomas scratched his oily head again before flipping a dirty hand at the three men.

"Mount the army," he ordered. "We ride for Erith to clear up this mess before Braxton gets himself into trouble."

Steven and Davis were on the move, racing from the great hall and calling to the sergeants. Robert, however, remained behind. He went to his father and clapped the man on the shoulder.

"You make excuses," he teased quietly. "Your true motivation in riding to Erith is to meet Braxton's wife. You want to see how well he did for himself."

Thomas growled at him and stomped away, leaving Robert laughing silently. But Niclas was still standing there and Robert went to him, eyeing the man thoughtfully. He sobered.

"Tell me the truth," he lowered his voice. "What was Braxton doing when you last saw him? Did he mention anything about

Erith Castle?"

Niclas shook his head. "I met your brother at a tournament in Milnthorpe," he said. "He competed briefly until one of his men was gravely injured. When last I saw him, he and his wife were camped outside of Milnthorpe. That is all I know, my lord."

Robert's eyebrows lifted. "Compete, did he? How did he fare?"

"Only one bout. He unseated his opponent and gained his horse."

Robert grinned. "That sounds like my brother," he agreed. "And his wife; is she truly lovely?"

"As a new spring morning, my lord."

"But there was no hint that she might have been married to him against her will?"

"Absolutely not. It was clear to me that she adored him."
Unfortunately for me.

Robert nodded, digesting the information. "And my brother is well these days?"

"Well and rich. He travels like a prince."

Robert's grin was back; he had a special fondness for Braxton, the only brother out of the four who had enough drive and ambition to create his own life away from Black Fell. The man had done exceedingly well for himself over the years, something that Robert was proud of. He admired Braxton for not following the path that the rest of the family chose. Braxton was, and always had been, his own man.

"I miss my brother," he muttered in reflection.

Niclas smiled faintly. "He said the same thing about you."

Robert glanced at him, his grin broadening. Then he looked at his hands, disfigured by the disease that twisted and enlarged his joints. He flexed them, feeling the pain that was his daily companion. He could hardly hold a cup these days much less a sword, but he had once been a very skilled knight. He missed those days.

"It is not my normal routine to ride with the army," he said softly. "But to see Braxton, I would ride to the ends of the earth. Have my charger saddled and waiting."

Niclas nodded. "Aye, my lord."

"And then you will ride ahead and tell Braxton that we are coming."

"By your command, my lord."

The big black knight quit the hall, leaving Robert and the messenger as the only two occupants. Still flexing his fingers, Robert turned to the de Vesci messenger.

"You will return to the earl and tell him that Gilderdale rides for Erith," he said. "Have no doubt we shall seek the truth of the situation, whatever it may be. Where is Erith, anyway?"

"West of the town of Levens in Cumbria, I am told."

"Very well. Go, then; do as you are told."

The messenger saluted sharply and left. Robert watched the man go, his mind moving to the adventure ahead. The messenger was correct; Braxton was a well known mercenary and mercenaries were only out for profit. He wondered if Braxton had married the lady of Erith to gain wealth or if there was some other reason. At this point, he was as confused as the rest of them. But he fully intended to know the truth.

***

For five weeks, Erith was a fortress under construction. There was a frenzied pace about it and the work went on day and night. Dallas and Braxton took turns overseeing the rebuilding, hardly sleeping a few hours in between shifts; they were both master builders, precise in their measurements and plans. Braxton could do the most complicated arithmetic in his head, which translated into stronger walls and a stronger outer gatehouse. The man was a talented architect.

They had sent the bodies of Roger and William de Clare back to Roger's stronghold, Elswick Castle. Braxton and Dallas knew, without question, that the death of the earl's cousin would not be well met but there wasn't much they could do about it. The wheels were in motion and they knew that sooner or later Gloucester would seek revenge. Their best hope for protection was to be prepared.

The past few weeks saw other changes as well. Braxton and Dallas now worked more as a team rather than a commander and his subordinate. The marriage of Dallas to Brooke had created a familial relationship and Braxton relaxed his usual strict standards of conduct with the man, although it was still very clear who was in charge. Still, Dallas seemed to be growing as both a knight and a man. Something about Brooke brought out another side of him and Braxton watched the transformation with approval; Dallas had always been obedient, wise and talented, but now he had added something deeper to the mix. He smiled more, seemed more apt to go the extra effort in all things; the men, a word of approval, assistance with rebuilding his fortress. Dallas was moving from obedient knight into a man of depth and character.

And then there was Brooke; since the day she had chased Edgar out onto the main road, there hadn't been a harsh word between her and the young squire. In fact, she had nearly stopped paying attention to him altogether because her focus was fully on her new husband. She had always been rather careful with her appearance, at least as careful as their meager surroundings would allow, but now she was positively intense about how she looked. Dallas would praise her for the way she arranged her hair or the loveliness of her eyes, which only seemed to make her more conscious of how she looked. It was evident that she wanted to please her husband, and please she did. In spite of any reservation Dallas might have had in the beginning, he was completely smitten with the lovely young lady. The beautiful wild rose was becoming a gorgeous, cultivated one.

During this time of building and romance, there were other things going on as well.; Geoff, for instance, was healing admirably from his brush with death and was trying his best to resume a normal routine. Braxton hadn't gone so far as to order Geoff to remain in bed but he had spent a good deal of time trying to reason with him. Geoff managed to stay down for another day and night before rising early one morning and making his way, however slowly, to the inner bailey. Braxton knew that there was no keeping the man down, so he gave him a job supervising the rebuild of the inner portcullis, the one so badly damaged by Garber's trebuchet practice. Geoff supervised the builders, making him feel useful without actually exerting himself.

Gray was also on the mend from her run-in with her mother and as the days passed, she watched Brooke transform from a silly young girl into a responsible young woman. They hadn't spoken of the day when Constance had been forcibly escorted from the keep and, as time passed and their new lives unfolded, it was easier to forget about the vicious old lady and get on with their lives.

Even now as Gray sat in the great hall after the morning meal, she watched Brooke rush around to make sure the nooning meal was in full preparation. It took foresight and thought, which Brooke was trying very hard to do. Even the keep itself was transforming under her hand and Braxton's money. As a mother, Gray found herself moved by the sight of her daughter growing up and thanking God that Constance was no longer around to poison her. They were happier than they had ever been.

As Gray sat and watched Brooke direct some servants to clear out the stale rushes, big arms suddenly embraced her from behind. Braxton gently enfolded his wife into his arms, kissing the side of her head and being mindful of her sore ribs. Gray smiled, placing a warm palm against his stubbled cheek as he kissed her.

"Greetings, wife," he purred into her ear, kissing her again. "I am pleased to see that you are learning to be a lady of leisure."

She gestured at Brooke, helping one of the old servants with a particularly large branch. "I was watching my daughter," she said. Then she sighed. "My little girl seems to have grown up all in the past few days and I am not quite sure how I feel about it."

He sat down on the bench next to her, holding her close and watching Brooke move about quite capably.

"Odd," he said softly. "I have been thinking the same thing about Dallas. I have known the man since he was twenty years and one, when he was newly knighted, and although he has always proven himself extremely capable and responsible, our lovely young daughter has done something to him. He's a changed man."

Gray turned to look at him, her amber eyes soft. "*Our* daughter?"

His blue-green eyes twinkled. "She belongs to me, as do you," he whispered, kissing her cheek. "She was mine the moment I married you."

She smiled at him, touching his handsome face. "You are as compassionate as you are generous. There are not many men who would happily accept two destitute women."

"They are fools."

She laughed softly and kissed him, to which he readily responded. When he pulled away, it was to cup her face in his enormous hands and study her fine features intently.

"I have been thinking something else along those lines," he murmured.

"What is that?"

"I would like to make Brooke and Dallas my heirs."

Gray nodded in serious consideration. "Although I do not question your judgment, would you not want for a child born of your blood to be your heir?"

He shrugged. "I do not have any children of my blood."

"Not yet," she smiled when he looked rather surprised at her. "I am not beyond my childbearing years, Braxton. It is entirely possible that you and I will be blessed in the future."

He just stared at her. "Although I have always hoped...," he trailed off, not sure what to say. "The thought of bearing another child does not distress you?"

Her smile broadened. "Of course not. Why should it?"

He half-shrugged, half-scratched his head, suddenly looking nervous. "You had Brooke at such a young age," he stumbled through his words. "You are now... well, were very young then."

"Aye, I was," she laughed softly. "'Tis well enough for you to mention my current age. It does not offend me. I am not exactly a young woman anymore, but I am certainly not too old to bear a child."

He snorted, relieved that she wasn't offended by what could have been slander against her age. "Nay, you are not."

"But I am not getting any younger. Perhaps we should make all due haste to conceive a child quickly so I do not die of old age before your son is born."

He gazed at her, his hands moving to her face again. There were a thousand unspoken words that he could not seem to bring to his lips; it seemed as if each day with the woman brought about greater pleasure and surprise. He could hardly believe this side of life existed, one where he was wildly content and with everything he had ever wanted. After a moment, he simply shook his head.

"We have not yet known each other a full month," he murmured. "Speaking of children seems so premature, so... aggressive. I did not marry you in order that you should bear me a child right away."

"I know," her smile remained. "I brought it up, after all. Every man wants a son and it would be my deepest honor to bear yours."

He was truly speechless for a moment. "A son would be the greatest gift, madam," he finally said, sincerely. "Yet I am already the most blessed man in England."

"Why do you say that?"

He kissed her. "Because I have you."

Gray smiled, wrapping her arms around his neck and laying her head on his shoulder. It was a sweet moment broken up by Brooke as she suddenly appeared with a broom in her hand. She thumped the end of the broom on the floor to get the attention of the cuddling adults.

"Sir Braxton?" she asked crisply. "May I ask you something?"

Braxton looked at her as Gray unwound her arms from his neck. "You may," he said. "But first, I must tell you something."

"What?"

"Do not call me Sir Braxton."

Brooke cocked her head. "What should I call you?"

"I am your mother's husband," he informed her of the obvious, "and, I might mention, your new father. You do not need to be so formal with me."

Brooke grinned, a charming smirk that emphasized the dimple in her left cheek. "Shall I call you Dada, then?"

Braxton gave one short, big guffaw that set both Brooke and Gray to giggling. "You cheeky girl," he rumbled, lifting an eyebrow at Brooke. "Call me whatever you wish but do not call me Sir Braxton ever again."

Brooke was still snorting; she leaned down and pecked Braxton on the cheek. "As you command, Dada," she said lightly. "Now, may I ask my question?"

She was taunting him; he could see it. But he was also quite charmed by it and pleased that she felt comfortable enough with him to show some affection. After their tumultuous beginning, he wondered if they would ever reach that state.

"Very well," he sighed. "What is it?"

"Would it be too much trouble to procure a few more servants for the keep?" she asked. "What I mean is that our servants are very old. It is difficult for them to do the amount of work that is now required with all of the people living in the keep. I believe we need some strong, young peasants to help us."

"Brooke," Gray shook her head admonishingly, but Braxton stopped her. He looked as if he was seriously considering her request.

"What would you suggest, Lady Aston?" he asked her.

Brooke cocked her head thoughtfully, leaning on the broom. "We need at least two strong men to help in the kitchens and in the hall. It is too much work for the women with all of the additional people we now have eating and living in the keep," she replied. "I believe we also need at least two or three more women to help out. There is much to do around here and not enough people to do it. Why, I myself must sweep the floor because everyone else is busy."

She suddenly shook the broom at him. Gray was moving to her

feet in outrage but Braxton stood up with her, putting his arm around his wife and giving her a good squeeze to silence her; Brooke was now lady of the keep and must be given that confidence and control.

"I will see what I can do," he assured Brooke patiently. "For now, I will have one of my men do the sweeping. You do not need to do it."

"Oh, good heavens," Gray rolled her eyes and yanked the broom from her daughter's grip. "This conversation is ridiculous. Give me that broom and I shall do the sweeping."

Braxton snatched the broom from her and held it out of her reach. "Nay, Lady de Nerra, you will not," he moved away from her as she swiped at the broom, trying to snatch it from him. He made haste towards the door with Gray following. "Go away from me, woman. You cannot have the broom."

Brooke was laughing uproariously as Gray went after Braxton and he made every effort to stay out of her way. He was too big, fast and agile for her but Gray wasn't make a very strong attempt; her ribs were still sore so she finally surrendered as he gave her a flashy grin and darted out of the front door. Gray stood there with a smirk of her face, shaking her head, as Brooke came up beside her.

"He is funny," she turned to her mother. "Do you really think he is going to find someone to sweep?"

Gray gazed at her daughter, tucking a stray piece of blond hair behind her ear. "Aye, I believe he is going to find someone to sweep," she winked at her child. "Returned to your duties, sweetheart. You are doing a marvelous job."

Brooke flashed a happy grin, thrilled with her mother's approval. "What are you going to do now?"

Gray sighed, her amber gaze lingering on the bailey beyond the door in the hope that she might catch a glimpse of her husband with the broom. "Rest, I suppose," she said. "There isn't anything for me to do and I feel rather useless."

Brooke's smile faded. "You are not useless, mama. Braxton simply doesn't want you to work. This is my keep now and I should be doing all of the work, anyway."

Gray smiled faintly at her daughter, stroking the young woman's blond head before moving to the stairs. Just as she did so, Dallas suddenly came bolting through the keep door with the broom in his hand. He smiled sweetly at his wife, completely ignorant of the fact that his mother-in-law was standing on the stairs just to his left. He had eyes only for Brooke.

"Greetings, Lady Aston," he said jovially. "I have come to sweep your floor."

Brooke blushed furiously as Gray chuckled. "Is this the type of strong, young help you had in mind, Brooke?" she asked.

Brooke's gaze moved between her mother and her husband. "Well... aye, I suppose," she was growing increasingly embarrassed. She focused on her husband. "You do not have to sweep the floor. I can do it. I thought Braxton was going to have one of his soldiers do it."

Dallas winked at her. "I *am* one of his soldiers," he said, glancing over at Gray on the stairs. "Good morning to you, Lady de Nerra. 'Tis a fine day."

He was far too cheerful, more so that Gray had ever seen him. The serious young knight had sprouted a lively personality and bright grin in the past few days. She repressed the urge to laugh at his giddiness which she could only assume had been brought on by the appearance of his wife. It was sweet and hilarious. She smiled at the young knight as she continued her trek up the steps.

"Aye, it is," she replied. "Enjoy sweeping the floor."

Dallas watched the beautiful woman disappear up the stairs before turning to his wife. She gazed up at him adoringly with her luminous blue eyes.

"You really do not have to sweep," she said quietly. "I can do it just as well."

His smile grew warm. "But I want to do it. It gives me an excuse to be close to you."

She batted her eyelashes sweetly at him and he took her hand, leading her back into the hall which was now completely empty.

The dogs were snoring in the corner and the hearth was snapping dully with a low fire. Dallas took her over by the hearth and sat her down on the great table that had been strongly reinforced in the past few days.

"Sit ," he commanded softly as he began to sweep. "Tell me how your day has been so far."

She sat obediently and watched him sweep."It has been well enough," she told him. "The cook and I inventoried the stores this morning. I fear we will be out of white flour in a few days."

He glanced up at her as he swept the old rushes and food into the hearth. "We must remedy that."

"Can we go to town?"

He shook his head. "You will stay here," he said. "I want you here where it is safe."

She was disappointed, sitting somewhat dejected as he continued to sweep. "It is not *that* safe here," she said pointedly. "The walls are falling down and if someone was truly intent on breaching this place, they could."

His eyebrows lifted. "Have you not seen the grounds lately?" he asked, incredulous. "My soldiers have been repairing night and day. The walls are being rebuilt, madam, along with everything else. Both portcullises are now working. Erith is returning to her former glory as we speak."

She made a face. "I have not been outside as of late," she admitted. "I have spent most of my days in the kitchen or here in the hall. Have you seen how nice the keep looks?"

He could see that the rebuilding of the castle didn't impress her nearly as much as the living space that she was in charge of. He smiled at her. "It is an amazing transformation," he assured her. "You have done an exceptional job."

Brooke smiled bashfully. "Do you think so?"

"I do."

Her smile deepened. "Do you think it would be too much if we were to get some fine chairs for the hall? And perhaps even rugs if we have enough money?"

He nodded. "Perhaps," he replied, sweeping briskly. "We shall have the finest keep in all of Cumbria someday."

She looked down at her fingernails, picking at them. "I was hoping that... well, hoping that...."

He looked at her when she didn't finish. "Hoping what?"

She shrugged, suddenly looking uncomfortable. "Well, I was hoping we could go shopping in town together to purchase flour and other fine things for our keep," she continued picking at her nails. "I do not see much of you while we are at Erith. When we travel, it seems as if I see you a great deal. You always seem to be near me."

He paused after sweeping a pile of crumbs into the hearth. "I am sorry," he suddenly didn't feel like sweeping anymore and went over to sit next to her. "Things are very busy at Erith these days. If I had a choice, I would certainly not spend my time away from you. But it is necessary. The castle and her walls must be fortified."

She gazed up at him, smiling faintly. "I know."

He lifted an eyebrow. "We must repair the fortress as much as possible before Gloucester comes."

She suddenly looked fearful. "Will he really come?"

Dallas shrugged, realizing he didn't want to frighten her more than she probably already was. "It is entirely possible. In any case, we must be prepared."

She looked up at him a moment longer before timidly laying her head against his broad shoulder. Dallas dropped the broom and wrapped both arms around her fiercely. He hadn't even been married to her for a week yet he felt such excitement and contentment when she was in his arms, it was as if he had been dreaming of it all of his life. Brooke's innocence, her beauty, her sweetness touched him like no one else ever had. The beautiful wild rose he had once imagined her to be was taming admirably. He still had trouble believing it.

"Do not fret, love," he murmured into the top of her blond head. "Erith will be strong. Our fortress will not fall."

She responded by wrapping her arms around his waist, tightly. "I do not care about Erith so much as I care about you," she whispered. "I have never seen a battle before until the day we returned from Milnthorpe. I am afraid for you."

He smiled faintly, pulling her closer. "No need," he said softly. "All will be well."

She lifted her head and looked up at him. "But how do you know? Those men will be trying to kill you."

"Men have been trying to kill me for five years. No one has yet succeeded."

She frowned at him, unhappy. "That does not mean that your luck will hold out forever," she was sorry she said it even as the words left her mouth. She climbed onto the bench, her knees on the wood and her body pressed up against her husband. While she toyed with his shoulder-length hair, Dallas kept his arms wrapped around her slender torso.

"I just do not want anything to happen to you, 'tis all," she insisted softly. "I am worried."

He sighed faintly as he rubbed her back affectionately. "I appreciate that, but you must not worry," he assured her. "I can do well for myself."

She smiled timidly, accepting his kiss by throwing her arms around his neck and strangling him. It was becoming quite a habit with her and he laughed softly in his throat even as his lips fused to hers.

"Can I please come to town with you?" she asked, her mouth against his.

"Nay," he murmured as his lips suckled hers.

"Why not?"

He was becoming upswept in the lust and passion that seemed to explode whenever he took her in his arms. He was in the process of tasting heavily of her when he heard a soft cough behind him. Somewhat startled, he turned around swiftly to see Braxton standing several feet behind him.

Braxton's expression was grave, a far cry from the jovial man from just a few minutes prior. "I am sorry to intrude," he said, looking at Dallas. "You will come with me."

Simply by the man's tone, Dallas didn't ask questions; he went immediately to Braxton's side, followed by Brooke. But Braxton grasped her by the elbow before she could follow them.

"Nay, lady," he said softly. "You remain here. I only require your husband."

Brooke's big blue eyes followed her husband and Braxton from the keep. When they had quit the keep, she reckoned it would not hurt if she were to go to the door and see where they were going. So she moved to the open entry and stood there, watching them as they disembarked the staircase and headed towards the inner gatehouse.

Brooke watched them move towards a cart that was parked just inside the gatehouse, surrounded by several of Braxton's men. There was a buzz going about as more men dropped what they were doing to come and view the contents of the cart. As men moved aside to allow Braxton and Dallas access, Brooke suddenly saw what had them so interested.

The cart was full of dismembered body parts; arms, legs, torsos and heads. It was blood and carnage like she had never seen and Brook's horror was full blown.

Dallas heard her scream from the keep.

***

"What do you plan to do, Braxton?" Gray's voice was soft with concern.

Braxton gazed down at his wife and daughter; Brooke was cradled against her mother's chest, sobbing softly. Gray was composed as she comforted her daughter but there was fear in her expression. She was remaining strong for Brooke's sake; the young woman was positively distraught and for good reason. Gloucester had sent back the men who had escorted the bodies of Roger and William home back in pieces. The mood surrounding Erith was now dark and somber; bad tidings were in the air. What they had feared was upon them.

"You will not like my answer," Braxton sighed faintly. "Gloucester sent three of my men back dead but left the fourth man alive to deliver a message. I am not going to sit here and wait for Gloucester to come down around us."

Gray lowered her gaze, rocking her daughter gently as the great hall filled with pregnant, horrible anticipation in the wake of Braxton's statement. She could hear men outside shouting and sounding extremely busy; she didn't want to look outside to see what they were doing. She had a suspicion. Braxton's reply only increased her anxiety.

"Tell me what you are planning," she begged quietly.

Braxton heard footfalls entering the hall, glancing to Dallas as the man entered the room in full battle armor. He turned back to his wife.

"I ride for Elswick Castle, the seat of Roger de Clare," he said quietly. "I will lay siege and take the castle a prize."

Gray didn't say anything; she simply closed her eyes and held her daughter tightly. She knew of Elwick Castle, the formidable bastion inhabited by the de Clares. As Dallas reached down to gently pull Brooke from her grasp, Gray stood up to face Braxton.

"Braxton," she murmured. "I would never dream of interfering in military matters, but you surely know that an attack upon Elswick is a critical undertaking."

He put his arm around her, leading her away from where Dallas was comforting Brooke. What he needed to say was for her ears alone.

"You must understand something so there is no mistake," he lowered his voice as they made their way towards the keep entry. "The bodies of those men returned from de Clare were only the beginning. Gloucester plans to attack and he will do to every man and woman at Erith what he did to my soldiers. He will destroy us."

By this time, Gray had come to a stop, gazing at him with incredible fear. She was struggling to keep the tears at bay. "So you plan to attack them first?" she hissed. "How will attacking Elswick make any difference?"

He lifted an eyebrow. "It will make a difference because I intend to confiscate Elswick and hold the remainder of Roger's family hostage as a guarantee that Gloucester will leave Erith alone." As Gray watched, Braxton suddenly turned into the calculating mercenary before her very eyes. She had never seen this side of him, ever. "I might return the wife at some point, but I will keep the children as insurance against de Clare's good behavior."

She stared at him. "Oh... Braxton," she sighed heavily, feeling ill and saddened. "You would do this? They are only children, after all."

"Gloucester would do the same and not give it any thought. The man will know the meaning of what it is to be ruthless before I am finished with him."

Gray could see the cold blooded killer in his eyes and it frightened her; she'd only known the man to be sweet, warm and generous. The transformation was shocking. But upon reflection, she knew that Braxton was the most feared mercenary in England. She was beginning to see why. After a moment, she sighed heavily and looked away.

"I will not tell you how to conduct your business, for these are matters of which I know little," she said quietly. "But I do ask that you remember the children are innocent in all of this, just as Brooke and I are. War is a man's domain. I would plead with you to deal mercifully with the children."

Braxton wasn't oblivious to the way he sounded; he could see in her expression how fearful and disappointed she was. He was well aware she had never seen this side of him, the battle-hardened and brutal warrior, because he had meant it that way. But now the time had come for her to see what he was capable of. He took a couple of steps towards her, taking her hand in his and bringing it to his lips.

"I have always considered myself a merciful man when the situation called for it," he whispered as he kissed her fingers. "I realize this is distasteful to you but you must understand that it is necessary. I will kill, maim and destroy whoever stands in my way in my quest to protect you and Brooke. And that is what this is about, Gray; protection and survival. I intend that Erith and her inhabitants will survive."

She looked at him, understanding what he was telling her. But understanding brought greater fright. "Then you ride to battle," she whispered. "This is all so new to me and I am not ashamed to admit that I am terrified for you."

Braxton could see the tears forming in her eyes. He put his arms around her, holding her tightly and whispering soothingly in her ear.

"Shush," he murmured, rocking her gently. "Have you so little faith in my military prowess?"

The tears were coming now as she felt his warmth, his strength, against her and struggled not to imagine what it would be like without him.

"Oh, Braxton," she whispered against his ear. "I have only just found you. I could not bear it if you were taken away so swiftly. I could not live without you."

He took her face in his hands, kissing her cheeks. "You will not have to," he assured her softly. "But I must make a preemptive move against Gloucester. I have no choice if we are to know a measure of peace."

She gazed back at him, her eyes brimming with unshed tears. "If you feel it is the right thing to do, then I trust you," she whispered. "When must you leave?"

"Before dawn."

"Then we still have tonight."

He nodded faintly, thinking ahead to the emotions, joy and sorrow, that the night would bring. "We do indeed."

She leaned forward, kissing him tenderly, gently suckling on his lower lip before releasing it. "Then perhaps tonight you will give me your son," she breathed. "A child worthy to bear your name."

Braxton closed his eyes as she suckled his lower lip again, feeling his chest tighten with the thought of a future he might not see. He remembered looking in Gray's eyes once and seeing a daughter with her beautiful features and a son with his strength. He wanted with all of his heart to live a long life by her side, raising their children, watching his family grow. He'd never wished such a thing until this very moment. Without another word, he took her upstairs to their chamber.

Back in the great hall, Dallas had hold of Brooke as she clung fiercely to him. Oddly, she wasn't crying any longer; she simply wrapped her arms around Dallas' waist with her head against his chest, eyes tightly closed. He held her close, trying not to jab her with his armor. His mouth and nose were pressed into the top of her head.

"I must make preparations to depart," he said softly. "I will not see you until late tonight, if at all."

She craned her neck back, looking up at him. "I do not want you to go," she breathed. "They will cut you up like they did those other men and send you back to me in pieces."

The corners of his mouth twitched with a smile. "Not if I cut them into pieces first."

Her brows drew together and her lips molded into a pout. "You jest with me and I am serious."

He kissed her forehead. "I am serious as well," he said. "You worry overly, wife. I will return to you whole."

"Can you swear this to me?"

"I can."

Some of the tension seemed to drain from her expression and Dallas took her hand, leading her over to the dining table. He sat down and pulled her onto his lap, all the while thinking of what more he was going to say to her. He'd never faced a situation like this before, leaving someone behind that he deeply cared for. He didn't want her to worry and he very much wanted to return to her safely. He wasn't sure how he could explain everything to her so that she would not panic when he left. When he finally looked up at her, he could see that she was studying him intently.

"Why do you stare at me so?" he asked, smiling faintly.

Brooke cocked her head, a gesture she seemed to do quite often. A finger came up, delicately tracing the shape of his eyebrow, his nose, as her expression remained thoughtful. "Because you are not the husband I imagined I would have," she said softly.

He lifted an eyebrow. "Nor are you the wife I would have imagined to have."

She stopped tracing the shape of his nose. "What do you mean?"

He could see she was verging on insult and his smile broadened. "I simply meant that I never imagined I would marry such a lovely woman," he replied. "And the first time I saw you those weeks ago, I certainly never imagined that I would marry you."

She lowered her hand from his face, smiling because he was. "Do you remember the first time you saw me?"

He nodded firmly. "Absolutely," he replied. "You were hanging over a cliff, screaming."

She puckered her lips, disappointed. "Is that all you remember?"

He shrugged. "I remember that I saved you from certain death."

She slapped him playfully on the shoulder and he laughed low in his throat before growing serious. "To be perfectly honest, my first clear recollection of you was the first night we dined at Erith when you entered the great hall in your grandmother's company," he said, gazing into her blue eyes. "I remember thinking how lovely you were. And how young."

His attempts not to insult her weren't working. "I am not too young," she insisted. "I am fifteen years old. I am a woman."

He lifted an eyebrow, his gaze moving down her delicious torso. "Aye, you are that," he confirmed in a rumbling tone. "You are very much a woman."

She heard the sexual undertones and blushed furiously; she still wasn't used to the games played by men and women. Dallas saw her discomfort and laughed softly, cupping her face and kissing her hot cheek as she averted her gaze.

"You are sweet," he murmured. "And you are distracting me from my duties."

She looked at him. "Can you not stay with me a few more

minutes?"

His smile faded. "The longer I stay with you now, the less chance there is of finishing my duties in a timely manner and returning to you tonight."

She jumped off his lap and yanked on his arm, pulling him to his feet. "Hurry up, then," she began to drag him towards the door. "I will see you this eve."

Dallas let her pull him towards the entry. "I will do my very best," he told her, then grew serious as they neared the door. He finally came to a halt and took hold of her arm, facing her as they stood in the entryway. His expression grew serious.

"Brooke, I know you are fearful with what we may be facing," he said quietly. "But I want to reassure you that I will do everything in my power to keep you, and Erith, safe. It is our castle now, the place where we will raise our family and live out our years together. For that reason alone, I will defend it to the last stone. But for you, I will defend you to the death. That is why we must strike against Gloucester; he threatens you personally and this I will not tolerate. Do you understand?"

She nodded solemnly. "Aye," she said softly. "I... I think that I shall thank you. My mother and Braxton said that you were a good man but I did not understand what they meant until now."

He smiled faintly, reaching out to touch her cheek. "Good can mean many things," he replied. "To me, it means a sense of responsibility and honor, and protecting and caring for those close to me."

She cocked her head again; he loved the gesture. She looked so sweet and innocent. "Am I close to you?"

His smiled widened. "You are the closest. You are my wife."

She smiled faintly. "You told me something once, the day we were married," she said. "You told me that you had not yet given your heart to anyone and that you had saved it for your wife."

He nodded, eyes twinkling. "I recall."

She began to look uncomfortable in the slightest. "Am I on my way to earning it? I am trying, you know."

He laughed softly and pulled her into his arms, rocking her

sweetly. "That you are, sweetheart," he kissed the top of her head. "That you are."

She squeezed him tightly, loving the feel of his embrace. Until she had met Dallas, she'd never knew a man's embrace and was coming to understand what she had been missing. It was all she could have imagined it would be.

"Good," she whispered. "Because you already have mine."

Dallas' smile faded and he pulled back to look at her. He studied her features a moment before replying. "I thank you for that, Lady Aston," he murmured. "It fortifies me more than you know."

Brooke didn't know what else to say; she simply gazed up at him with a timid smile on her face, full of all of the hopes and dreams that a young wife possesses. She was navigating her way through unfamiliar territory and loving every minute of it. Dallas, of course, made things as smooth as they could possibly be. She was truly coming to appreciate him.

"Go now," she urged. "I will see you later this eve. Shall I send sup out to you?"

He was about to reply when shouting from the inner bailey caught his attention. He bolted out on to the stair landing just outside the entry, bellowing to the men on the walls. Startled, Brooke instinctively followed him out onto the steps, watching as men began racing in from the outer bailey.

There was a huge amount of commotion as men began scrambling for their weapons. The portcullises were beginning to grind. Whatever was happening, they were struggling to prepare. Brooke stood next to Dallas, her mouth open with surprise and some fear, when he abruptly turned to her and shoved her back inside.

"Get inside and bolt this door," he commanded. "Do not open it for anyone other than Braxton, me or the other knights. Is that clear?"

She almost stumbled as he thrust her back into the keep. She opened her mouth to reply but was interrupted when Braxton suddenly bolted past her from the upper floors. He didn't say a word; he took the stairs down to the bailey far too quickly and began issuing commands in a hurry. Brooke's measure of surprise was replaced in whole by fear.

"What is happening?" she begged. "Tell me what is wrong."

Dallas didn't have time to explain; he grabbed her face between his big hands and kissed her firmly. "Go inside," he jabbed a finger at her as he began to rapidly descend the stairs. "Bolt the door and stay there."

Brooke watched him go with tears filling her eyes but she did as she was told. She slammed the door and threw the big iron bolt, turning just in time to see her mother descending the stairs from the upper floor. The two women stared at each other, wide-eyed, as the sounds of commotion in the bailey filtered in through the slit windows.

"What is wrong?" Brooke went to her mother. "Did Braxton tell you?"

Gray was a little dazed; she and Braxton had been in the midst of passionate lovemaking when he had heard the shouts from the walls. He had bolted from their bed quickly, telling her to stay to the keep. Gray dressed quickly, peering from her window only to see a measure of the road beyond Erith. Upon it, she clearly saw soldiers that did not belong to Braxton and her heart surged into her throat. Whatever was occurring she knew, instinctively, that it was not good.

Therefore, it was difficult to answer her daughter. She could read the panic in Brooke's face and did not want to frighten her further. But a volley of arrows over the walls came crashing into the keep, two of the arrows finding their way inside the small lancet window just to the right of the entry door. Brooke screamed and threw her arms around her mother as Gray pulled her daughter away from the open window. They began smelling smoke, having no idea at the time that Graehm was at the base of the stairs leading into the keep, burning them. Braxton had ordered all access to the keep cut off; no matter who was attacking Erith, they would not get the women under any circumstances.

Erith, the recently rebuilt fortress, was under siege.

CHAPTER SEVENTEEN

Brooke remembered the days of quiet at Erith, days that brought with them the uncertainty of where their next meal was coming from. She clearly remembered weeks upon weeks, especially in the winter months, when they had gone without meat. Life at Erith had been difficult, quiet, forgotten by the world. She had not been content in the least. With the introduction of a new husband over the past few weeks, Brooke was coming to see what treasures and wonders life truly held for her. She hadn't wanted to marry Dallas but now she couldn't remember when the man had not been with her. And she didn't know what she was going to do without him.

The sounds of battle had been going on for three days. Heavy smoke filled the air as the sounds of screaming and fighting filled the ambient air like a surreal backdrop. Brooke and Gray stayed to the hall, comforting the few servants that had managed to be inside the keep and trying not to starve to death in the process. The kitchen stores were on the ground floor below them but the only way to get to them was outside. By the end of the second day, they had been out of wood for the hearth. Now, they were nearly out of what food they had managed to scrounge.

Gray was going without food again simply so the others would have something to eat. She hadn't eaten in almost two days and was looking pale and very weak. Brooke tried to coerce her into eating some stale bread crust, but Gray simply smiled and insisted that her child eat instead. The three servants sat huddled in the corner with the whining dogs, whispering among themselves about the virtues of dog meat. As night fell on the third day and a dog in the hall suddenly yelped and went silent, Brooke stood near the lancet window in the entry and cried. She knew the servants were eating the dog and soon her mother would insist she partake. She didn't want to do it. She wanted to see Dallas and she wanted to get out of the keep.

She couldn't even see the bailey beyond very well; Gray wouldn't let her get too close to the window so the best she could do was stand there and listen to the chaos below. So she stood there, pale and drawn from weeping and hunger, wrapped in one of her lovely new cloaks and praying for any sign from her husband. It seemed to her that the fighting had shifted for it didn't seem as loud as it once was; perhaps the armies were taking a rest from their marathon battle and perhaps that meant Dallas would soon appear with food and wood for the hearth.

As Brooke stood near the lancet window and dreamed of a better time, a body suddenly appeared in the window. Brooke shrieked and rushed at it, trying to push it through, but the body in the opening protested vehemently.

"Brooke, stop!" It was Edgar, wedged into the skinny window. "Stop pushing! You are going to kill me!"

Brooke shrieked again when she realized who it was and she grabbed hold of Edgar instead, pulling him through the window. The youth fell to the floor with a thud, drawing Gray from the other room. Gray came running into the entry, her eyes wide at her husband's squire.

"Edgar!"she exclaimed. "Why are you here?"

Edgar was filthy and had a nice cut on his right forearm but was otherwise unharmed. He stood up and rubbed his elbow where he had smacked it against the floor.

"Sir Braxton sent me," he said as he dashed between the women and threw the big iron bolt on the entry door. He yanked open the door and shouted to those below. "Up here!"

Gray closed her eyes tightly at the sound her husband's name, fairly close to collapse. "Braxton is well?" she asked the boy.

Ladders were being propped up against the keep, coming to rest just beyond the bottom of the door frame. Edgar steadied them as he answered.

"Aye, m'lady," he said. "He is well. So is Sir Dallas. But Sir Graehm took an arrow to the chest yesterday and died."

Gray murmured a prayer for both Braxton's safety and Graehm's death. "What of Geoff?" Gray wanted to know. "He was caught outside when all of this happened and he is not nearly healed from his neck wound."

A ladder was being raised to the edge of the door from the bailey below. Edgar held the vertical post firm as men began to mount the ladder from below.

"He is well, too," the lad said. "Not a scratch."

Gray was relieved beyond words. She stood there, pale and trembling, as Braxton was the first one to reach the top of the ladder. One look at his wife and he propelled himself off the ladder and into her arms. He was grimy, sweaty, smelly and exhausted, but it didn't matter. Gray clung to him, weeping softly.

"All is calm, sweet," he squeezed her so tightly that he was sure he heard bones crack. Then his lips began moving over her ears and cheeks. "Are you well?"

She sniffled, wiping away the tears of joy and relief. "Fine," she murmured. "Just a bit hungry. We've not had anything to eat for a day or so."

He was already nodding even as the words left her mouth, snapping orders to Edgar, who leapt out the lancet window and took the rope down to the bailey because Dallas was on the ladder.

"Edgar will bring some food," Braxton told her, holding her face in his dirty hands just to get a look at her. "You appear tired. Have you not slept?"

She was more concerned with him than with her own needs. "Do not worry about me," she turned the subject around. "Are you well? What is happening out there?"

Braxton kissed her, gently and with great emotion, before putting his arm around her shoulder and leading her towards the great hall.

"Come and sit," he murmured. "There is much to discuss."

As Braxton led Gray into the cold and dank hall, Dallas reached the top of the ladder. Brooke was standing there, jumping up and down with excitement, and he swept her into his arms as one would carry a child. She threw her arms around his neck, joyfully strangling him, as he carried her towards the hall without a word. Brooke didn't utter a sound; she simply squeezed him tightly, eyes closed and face pressed into the side of his head. Dallas was so exhausted and emotional that, for a moment, he didn't trust himself to speak. He could see that Braxton was taking Gray into the hall and he knew why; he and Brooke would join them.

Braxton was helping Gray sit on the bench just as Dallas approached carrying Brooke. He set her down opposite her mother, removing his helm and setting it on the table as he called for water from one of the servants. One of the three who had dined on dog meat went running to do his bidding. Meanwhile, both Braxton and Dallas began to remove various piece of armor, like gloves and helms that had been on their bodies for three days. There was great weariness to their movements.

"What is happening, Braxton?" Gray asked softly. "Has the fighting stopped?"

Braxton raked his fingers through is dark blond hair, scratching his scalp with some satisfaction. "For now," he told her. "But it is a temporary lull. They will be back."

The fear returned to Gray's expression. "How do you know?"

Braxton was still in battle mode, trying not to be harsh or abrupt with her. "Because they have not left the area," he told her. "They have simply pulled back to regroup and, I suspect, await reinforcements."

Gray's eyes widened. "Reinforcements?" she repeated. "From where? Who has attacked Erith?"

"Gloucester," he told her the obvious. "When they sent the bodies of my men back, the entire army had come as escort, only they were hiding to the trees and I did see them. Stupid in hindsight; I should have suspected something like that. In any case, they could not breach Erith's inner wall and they have retreated to try again another day."

Gray was stunned, frightened. She didn't dare look at Brooke. All she knew was that her entire life was at stake and especially her daughter's. It made her terrified and angry at the same time, her mind brittle from lack of food and sleep. She abruptly stood, pacing over to the cold hearth where a servant was laying out peat and wood. As the man attempted to start a fire, Gray came to a halt, her gaze moving over the great hall of Erith, the only home she had ever known.

"What doom has been brought upon us?" she whispered rhetorically. "Are we to now know a greater measure of horror than we have ever experienced?"

Braxton could hear the desolation in her voice and moved to comfort her. "I would not worry so," he told her quietly. "Gloucester sent a few hundred men, thinking they could easily raze Erith. But they had no idea that we had reinforced and rebuilt so much of her, which is why I suspect they are waiting for reinforcements. It was not an easy task as they originally thought. That gift of time will allow us to prepare a reception for them when they come again."

She looked at him. "I do not understand your words," she said. "What do you mean?"

Braxton's blue-green eyes twinkled. "Now that I know they are returning, I can formulate a plan of resistance and counter attack. Erith will not be an easy target, I assure you, but I am greatly concerned that you and Brooke will be within the walls when Gloucester returns."

Gray cocked her head as if having no idea what he was getting at. "This is our home. We will stay here."

He went to her, putting his hands on her arms. "Sweetheart, listen to me," he said softly. "I want to remove you and Brooke and send you somewhere safe. I do not want you here when Gloucester returns."

Gray stared at him. Then she pulled from his grasp, her amber eyes blazing. "I am not leaving my home and neither is my daughter," she was angry, exhausted and unbalanced. "I am not leaving."

Braxton was exhausted, too. He struggled to maintain his calm with her, having been in battle mode for days. His usual patience was slipping.

"Please, sweet," he was laboring not to come across as hard

and commanding with her. "If you remain at Erith, my focus will be divided and I must maintain all of my focus on the battle. Your distraction could prove deadly if my mind is not where it should be."

She gazed at him, looking horrified and accusing at the same time. "Are you saying it would be my fault if you were killed because I do not want to leave my home?"

Braxton pushed himself to calm before things got out of hand, reaching out to grasp her again and put his arms around her. "I am simply saying that removing you from Erith would relieve my mind considerably," he kissed her pale cheek, noticing that Edgar was back with a sack full of food. He pulled Gray to sit once more. "Sit down before you fall down. Come have something to eat and we shall continue this conversation when we are both feeling better."

Shaking, pale, Gray allowed him to sit her back down at the table as Edgar rushed up and began to pull food out of the sack; he put three big loaves of bread on the table plus two chunks of white cheese, three small apples, several handfuls of walnuts, and a bundle of dried jerky that was tied off with dried grass. As Braxton and Dallas began dividing the food up for the women, Norman suddenly popped up through the floor from the lower level kitchens with a hogshead barrel of wine in his grip. He rolled the barrel out onto the floor, leapt off the ladder, and reclaimed the barrel as he made his way over to the table. Servants and two soldiers were following him with cups and other morsels of food.

Braxton's first order of refreshment was the wine. He poured, and drank, two big cups before pouring himself a third and slowing down his intake. He sat next to Gray, his focus on the open entry door and the commotion going on down in the bailey as he slowly swallowed his third cup of wine. He was thinking on the siege engines his men were quickly constructing, wondering if they would do the damage to de Clare's incoming army as he hoped, when he glanced over at Gray and noticed how the woman was wolfing down her bread. Her starving actions

281

brought waves of remorse, of guilt and sadness, and he reached up a big hand and put it gently on the back of her head, affectionately, as if to silently apologize what she had been through.

He glanced over his shoulder, looking across the table to Brooke and Dallas; his knight was perched on the table next to his wife, cutting off only the best pieces of jerky for her. Brooke gobbled them up like a little bird, fairly starving herself. His gaze met with Dallas' and the younger knight wriggled his eyebrows as if to acknowledge what horrors the women must have endured closed up in the keep while the men were down in the ward fighting off de Clare's army. It frustrated Braxton all the more; he only wanted to spoil and pamper his wife and daughter, not force them into hardship. He found himself cursing Constance yet again for bringing all of this upon them; even though she was no longer present at Erith, she was still wreaking havoc. Like ripples on the water, the repercussions kept coming and coming.

But Braxton was still determined to emerge the victor, no matter what the old woman had started. He began to rethink his strategy of forcing Gray away from Erith. Perhaps if he put it to her another way....

"Sweetheart," he leaned over, kissing her on the temple. "Can I make a suggestion?"

Gray was chewing on an apple. "What is that?"

He watched her cut pieces of apple with a small knife. "Well," his free hand began to stroke her shoulder; he wanted to come across gentle and persuasive, which seemed to be the best way to deal with her. "I know of a wonderful place in Lancaster where you and Brooke could go for a time until this madness is over. It is an inn built on the foundations of an old Roman bathhouse and they have the most marvelous amenities. "

Gray was looking at him curiously but across the table, Brooke had heard him also. She perked up. "Amenities? What does that mean?" she asked.

Braxton was smart enough to capitalize on Brooke's interest;

he thought that if perhaps he got the young woman interested, then Gray would surely follow.

"It means services and features," he told her. "First of all, every bed chamber is luxurious with silks and furs, and the food is the best in the city. They serve things like baked fish with raisins and onions, and sweets made from pears and honey. They also have women whose only job is to bathe you, massage you, dress you, and tend to your every need. If you want them to scratch your back all day, they will do it without complaint."

By this time, Brooke's eyes were alive with delight. "Truly?" she sighed.

"Truly."

"Have you been to this place?"

He nodded. "I was there once for a meal," he said. "I met a baron there who... well, suffice it to say that we supped together and the food and accommodations were remarkable."

Brooke shoved a piece of cheese into her mouth, chewing as she hung on his every word. "What did you have to eat?"

He thought a moment. "I had beef soaked in wine with peppercorns and pine nuts, and apricots with mint and honey, and other delights," he cast a glance at Gray to make sure she was listening. "But the accommodations were surely the best in the world. I slept on a bed of silk, bathed in an enormous bath with painted tiles, and was surrounded by a half dozen servants. I never had to lift a finger for any want or need; they ensured every wish was fulfilled."

Brooke swallowed the food in her mouth, obviously entranced by his description. She looked at Dallas. "Have you been there also?"

Dallas nodded, looking drolly at Braxton. "I was there, but I remained outside while Braxton lived like an emperor. I was not fortunate enough to be treated to such luxury."

Brooke giggled. "Do... do you think we can go there someday? I want to see the Roman baths."

Dallas smiled, stroking her soft cheek which was starting to regain some color to it. "Of course," he said. "If that is your wish."

"Perhaps you would like to go now until this business with de Clare is finished," Braxton suggested. "You and your mother could live the life of luxury while your husband and I finish off Gloucester. We will come and join you when we are finished."

He threw out the big bait and held his breath as Brooke looked at Dallas and then to her mother. In fact, he turned to look at Gray, too, as if she was the deciding factor in the vote. But Gray remained focused on her apple, chewing slowly and thoughtfully. Gently, Braxton collected her free hand and kissed it.

"I am sure you would enjoy it," he said softly. "It would be much better than staying here in this dank place, starving for days on end while a battle goes on around you. You could be treated to the finished luxury England has to offer; food aplenty, soft beds, fine clothes, and servants tending to your every whim. And you and Brooke could go shopping daily and buy more finery than you know what to do with; a new surcoat for every hour, a new necklace for every mood, and perfumes for every day of the week. Does that sound appealing, sweetheart?"

With all eyes on her, Gray could see what he was doing; she wasn't stupid. She knew he was very nicely trying to convince her to leave Erith. She looked at him, her amber eyes glimmering.

"It does," she said quietly. "And you are most sweet and generous to suggest it. But I would be living like a queen, wondering if I still had a husband. Braxton, none of that means anything without you. I could not be living a carefree life knowing that you were fighting for your every existence. What kind of wife would I be if I could forget your peril so easily?"

Braxton could see that she wasn't being deliberately stubborn; she truly meant what she said. He kissed her gently.

"You would a wife giving her husband peace of mind," he whispered. "If I know you are happy and well, I can move mountains. Please do this for me."

She set the apple down on the table and hung her head. Braxton put his arms around her, his forehead to hers, feeling her body as it began to shake with soft sobs. He knew she was distraught; he was distraught, too, but he truly believed it was best for her. The mood of the room turned painful, uncertain, as Braxton tried to comfort his wife. Across the table, Dallas suddenly spoke.

"Although I will respect Lady de Nerra's decision to remain or to leave, I intend to make the decision that I feel best for my wife and I," he cleared his throat as he looked at Brooke, taking her soft hand in his. "I, for one, do not want you here when Gloucester returns. I intend to send you away until I can come for you. If you wish to go to Braxton's inn in Lancaster, I will send you there happily. It would bring me comfort knowing you are content and well cared for."

Brooke's luminous blue eyes bulged. "You... you would send me away?" she looked at Gray, almost in panic. "But what about my mother?"

Dallas was firm but not unsympathetic. "What she and Braxton decide is their own affair," he said, caressing her hand. "But I must do what I feel is best for you."

Brooke bolted to her feet. "I am not leaving without my mother."

By this time, Gray had lifted her head to look at what was transpiring between her daughter and Dallas. "Dallas, she is my daughter and...."

"It does not matter if she is your daughter," Dallas cut her off, his attention returned to Brooke. "She is my wife and I will make the decisions for her. She will go to Lancaster until this madness is through."

Brooke burst into tears and Gray looked to Braxton in a panic. "I do not want her away from me," she said, her lower lip quivering. "Please do not let him send her away."

Braxton tried to soothe her even though he completely agreed with Dallas. "Then your only choice is to go with her. Dallas says she is going and she is."

"But...."

"Go with her, sweetheart. It is what I want."

Gray hung her head and now the men had both women in tears. Braxton cast a long glance at Dallas, silently urging the man to take Brooke away. As it was, the two women were playing off each other's emotions and Braxton needed Gray's full attention. He knew that ultimately she would do as he asked but he didn't want her being hysterical about it.

Dallas stood up from the table he had been perched on and put his big arm around Brooke's shoulder, leading her away from the table. But Brooke resisted so he swooped down and picked her up, carrying her off towards the spiral stairs that led up to the bed chambers. When Dallas and Brooke were free of the hall, Braxton put his big hands on Gray's face and forced her to look at him.

"Listen to me," he murmured, kissing her wet cheeks. "I will send you to Lancaster with Edgar and a few soldiers as escort. I will also send you with enough money to keep you well supplied for months. You can stay at the inn and indulge yourself until I come for you. All that matters to me is that you are safe, happy and whole. It will ease me tremendously so I can focus on more important matters. Do you understand?"

She nodded, wiping at her eyes. "But I do not want to leave you."

"And I do not want to leave you. But I must have you safe. You are the most important thing in the world to me, Gray. Without you, there is nothing to live for. I could not bear it if something happened to you."

She looked at him, the amber eyes spilling over, silently conveying all of the emotions that a thousand words could not adequately express. After a moment, she wrapped her arms around his neck, holding him tightly, her mouth by his ear.

"I love you, Braxton," she whispered. "My life was reborn the day I met you. Please… please do not leave me."

He held her tightly, the pain of their impending separation already filling him. "I will never leave you," he murmured. "I will always been with you, until the end of time, in this life or in the one beyond. I will always be there."

His words brought her sweet and painful comfort. Gray knew there was nothing more to say. Nothing would change his mind and the decision had been made. She was distraught, exhausted and ill, her head eventually coming to rest on his shoulder as Braxton held her tightly. Eventually, he stood up and scooped her into his arms as Dallas had done with Brooke. Gray simply wrapped her arms around his big neck and lay her head on his shoulder as he carried her towards the spiral stairs.

Just as Braxton mounted the bottom step, Geoff mounted the top rung of the ladder and appeared in the entry. His pale face was lined with exhaustion and there was a big, dirty bandage on his neck, but he was surprisingly alert and strong. Braxton caught sight of him and paused before he took the stairs.

"What is it?" he asked.

Geoff had an odd expression. "We have a rider, Braxton," he said, moving to scratch his red head as if greatly confused. "De Aughton is here. He says he needs to speak with you."

Gray's head shot up and she focused on Geoff with surprise. Then she looked at her husband fearfully. "De Aughton?" she repeated.

Braxton wasn't particularly surprised but he was curious. "Did he say why he needs to speak with me?"

"He did not. Shall I bring him to the hall?"

Braxton nodded. "Bring him in," he said, swinging back around for the stairs and beginning to mount them. "I will settle my wife and be down shortly."

Geoff nodded sharply and was gone. As Braxton mounted the steps to their third floor chamber, Gray watched his expression with a mixture of curiosity and fear.

"Why do you suppose he is here?" she asked.

He reached the landing and moved to their chamber door, kicking the panel open as he entered.

"I could not guess," he set her down gently, realizing that their small bed with its warm linens looked quite inviting; he was absolutely exhausted. "But I intend to find out. Now, I want you to lie down for a time. I will be back shortly."

"But...."

He looked at her sharply, his expression laced with fatigue.

"Please, Gray," he snapped softly. "Does everything have to be an argument with you today?"

She blinked, hurt by his tone but realizing he was right. She had done nothing but argue with him since the moment he had climbed off the ladder from the bailey. She didn't want any more harsh words or bad feelings between them. She hadn't seen the man in days. Contrite, she shook her head.

"Nay, Braxton," she said obediently. "It does not. I apologize."

He looked at her, realizing he'd been snappish, and leaned over to kiss her cheek. "As do I," he murmured, kissing her again. "I did not mean to be curt. Please lie down and I will return as soon as I know why de Aughton is here."

She smiled at him and he returned the gesture, winking at her as he quit the room and quietly closed the door behind him. Gray stood there a moment, her thoughts going with him, wondering with increasing trepidation as to why Niclas de Aughton had reappeared. But her curiosity wasn't enough to overcome her fatigue and she obediently took to her bed just as she had promised him.

She was asleep before her head hit the pillow.

In Brooke and Dallas' chamber on the floor above, it was anything but still and quiet. After a temper tantrum and tears, Dallas had made up with his wife the only way he could think of; he was preparing to make love to her. But he wasn't moving fast enough pulling off his armor and Brooke almost ripped his ears off again removing his hauberk. They laughed as the hauberk hit the floor, he rubbed his ears, and pulled Brooke into his arms once more, kissing her amorously. But there was more clothing that needed to come off so in between heated kisses, they managed to rip off every last stitch of clothing and fall together on the bed.

Dallas was grimy and sweaty, but it didn't matter to Brooke. She was just glad to have him warm and alive in her arms. Over the past several weeks, she had become sexually insatiable and

Dallas, although understandably overjoyed, found himself aroused in the oddest situations; he'd taken her several times in the stables, in the kitchens, once in Erith's big armory in the southwest tower, and at least twice a day in their bedchamber. Her young, nubile body was agile and responsive, so much so that Dallas was finding himself a slave to her desires. All she had to do was look at him or touch him and he was instantly aroused, visions of mounting her sweet body filling his brain. He couldn't get enough of her.

But it was more than that now. Even as he pushed her onto her back and suckled her tender nipples, he felt more emotion for the woman than he had ever felt in his life, for anyone. He tasted her flesh, listened to her soft grunts of pleasure, and it overwhelmed him. When he rose to his knees and wedged himself between her slender legs, pulling her pelvis against his, all he could think of was how beautiful and sweet she was. And when he finally buried his manhood deep inside her slick body, all he could think of was how much he loved her.

Dallas thrust into her repeatedly, feeling her body respond to his as if God had made her for him exclusively. She wrapped her legs around his buttocks, keeping him buried tightly inside of her as their bodies moved together as one. In little time, he could feel her multiple releases and it threw him over the edge, spilling himself deep. He lay against her afterwards, feeling their hearts pounding, smelling her gentle musky scent and wishing that he could spend the rest of his life with her just as they were.

Brooke's small hands caressed him, moving over his back, his arms, finally coming to rest on is buttocks, which she stroked gently. He could tell by her touch that she felt for him as he felt for her. Their feelings for each other were strong and enduring, growing more solidified by the day. In little time he was hard again and he resumed making love to her as the day began to wane.

After the third round of lovemaking, they lay sweaty and intertwined in each other beneath the linens. Brooke's eyes were closed and he was sure she was sleeping, but he couldn't help touching her face as he studied her. She was such a lovely creature. When he touched her nose, she wrinkled it up and scratched at it. Then her blue eyes opened, fixing on him.

Dallas smiled at her. "Did I wake you?"

She returned his smile. "No," she whispered, taking the hand that was on her head and putting it on her bare breast. He squeezed and she wrapped her legs around him, arching her pelvis against his. "I have missed you."

He fondled her pert and perfect breast gently. "And I have missed you," he murmured. "In fact, there is something you should know."

She closed her eyes as he began to play with a taut nipple. "What is that?"

"You have my heart, Brooke."

She paused in her pleasure, opening her eyes to look at him. Her expression morphed into one of surprise.

"I do?" she asked, amazed.

He nodded, smiling at her reaction. "You do," he whispered. "I love you very much."

She stared at him. Then, the most miraculous smile came over her lips and she threw her arms around his neck, enthusiastically strangling him. "Oh, Dallas," she murmured. "I love you also. I love you more than anything."

He laughed low in his throat, holding her close. There wasn't much more he could say at that point so he let his body do the talking for him. He made love to her once more, every move and every sensation infused with the deep love they felt for one another. Dallas had never been happier or more content, knowing he shared something with Brooke that few people ever experienced in their lifetime. He felt blessed. But he refused to think on the upcoming separation, knowing it would probably hurt him more than it hurt her. Already, it was killing him.

Exhausted, content, he fell into a deep sleep next to his wife.

CHAPTER EIGHTEEN

"Your father is less than a day behind me, my lord," de Aughton said. "He told me to tell you that Northumberland has sent him to discover the truth about your association with Lady Gray."

Seated across from de Aughton at the table in the banqueting hall, Braxton's eyebrows slowly lifted. "Association?"

Niclas's black eyes flickered; for a moment, he looked uncomfortable. "A missive was delivered to your father from Lord de Vesci on behalf of the Lady Constance Gray de Montfort. Apparently, Lady de Montfort feels that her daughter is with you against your will and has asked Lord de Vesci to intervene. Your father rides to Erith to sort out the situation."

Braxton, exhausted as he was, found that he wasn't as in control of his emotions as he usually was. He scowled at de Aughton.

"That is madness," he hissed, wiping both hands over his face as the news sank in. "I exiled the woman from Erith and somehow she has made her way back to her family in Northumberland, now to spread more lies about me."

De Aughton wasn't privy to the politics that had gone on between Lady Constance and Braxton and was unsure how to reply.

"De Vesci is very concerned, apparently; enough to send your father to investigate."

Braxton just looked at him, sighing heavily. "Lady Constance is a cunning liar and a grand opportunist," he snapped softly. "That woman has been seeking to destroy me since nearly the moment I met Gray."

Niclas could see the man was genuinely upset. "I told your father that, from what I witnessed, Lady Gray was not with you against her will," he wriggled his eyebrows. "I can attest to the fact that she will not be separated from you and I sincerely doubt it is because she is afraid of you or being held hostage."

In the midst of his outrage, Braxton saw humor in the statement. Whereas before he would not let himself succumb to any emotion in front of Niclas, now, he wasn't so careful about it. There was no reason to be. He eventually shook his head as if baffled by the entire circumstance.

"Gray and I married because we love one another," he said simply. "Gray's mother has been trying to sell off her granddaughter to the highest bidder since the girl came of marriageable age and she is furious that I interrupted her plans by marrying Brooke to one of my knights. That old bitch has been trying my patience since the moment I met her; all of the chaos you saw out in the bailey, the battle scars and damage, are because of her."

De Aughton toyed with his cup of wine, a better quality product since Braxton and his money had overtaken the keep.

"I saw an army camped about three miles to the east," he said quietly. "I would assume they are your antagonists?"

Braxton nodded faintly. "They are," he looked at de Aughton and thought the man might deserve some explanation. "It is Roger de Clare's army. They are awaiting reinforcements from Gloucester."

Niclas' eyebrows lifted. "Gloucester?" he repeated, incredulous. "Why on earth are they harassing you?"

Braxton took a swallow of the Spanish Port wine. "Because Gray's mother sent a missive to them promising Brooke's hand in marriage, only Brooke was already married by the time they arrived here to negotiate the contract," he sighed, glancing around the walls of the great old hall. "In the confusion surrounding that, Roger and his heir were accidentally killed. Gloucester is understandably upset about it and, I would assume, is planning on razing Erith in punishment."

Niclas understood a great deal in that quiet explanation. Braxton seemed angry more than anything, a fury to which he was indeed entitled. It was an extremely serious matter. But it also brought up another serious issue, one he was hesitant to mention but felt, for the sake of them both, that he must.

"Gloucester and Northumberland are allies," Niclas' voice was quiet, hesitant. "Your father serves Northumberland. If he is ordered to support Gloucester, then we have a problem on our hands."

Braxton looked at him. ""My father is sworn to Northumberland but I doubt that it will supersede family ties, and at such time we will indeed have a problem because I am sure my father will support me. It is therefore my father with the problem and not me."

De Aughton understood that completely. "May I offer advice, my lord?"

Braxton lifted his hands in a helpless gesture. "Please."

Niclas set down the cup, his obsidian eyes intense. "Remove Lady Gray and her daughter from Erith immediately," he said. "The longer you delay, the more chance there will be that you will never be able to remove them from Erith. If Gloucester returns with reinforcements as you have said, then your wife and her daughter will be in mortal danger. I am not sure how your father is going to react to all of this so it is better to remove the women. We could have a bloodbath on our hands with all of these politics converging."

Braxton nodded slowly, finishing off his wine. "I realize that," he said. "And I have already made plans to remove them. In fact, they will be vacated from the castle before the day is through."

Niclas nodded, in complete agreement. "Where are you sending them?"

Braxton wriggled his eyebrows. "You should know that my wife is an exceptionally stubborn woman," he said. "She does not want to leave Erith no matter how much I plead or threaten, so I resorted to bribery. I am sending her to Lancaster with promises of shopping trips and luxurious accommodations."

Niclas' brow furrowed. "You are sending her to the city?"

"Aye." Braxton noticed an expression of doubt on Niclas' face. "And why not?"

Niclas realized that Braxton had deciphered his slightly

confused countenance and hastened to recover. He didn't want to seem critical or superior. "I would assume she is staying some place fortified?"

Braxton shook his head. "A very luxurious inn where her every whim will be catered to. I fear it is the only way I could convince her to leave, mostly because her daughter very much wants to go there. If Brooke goes, then Gray will follow."

Niclas stared at him a moment before shaking his head and averting his gaze. It was clear he disapproved. Braxton caught on and he leaned forward on the table.

"Why do you look so? You disagree?"

Niclas shook his head. Then he shrugged. "In my humble opinion, if Gloucester tracks her to such a place, there will be no protection for her at all. They will be able to take her without a fight and you will find yourself at their mercy."

Braxton lifted an eyebrow. "I realize that," he said. "I am sending her with a contingent of men, designed to protect and watch over her," he said as if Niclas had pegged him for an idiot. "The men understand that if my wife is followed, they are to remove her immediately. These men are cunning and seasoned; they will not allow her to come to harm."

Niclas could see that Braxton was riled so he maintained his cool demeanor. "I have no doubt of your foresight, my lord," he said. "However, if it were me, I would send her to an allied fortress. At least there, you know she would be amply protected and you would not have to worry. Do you not have an ally you can send her to?"

Braxton thought a moment. "Aye," he said slowly. "There is a castle to the north, near Kendal, called Creekemere. Baron Wenvoe and I have an understanding."

"Then send her there until this is over. If it were my wife, I would not send her anywhere else for my own peace of mind."

Braxton stared at the man a moment, digesting his advice, realizing as the fog began to clear that he was absolutely right. Braxton had been trying so hard to appease his wife and daughter that he had been lax in their security, the very reason he was sending them away in the first place. He had let his emotions get the better of him, not the facts that he knew so well. Niclas was correct; if Gloucester caught wind of Gray and Brooke somewhere they could easily breach, then the ladies' lives would be in far more danger. He would have to suffer through their tears and denials and do what he felt best; send them to a fortress where they would be protected, even if it was tiny Creekmere.

Braxton finally stood up, realizing he had a lot of work ahead of him, things he had to fix as a result of his own short-sightedness. The time for pleasantries was gone.

"Find my father and tell him the situation," he said. "Let him know that Gloucester is about to hammer us. Meanwhile, I will send my wife and daughter someplace safe. I thank you for your prudent advice."

Niclas rose quickly, collecting his helm and heading for the door. "Do you wish for me to escort them, my lord?"

Braxton looked at the man; although he had proven himself reliable and wise since the incident outside of Milnthorpe, he still didn't trust the man completely where Gray was concerned. Niclas still had that hunger to his eyes when discussing Lady de Nerra and Braxton wasn't so sure if he sent Gray with the man that he would ever see her again. Still, the coming conflict left him unable to spare Dallas or Graehm to escort the ladies; it would have been desirable to have at least once seasoned knight as their protection. But not de Aughton.

"Nay," he said after a moment. "I am sure my father will require your services should this situation get out of hand."

"Your father has ten knights under his command," Niclas told him. "I can be spared should you require my assistance."

Braxton's gaze lingered on him. "You will understand if I decline your offer, de Aughton. Although I appreciate your generosity, I will again say no. Go now and tell my father the situation."

"By your command, my lord."

"And tell him to hurry."

"Aye, my lord."

Braxton watched Niclas dash from the keep, all the while just the least bit frustrated with himself for not having seen the situation with his wife as clearly as he should have. As he ascended the stairs to their second floor chamber, he ran into Dallas descending from the top floor where he and Brooke slept. A few words to Dallas relayed the situation, the decision, and Dallas heartily agreed.

As Dallas retraced his steps back to the top floor to prepare his wife for her journey to Creekmere, Braxton entered the chamber he shared with Gray only to find her sleeping peacefully. He paused a moment, gazing at her, thinking he'd never in his life loved someone, or something, as much as he loved her. She was everything to him, his very reason for living and breathing. He didn't want to be separated from her and he didn't want her to be miserable, but life wasn't always the ease one hoped for. Just when Gray was beginning to experience the life of love and luxury she deserved, her happiness was about to take another downturn.

So was his.

***

Thomas de Nerra entered the outer gatehouse of Erith Castle, looking around the place with great curiosity. He'd heard of Erith, of course, one of Simon de Montfort's holdings and knew that the castle had seen great men of history pass through her halls. But the castle around him, though big and bulky and marginally fortified, still seemed like a shell of its former reputation. To him, it looked like a ghost.

Gray stone and much rebuilding met him as he entered the inner bailey. Several of Braxton's men came out to greet the party, having been told of their impending arrival. A tall, blond knight greeted them formally in the dusty, cluttered inner ward.

"My lords," Dallas said to the general group dismounting their expensive chargers. "I am Sir Dallas Aston, Sir Braxton's second in command."

Thomas turned to the young knight, inspecting the man just as he had inspected the keep; the blue-green eyes missed nothing, as sharp as a hawk.

"Where is my son?" he asked, removing his mail gloves.

Dallas could immediately see the resemblance between father and son. "He will join you shortly," he replied. "He asks that I escort you to the banqueting hall."

Thomas grunted, perhaps in disapproval that his son had not been in the ward to greet him, but kept silent on the matter. Leaving de Aughton and his three grandsons in charge of settling the men, he tossed his mail gloves back onto his saddle as he began to follow Dallas across the bailey and towards the newly re-built stairs that led to the keep. It had taken twenty men less than a day to build the flight, which was far sturdier than the original stairs.

The rest of the men were concentrated on building three enormous mangonels, great monstrous sling-shot devices that were positioned in the inner bailey at regular intervals. Erith Castle was built so that the north and west walls were facing a mountainous crag and between the crag and the outerwalls were big ditches that had been dug long ago. Great boulders and remnants of obstacles remained in the ditch, and a military approach from those sides was not the wisest of choices. There were too many obstacles and pitfalls, making the going treacherous.

Therefore, the best manner in which to approach Erith was on her south and east sides where the ground was more level. There was still a big ditch, partially filled with great jutting boulders and swampy water, but it made for a better tactical approach. Based on this, and the fact that Gloucester had come from the south, Braxton had the three mangonels covering the south and west walls.

Men were building furiously and gathering their supply of crude oil in great barrels. They also had a huge supply of quick lime, sulpher and salt peter from one of Braxton's enormous supply wagons, creating incendiary devices that they intended to shoot at the enemy. Braxton de Nerra was, if nothing else, legendary for his military cunning and tactics. As Thomas, Robert, Davis and Steven de Nerra watched the extremely precise placement and planning of the defenses, Braxton suddenly appeared at the top of the keep's stairs.

Davis was the first one to notice him and he suddenly bellowed like a madman, charging up the stairs and grabbing his youngest brother around the waist. He lifted Braxton up, shaking the man as if to shake him to death. Laughing, Braxton clipped his brother on the Adam's apple and was promptly dropped.

Robert and Steven practically shoved their father aside to get to Braxton. The brothers came together in a clash of joy and affection, handshakes and brotherly hugs going all around until Thomas pushed his way in.

"Braxton," he demanded in a very fatherly-way. "What goes on at this place? What are you doing?"

He was pointing to the mangonels. Braxton went to his father, taking the man's hand affectionately; it had been years since he'd seen the man, now much older than he had remembered. He let his gaze linger on the man fondly.

"It is good to see you, too, Father," he said.

Thomas grunted; he'd never been particularly affectionate with his boys but they all adored him and he adored them. Especially Braxton; the man resembled his mother to a fault, the fair Regan, and Thomas was very fond of his youngest. Braxton had always been the strong one, the brilliant one, something that Thomas had missed a great deal when the man had decided not to remain at Black Fell. But he respected his decision, or at least he had until Northumberland send the missive regarding Lady Gray Serroux. Thomas gazed into his son's eyes, so full of wisdom and life, and finally relented to the emotions with a pat to his son's rough cheek.

"You look well enough," Thomas said; it was as close to an affectionate greeting as he could get. Uncomfortable with the emotions he was feeling, he pointed at the mangonel again.

"What is all of this?"

Braxton lifted an eyebrow, looking out over the inner bailey and his three big war machines.

"We are preparing for Gloucester's arrival," he turned back to his father. "Did de Aughton not tell you everything?"

Thomas nodded. "He told me that you are having some difficulty with Gloucester."

Braxton lifted an eyebrow. "Difficulty indeed. The man is trying to kill me."

Thomas slapped him on the shoulder and turned him for the entry. "Take me inside and feed me. We will speak more of this inside."

Braxton did as he was told. His brothers brought up the rear, inspecting Erith's keep as it opened up into a two-storied banqueting hall. Due to Braxton's money and the on-going repairs, it looked far better than it had in years, including a roaring fire in the enormous hearth. Robert made his way up to Braxton, a big, gnarled hand on Braxton's shoulder as they walked.

"So tell me of your acquisition, Braxton," he said. "Erith Castle used to belong to de Montfort years ago. How did you come by it?"

Braxton looked at his brother. "I did not 'come by it'," he said. "I married it."

"And that is something else!" Thomas suddenly barked. "What is this we hear about you taking a wife? Why did I have to hear about it from another?"

They had moved through the small entry and passed under the great Norman arch that led into the banqueting hall. Just as Thomas boomed his question, an exquisite woman suddenly appeared from the alcove near the kitchen entrance. Dressed in a lovely green surcoat, she had a big earthenware pitcher in her hand. All four men suddenly came to a halt, fixed on the blond beauty with the angelic features. Braxton, fighting off a grin at their astonishment, went to his wife.

"Gentlemen," he put his arm around Gray's shoulders and

pulled her before his family. "This is my wife, the Lady Gray de Montfort de Nerra. Gray, this is my father, Thomas, and my brothers Robert, Davis and Steven."

The men were staring at her with some shock and Gray smiled politely, looking into faces that faintly resembled her husband to varying degrees.

"My lords," she said in her soft, sultry voice. "Welcome to Erith. I am so pleased to meet you all."

Robert was the first one to push forward and take her hand. "Lady de Nerra," he said politely. "You have little concept of just how thrilled we are to meet you. We had no idea that Braxton had taken a wife and already I can see that you are far too good for him."

Gray smiled sweetly at her husband before returning her focus to his brothers. "I am the fortunate one," she said, then indicated the banqueting table, which was laden with several dishes and great pitchers of wine. "Will you please sit? Let us become acquainted."

Braxton took the pitcher from her and set it on the table as his brothers and father began commandeering seats. Braxton helped Gray to sit down opposite his father, taking his seat beside her while Davis tried to sit on her opposite side. But Steven slapped Davis on the head and yanked him out of the way, taking the seat for himself. Dejected, Davis plopped his big body on the table top and tore into a huge loaf of white bread.

Braxton poured his father a cup of wine before serving Gray and them himself. Robert, seated across the table next to Thomas, poured himself a cup also.

"We have not seen Braxton in several years," Robert said, passing the pitcher to his father. "Much has changed with him. I never thought I would see the day when he would settle in one place."

Braxton has his arm around Gray. "I still have not settled in one place," he told his brother. "Erith does not actually belong to me; it belongs to my daughter and her husband."

The de Nerra brothers looked doubly shocked for the second

time that day. Thomas' bushy blond eyebrows lifted. "A daughter?" he sputtered. "What daughter?"

Braxton and Gray laughed softly. "My wife's daughter, the Lady Brooke," Braxton replied. "You should see her; as beautiful as a new spring morning."

"And her husband?" Thomas demanded.

"The knight who greeted you in the ward, Sir Dallas," he replied, catching sight of the Dallas as the man entered the keep. "Ah, here he comes now. I suppose you could say that he is your grandson."

Thomas' expression was one of shock and outrage as Dallas approached the table, but the old man's expression didn't hold for long as Braxton formally introduced Dallas to his new family. Dallas projected a strong, well-spoken and intelligent demeanor as he took his seat next to Braxton and Braxton realized that he was very proud of the man. Their relationship had changed since he had married Brooke and now Braxton took pride in him as a son and not just a knight in his service. It was a pleasing awareness.

Thomas and the brothers couldn't decide whether to focus on Gray or on Dallas; there was too much information coming forth and they were understandably befuddled. But Robert kept his head in the face of all of the new information; he remained focused on Gray, his new sister, simply because she was much prettier than Dallas. He wanted the chance to know her.

"Your family is de Montfort, Lady Gray?" he sipped at his wine. "'Tis a distinguished heritage you bear."

Gray smiled faintly. "It is kind of you to say so," she replied. "Not many do."

Robert cocked an eyebrow. "I have always admired Simon de Montfort. There are many who do in spite of the general opinion of his actions."

Gray again smiled her thanks, not sure what more to say as Braxton came to her rescue. In fact, he came straight to the point of his father and brothers' visit.

"Speaking of de Montfort," he said to her. "You will not believe why my father is here. Your mother has apparently sent him to save you from me."

Gray's eyebrows flew up. "Save me?" she looked confused. "What are you talking about?"

He grinned, taking her hand and toying with her fingers. "Your mother evidently made it back to Northumbria, whereupon she asked the Earl of Northumbria, Yves de Vesci, to send help back to Erith to save her daughter from the clutches of the horrible mercenary Braxton de Nerra. My father, being a vassal of Northumbria, was asked to come and intervene."

Gray looked at him as if he was mad. Then her gaze moved to Thomas, to Robert and Steven, shocked by the circumstance of their appearance. Her wide-open gaze ended up back on Thomas.

"Is this true?" she asked, her voice barely above a whisper.

Thomas nodded slowly, studying Gray just as she was studying him; he was trying to discern if the woman really was in danger from his son but, so far, all he could see between them was great happiness.

"It is," he replied. "Is my son holding you against your will?"

"Absolutely not!"

"Did he force you into marriage?"

"He did no such thing!"

"Then why would your mother say such things?"

Gray's face began to turn shades of red. "Because my mother is a miserable, deceitful person who cannot stomach the fact that my daughter and I are no longer under her control," she hissed. "She has used lies and manipulation to gain her wants and even now, she continues to cause trouble. The army that attacked Erith two days ago was a direct result of my mother's underhanded actions. She has done all she can to try and destroy me, and Braxton, and your presence here shows me that she is still trying."

Thomas remained calm, although he believed her explanation completely. He didn't sense any fear or treachery from the woman in the least.

"Why is Gloucester here to destroy you?" he wanted to know.

Gray told him everything she knew, followed by Braxton elaborating on the more critical issues. They heard of Constance's lies against Braxton, of her attempt to sell Brooke's hand to the highest bidder, and of Braxton's solution to marry off both Gray and Brooke so that Constance could no longer control them. Thomas, Robert, Steven and Davis sat quietly through the explanation, drinking their wine and feasting on warmed over venison and bread.

Braxton finished his tale with the deaths of Roger and William de Clare, bringing them up to date on everything that had happened, and Thomas poured himself another cup and drank the entire thing in two swallows. It was evident that he felt the situation was indeed dire. Robert and Braxton exchanged concerned glances as Thomas seemed to lose himself in deep thought and another cup of wine. Finally, the man stirred back to life.

"Then it would seem that we have a problem," Thomas finally said. "I cannot leave here with Gloucester an impending threat, but Gloucester is a strong ally of Northumberland. If I fight Gloucester, then I will do great damage to that alliance."

"I will fight with Braxton, Father," Robert said decisively. "I have one hundred and fifty men sworn to me. They are at Braxton's disposal."

Thomas held up a hand to quiet him as Davis, the biggest brother, checked in with his opinion.

"And I will fight with him also," he boomed. "No man will attack my brother and get away with it. I will kill them all."

Thomas waved a hand in Davis' face as the man began to argue with him. Robert began to interject his very strong opinion and soon, the table was filled with men shouting to be heard. Gray looked at Braxton with concern, who merely shook his head at the sight of his father and brothers going at one another. Some things never changed. The only one not shouting was Steven and that was because his temperament was more like Braxton's, quieter and calmer. Like Braxton, he was watching the explosions until he finally turned to his brother and shook his head with exasperation.

"Braxton," he said in his calm, cool tone. "I believe I have a solution to all of this."

Braxton, his arm around his wife, sat forward with interest. "What is that, Steven?"

Steven ducked when a cup, slammed to the table by Davis, shot up over his head before clattering to the floor several feet away.

"I would suspect that Gloucester's army has spies watching Erith and undoubtedly saw us arrive," he said. "But you know that it is Father's custom not to fly banners when we travel. Knowing we are Gilderdale can attract those wanting to make a name for themselves against our might force. We therefore arrived with no fanfare or colors. Even if Gloucester is watching, they will not know who we are."

Braxton was starting to guess what his brother was suggesting. "For all they know, you are reinforcements for Erith," he said. "They do not have to know you are Gilderdale."

Steven lifted an eyebrow. "Exactly," he said. "Especially if we remove all tunic, colors or banners that even remotely suggest such a thing. We will replace our colors with yours and they will believe we are simply part of your army."

By this time, Thomas had stopped shouting at Davis and Robert and was listening intently to what Steven was suggesting. He finally smacked at the table, startling Gray with the noise.

"A brilliant suggestion, Steven," he said, looking to Braxton. "I have brought six hundred men with me, Braxton. Can you accommodate us?"

Braxton was coming to feel like he now had a great chance of success against a Gloucester offensive. In spite of alliances and lieges, he knew his father would not abandon him. He felt more relief than he would admit, squeezing Gray affectionately as he replied to his father.

"With my one hundred and eighty men, that gives us a sizable force," he said. "Erith is a massive beast of a castle; of course we can accommodate you. Dallas will see to it immediately."

Dallas nodded firmly and rose to his feet. There was a sense of hopefulness in the air now, as if they were not about to fight a losing battle. Dallas' spirit was renewed. But there was still the matter of removing Gray and Brooke until the madness was over.

"Braxton," he said. "This is all well and good, but we still must remove the ladies immediately. I do not want Brooke in a castle under siege."

Braxton nodded, hoping he wouldn't set Gray off with the touchy subject.

"Indeed," he agreed. "The sooner the better. But plans for their destination have changed."

Gray looked at him, surprised and concerned, as Dallas sat back down on the bench beside him. The young knight's expression was somewhat wary.

"Where are they going?" he asked hesitantly.

Braxton told him. Dallas, not surprisingly, agreed. Gray, not surprisingly, did not.

CHAPTER NINETEEN

Gray had never been to Creekmere Castle, although Garber had spent some time there in the past. Baron Wenvoe was a known gambler, a man who had prospered from the sport, and his castle reflected that. It was small but well built and well maintained, and as the party from Erith entered the main gates, men went running into the keep to summon the baron. Astride their two big warmblood mares, Gray and Brooke inspected their surroundings cautiously.

A wagon, ten men at arms and Edgar had accompanied the women from Erith on the morning following the arrival of Gilderdale. Gray had known of a way north that kept them out of the line of sight of Gloucester or her spies, so the party had stayed to a small, less-traveled road to the northeast that kept them shielded by forests and dales. It took just a few hours to reach Creekmere, now as clouds were beginning to waft in from the sea and gather ominously overhead. As the portcullis dropped in behind them with a resounding boom, Gray was coming to feel as if she was a prisoner in this tiny castle.

Edgar, riding at the head of the column quite proudly on a fluffy brown destrier that was too old to do much fighting or competing, dismounted his steed and very impressively announced Lady de Nerra and Lady Aston to Baron Wenvoe's servants.

Even now, he stood at the head of the group, waiting expectantly for the baron to appear. Braxton had put him in charge of the ladies even though a senior sergeant was in charge of the soldiers, but still, Edgar was coming to feel as if he was finally being appreciated. Norman so often overshadowed him that it was rare when he had such opportunity to prove himself. As he turned back to look at Gray and Brooke, just to make sure they were looking at how officious he was, Brooke made a face at him. So much for being officious; he stuck his tongue out at her.

Baron Wenvoe emerged from the small keep several minutes later, looking rather flustered, as if he had just been awakened in his bed. His white hair was standing up and he had a crease on one side of his face as he stumbled down the stairs from the keep, his fat face fixed on the small party from Erith. He approached Gray somewhat timidly.

"My lady," he semi-bowed, not an entirely mannerly man. "To what do I owe the honor of your visit?"

Gray dismounted the mare as a soldier grasped the reins to steady the beast. She approached Baron Wenvoe, struggling against the memories that the man provoked. Garber and Baron Wenvoe had been as thick as thieves with their gambling habits and she had tried to explain that to Braxton, but he was less concerned about old memories than he was about getting his wife and daughter to safety. She didn't agree with him but she respected him enough to do as he asked.

Facing Wenvoe, however, she was coming to feel some disgust. She simply didn't like the man.

"Greetings, baron," she said with more pleasantness than she felt. "My daughter and I must beg refuge from you for a few days, at least until my husband sends for me."

Wenvoe peered at her curiously. "Husband?" he repeated, well aware that Garber Serroux had been dead for years. But then it occurred to him that she had been announced by another name. "Are you... are you now Lady de Nerra?"

Gray nodded. "Braxton and I were married last month," she said. "I am now Lady de Nerra and my daughter, Brooke, is now Lady Aston. She married one of Braxton's knights."

Shocked, Wenvoe looked between Gray and her lovely daughter. His jowls quivered as he attempted to straighten out his line of thought.

"I see," was all he could manage to say. "You said you are seeking refuge? What has happened to Erith?"

Gray's pleasant expression faded. "Erith is under threat of attack from Gloucester at the moment," she said evenly. "My husband wishes for Brooke and I to be away from the compromised fortress until the matter is settled. I hope you will be able to accommodate us."

"Accommodate you?" he scratched his head, looking back at his tiny keep before nodding. "Of course I will show you hospitality. An attack, did you say?"

"Aye."

"But... but Erith is already a crumbling wreck. Surely Gloucester and all of its might will have no problem breaching the castle."

Gray smiled thinly. "You have not see Erith recently," she replied. "The fortress has been rebuilt. She is back to her former glory, make no mistake. She will hold."

"Is that so?" Wenvoe was genuinely surprised. "Erith has been derelict for years."

Gray thought of Braxton and his massive rebuilding project, trying not to let the depression of their separation swamp her. "My husband has virtually rebuilt the castle," she said. "It is truly remarkable. Hopefully you will have the opportunity to see what he has accomplished when this difficulty with Gloucester is over."

Wenvoe couldn't decide how he felt about that. Once, the fortress had been promised to him. Then de Nerra came along and basically threatened him into selling his rights. Now de Nerra had it and had stirred up problems with, of all people, the mighty force of Gloucester. Wenvoe didn't understand any of it, but he was coming to think some evil thoughts about the situation. It was simply his nature.

Lazy and slovenly, Wenvoe was no fool. Money and greed were his livelihood. As he looked at the two women, he could suddenly see how he would be able to capitalize on the situation. Damn de Nerra for forcing him to sell his rights to the young Serroux girl and the castle along with her; Wenvoe wanted it back. He couldn't do anything about the girl, but perhaps he could do something about the fortress. And with that, his mind began to work.

As he called his servants to collect Lady de Nerra's belongings, he began to think very wicked and calculating thoughts. He was a gambler, after all; with his very precious guests, he began to see monetary possibilities in all of this. Gloucester was mad enough at de Nerra to attack Erith; de Nerra was trusting enough to send his wife and daughter to Wenvoe, who had had claimed as an ally those weeks ago when he had purchased Wenvoe's rights to Erith.

Wenvoe wondered how much Gloucester would pay him for Lady de Nerra and her daughter. It would make them extremely valuable hostages and de Nerra, for whatever he had done to Gloucester, would be at their mercy. But best of all, Wenvoe would make an ally of Gloucester, giving de Nerra pause should he consider vengeance for the betrayal. The man would be foolish to tangle with Gloucester, and Wenvoe. Retribution was a sweet and awful thing.

As Wenvoe watched the women mount the stairs into the keep, he grabbed one of his trusted male servants and whispered words of treachery into the man's ear. The servant, stupid and strong, slithered off to accomplish his lord's bidding with the promise of a great reward when all was said and done.

As Gray and Brooke settled in to the tiny keep at Creekmere, they had no idea that the man who had humiliated Garber Serroux was about to do the same thing to them.

CHAPTER TWENTY

Nine days later

The night was cold, clear and crisp. There wasn't a cloud in the sky and the brilliant white moon bathed the landscape in an eerie silver glow. Upon the rebuilt battlements of Erith, Dallas and Norman made their rounds, checking on the sentries, looking out for any activity to the east where Gloucester's army had once been encamped.

Oddly enough, they hadn't seen any sign of the army for a couple of days. Scouts had been sent out but they had returned with the news that Gloucester's army was nowhere to be seen. Braxton had assumed they had moved simply to throw them off their guard but the past two days of searching failed to show up any Gloucester encampment in the immediate area. Braxton was coming to think they had simply gone home, but Thomas and Robert were convinced that it was a ruse. Based on their opinion, Erith remained on high alert until the oddity could be sorted out.

The night around them was still; too still. Not a dog or night hawk filled the sky. Dallas couldn't decide how he felt about it, if it was simply peaceful or a prelude to something ominous. He remained away from the parapet, out of the range of any archers that might be lingering in the trees, going about his rounds but thinking on his wife. She filled his every moment, awake or asleep. He never knew it was possible to miss anyone as much as he missed her, but he did. He missed her so badly that it hurt.

While Dallas was in physical pain from his longing, Braxton was worse. Although he didn't show it, his pining for his wife had manifested itself into a dull ache that throbbed more painfully with each passing day. He would sleep a few hours when he had the chance, clutching her pillow and smelling her upon it. It was both comforting and painful, awaking in the morning only to realize she was not by his side.

He knew she had arrived at Creekmere safely because a soldier had returned the same day they had departed for the castle to tell him that Lady de Nerra was safely inside the fortress. That should have brought it comfort but it only made him miss her more. He took to carrying around a fragment from one of her old surcoats, one she had worn the day he had met her, because it was the one thing that kept his sanity intact. Without the faded scrap of yellow linen, he would surely wither away and die.

Braxton joined Dallas this evening upon the battlements in the stark moonlight, his blue-green gaze moving over the muted countryside. Dallas heard him approach, turning to see Braxton's weak smile. Dallas returned the gesture as the two settled in next to one another, their trained eyes on the moonlit land beyond.

"I thought Geoff had the night watch," Braxton said casually.

Dallas grunted. "He does," he replied. "He and de Aughton are supervising the walls."

Braxton grunted. "Geoff does not seem troubled to be serving with the man who nearly killed him."

"Geoff is a better man than I am," Dallas sniffed. "I am not sure I would be so forgiving."

Braxton smirked to that statement. "Aye, you would. You underestimate yourself," he said, turning to look at him. "So why are you here if Geoff and Niclas have everything in hand?"

"I could not sleep."

"Do you miss her that much?"

Dallas looked at him, an eyebrow raised. "Do you?"

"I asked you first."

Dallas pursed his lips and shook his head, turning away. Beside him, Braxton snorted softly.

"I miss her so badly that I can hardly breathe," Dallas finally said. "Whose foolish idea was it to send the women away?"

Braxton continued laughing, softly. "It was yours. I hold you personally responsible for my misery."

Dallas rolled his eyes. "Of course you do."

Braxton's laughter faded and he folded his muscular arms across his chest. "Nonetheless, it was the right thing to do," he said quietly. "But it is my sense that if we still do not find any sign of Gloucester's army by tomorrow, we will ride to Creekmere and retrieve the women. If Gloucester is gone, there is no reason for us not to return to some semblance of normalcy."

Dallas looked at him. "Do you truly believe they are gone?"

Braxton inhaled deeply, thoughtfully. "There is no sign of them," he said. "But if they are truly gone, I would like to know why. What chased them off?"

Dallas shrugged. "Perhaps it was the reinforcements from your father," he said. "Perhaps it was because they attacked us for days on end and were unable to make headway. Perhaps they were discouraged."

Braxton shook his head. "I would not believe that, not from Gloucester," he said firmly. "It must have been something else, something...."

He suddenly trailed off, his gaze finding something of interest in the land beyond the walls. Moving swiftly to the parapet, he studied movement in the trees about one hundred yards from Erith's eastern wall. There was a small river that ran in that direction and he could see movement in the trees. As he and Dallas struggled to make sense of what it was, a lone body suddenly burst through the brush and began stumbling towards the castle.

"What in the hell is that?" Dallas wanted to know.

Braxton watched the figure stagger and struggle, falling on the grass and then picking itself up again. He shook his head, feeling an odd sense of concern. As the seconds ticked away and more soldiers joined them on the wall, watching, Norman was suddenly beside them, having come from the south wall to see what all of the fuss was about. Dallas pointed at the approaching figure.

"Can you make that out?" he asked the young man.

Norman squinted, trying to make out the detail in the silver glare of the moon. Ever since that day in Milnthorpe when he had protected Lady Gray from de Aughton, Braxton had elevated Norman from his squire duties to those of a knight. He wasn't sworn yet but that would come. At the moment, he was learning the intricacies of such a position and taking to it admirably. Braxton knew he would have a fine knight on his hands when all was said and done.

"It looks like someone beaten half to death," Norman strained to catch a better glimpse as the figure staggered to its feet once more and limped towards the castle. "In fact, it looks like...."

His eyes widened and he trailed off. Suddenly, he was bolting for the ladder that led down to the bailey, taking it so fast that he practically fell the last six feet to the ward below. Braxton and Dallas bolted after him, calling his name, wondering what had the young man so startled. Norman was screaming for them to open the outer portcullis, waiting until it was lifted by only a few feet before dashing underneath it and tearing out into the landscape beyond.

Dallas was fast and on his heels, racing after him at top speed as they tore in the direction of the staggering figure. Dallas stopped yelling at Norman as they drew close, for he could finally see what Norman saw.

It was Edgar.

The lad saw them coming and finally fell face first into the grass, as if his strength had finally left him now that he had been spotted. Normal fell to his knees beside his brother, rolling the young man over onto his back and being greeted by a terrible sight; Edgar had been horribly beaten. His right eye was swollen shut, his nose broken, and he had welts and bloody cuts over every inch of skin that was exposed. He was a mess.

"Edgar!" Norman breathed. "What has happened?"

Edgar was miserable but he was struggling to stay strong. He reached up and grabbed his brother's hand. "They... they took them," he gasped.

Dallas felt so much horror that he nearly vomited from the

stress of it. He swallowed hard, struggling to maintain his calm. "Who?" he almost barked. "Who did they take? Edgar, what happened?"

By this time, Braxton had joined them, bending over Edgar to get a good look at the lad. He hissed when he saw all of the damage.

"Edgar," he said quietly, urgently. "What happened to you?"

Edgar looked up at Braxton with his one good eye, the only father he had ever known. His eyes began to well with tears.

"I am sorry," he whispered through his swollen lips. "I tried to stop them but I could not."

Braxton knelt down beside the distressed lad, putting his big hand on his dark head. "Stop who?"

Edgar swallowed, feeling like such a failure. He had been put in charge, after all. It was all his fault.

"Gloucester's men," he whispered, closing his eyes. "They came for Lady Gray and Lady Brooke. They took them away."

Dallas bolted to his feet unsteadily, hands over his mouth as if to hold back the shout of horror. Braxton had more control over himself, but only slightly. His heart was beating so hard that he was sure it was going to slam right out of his chest.

"How do you know they were Gloucester?" he asked, his voice quaking. "Where is Baron Wenvoe? What happened to him?"

Edgar opened his eye and look at him. "Baron Wenvoe let them in," he said. "I recognized the Gloucester tunics of yellow and blue. He let them take the women. I heard the baron say they could have anything for the right price."

A look of complete horror crossed Braxton's face. "He said *that*?"

"Aye, my lord. But Lady Gray and Lady Brooke did not go without a fight. It was an awful battle."

Braxton's chest seized up as he thought of his wife doing battle against faceless, ruthless knights. "And you?"

"I tried to protect them, my lord. So did the other soldiers you sent to escort them. But Gloucester's men were too many; they overwhelmed us."

"Where are my soldiers?"

"I was the only one that survived."

Braxton gazed at the young man for a few painfully lingering moments before hanging his head in total, utter desolation. He could hardly believe what he was hearing but suddenly, it all made a great deal of sense. Gloucester's army pulled out because they didn't need to be there any longer; all of the sieges in all of the world wouldn't accomplish against de Nerra what the captivity of two small women could. Wenvoe, the man he had bullied into surrendering Erith and Brooke for a price, had betrayed him.

He stood up, uneasily, struggling not to explode in all directions at the news. It was the most difficult struggle of his life, made worse when he looked at Dallas to see the man glaring daggers at him.

"You sent them there," Dallas snarled. "You said Wenvoe was an ally. He sold them; he sold them to Gloucester!"

Braxton had never heard that tone from Dallas, ever. His jaw flexed dangerously as he faced off against his furious son-in-law.

"It was not my fault that Wenvoe turned them over to Gloucester," he replied steadily. "But it will be the baron's last mistake. He will rue the day he was born, I assure you."

That seemed to calm Dallas somewhat and he took a few deep breaths, struggling to calm himself further. He ran his big hands through his long blond hair, nervously, as if suddenly realizing how he had verbally attacked Braxton. He looked at the man.

"I am sorry," he muttered, deeply contrite and upset. "I should not have... I did not mean to accuse you. I let Brooke go also. It was my decision as much as yours."

Braxton went to the man, putting his hands on his shoulders in a fortifying, comforting gesture, before turning back to Edgar. Norman had his brother propped up now, inspecting the bruises on his face.

"How long ago did this happen, Edgar?" Braxton asked, trying to be somewhat gentle with the battered lad.

Edgar gazed up at him. "Four or five days ago, I think," he

shook his head. "I do not know, exactly. They beat me and threw me into a room. I do not know how long I was there."

"But you escaped," Braxton continued. "Did someone help you?"

Edgar shook his head. "I just left. I walked out in the middle of the night. Creekmere Castle isn't watched very well."

Braxton's jaw ticked as he thought on that. He looked at Dallas.

"If they realize that Edgar is gone, then I have a feeling they will heavily fortify it, knowing he returned to me to tell me what had happened." His calculating mind began to plan the next step, keeping a rein on his sanity which would have undoubtedly left him had he allowed himself to think on Gray's fate. "Go back and find my father and brothers. Meet me in the great hall. We have a battle to plan."

Dallas hesitated. "Edgar said yellow and blue tunics," he said. "That is Roger de Clare's colors."

"I know."

"Then he must have taken them back to Elswick Castle."

"That is my sense as well," his gaze turned deadly. "They have called forth the Devil and now, he shall appear. *I* shall appear."

Dallas had heard that tone before. He knew that, indeed, Hell was on the approach.

Hell hath no fury like a husband betrayed.

CHAPTER TWENTY ONE

Creekmere Castle never stood a chance.

Braxton's army, mingled with the Gilderdale force, razed Creekmere in less than two days. Braxton brought his mangonels, the same war engines he had built for his battle against Gloucester, and destroyed Creekmere with barrages of flaming-tar projectiles that burned the outbuildings and killed most of Wenvoe's men. After burning the wood and iron portcullis into ashes and twisted remains, Braxton entered the bailey and ordered his men to kill everything that moved.

The rich keep was looted of all of its finery; furs, tapestries, plate and gold pieces were all confiscated by Braxton and his men. He took back every pence of the thirty thousand gold marks he had paid for Brooke and Erith and then some. The true heart of the mercenary came to pass and Braxton was ruthless in his conquest. Those who did not flee were put to the blade; those who resisted were also put to the blade. Wenvoe himself was dragged from a closet by Dallas, who gutted the man from his throat to his groin and took great pleasure in it. In the heat of his fury, his sense of vengeance knew no limits. Every stroke had Brooke's name on it.

As de Aughton and the soldiers from Gilderdale began systematically destroying the walls with projectiles from the mangonels, Braxton, his brothers and father were brutal in their conquest of the keep. When the entire thing was stripped bare, a fire of dead bodies was lit on the bottom floor and the heavy, greasy smoke of human corpses began billowing in great black tides from the windows. Wenvoe himself was cut into several different pieces and put into a wagon with his head stuck on a pike jutting from the front of the wagon. Braxton ordered four of his men to take the wagon to Elswick and leave it at their doorstep as a promise of things to come if Lady de Nerra and Lady Aston were not immediately released. It was Braxton's calling card.

With Creekmere obliterated, Braxton's next move was Elswick Castle and Roger de Clare's family. He fully intended to do to Elswick what he had done to Creekmere. He spent a restless night watching Creekmere burn and at dawn the next day, his seven hundred man army began to move south towards Elswick. It was a thirty mile journey and he knew they could easily make it in a day; he was fully prepared to begin the siege the moment they arrived. Even if they handed Gray over, he was still going to burn the place in vengeance. He could think of nothing else. The closer he drew, the more obsessed he became. The more obsessed he became, the more obsessed his father and brothers became. It was a vicious cycle.

Riding at the head of the enormous army, it was the de Nerra men – Thomas, Robert, Davis, Steven, Braxton and the Thomas' three grandsons Dair, Laurence and Roderick, united for one cause, one purpose. Dallas rode among them, one of the family now and accepted as such, as Geoff and Niclas flanked the army, keeping the men in line. The trek south was filled with a tremendous sense of purpose and hardly a word was spoken as they covered the road to Elswick in less than a day, arriving at the castle with the sun sitting low on the horizon.

Elswick was a Gloucester stronghold that covered quite a bit of ground. It was a big castle with an enormous bailey, huge ditches surrounding it, and fifteen foot walls. It had a big gatehouse and an enormous keep in the center of the complex along with all of the usual outbuildings like stables and smithy shacks. It sat on a rather flat plain, a beacon of Gloucester strength that could be seen for miles in all directions.

Braxton and Robert didn't waste any time moving the army into position. They surrounded the entire castle, keeping out of range of the archers as they moved the great mangonels into position. Braxton's plan was to fire flaming projectiles into the bailey to cripple it before moving in on the gatehouse. Assuming his wife and daughter were being held in the keep, it was his intention to leave it untouched, at least until Gray and Brooke were safe. Then he would burn it to the ground and everyone in it.

It was close to midnight by the time the army was completely situated. The army had stripped wood from the nearby forests, building a fourth mangonel as well as creating massive bonfires on which to heat the thick, gooey tar. Only when everything was set did Braxton turn his attention to the castle, which had been on extreme alert since their arrival. He could see men walking the walls, fully alert, waiting for the onslaught.

Braxton stood by the light of one of the gigantic bonfires, watching the castle in the distance. He was in full armor, heavy chain main and weapons slung about his body. There were dark splotches on his mail, bloodstains from the destruction of Creekmere, and his face was drawn and stubbled. He literally had not slept since receiving the news that Gray had been abducted by Gloucester and it showed in every expression, every movement. The man looked like the walking dead.

He stood, staring at the distance castle as if he could see his wife through the great stone walls and tightening up his gloves. Robert walked up beside him, his gaze moving between his brother and the distant castle. He knew how badly the man felt; they all felt badly. But Braxton's brutality to those who had betrayed him had been nothing short of astonishing to watch. He knew his brother was sharp, cunning and ruthless, but his actions over the past three days had surpassed with even Robert thought he was capable of.

The rest of the knights were spread out with the soldiers; Thomas was supervising the building of the mangonel, Steven and Davis were positioning the archers, and the rest of them were mingled with the infantry. Geoff and Niclas' commands echoed over the darkened landscape as the senior knights in command. Everyone was prepared, waiting. Robert faced his brother expectantly.

"Your orders, Braxton?" he asked quietly, watching the man as he fussed with his gloves. "The men are prepared when you give the word."

Braxton didn't look at his brother; he was still looking at Elswick.

"In a moment," he said. "I will give them the opportunity to deliver my wife and daughter unharmed first."

Robert nodded. "Shall I accompany you?"

Braxton shook his head. "Nay," he replied. "You will stay here and keep Dallas at bay. I am afraid of what he will do if Elswick denies my request. He may charge in there and get himself killed."

Robert nodded again, his gaze moving to the enormous castle, illuminated in the dark night by hundreds of torches against the sky. It was an eerie sight.

"You realize that they will probably not turn her over," he said softly. "She is the only guarantee that you will not completely raze the place."

Braxton shrugged and finished with his gloves. "I am going to completely raze it as it is," he said. "I will kill any remaining de Clare relatives and post their bodies on poles for all to see."

Robert knew that. He wasn't going to try and talk him out of anything so he looked around, spying Dallas several feet away, using a pumice stone to sharpen the smooth blade side of his sword. With a lingering look at Braxton, he made his way over to Dallas to await the signal to battle. Everything was dependent upon Braxton's interaction with the inhabitants of Elswick.

Braxton didn't waste any time. He mounted his big black charger and spurred the beast forward, thundering towards the gatehouse of Elswick. As he cantered towards the lifted drawbridge, he could hear shouting upon the walls of Elswick as the men inside realized that something was happening. Someone in de Nerra's army was about to make contact. Everyone who was able ran for the gatehouse, waiting for the first barrage of words that would determine their future.

Braxton kept calm, focused. He thought about what he was going to say. He wanted to stress upon the commanders of Elswick that they had little choice in surrendering Gray and Brooke but he didn't want to provoke them to the point where they might actually harm the women. That was his greatest fear, in fact, that Elswick would not surrender his wife and daughter and, instead, punish them because de Nerra was intent on destroying their castle. Time would tell. He braced himself for what was to come.

He pulled his charger to a halt when he came within range of the mighty gatehouse of Elswick. Dozens of torches lit up the structure and he could see many soldiers upon the gatehouse battlements. Everyone was scattering back and forth, orders being relayed as men showed their fear of what was to come. Braxton could feel their terror and it both pleased and concerned him. Used properly, terror was a good motivator, but men that were overwhelmed with panic could do stupid things. He didn't want his wife or daughter to fall victim to stupidity.

"My name is Braxton de Nerra," he bellowed for all to hear. "I have come to secure the release of my wife and daughter. Failure to give me what I have come for will have deadly consequences for the inhabitants of Elswick. Do I make myself clear?"

More scuttling and shouting upon the battlements. Torches flickered as men ran about. Braxton's charger danced around excitedly, sensing a battle, and he sat patiently astride the beast, trying to calm it. After several tense and uneasy moments, a knight suddenly appeared on the wall where it joined with the enormous gatehouse. He held up his gloved hand to Braxton.

"I am Blakeney de Milne, husband to Lord Roger and Lady Anne's eldest daughter," he called down to him. "Your wife and daughter are in my custody. Such is the punishment for the deaths of Lord Roger and his son William."

"Lord Roger and his son William's deaths were unintentional, I assure you," Braxton shouted steadily. "They attacked me first and were killed whilst we defended ourselves. If anyone was wronged, it was me. Had you not murdered my men and sent them back to me in pieces, perhaps you would have heard the entire story. Instead, you made an uneducated and deadly decision, made worse with the capture of my family. Turn them back over to me now and I will be merciful. Resist my demand

and every man, woman and child at Elswick will die. This I vow."

De Milne remained cool; he was a seasoned knight, skilled and calm, but he knew who Braxton de Nerra was and had little doubt he meant what he said.

"Make a move against us and I will send your daughter and wife out to you in pieces," he threatened. "If you return your army to Erith this night, I will not harm them."

Braxton sighed slowly; he was losing patience. "You do not make demands," he countered. "I want my family returned to me. As an honorable knight, you will do as I ask. Resist and die."

De Milne wasn't stupid; he knew the only reason Braxton hadn't let loose on them was because they held his wife and daughter. But he also knew that sooner or later, de Nerra would begin a siege to regain them that would end up destroying everyone at Elswick. He had a wife and children in this castle himself; he didn't want to see them come to harm. He knew that, at some point, he would be forced to negotiate. He thought carefully on his offer before speaking.

"I will make you a proposal, de Nerra," he said. "I will return one of your women to you. You will take her and return to Erith and, when I see that peace has settled between Erith and Elswick, I will return the other woman to you as a reward for your good behavior. Attack me now and the first bodies I throw over the wall at you will be your wife and daughter; this I swear. Agree to my terms and they will live."

Braxton's patience was evaporating and he could feel his temper rise. The threats against Gray and Brooke infuriated him.

"Are you truly so bold and foolish?" he wanted to know. "Roger de Clare and his son were killed when they attacked me. It happened so quickly that I had no idea who they were until after it was over. I did not make the first move against them, I assure you. Although I understand your grief at the loss of your lord and his heir, to attack Erith and then steal my wife and daughter in punishment is beneath honorable men. I would not say this if it were not so; I do not lie. On my oath, I tell you that Roger and William's death were an accident. Now return my wife and daughter to me and I shall forget my vengeance against you. If you kill them, know that there will be nothing stopping me from capturing you and forcing you to watch as I murder your wife and children right before your very eyes. Their deaths will be as painful and horrific as you can imagine. The choice is yours."

De Milne fell silent, watching de Nerra down below, just out of the range of the archers. He turned to the man next to him, whispered something, and the man took off running. Braxton waited for a reply; a minute passed, and then another and another. Soon several minutes had passed and Braxton was beginning to get anxious. Just as he opened his mouth to shout up to them again, the drawbridge suddenly lurched.

Unsure what was happening, Braxton backed up. He lifted his hand to his waiting army and the archers got into position, followed by the infantry. For all they knew, screaming hordes of Gloucester men were about to come leaping out at them and they would not take any chances. Every man in Braxton's army was poised at the ready. Dallas, having shaken his shadow Robert, came thundering up to Braxton, taking his place beside him. If there was going to be a fight, he was going to fight alongside Braxton.

The wait was beginning to become excessive but it was clear that something was in the works. Braxton could hear men shouting on the other side of the wall and he prepared to unsheathe his broadsword. He could feel a fight coming.

The enormous drawbridge suddenly began to move. It jerked on its chains, lowered unsteadily by a host of nervous soldiers deep in the walls of the gatehouse. As the thing slowly lurched downward, Braxton and Dallas could see that the portcullis was slowly lifting as well. They could see a cluster of soldiers on the other side, shadows shifting about in the darkness of the gatehouse passage. Braxton's grip tightened on his reins, waiting for the charge. But suddenly, something unexpected caught his attention.

It was a spot of color in a sea of shadows. He could see it, a pale blue flash now and again. But suddenly, the pale blue flash had become solid and steady, approaching the portcullis, which by now had stopped only half-raised. As Braxton watched, curious and apprehensive, it took him a moment to realize that Brooke was being released.

She skittered beneath the half-raised portcullis and began to run. Dallas, startled, suddenly spurred his charger forward as Braxton screamed at him to stop; the man was heading into the optimal range of the archers and Braxton was terrified that Dallas was about to get himself mowed down. But Dallas must have realized it, too, because he suddenly yanked his charger to a halt and raced back to where Braxton was still positioned.

Braxton glanced over at the young knight, seeing utter and complete relief and terror on the man's face. Then he returned his attention to Brooke, racing across the damp, dark earth at top speed. He could hear her sobbing as she approached. Dallas bailed from his charger and held out his arms, softly encouraging her to come to him. Brooke picked up the pace and threw herself into her husband's open arms, so hard that Dallas nearly toppled over with the force of her hit.

Hysterical sobs filled the air as Braxton dismounted his charger and went to Dallas and Brooke, a mass of hugging warmth in the dark of the night. Braxton could feel the emotion radiating from the pair; in fact, he had quite enough of his own as he reached out and tried to separate them.

"Brooke, sweetheart," he got his big hands around her head, forcing her to look at him ever though she was in her husband's arms. "Where is your mother?"

Brooke was a sobbing mess. "She is inside," she sobbed, reaching out to grab his forearm as he gripped her. "Braxton, she is sick. I do not know what has happened to her because they will not let me see her, but I have been told she is very sick. They told me to tell you to return to Erith or you will never see her again."

Braxton stared at the girl as she collapsed back into Dallas' arms. By this time, Thomas, Robert, Davis and Geoff had made their way over to him, glad to see Brooke but wondering where Gray was. Some of them had caught the tail-end of her sobbing explanation. After taking a few shocking moments to digest her news, Braxton suddenly reached out and yanked her from Dallas' grip, so hard that her neck nearly snapped. That set off Dallas and Geoff had to throw a big arm around Dallas to keep the man from charging Braxton.

"Brooke," Braxton was as close to losing his composure as he had ever been in his life. "You will tell me what has happened from the beginning. What happened when they took you from Creekmere?"

Brooke sniffled and wept. "They came on our fourth day there," she sobbed. "Baron Wenvoe let them in. They tried to take my mother first but she would not let them; she ran and hid from them, and then beat those who found her with a roasting iron. I heard someone say that she put a man's eye out."

Braxton realized he was shaking as he kept his grip on her arms. "And then what happened?"

Brooke was calming somewhat now that she was in familiar hands, with familiar people. "They took us both back to Elswick," she said, gazing into Braxton's blue-green eyes. "But Mama was not feeling well along the way. I think that fighting those men off must have hurt her somehow. By the time we got here, she could barely walk and they took her away from me. I have not seen her since our arrival."

Everyone heard the softly-uttered information, but no one more clearly than Braxton. He struggled to remain collected, knowing that if he let himself go, he would surely destroy all in his path. There would be no return.

"And you do not know what is wrong with her?" he asked.

Brooke shook her head. "Nay," she replied, her eyes beginning to well again. "I am afraid she is dying."

Braxton let go of her, turning to face the black, shadowed bastion of Elswick. Thomas moved to his son, seeing his distress.

"They sent the girl out as a good faith measure," he rumbled. "They are hoping you will do the same."

Braxton grunted. "By returning to Erith without my wife?" he growled. "I think not. If they...."

He was cut off by shouting from the dark, torch-lit wall. It was de Milne again.

"You have your daughter back, de Nerra," he hollered. "We have showed a measure of mercy. Now you will do the same."

Braxton was losing his mind. His nerve, his gut, and everything else was starting to go. The knowledge that Gray was ill, perhaps dying, swamped him until he could think of nothing else. He heard de Milne's offer but he couldn't agree with it, not in the least. He could hear Brooke weeping softly as he faced the darkened walls of Elswick.

"I appreciate your show of mercy," he shouted up to de Milne. "But I am told that my wife is very ill. Surely you know that I cannot leave without her."

De Milne didn't reply for several long and tense moments. "It would be better if she is not moved," he replied. "I have a physic with her. She is well tended."

The news should have made Braxton feel better but it only made him feel worse. He lost everything at that moment; his guard went down completely and he was stripped of his vengeance. All he wanted was to see Gray no matter what the cost. If they would not turn her over to him, then he would go to her. It was the only choice.

"I will send my army home," he told de Milne," but you will take me a hostage. I want to be with my wife. If you will not release her, then you will take me also. Please, de Milne; as one husband to another, surely you can understand my desire. I beg of you."

Dallas, Thomas, Robert and the rest of the brothers heard him, turning to look at Braxton with varied degrees of astonishment and horror. Dallas even let go of Brooke, rushing to Braxton in denial.

"Nay, Braxton," he hissed. "They will kill you."

Braxton pretended as if he hadn't heard him. He yelled up to de Milne again. "I am surrendering to you, de Milne," he said. "You will accept me as a prisoner and take me to my wife."

De Milne was off-balance by the offer, evident in his manner.

He was no longer hard as nails; he was edgy in his reply. "Send your army home now and I will consider it."

"They will leave before sunrise. You will take me to my wife."

De Milne was still hesitant. "If you enter Elswick, I cannot vouch for your safety, de Nerra. There are many here who seek vengeance for Lord Roger's death. It is possible that you may not live long enough to see your lady should you venture into Elswick."

"I will take that chance. My life is in your hands, de Milne. As an honorable knight, I will trust you."

He began to pull off his weapons, casting them to the ground as Dallas and the others watched in horror. Thomas tried to plead with his son as he continued to remove his armor, his mail, throwing them into a pile on the cold, dark ground. Robert tried to talk to him, as did Davis. They all begged Braxton not to do it, but Braxton wasn't listening. By the time he was finished, he was clad only in his breeches, boots and damp, dirty tunic. Everything else was on the ground in a pile.

The only person who didn't seem to be begging him not to do it was Brooke. She watched Braxton as he stripped down to his clothing, standing vulnerable before an entire fortress. As Dallas and Thomas suffered through the throes of anxiety and Braxton's brothers collective tried to dissuade him, Brooke went over to Braxton.

She was coming to understand his logic where no one else did, this young woman who had grown up so much over the past several weeks. Perhaps it was her love for Dallas that had helped her reach new heights of maturity; perhaps it was because she was coming into her own and developing her own sense of wisdom. Whatever the case, she was the only one who wasn't fighting Braxton on the matter of his surrender. She understood.

She stood in front of him, smiling faintly at the war lord, the mercenary, who was now at his most vulnerable. He was such a mighty man, someone she respected most in the world. But he was also the gentle man who had made her mother so very happy. Her voice was soft as she spoke.

"Once, Dallas came to my rescue and saved my life," she murmured. "It was a great sacrifice; I understand that now although I did not at the time. I did not see how close he came to losing his life, too, and that he was willing to do it for a woman he did not even know."

Braxton gazed at her, suddenly seeing a good deal of Gray in the young woman. The beauty, the gentle wisdom, was the same in both women. Reaching out, he took her hand and brought it to his lips for a gentle, fatherly kiss.

"Sometimes, one must do as he must without thought to personal safety," he whispered. "This is something I must do."

Her smile broadened. "I know," she reached out and touched his rough cheek. "But before you go, please know that although I did know my real father, I did not love him half as much as I love you. He did not teach me half as much as you have or show such concern for me. You are the father I always hoped for, Braxton, and I thank you for that. Without you, I would not know such happiness or such love. You have made all things possible for me and for my mother. That day at the falls of Erith, my life changed forever because of you."

Braxton gazed at her with tears in his eyes. "I am very proud of you, Brooke," he murmured, kissing her on the forehead. "I could not love you more if you were my own flesh and blood. Please know that."

She clutched his hand, smiling up at him. "And I love you also," she whispered. "I will walk you to the gates."

He simply nodded, putting a big arm around her shoulders as they began their trek towards the gatehouse of Elswick. Dallas watched them go, tears streaming down his cheeks; a greater self-sacrifice he had never seen, coming from a man who had been like a father to him. Braxton knew full well that he may never make it out of Elswick alive, but that didn't matter to him. It was more important that he be with Gray, the very center of his world. It was selflessness of the greatest magnitude.

As Braxton and Brooke faded off towards the torch-lit castle, Dallas turned to Thomas.

"My lord," he said hoarsely. "Your son is the finest man who has ever lived."

Thomas' blue-green eyes watched his youngest son in the darkness, drawing closer to the portcullis of Elswick. He understood the depth of the self-sacrifice; they all did. Thomas could barely put his feelings into words but, for Dallas, he tried.

"He is his own man, lad," he murmured. "What he is has nothing to do with me. But I will tell you this; a prouder father has never walked this earth."

Dallas glanced at Braxton's brothers, all in varied degrees of anguish. Robert's cheeks were wet with tears as he turned away and headed off into the darkness. Eventually, they all turned away and headed off into the darkness. Braxton was doing what he felt he must do and they respected that. But Dallas stood there, waiting until his wife returned to him.

Then they, too, disappeared into the darkness.

CHAPTER TWENTY TWO

August 1306
Erith Castle

It was just after the nooning meal and Geoff was watching Brooke as she furiously swept the floor, pushing every crumb and every piece of dust into the hearth to be burned. He also knew that, once her husband arrived, she was going to be in a good deal of trouble. Dallas didn't like her sweeping, especially now.

But Brooke had ignored her husband's wishes for months. Any time he told her not to do something or to rest, she soundly resisted. Geoff watched her as she stood up from having been bent over the hearth, stretching out her back and exposing her enormous belly. Broom in one hand, she alternately rubbed at her back and her belly as if she couldn't decide which one to massage first. Spying more crumbs in the corner, she hustled over to the spot and began to sweep furiously.

"Dallas will be here any moment," he told her. "You had better turn that broom over to me."

Brooke scowled at him. "I will not," she said firmly. "You do not sweep as well as I do."

Fighting off a grin, Geoff shook his head and looked away just as Edgar and Norman entered the keep. Both young men had grown by leaps and bounds over the past year; Norman had grown up and outward, now taller and wider than Dallas was. As a new knight, he was performing admirably. Edgar, too, had shot up and was now nearly as tall as his brother, although he hadn't filled out quite as much. He, too, was in the midst of his knightly training and doing exceptionally well.

The one thing that hadn't changed, however, was his relationship with Brooke. They were still like a brother and

330

sister, antagonizing each other, although it was much more discreet now that Dallas was around. As he entered the hall and she realized who it was, she stuck her tongue out at him. He balled a fist and shook it at her.

"Edgar," she snapped. "Come here and sweep the floor. I should not be doing this."

He lifted an eyebrow at her. "I am not a house servant," he sniffed, making his way to the table. "Find someone else to do it."

"What was that, Edgar?" Dallas was coming in through the hall entry. "Did I hear you refuse my wife?"

Edgar bolted over to Brooke and snatched the broom from her. "Not at all, my lord," he began to sweep furiously. "I am happy to help Lady Aston."

Geoff lowered his head lest Edgar and Dallas see him laughing. Dallas reached the table, leaning over to kiss his wife as he removed his heavy gloves.

"If I catch you sweeping again, I am going to blister your backside after this babe is born," he told her. "You are not to exert yourself like that. Last night, it was cleaning out our chamber and the day before, it was washing linens."

Brooke gave him the big pouty face. "But I cannot sit still."

"Why not?"

"Because I cannot. I feel nervous, as if I have to be doing something."

He lifted a warning eyebrow at her. "Nothing strenuous," he ordered softly, giving her a swift kiss. "Now, I must meet with my men. Will you please give us some privacy, sweetheart?"

Her pout grew. "Why can I not stay? I will behave. I will not say a word."

He shook his head. "It would not interest you."

She grabbed his arm. "Please?" she begged. "I have not seen you all day. May I please sit here with you, quiet, quiet, quiet like a little mouse?"

He didn't want to get in a big battle with her; she was incredibly sensitive these days, raging one minute and weeping the next. Her pregnancy had been extremely easy but for the mood swings, something Dallas lived in fear of. So he nodded with resignation and sat her down on the bench beside him. Just as they were settling in, another figure came in from the bailey.

Niclas brushed the dust off his breeches as he moved towards the banqueting hall. Lady Aston had a great revulsion to dust and dirt and would yell at any man who entered the hall and got her swept floors dirty. Niclas wasn't used to a clean keep; having served for many years at Black Fell, which was a filthy pit of man stink, he had to retrain himself to behave around a clean and tidy woman.

He made his way to the table, hoping that Lady Aston would screech at him for bringing dust into the hall. He'd come to know her over the past year, since being gifted from Thomas de Nerra to Dallas to help fill the void of Braxton's absence, and she was a very young woman with a keen sense of humor. Truth was, Niclas was much more content being a mercenary. He had taken to it easily. Now, he served Aston as a member of the mercenary army.

Fortunately for Niclas, Brooke did nothing more than glance at him as he took a seat next to young Edgar. With all of his knights seated at the well scrubbed table, Dallas settled down to business.

"Now," he began. "As you know, I received a missive some time ago from Baron Portington in Humberside soliciting our services for a land dispute he is having with his neighbor. I received another missive from him this morning pleading for negotiations. He is offering a great deal of money and I fear I would be remiss to refuse him."

"How much money?" Niclas wanted to know.

Dallas looked at him. "He is offering us five thousand gold marks simply to come and speak with him," he replied. "It is a tidy sum. Even if we do not take the job, we will still make money."

The knights nodded in agreement. "We made a great deal of money off of the dispute between North Cliffe and South Cliffe in the spring," Norman said. "Who ever heard of two villages going to battle against one another? I believe that is the first time an entire village hired our services."

Dallas had to agree. "We received enough goods and coin from that venture to start our own country," he glanced over at his wife, noticing that she was staring at her hands folded over her belly. She seemed distracted and he put his big hand over hers. "And you received more clothing and jewelry than you know what to do with."

Brooke nodded and he squeezed her hands gently. "What is wrong? You do not seem pleased by it."

She lifted her head, looking around the table at her husband's knights. Then, she shrugged and lowered her gaze again.

"You have fought four battles since Braxton and my mother went away," she couldn't even bring herself to tell the truth; all she ever said about them is that the 'went away'. "You do not tell any of these people that Braxton is no longer head of his army. Everyone still thinks he is in charge."

Dallas' jovial mood was fading as he squeezed her hand again. "It is better this way," he said quietly. "I told you that people know Braxton's name. It commands respect. No one would know Dallas Aston's name as a terrifying mercenary. It makes better business sense to keep all as it has been, including keeping Braxton's name, because he may very well return someday. The army is bigger and stronger now than it has ever been, and we continue to fight under Braxton's banner because it *is* his army."

She looked at him. "If the army is bigger and stronger, then why not go back to Elswick and demand to know what became of my mother and Braxton?" she asked; it wasn't the first time she has asked such a thing. "It has almost been a year and we still do not know."

It was an extremely delicate subject with Brooke and Dallas put his arm around her, kissing her temple.

"Sweetheart, you know that we have done all we can," he said softly. "We did as Braxton wanted; we returned to Erith. I have sent a missive to Elswick every week since then asking to know the condition of Braxton and your mother, and every week I get no response. If Braxton is still alive, I do not want to jeopardize anything by riding back to Elswick and demanding answers. They would perceive it as a threat and Braxton, and your mother, could be put in grave danger. All we can do is wait to be contacted by Braxton. You know this."

She was staring at her belly; as he watched, she frowned terribly and burst into tears.

"I do not want to wait," she struggled to stand up from the table with her big belly; she was weary and off-balance. "I want you to take the army back to Elswick and beat down the walls if they do not tell you what became of my mother and Braxton."

Dallas tried to steady her as the knights thought this was their opportunity to retreat. Lady Aston went through this same fit about every other day, and every other day Dallas would gently soothe her. He was trying to do what he thought Braxton would want and his wife disagreed. It made for a touchy situation at times.

"Sweetheart," Dallas stood up next to her as she tried to pull away. "Do not upset yourself so. I know you do not understand, but you must trust me that I know what is best."

Brooke moved away from the table, sobbing unhappily. Dallas needed to finished his business with his knights but he needed to soothe her more. With a glance to his men, giving them a brief shake of the head to let them know they would have to discuss the Portington issue at another time, he followed Brooke to the spiral stairs that led to the upstairs chambers. He caught up to her about the time she took the first step, reaching out to pull her into his arms to comfort her. But his efforts were thwarted by a soldier as the man abruptly burst into the keep.

It was a young soldier, one of those gifted to Dallas by Thomas when he had also gifted Niclas. In fact, Thomas had gifted Braxton's army with another one hundred men, bringing his total army to nearly three hundred. Dallas paused as the soldier entered, spied his commander, and made his way to him.

"My lord," the soldier tried not to notice when Brooke slapped Dallas' hands away as she made her way up the stairs. "We have sighted an incoming party about a half a mile away."

Dallas nodded, not particularly concerned. "Banners?"

"None, my lord."

"How big?"

"We can make out a wagon and four riders." As Dallas nodded again and prepared to give an order, the young soldier interrupted him. "I have heard... my lord, that is to say, I have heard some of the more seasoned men say that one of the riders looks like de Nerra."

Brooke froze on her ascent up the stairs, staring at the soldier, as Dallas' brow furrowed.

"Which de Nerra?" he asked.

"Sir Braxton, my lord."

Brooke gave a hoot and quickly came off the stairs. The other knights, who were in the process of vacating the hall when the messenger entered, heard the man's words also and they began barreling out of the keep. Dallas moved to follow, trying to keep a rein on his excited wife so she wouldn't overly strain herself or, worse, fall down the stairs in her excitement. He held on to her all the way down the stairs that led from the keep into the bailey, pleading for calm from her even as he bellowed orders to open the gates on the outerwall.

Long since repaired to her former glory, Erith's great gates yawned open as soldiers cranked the wheel that reeled in the chains. As Dallas had good hold of Brooke, chargers suddenly bolted past them and he looked up to see Norman, Edgar and Geoff thundering out onto the road. Niclas was on foot, standing at the outer gate house as the gates cranked all the way open. He bellowed to the men to take up the slack and secure the chains.

Brooke stood between the inner and outer wall with Dallas, whimpering softly as the wagon finally came into view down the long expanse of road. She could clearly see when the three chargers met the wagon and she could see the ensuing commotion, but she couldn't see who was actually approaching. They were just too far away. Dallas had his arm around her shoulders, holding her fast, his blue eyes riveted to the incoming party. He didn't want to hold out hope that what the men said was true. But as time passed and as the party grew nearer, he began to recognize one of the mounted men. A slow smile spread across his face, joy and excitement filling his veins. He kissed his wife on the temple as the party drew closer.

"It is him," he whispered to her. "It is Braxton."

Brooke burst out into loud sobs. "Where is my mother?"

Dallas' joy and excitement tempered dramatically; he didn't have an answer for her and the only one he could come up with was not a pleasing one. He squeezed her gently.

"I do not know, sweetheart," he said, trying to comfort her. "Perhaps she is in the wagon and we cannot see her."

Brooke was weeping loudly. Suddenly, she broke away from him and began running down the road towards the wagon. Dallas easily caught her and stopped her from running any further, terrified she was going to injure herself and the child. But Brooke struggled against him, crying and smacking at his hands, as he prevented her from running any further. The wagon drew closer and Braxton, in all his glory, came into focus. It was an amazing and awesome sight.

Without armor, he rode the cream-colored charger with ease, clad in simple breeches, tunic and boots, the same clothing they had last saw him in. He could hear Brooke crying loudly from several dozen yards away and even as Geoff and Norman milled around him, he spurred his charger forward at the sight and sounds of Brooke's fit. He was on her in an instant, noticing her advanced pregnancy. His eyes widened.

"Brooke?" he drew the charger to a halt, vaulting off the animal as he moved quickly to his daughter. "Sweetheart, what is the matter?"

Brooke pulled free of Dallas and threw herself against Braxton. Her arms went around his neck.

"Braxton," she wept dramatically. "I thought you were dead!"

He hugged her, trying not to quash her big belly. "Nay, sweetheart," he kissed her on the side of her head. "I am not dead. I am very much alive. And you are pregnant."

He said it with such surprise that her sobs turned into weepy giggles as she pulled back to look at him; he looked healthy and whole, just as she remembered him. Like a vision from a dream, she could hardly believe what she was seeing.

"I am," she said, seeing his amazement. But it didn't deter her terror and grief and the tears returned with a vengeance. "Where is my mother?"

Braxton realized what had her so upset; he took her by the arm, passing a glance at Dallas and smiling at his son-in-law.

"I can see you are taking great care of her, Dallas," he grinned. "And you are looking well yourself."

Dallas smiled broadly. "As are you, for a dead man," he said, moving up behind Brooke and putting an affectionate hand on Braxton's shoulder. "You have no idea how glad we are to see you."

Braxton wriggled his eyebrows as he began to lead Brooke and Dallas toward the approaching wagon. "As I am very glad to see you," he said. "There is much to tell."

Before Dallas could respond, Brooke looked up at him with her big, watery eyes. "What happened after we left Elswick?" she wanted to know. "Dallas sent a missive every week asking for information on you and Mama. We never received an answer. We did not know what happened to you."

Braxton held her hand, squeezing it gently. "I know," he said. "There was much going on at Elswick. I was much occupied taking care of your mother."

Brooke started to well up again as they approached the wagon. "Where is my mother?" she wept, pleading. "What happened to her? Why was she so sick?"

"Because your brother was making himself known."

The soft, female voice came from the wagon as it came to a stop. Startled, Brooke's tears vanished as she gazed into the wagon bed and immediately spied her mother. But Gray wasn't alone; she was propped up against the side of the wagon, holding a downy-haired infant in her arms. Gray smiled at her daughter as Brooke nearly came apart.

"Mama!" she gasped. "Wha... what....?"

Gray laughed softly. "Slow down, sweetheart," she looked at Braxton. "Help her into the wagon so she can see her new brother."

Both Braxton and Dallas lifted Brooke up into the wagon bed and it was Gray's first glimpse of her daughter's advanced state of pregnancy. She reached out as Brooke scooted over to her, putting her hand on Brooke's belly and biting off tears of her own. She felt the warm firmness of her daughter's belly with the greatest of reverence, startled in her own right at the sight of her daughter.

"Look at you," she gasped, gazing up into her daughter's rosy face. "Are you well, sweetheart? How do you feel?"

"She is fine," Dallas was standing at the edge of the wagon, beaming from ear to ear. "She eats more than I do, runs around like a madwoman, and refuses to slow down. I have my hands full with her. She is as healthy as a horse."

Gray laughed softly, tears finding their way onto her cheeks as she returned her gaze to her daughter. "You really should ease up," she said softly. "You must take care of yourself and my grandchild."

Brooke waved her off, peering at the tow-headed baby in Gray's arms. "I am fine, truly," she smiled at the round-cheeked, blue-eyed infant. "Oh, Mama, he is wonderful. He looks just like Braxton. What is his name?"

Gray looked down at the baby, cuddled and content in her arms. "Meet your brother," she murmured, stroking the velvety cheek. "This is Deston de Nerra, a big and healthy boy who very nearly drained the life from me."

Brooke was cooing and touching the infant, who smiled back at her. She crowed in delight. "He is beautiful! Can I hold him?"

By this time, Braxton and Dallas had moved to the side of the wagon where the women were sitting. Dallas helped his wife to sit on her bottom while Gray handed the baby over to her. Brooke happily cuddled the boy with the white-blond hair.

"He is so sweet," she crooned, then looked to her mother. "Is this why you were so sick?"

Gray nodded, peeling back the swaddling from the baby's head and exposing him to the warm sunlight. "He made me ill day and night," she replied. "I could not eat and could barely keep water down. He was just starting to announce himself when the Gloucester soldiers took us from Creekmere and when I fought with them, I very nearly killed myself from the strain. "

Brooke nodded in understanding, turning back to look at the baby. "It makes sense now," she said. "But why did you not send word to us before now? We did not know if you or Braxton were dead or alive."

Braxton's big hand came to rest on Gray's shoulder. "Your mother was quite ill for the duration of the pregnancy," he said. "I spent my time at Elswick keeping both myself and your mother alive. I could not attempt escape because she could not be moved, so my only choice was to stay with her. Moreover, I did not have the type of relationship with de Milne where the man would allow me to send missives; we were, essentially, prisoners. But that all changed when Deston was born. De Milne's wife, who helped me tend your mother for the duration of her pregnancy, convinced her husband to let us leave. As soon as your mother was strong enough and the baby old enough, we did."

It explained a great deal. Brooke realized she wasn't perturbed about it any longer; she was just grateful to have her mother and Braxton back. All of the anguish and grief she felt over the past year suddenly vanished as she gazed at her mother.

"I am so glad you have come home," she looked at Braxton. "It simply was not the same without you."

Braxton kissed his wife. "I have always been a wealthy man," he said softly, his gaze moving to his beloved son, the one he had seen once reflected in Gray's eyes. "But suppose I never truly understood what it was to be truly rich. If happiness and a family makes a man rich, then I am indeed the richest man in the world."

Dallas clapped him on the shoulder. "You are very rich," he agreed. "And we are glad to have our liege back."

Braxton wriggled his eyebrows. "My time in captivity has taught me something, Dallas," he looked at the young man. "It has taught me that it is my time in life now to enjoy my wife and children and leave the warring to the younger men. I have put in my time as a knight and commander; now it is my time to enjoy the fruits of my labor."

Brooke looked at Braxton. "Dallas has been commanding your army for the past year. He has done a wonderful job. He has made a lot of money."

Braxton grinned. "And he can keep on commanding it, for I am going to stay home and grow fat and lazy with my wife by my side."

Brooke laughed softly, returning her attention to the infant in her arms. She kissed his little cheek happily.

"I have never had a brother," she murmured, watching the baby grin. "Welcome home, Deston. Soon you will have a little playmate."

And soon he did. Fat, healthy Matthew Aston was born on a cool September night, so easily that it was over almost before it began. Brooke hardly broke a sweat while her husband's light-headed reaction was decidedly different. The following year, Deston was joined by brother Auston and Matthew was joined by twins Andrew and Alexandra. Erith, once a place of doom and hopelessness, was now a place with joy and children. The old de Montfort castle began to live again.

Life went on. Dallas went on to assume the mantle of commander of Braxton's army but with three little ones at home, he mostly sent Geoff and Niclas out instead, carrying on the legacy of the great de Nerra mercenary army. Like Braxton, Dallas wanted to watch his children grow up. In the years to come, he and Braxton would sit in the great hall of Erith before a roaring blaze, watching five tow-headed youngsters play and grow, thinking that these were the best years of their lives. But then Deston would clobber Matthew, Auston and Andrew would squabble, and screams would fill the air. After the fathers broke up the fights, they still thought it was the best time of their lives.

340

There was no doubt about it.

Sometimes, when all was still and peaceful and the children were in bed, they would discuss that day at the falls of Erith that changed their lives forever. A happenstance on that day turned out to be platform through which greater things were achieved. Dallas admitted once that he thought, as he held tight to the girl clinging precariously on the wet rocks, that he was certain he would lose his grip on her. He even remembered at the time feeling her wet flesh slip away from him, increment by increment, and thought for certain that her life was about to end.

But it didn't end. He had no idea at the time that his, in fact, had just begun.

ABOUT THE AUTHOR

Kathryn Le Veque has always been a writer. From her first 'book' at the age of 13, Kathryn has been writing prolifically. A strong interest in History and adventure has added to her stories, most of which take place in the Plantagenet period of England. She also writes contemporary romance and adventure, as evidenced in the Kathlyn Trent/Marcus Burton Adventure/Romance Series.

When Kathryn isn't writing, she is volunteering her time with the local high school as the booster president, gardening, golfing, or watching old black and white movies. Her daughter, currently in college, is following in her mother's footsteps with a love of creative writing and Medieval History.

Visit Kathryn's website at www.kathrynleveque.com for more novels and ordering information.

Made in the USA
Middletown, DE
16 March 2018